WITHDRAWN

D0045979

WITHDRAWN

Eve

ELISSA ELLIOTT

Delacorte Press

Eve

YOLO COUNTY LIBRARY
226 BUCKEYE STREET
WOODLAND, CA 95695

A Novel

of the

First Woman

EVE: A NOVEL OF THE FIRST WOMAN
A Delacorte Press Book / February 2009

Published by Bantam Dell
A Division of Random House, Inc.
New York, New York

This is a work of fiction. Names, characters, places,
and incidents either are the product of the author's imagination
or are used fictitiously. Any resemblance to actual persons,
living or dead, events, or locales is entirely coincidental.

All rights reserved
Copyright © 2009 by Elissa Elliott

Book design by Virginia Norey

Delacorte Press is a registered trademark of Random House, Inc.,
and the colophon is a trademark of Random House, Inc.

Library of Congress Cataloging in Publication Data
Elliott, Elissa.
Eve : a novel of the first woman / Elissa Elliott.
p.   cm.
ISBN 978-0-385-34144-8
1. Eve (Biblical figure)—Fiction. 2. Women in the Bible—Fiction.
3. Religious fiction. I. Title.
PS3605.L447E94 2009
813'.6—dc22
2008027583

Printed in the United States of America
Published simultaneously in Canada

www.bantamdell.com

BVG   10 9 8 7 6 5 4 3 2 1

For Daniel — my Adam

The world was all before them, where to choose
Their place of rest, and Providence their guide:
They, hand in hand, with wand'ring steps and slow,
Through Eden took their solitary way.

—from John Milton's *Paradise Lost,*
Book XII, Lines 646–649

Eve

Prologue

Belief is not always easy.
Even when you have seen and heard the thing
you are supposed to believe in.

Come, my child. You heard my crying and did not wish to intrude upon your old mother. I heard your footfalls outside my door and waited, but you did not enter. No doubt you were afraid, since I was the one who sent you away, doomed you to a life of aimless wandering with a cursed husband. My cursed son.

Closer now, let me look at you. Too many moons have passed since I saw you last. So beautiful you are, yet your eyes are restless, your cheeks are loosened like waterskins. Your shoulders curve like a sickle, and when you walk, it's as though you are mired in a riverbed.

My child, rest, sit awhile, and listen. The day is almost done for us. The oil lamps are lit. The frogs rasp from the desert sands, and the spiders and scorpions have been brushed from the corners. The mice have been lured elsewhere, to forgotten bowls of wheat and barley. The cock will not disturb us until daylight shouts.

Where is Cain? Does he still bear the mark upon his brow?

Do you have many children, a quiver full of arrows?

You make to speak, but your lips are parched. Perhaps you need wine with a little milk? Here, take this cup and drink. I see you have come a great distance, rods upon rods, to be with me, and I am here to greet you and bless you and tell you how your presence gladdens my heart and puts a smile on my lips. A daughter can cure any ill.

I was once as beautiful as you. You would not know it to look at me, but I have lived most of my life as grass beaten down by rain, broken and trampled as you are. It is no way to live; I've come to know that.

Adam, your father and my lover and my friend, has returned to the earth. Your siblings are grown and have children of their own. They grew weary of my storytelling long ago, though had one of them listened, really listened, I would not need to tell it again, to you. That is how I see it: A tale needs only to be told as many times as it finds its way home.

Give me your hand. I say to your weary soul, Elohim is near to the brokenhearted, the crushed in spirit. Go ahead, cry, and breathe deep. Incline your ear to me, dear Naava.

I know that to some my name sours on the tongue and twists in the ear, but understand this: Remembrance is holy, blame is not.

Look here, look what I have kept all these years. After your bitter and rapid flight in the night, the three of us, your sisters and I, could only hunch next to the fire and press our emotions, our memories, into clay. Now they are only shards, crumbling in an old jar.

Now they are like me, tired and brittle and full of recollections.

My child, these are our lives. Even as Elohim dug up the red earth and breathed life into it, so we, also, scooped up river mud and breathed life into it.

Each one of these clay fragments tells a story.

Each one represents a season in this grand and cruel world of Elohim's.

Listen. Can you hear them?

PART ONE

Strangers
in the
Land

Eve

I came upon my son's body by the river. The morning was no hotter or drier than usual, but as I crossed the plains between the house and the river, the wind kicked up the dust clouds, and I had to hold my robe over my nose. Dust clung to my wet face and marked the crooked trails of my tears. Behind me, the sky was the color of lettuce. The sand chafed my swollen feet, and my groin ached with the pains of Elazar's birth—was it just last evening I had borne him?—and my heart, oh, my heart's deep sorrow was for the travesty Cain had committed, then confessed to me like a blubbering child.

The body was not hard to find. The flies and vultures led me to him, fallen under the date palms, alongside the marshy river. His face was unrecognizable; Cain had seen to that. I don't remember if I was sad or grieving just then. I was more astonished than anything. I had seen animals killed, their throats slashed and their viscera splayed out on the ground, and certainly there were my babies who were lost. But nothing prepared me for the sight of Abel, my precious son, as still as a rock, his head bloodied and his neck arched back, stiff, at an unnatural angle. His eyes—I realize now that it was a miracle they had not yet been pecked out!—once full of his vigor and brooding and planning, were empty. They said nothing to me. Of course, Abel had said little to me ever since he took to the fields to tend his goats and sheep, but that is no matter. He was still my favorite. Is a mother permitted to say such things about her children?

I fell to my knees and threw my body over his. I lifted his head, cold and broken, to my breast, and cradled him there, as I had done so often when he was a baby. Fresh tears refused to come, which was strange. It was as though I had been thrown out of the Garden once again, rejected and abandoned, and, as only Adam can testify, they flowed like a river then. And where *was* Adam, my husband? Did he not care about our son, the one kissed by Elohim for his magnificent sacrifice? Or had Adam's deafness prevented him from hearing my anguished cries when Cain told me what he had done?

Softly, I sang the Garden song into my dead son's ear. I knew he would hear it, wherever he had gone off to. He had been the only one to understand its message and allure.

Abel's flesh was cold and clammy, and all I could remember was the vision of loveliness he was as a child—soft chubby skin folds and eyes only for me. He was the first to bring me gifts—poppies and ranunculus and clover, discarded feathers, and pebbles worn smooth by the river and carried down from the mountains. Cain would not have thought of it. He was too busy traipsing after his father—digging, planting, terracing, and experimenting with anything green.

What sorrow there is in having children! At first, they tickle your heartstrings. They linger for your words, clutch at your skirts, feed on your breath, and then one day they lurch to the edge of the nest and flutter out. They never return, and the empty space yawns impatiently, demanding more. It is a never-ending ache, one that I continued to fill as long as I was able.

The vultures hissed at me and made loud chuffing noises. They spread their mighty wings and danced about.

"Get!" I shouted, half rising and waving my arms.

They did not budge.

Where was my Abel? Where had he gone? Was he wandering somewhere, looking for his mother? I wondered if he would weep at not finding me. I remembered Elohim's words to Adam and me, "For you are dust, and to dust you shall return," but still, I did not believe it, did not *want* to believe it. What good were our lives if, in the end, we simply returned to earthly particles?

To make sense of this tragedy, I shall have to go back to the beginning of that hot summer, preceded by the spring harvest and sheep plucking, when our family's unraveling began. Unfortunately, it is always in hindsight that we see our mistakes, like a wrong color in the loom or a foreign stalk in our fields, but by doing so, I try to account for my life and change that which I can. It provides a bit of solace.

Imagine then: The sun hung low and orange on the horizon, and Naava, my eldest daughter at fourteen years, was lighting lamps in the courtyard. There was the usual bustle of the men coming in from the fields—Adam, my husband, from the orchards and Cain, our eldest son, from plowing. Adam, his robes caked with dirt and sweat, hung his arms across my shoulders and squeezed. "Wife," he said, pecking me on the cheek. "How is my woman?" He said this laughing, as though he had said the most humorous thing, and I grinned back, glad of his presence.

"Your woman is exceptional," I said.

On this particular occasion, Abel was absent. Frequently, he claimed that sleeping among his flocks gave him solitude and peace. Even after Jacan's discovery that morning.

Jacan, my youngest son, had been trembling when he returned at dawn from collecting water at the cistern. We could barely make out his words— he was gulping in so much air. "Lion tracks," he said. "This big." His little arms stretched wide, and his fingers tried to frame a large circle in the air. "Abel," he said. "You should stay here today."

Abel had laughed and ruffled Jacan's hair. "Who will kill the lion if I sit at home?"

Jacan's eyes grew as round as onions, and he stared at Abel. "It's a big one," he said, doubtful that Abel understood.

Our tools and weapons hung on our courtyard wall—adzes, sickles, scythes, hoes, throwing spears, daggers, and bows and arrows. It was to this wall that Abel went. He reached up for a slingshot and a bag of clay pellets. He turned to Jacan and said solemnly, "My aim will be true the first time." And towheaded Jacan went to him and hugged the huge trees of Abel's legs, Jacan's arms seeming so frail to me, like vines trying to find purchase. Oh, how I wanted to grab both of my sons and hold them tight!

Now, the long day over, the purple-gray evening skies pressed in from all sides. Inside the waist-high clay walls of the courtyard, moths and flies were drawn to the flames and danced shadows upon our faces. Aya, my crippled middle daughter, ladled meat into wooden bowls and plucked hot and steaming flat bread from the walls of the *tinûru*. I smiled to watch her kiss each piece of bread before she placed it on a platter. It was something she had always done from the time she was small and just learning to cook. I asked her about it once, and she said, "But, Mother, all things must be blessed. You said so yourself that Elohim blessed each thing He made." It was true. I had told her that, although I was beginning to doubt there was a personal Elohim who enjoyed my company. That had been a truth for the Garden, something sweetly shared between Adam and me.

Dara and Jacan were in their seventh year. As the sun slipped over the plain's flat edge, Jacan came running in from the river, knees churning, shouting, "Dara, Dara, Dara!" as though he were mad. He carried a box turtle from the marsh, and although I was convinced he had squashed it in his hand in his eagerness to show Dara, it was still alive and moving when he gave it to her. She squealed, of course, then grew morose when the turtle refused to poke its head out. "Mama," she cried. "Do something!"

I told her to be patient. "The turtle is probably frightened," I said. "Wouldn't you be too, if someone was throwing you about?"

So they hovered, squatted down on their haunches, and waited for the turtle's glorious head to emerge in the twilight. Such is the life of small children! It never failed to delight me, watching them involved with a task so simple, yet they remained so wonderfully curious and happy.

I do not recall what my family talked about that night as we filled our bellies, but I do remember what it was that made us all *stop* talking. There was a sharp cry in the distance, then a *thud*. To the north, maybe. Cain was the first to scramble up, because Adam, who was deaf in his left ear, hadn't heard. I'm sure we all looked like baby birds, mouths open, food suspended, for a moment, waiting, waiting, for another noise. *What could it be?*

"Father," Cain cried, as he rushed to the courtyard wall and disappeared into the edges of night.

Adam, accustomed to this disconnection between his inner and outer world, took his cue from Cain. He jumped to his feet, setting down his bowl. He reached for my hand and held it for a moment. "Stay," he said to us, and then he, too, was through the courtyard gate.

I daresay his command was ignored. Naava had a nose for adventure and for everything else out-there, a desire I could never quite understand. It was a compulsion that neither of my other girls seemed to possess. She rose, and though I called sharply, "Naava, wait," she dashed out too and vanished.

"What is it, Mama?" said Dara.

"The lion!" said Jacan, yanking on Dara's arm, then looking at me, fear solid in his eyes. "Abel!"

Aya's voice was calm and contemptuous. She had no time for silly conjectures. "Abel is in the hills. How could we hear his voice from here?"

Jacan's face registered confusion for a moment, then he rallied. "Maybe he was on his way home because he was lonely, and the lion attacked him." He turned to me. "Father will save him, right?"

I waved his worries aside and began collecting the bowls to scour with sand, but Jacan's words gave me goose skin. *What would happen if I lost my son?*

I tended a small collection of burial mounds in the garden that Adam had planted for me—a son whom I had borne before his time, a daughter with a malformed head, and another daughter who had emerged, dead, with knots in her cord—but this was different. Abel was a grown man, with curls of hair on his chest and a gruff voice and somber moods. He did not belong in the ground, away from his family, silent, covered with dirt and thistle and mesquite.

Because I have given life to each of my children, I love each one. Cain—for his ingenuity. Abel—for his sweet ways. Naava—for her feistiness. Aya—for her resourcefulness. Jacan—for his tender heart. Dara—for her compassion. But in times like these, a mother's mind flashes to—oh, think me not cruel!—whom of her children she would most like to hold fast, if given the choice. Although I strive to treat each equally, my heart cannot be led like Abel's sheep. It is stubborn and goes where it likes. I do not find any solace in this truth; in fact, it causes me much turmoil.

My love comes in shades of color. There is a bright pulsing red, and there is a weakly washed pink. I do not know why; I only know that it is so.

So, truth be told, it would have been Cain I would have sacrificed, if I had been forced to choose. Cain always grappled for his significance with the universe, his superiority over all of us, even his disgust with us. It was as though he were made in the starry heavens yet housed in a fragile warm shell that was susceptible to injury and ache and decay, and the frustration for him was too much.

As a child, Cain tortured and killed frogs, birds, and lizards. He baited the ducks at the river by hooking a bit of bread and waiting for an unfortunate one to pluck at the morsel and swallow it. He sliced open their throats, then cut them apart, determined to find out what made them breathe or walk or fly.

Everything was a torment when they were boys, even such a small thing as splitting a pomegranate between him and Abel.

"You've given him more," Cain would squeal in fury.

"Here's a bit more then, from mine," I would say, and give him another section.

"I want it from *his*!" Cain would say between clenched teeth.

"That's enough," I would say.

From Abel, there was nary an unkind word or threatening look.

He was a summer rain.

That night, I quelled a gasp in my throat. *Not Abel, please not Abel,* I prayed. I prayed to the One who had formed us in the Garden, the One whom I had talked with there, and the One whom I did not believe cared for me anymore.

The reason I prayed was simple: I prayed to Him because it was the only thing I could do. True, my energy was irrational and ill-founded, but nonetheless I invoked Elohim my Creator.

Hear my cry, O Elohim, and give heed to my prayer. I shall shout Your praises to the sky. Let me not be ashamed.

And so it came to pass that, as I prayed, the winds of my heart blew no more. It was quiet, and I sat to hear what He would say to me.

His words never came.

Naava

Eve closes her eyes and rests. She's been holding her head up this whole time, straining to make herself heard. Her hair is white now, splayed out like a sun-bleached starfish upon her pillow.

Naava places a cool cloth on her mother's forehead. "Shhh," she says. "Lie back." She stares at Eve's face, the bear-clawed scars on her right cheek, the irregular brown spots on her hands and arms, the deep lines in the skin around her eyes and lips, and the frown cracks between her eyebrows. Naava wonders why her mother is so dramatic, so wrong about the past. *Is it possible that two people can experience the same thing and come away with two different stories?*

Naava takes Eve's hand, knobbed like a piece of gingerroot. She traces the swollen rivers of blood in Eve's veins, shutting them off, then letting them rush forth under the skin. She remembers: sitting with Aya and the younger children by the pond, under the shade of Eve's beloved Garden of Eden tree, telling Eve's stories to one another in the heat of the afternoon, while the asps warmed themselves and the bees buzzed above their heads. They played the parts—the serpent, Eve, Adam, even the cherubim and the wavering lights. Once, Aya insisted they all chant to Elohim, asking that they be able to return to the Garden, to see where their mother and father had come from. Elohim answered in a breeze; His words sounded singsongy and soft. *What's done is done, my children.* His swift reply only encouraged Aya in her attempts at further conversation; it did the opposite for Naava. Naava was petrified. Voices should come out of people, not out of thin air. Really, she wasn't even quite sure she'd heard anything at all.

Naava felt this: Eve knew so little of what had happened because she saw only what she wanted to see and loved only what she wanted to love. She herself had said this in so many words, hadn't she?

On that night in question, Naava hadn't run out. She remembered it clearly, even if Eve did not. She had stayed with Eve and the children. While her mother and the younger ones argued about whether or not Abel was in serious trouble, Naava went to her loom in the front room off the courtyard, lit another lamp, and began to thread her shuttle and pull colored pieces of wool through the open shed. This was *freedom* for her, to design something spectacular and watch it bloom like a reluctant flower beneath her hands.

The desire to create was strong in her, as it was in her mother. Naava knew Eve was with child again, and Naava also knew by the low melon roundness of Eve that the baby would be born around the fall harvest. Naava smiled to herself. Her two favorite moments in weaving were at the beginning and at the end. In the beginning, wondrous visions danced in her head, and her fingers had only to step nimbly, turn gracefully, to translate the images—flowers and trees and rivers and sunbursts—into tangible beauty. At the end, she held the rough cloth to her face and traced the colors and the designs with her fingers, and the satisfaction was sweet, like honey. Naava had already decided to make a sling for the new baby her mother would bear. She had gleaned wool from Abel's goats, cleaned and washed it, boiled it with walnut husks to turn it into a rich wheat-brown color, rolled it upon her thigh, and pulled it into strands of yarn. After designing her warp—the latticework support for all those threads—she was ready to weave. She was ready to create.

Naava's helpfulness came in bursts then, in summer's early days.

As she concentrated on her weaving, Naava thought of Abel and how handsome he was, certainly more handsome than Cain. She had begun to notice, with delicious pleasure, his side glances at her when he thought she wasn't looking.

In fact, morning before last, she had been outside the courtyard, on her hands and knees, picking through her collection of cut plants—yarrow, marigolds, geraniums, madder, and chamomile—and sorting them by the colors they would produce when boiled with wool, when she lifted her face, wet around the temples from the morning heat, and looked toward the corral where Abel was shaking a clay jar full of seeds to get his flocks to follow him through the gates and out into the sandy fields. Except that Abel had been watching her, and when she looked up, he diverted his glance, then caught himself and waved, so she would think nothing of it. Naava grinned and waved back, then realized that the top of her robe was gaping and Abel had been staring into its dark recesses. Shocked, and slightly pleased, she blushed and looked down to put herself in exactly the same position she had been in when Abel—*what had he seen?* She glanced up, but Abel had vanished. She straightened her neckline and tucked the panel firmly under the sash—but not so tightly that he could see nothing.

Lately when Abel took to the pastures at night, she thought it was due to his fear of her—or fear of himself around her. He smelled of rain and earth and wet wool and starlight. How could he not? And how Naava loved that smell and wanted to smother herself in it.

She thought what a tragedy it would be if something should mar that beautiful face of his, for it would be sad to look upon a ruined countenance day after day. She wanted him whole, intact, and lovely. She did not want to give up her dream of having him to herself. For she *would* have him someday, at the right moment, and she would brush up against him, or place her hand in his, softly, tenderly, and whisper the words into his exquisite whorled ear, "I love you."

The shout had not been Abel's.

By the time Cain's slurred singing reached their ears, the oil lamps were sputtering out, and Naava's weft—her burgeoning piece of fabric—was the width of her smallest fingernail. Naava dropped her threads and ducked quickly out of her room. Eve and the children glanced up at the sudden movement, rising from their places at the sight of Naava's eager face.

"They're back," Naava said.

Eve tucked a strand of hair behind her ear and smoothed her robes. She grabbed the little ones' shoulders and pulled them back to her.

Naava opened the gate and disappeared into the night beyond the courtyard walls. Even in the darkness, she could see that Cain floundered like one of Abel's newborn lambs. Adam had one arm around Cain's waist and the other firmly locked on his forearm.

"Hold the gate," said Adam. His voice was stretched tight, like the knots he used to tie up his unruly grapevines.

Adam supported Cain through the entrance, and together they stepped into the yellow circle of lamps where Cain, with an ill-timed belch, held out a new wineskin to Eve. It was shiny and ready to burst. Eve half-laughed at the ridiculous sight before her, knowing Cain could not be so happy if there was trouble with Abel, and Naava saw the furrows in her mother's face grow smooth again.

"What is it, brother?" Naava called. "Surely you didn't go out to raid our storehouses."

Cain turned to her and gave a delighted snort. "We have guests! To the north of us. Real live people, just like us. They have tents, sheep, dogs, timber—you should *see* the building materials they've brought!—blue stones, and boats: these hollowed-out contraptions you put in the water, like floating logs, but better, more efficient!"

Naava paused. She wondered how she felt—thrilled or alarmed? The family, the whole lot of them, looked astonished, of course. Eve had her hand over her mouth, while Dara and Jacan examined the new wineskin with eager hands. They thought they were the only ones that Elohim had created. Maybe there was a mistake. Naava's first guess was that her family was no longer special. Elohim had made others, just like them, to work the land and be His laborers. He had no particular affinity toward them, ex-actly; He simply loved to create, and create He did, because, look, there were more of them. Her second guess was maybe He *did* love them after all and had seen fit to send them companions, or better yet, friends. More like themselves, more faces who could take away the infernal repetition of life in the desert, for it was outrageously dissatisfying to Naava, day after day, seeing and doing the same things over and over again.

"There will be problems," said Adam gravely. "They are very different from us. They look different, act different. Speak differently."

"Father's irritated," said Cain, his face unfolding like a newly lit star, fire and light at the same time. He pointed to his ear and said, "They wanted to know what happened to his ear."

Adam frowned.

Eve sidled up to Adam and slid her hand into his. Startled, Adam glared at her, shook his hand free, and said, "You too? Do you laugh with them, at my expense?"

Eve brought her fingers to her lips, then held them out, denying any misdeed, but Adam had already spit out what he wanted to say, what Cain had goaded him into saying, what he always said when the discussion circled and landed upon Adam's ear. "My ear would be whole if it weren't for you."

And then Cain, like a wildcat grown bored with a limp hare between its paws, said, "Mother, they've given me a gift for you." He reached into his leather bag and pulled out something white that looked like the figure of a woman—firm breasts, taut pregnant belly, and legs that were smoothed into a cylinder, nice for holding.

Adam sighed, shook his head, and sat down on the courtyard bench with his head buried in his hands.

Eve reached for the figure, puzzlement on her face, and traced her finger across its head, its neck, its belly. "It's stone," she said.

Cain shrugged his shoulders and gestured to Eve's swollen belly. "Alabaster. For the baby." He looked to Adam for help. "We're not entirely sure what it is, but when we tried to explain with our hands"—here he stretched his fingers over his belly—"that you were with child, a woman pushed this into my hands, rubbed her stomach, and folded her hands in front of it, mumbling a mess of words I couldn't understand."

"I think it's something they pray to, for help," said Adam, still not looking up.

Eve looked startled, and that's when Naava said, "There are men *and* women gods?"

"Elohim has a wife?" Eve said.

"It's *not* Elohim," Adam said. He lifted his face defiantly. He jabbed his hand at the statue. "Look at it. It's made of stone. Worthless, really. How could anyone expect something like that to help them?" He actually glowered at Eve's obvious interest in the stone woman, Naava thought. "I could eat a mule! Aya, where's my bowl?"

Aya brought Adam some olives and barley bread and sat next to him. "Father, do they have someone who knows herbs?"

Naava saw Adam's nostrils flare, which he did whenever he was on the verge of losing control. After all, this sudden intrusion of people had startled everyone, including him, and this fact seemed to only irritate him. "You're not going anywhere, do you understand? You're staying right here, with your mother." And to Eve, he said, "It's not safe. We don't know who they are or what they want yet."

Eve nodded but didn't answer. She was caressing the little stone woman with her fingers.

Naava let her mind concoct fabulous images of these strange people. She imagined they were beautiful. She imagined they were fascinating creatures, not a dull bone in their bodies. She imagined what they would think of her, upon first glance.

Right then, Naava resolved that Eve's baby sling would become a new robe for herself. For one could not visit such marvelous people in the rags Naava wore every day.

Aya

Hello, morning. Hello, sun, sliding up out of the blackness. I'm up here—invisible! This is partly because I'm up so high, like a bird in the sky, and partly because my family's just beginning to wake. Cain doesn't know I climb his date palms, and I don't intend to tell him. Besides, who would guess I could shinny up here?

If I had wings, I would swoop down from this tree and fly to the north. I would follow the green riverbanks of the great muddy Euphrates to the rugged mountains and shaggy pines where Mother and Father came from. There I would search for the flaming light that blazes the way back to the Garden. I would ask Elohim to let my parents come back, and I would beg Him for a good-as-new foot.

Father likes to joke that if anyone wants a view here in the Land between Two Rivers, just stand on a log. There are two giant rivers that wind down from the mountains in the north. When the snow on the mountains melts, the water tears through the countryside like a horde of locusts. Sometimes it overtops the riverbanks and drowns our crops and floods our house. Other times, it rushes on past and deposits silt and sand, which we have to dig out. There's no way to prepare for this. During the summer months, when the water trickles through, we cut trenches in between the willows and tamarisks and poplars so the river can water our crops.

And if the water doesn't destroy our crops, the mice, moths, snails, or fungi will. Believe it or not, it's the smallest vermin that do the most damage.

This is where I sit in the gray morning light, in one of Cain's date palms on top of a levee created by the melting snows. I am surrounded by forty palm trees, twenty-one fruit trees, a crop of baby emmer wheat and barley, and too many rows of vegetables to count—beets, turnips, leeks, onions, garlic, watercress, cabbage, and cucumbers.

Look. There go five gazelles, rumps flashing in the distance, their white flanks giving them away. And there. A flamingo stands on one leg, balancing its precious pink life.

Our house is set back a bit from the river. There are six rooms—Mother and Father's room, a pantry for dried herbs and preserved things, a store-room for wines and vinegars of all sorts, Naava's weaving room, a sleeping room for the girls, and a sleeping room for the boys. They are attached like arms and legs to the courtyard, which is where we eat and cook and labor when it's not raining. The cistern is on this side of the house, as is Mother's garden—a perfect haven of lush green vegetation and flowers abloom with brilliant color. Father planted it for her, to replace the Garden they left . . . or were banished from, however you look at it. Abel's pens for his sheep and goats are on the far side, away from the river.

Cain has come up with a plan, after the other night. I heard Father and him talking, in low voices, while I slapped dough onto the sides of the *tinûru* for the morning meal. Cain called the strange people "visitors," for that's what we thought they were—sojourners who would be moving on—because why would they want to share land with us when there was plenty for the taking? Cain tried to convince Father of the "learning possibilities" and "sharing capabilities" that we could have with them. He even suggested that he could teach these new people about flower dust. The way Cain described it to us the night they returned drunk to the courtyard was: "I couldn't believe my eyes, my tongue. Father and I were eating these things they were passing off as dates, but they were as scrawny and crisp as ants. I knew why. They don't know about flower dust!"

Father argued that we couldn't be sharing all our secrets, since that would mean we'd have no power and no leverage.

"Leverage for what?" Cain said, insisting they were nice people in an odd sort of way, but Father exclaimed, "Did you see the heavy yellow jewelry they were wearing? The shiny pots? The colored stones? They have more to offer than we do, my son."

Cain grew quiet then, but I could tell he was simmering like the broth in my cook pot.

"We'll keep to ourselves," said Father. "We don't know if they are friend or foe."

"But—" said Cain.

Father beetled his brow and glared at Cain. "You will do as I say. Is that so much? We don't know what they are capable of."

Cain stomped off like an angry boar and yelled back over his shoulder, "They'll think us simple!"

Father looked at me then, his fist halfway to his mouth and full of the barley bread I had made. I was the only one left in the courtyard with him. I scared him, I think, for he cast his eyes about him, like he was lost and a little embarrassed at our aloneness. Mother said that when she had presented me to him, his eighth child, after three others had been buried in Mother's garden, he made a face at me and said, "She will be of no use to us, her foot that way." But Mother said, "You'll see. She'll pull her weight."

That's how I came to be the cook, and I am eleven years now. My education began as soon as I could speak. I learned quickly, surpassing Mother's knowledge after only several years. I discover new plants and new weeds all the time, and I take great delight in bestowing clever names upon them. I collect bulbs—garlic, onion, and leek—and seasonings—nigella, anise, mustard, marjoram, cumin, coriander, and mint. I test the medicinal properties of plants like cassia and thyme, myrtle and asafetida. I catch fish with my bare hands. I dig up shellfish and crustaceans from the muck and scour them in the river. I churn butter from warm milk and press oils from the sesame seed and olive fruit, delicious for dipping and cooking. I harvest salt from the dry crusted soil and steal the thick sweetness found in honeycombs. I use a grinding stone to crush barley and wheat seed down to a sort of downy flour with which to make bread. By accident, I discovered that by soaking barley seeds in water I could make a beer that eased the tension between Cain and Abel, and recently I found that, miracle of miracles, the sap from the palm tree does this too.

All in all, if something happens to me, my family will die of starvation. Well, maybe not starvation, but serious deprivation. This is a comfort to me, strangely enough. Why should I feel secure in such a small kernel of knowledge? I'll tell you why. I am counting on them needing me too much to send me away or, worse, discarding me as easily as Abel does his crippled or flawed animals, even though *discarding* is such a clean word for what Abel actually does.

He calls it *culling*, and, in truth, it must be done—I know this—but it's still hard to watch.

Once, when I was in my fourth year, I begged Abel to let me help with the lambing. I, being a sentimental goose then, thought it would be pleasant and clean and easy.

It was not.

At the new moon, Abel had plucked the wool from the ewes, and now their bellies swayed with the weight of their babies. He interrupted my bread baking one afternoon.

"They're starting," he said.

I looked at Mother, who was churning milk.

"Go along," she said, smiling. "I'll watch your bread."

Abel turned to Mother. "I need oil."

Mother hopped up and ran to the larder. She came back with a delicate thin-necked clay jar with a knobbed stopper on it and gave it to him.

Abel nodded in thanks and held out his hand to me. His palm was like leather, and his fingers pressed firmly into my own. It was then I first felt his commitment to this thing he had to do, and another commitment to me, his younger sister, to show me how it was done. For a moment I felt privileged. To think: I could help Abel, my brother who was as steady as a tree, as accountable as the sun, as wise as the moon.

I smiled and hobbled after my thick-legged brother—I had often thought of him as a bear or an ox—and asked him *which one* and *how many* and *what can I do?*

There were two ewes down, their noses pointing up, their bellies heaving. One of them had expelled its purplish water bag; the second one was still straining. The other sheep *baa*ed.

"What's that?" I said, wrinkling my nose.

"The lamb's private sea," he said.

"Oh," I said, although I didn't understand.

Abel removed the stopper from the clay jar and poured oil over his right hand and arm.

"Hold this," he said, handing me the jar. He situated himself at the rear of the struggling ewe and shoved his hand and arm into her.

I cringed. I had not seen this done, not even in the one stubborn birth I had seen of Mother's, that of my sister Miriam, who came out like a shriveled grape with a knot in her cord. "Doesn't that hurt her?" I said.

"It'll hurt her more if we can't get her baby out." Abel grunted and turned his arm inside her. "I can't find—" he said. "Hand me that rope. On the wall."

The rope was thrown over a wooden nail, and I retrieved it.

By this time, the other ewe was licking her lamb's slick body clean.

Abel looked up at me and nodded over at the lamb. "Take the flint—no, to your left—and cut off the cord just a short way from the navel, about the length of your little finger. Think you can do that?" His hand was still in the ailing ewe, but this time the rope was too.

I took the flint in my hand and approached the newborn lamb cautiously. I looked at my little finger, then back at the helpless lamb. *Would the mother bite? Would I do it right? Would it hurt the baby if I didn't do as Abel asked?*

Abel cried out behind me and said something I didn't understand. I looked over to see him pulling a limp and wheezing lamb from his ewe. Abel wiped its nose and mouth clean. But still the lamb wheezed.

"What's wrong?" I cried, leaving behind my assignment and coming over to comfort the poor lamb. "What's wrong?" I said again, leaning down to touch it with my hands. "Hello, little lamb. Wake up. There, there . . ." I cooed.

"Its lungs are filled with water," Abel said. He sighed and knelt beside the ewe, who was now searching for her child. "I'm sorry," he said, stroking the ewe's head and face. "I tried everything." He picked up the sickly lamb and said to me, "Don't be frightened. It has to be done." He took the lamb a short distance away from the mother and laid it on the barley straw. He looked at me. "Have you cut the cord on that one?" he asked kindly.

I shook my head. I did not move.

I don't know what I expected. A miracle? That the lamb would get up and walk? That Abel would be able to mend the lamb's burdened breaths?

Oh, but I couldn't know.

Abel took the lamb's little head in his hands and twisted, fast, in one direction, and I heard a sharp *snap,* like the crack of a dry reed. The newborn lamb slumped. A blue hush fell over the pen. Mumbling a prayer, Abel gently released the lamb's head onto the straw. He stood up and came over to me. He wiped furiously at his eyes with a shrug of his shoulder. "Now," he said, "let's see if we can get this one taken care of." He took the flint from my trembling hand and severed my lamb's cord—there, like that, with the same swiftness he had used on the other.

"You *killed* it," I said, with accusation in my voice.

Abel said nothing.

"It could have gotten better. You'd see. I could have taken care of it, kept it warm by my fire." My voice rose to a cry. "It could have lived." Then, in disbelief and anger, I put my hands on my hips and said, in the most adamant voice I could muster, "*Someone* has to protect them."

Despite the evidence of his reddened nose and the wetness of his eyes, Abel laughed and said, "Aya, my sister, do you think everything is meant to live? Some babies die. Remember Mother's babies? The ones she buried in her garden? I will die one day. You will die one day. We will all return to the dust from which we were made." I had heard Mother and Father referring to this as one of the edicts Elohim had uttered upon their expulsion from the Garden, and here it was again, in the mouth of my murderous brother.

With that, he went back to the newborn lamb, who was now dry and sucking on the front knee of the ewe. "See?" he said. "This one could use your help. He can't find his mother's teat. Perhaps you could show him. Squirt a little milk into his mouth to get him going."

I contemplated this. Yes, certainly I was needed. I could see that. But this was a trap, to make me forget what I had seen.

What if Mother had done that to me? No one would have known. A quick jerk of the neck, *snap,* and she would have been rid of her mangled little daughter. A slight dusting—*smack smack*—of the hands, and back to cooking; that's how easy it would have been.

"Why are you pouting?" said Abel.

It came upon me suddenly, in a gush—a river of tears, like juice squeezed from Father's grapes.

"Why, whatever is wrong?" said Abel, reaching up to place his hand on my back. I imagined he felt the tiny bones between my shoulder blades, my tucked-in wings—for I had already dreamed of flying, me being Aya the Bird.

"Don't you see?" I whispered finally. "You would have killed *me.*"

Abel studied my face a moment and blew out a breath of air from his puffed-up cheeks. "Aya, you think too much. That lamb would not have lasted the night. He was too weak. You, however"—he looked me up and down—"are . . ." He paused, trying to find the right word, the right meaning.

"Crippled," I said.

"Yes," he said. He looked me straight in the eyes as he said this, searching for my response. He had agreed with me, acknowledged the label I placed upon myself, and had not immediately apologized for it, like Cain would have, in a quick attempt to cover an embarrassing blunder. Abel treated me as someone who was . . . well, whole. "But," he continued, "that is the way Elohim wanted you. Do you believe that?"

I nodded, half believing, half *wanting* to believe. But also I wanted to ask, *Why?*

In Abel's defense, he had given me a hobbling goat as a gift, and she follows me wherever I go, so I know he speaks the truth—he will spare a cripple once in a while.

So, as I stood in the courtyard that night, after Cain had stomped out, I saw an opportunity to impress Father, a small moment of time in which I might convince him to understand me just as I understood myself. I had no idea how to do it, though. Here I had been given a gift, and I couldn't, for the life of me, think of anything to say, to do. I stood, mute and unmoving.

Father's eyes shifted uneasily after Cain's squared shoulders and barrel of a neck, then shifted back to me. He laughed suddenly and said, "Aya, you've done it again. Delicious." In the withering light, his face was full of shadows. I could not read his eyes.

I bowed and scurried to remove his plate.

I scold myself when I act like a mouse. *Why do I care what Father wants?* Am I not Aya, the beautiful magnificent bird who can fly away from here in her dreams? Aya, the girl who holds the staff of life in her hands. Aya, Goat Owner.

Dara

I put my hand on Mama's fat belly, and I feel something go bump. I clap my hand over my mouth, surprised, and Mama says it's the baby inside her. She says that's how me and Jacan were—tiny tiny in her belly.

I ask, "How did we get out of you? Like the baby sheep get out of their mamas?"

"Yes," says Mama.

"Did we look that bad?" I say.

Mama laughs and says, "Yes."

I'm holding a turtle, a gift from Jacan. I'm jealous of Jacan because he gets to go with Abel and watch the sheep and the goats. Abel is a nice brother—he gave Jacan a horn to blow, and I always hear it, blasting in the distance, and Mama laughs and says, "That boy. I'm going to hide that thing from him one of these days!"

Mama is lying down on her back, on a bench in the courtyard. Her middle looks like a termite hill, and she holds one arm over her face, so the sun doesn't hurt her eyes. She says, "In the Garden, there was thick moss over the forest floor. To lie on it was divine."

"Why didn't you bring some of it here?" I ask, stroking the turtle's shell. That's it, I'll name him Turtle, like Aya's name for Goat.

"I didn't know how far we were going," says Mama.

"Oh," I say. "Look, Mama, a butterfly." I pick the butterfly up by its wings. It's got all sorts of colors on it, blue like Mama's eyes and yellow and shiny green. It tries to fly away, but I trap it between my fingers. I stuff it in one of my pots, the ones I make in the fire. I have a plan—it's a secret— to save special things for the baby. Already I have: number one, turtle; number two, butterfly; number three, swirly agate; and number four, pomegranate. These are all the things the baby will get from me, its big sister, when it comes out.

Aya's making lots of noise. She pours some grain onto a stone, then pushes another stone across it, back and forth, back and forth—*shup shup shup*—until it looks like the fluffy part of a dandelion. Her baby goat is black and has white ears and a white mouth, and it tries to eat her hard work. Aya shoves her away and says, "Find your own food."

I call out to Goat, but Aya frowns and says, "Make yourself useful and get me some dung for the fire, why don't you?"

Mama sits up and says, "That sounds good. Up we go."

Suddenly, the lapwing nesting under the eaves sings a warning.

There's a loud noise on the road. Donkeys, it looks like, with people— *other people!*—on them. So these are Father and Cain's people. *What do they want?* They're coming here, to our house. They have a lamb too, and they're leading it by a rope.

"Mama," I say. "Why are they coming here?"

Mama stands up and shields her eyes. She squints. Her forehead is wrinkled with worry, and she *tsk-tsk*s for me to come to her right now. Aya stops her grinding and comes to stand next to me. Mama stands me up on the bench and wraps her arms around me. I tippy-toe to see better. I remember Father saying that he doesn't know if the strangers are friend or *foe*. I don't know what that means. All I know is: There are four ladies— I can count them—and they're very pretty, like Naava.

The lady at the front clicks her tongue when her donkey reaches the courtyard gate. The donkey stops, and the lady gets off. She's wrapped in yellow robes that move like feather grass. Around her neck is a string of white shells. She has a yellow ring about her forehead and black lines around her eyes, and her nose has a funny yellow hoop in it.

I point to the lady's nose and say, "What's that?"

Mama slaps at my hand. Surprised, I move away from her and put my fingers in my mouth. *Why did Mama hit me?*

Yellow Lady kneels down in front of me and takes my hand and lets me touch the hoop in her nose. Oh, and see, she's got a hole in her nose too. I don't know how it got there, but the hoop is pretty, and I like it very much. Yellow Lady smells like cinnamon and aloe.

Naava comes out from her weaving to see the ladies. She grasps at the lady's robes shyly, and the lady smiles at her.

Naava says to Mama, "Feel them. They're so soft."

Mama claps her hands. "Aya, darling, will you bring some honey water and some figs?" But she never looks away from the ladies.

Yellow Lady looks at Aya, who is moving toward her pantry, and her face turns white like Goat's mouth. She makes some strange clicking noises at the other ladies, and they frown and chatter like crickets. Yellow Lady shoos Aya away with her hand, and Aya looks upset and all confused and limps into the shadows.

Yellow Lady smiles and bows. Mama bows too and shows the lady with her hands that she and her other ladies should sit on the reed mats. They do, except for a lady with big bosoms. She lifts her hands to the sky, like she's trying to hold it up. She tilts her face up to the sun and closes her eyes and begins to moan and sing at the same time. It sounds like sheep's bleating and crow's crowing, all rolled into one. Her chin wobbles. She sways back and forth, back and forth. After a long time, she puts down her hands and brings out a knife from the folds of her robe.

I can't help it. I gasp and move closer to Mama, and she pulls me tight against her. But the knife is flashing in the sun, and suddenly it slices across the throat of the lamb Bosom Lady has brought with her. The lamb's eyes grow still, its head flops, and blood spurts *everywhere*. I can't look. I hide my face in Mama's robe.

Mama squeezes my shoulder, then stands up. She holds her hand out and says, "Oh, that isn't necessary. I shall bring us some bread and dates."

The ladies ignore Mama. Two of them turn the lamb over on its back and stretch its legs out. Bosom Lady cuts right through the sheep's belly, and its insides poke out. They look like curled-up snakes. She reaches in and pulls out the sheep's liver, brown and steaming. Her hands are smeared with blood.

I scrunch up my face and whisper, "Mama, what's she doing?"

Bosom Lady lays the liver on the ground in front of her gingerly and plunks herself down in front of it. She sighs deeply. The lamb's carcass is forgotten.

Naava looks at Mama and says, "Should I get Aya to cook it?"

Mama shakes her head. Her eyes are as big as ostrich's eggs.

Naava gasps and says, "Does she expect us to eat it . . . like that?"

Mama looks like she might be sick. She says, "Please, let me get some figs."

Yellow Lady motions for Mama to sit, and she does. Naava and I do too. Mama holds me close. I can feel her heart beat fast fast fast underneath her robes.

Bosom Lady leans over the liver and grunts like a boar. She cuts into the liver, a long straight line, then looks up at Naava, at me, at Mama, and back down again. She studies that lump of liver for a very long time.

Yellow Lady puts her hand on her belly and points to Mama.

Mama nods and says, "With child."

"Wit chile," says Yellow Lady, like she's got something in her mouth.

Suddenly Bosom Lady claps her hands. A hawk calls from the sky. I'm afraid of Bosom Lady. Bosom Lady is big and ferocious and carries a long shiny knife. Mama squeezes me like Aya presses her dates.

Bosom Lady clucks like a pigeon and points to Naava.

Naava looks at Mama. Mama looks at Naava and crinkles up her forehead. She shakes her head at Bosom Lady and shrugs her shoulders.

Bosom Lady points to Naava again and makes a cradle in front of her like she's rocking a baby, but there *is* no baby.

Mama lets go of me. She waves her hands, no no no, and puts them on her belly. "She has to stay here, to take care of the baby," she says. "I cannot spare her. She does too much work around here."

"What?" says Naava, her mouth opening like a cave. "They want *me*?"

Mama hushes Naava and whispers to her, "I'm not sure."

Bosom Lady claps her hands again and frowns. She makes little circles in the air, and the other women bring out sacks of wonderful things from inside their robes, which they spill out onto the table—bracelets and jars and wine and cloth.

Mama says, "I think they want a caretaker . . . for their children, and I'm afraid what will happen if I say no. We'll stall them a bit and talk to your father."

Naava's face wrinkles up, then it's flat again. I hear her *hmmph,* a *hmmph* that means she is thinking about things. Then Naava grabs Mama's arm and says, "I'll go. Tell them I'll go." She's smiling and nodding and begging. "I'll learn how they make their cloth. *Please,* Mother."

"We don't even know them," says Mama. The ladies get more excited. They talk louder and reach for Naava. Mama wrings her hands. Then she turns to the ladies and points to me. She says, "Her. She's a hard worker, that one." To Naava, she hisses, "Leave this to me."

I stare at Mama, and my eyes get real big. *Why, what is Mama doing? She is giving me to them and not even asking me if I want to go!* I can see Mama talking with her hands, I can hear her words, but this is not good, not good at all, and I have a scary feeling, right here in my stomach, and I press down on it, to make it go away.

Naava is staring at Mama too. She grinds her teeth. "She's only a child," she says to Mama.

"Yes, Mama," I say. "I don't want to go. I have to get dung for Aya's fire, and, look, see?" I point to my collecting pot. "I'm making presents for the baby." I point to the clay pots around the fire. "And I have to keep making pots for Aya. She needs me."

Mama ignores me. She keeps her eyes on the visitors and says, "She knows how to milk a goat, pick up dung, make sturdy pottery. She'll do nicely."

I see Naava's eyes. They are like two points of fire. My words rush out of me, fast, like the water in the river. "Naava can go, Naava can go." Mama is getting blurry, and my cheeks are all wet.

Naava pulls on Mama's elbow again. "You *know* I can do a better job."

Mama looks at her and says, "Naava, not now. I will not discuss this with you now. Go on." She waves her hand across the courtyard toward Naava's weaving room.

Naava's mouth makes an O shape. She stands up and crosses her arms. She leans over and spits on me.

Mama turns and reaches up to grab Naava's hand. She squeezes it tightly, to hurt her.

Naava squeals and tries to pull away, but she can't.

Mama squeezes tighter and says, "You will do as I say." She lets go of Naava's hand, and Naava sighs loudly enough for everyone to hear. She keeps sighing as she goes back to her weaving room.

Mama is still pointing at me, and I want to hide so no one can see me. All of the four ladies are around me now. They smile and laugh and pinch my cheeks. They babble to one another, and I can't understand what they're saying.

With a stick, Bosom Lady makes the mark of a half-moon in the dirt at her feet and circles it.

"Half-moon," Mama says, and nods. "She will be ready."

I can't see all the gifts they give to Mama, but when Bosom Lady shoves a sparkly black stone in my hand, all shiny like a raven's wing, I remember Mama's precious black seeds in the jar under the ground. Mama's secrets, wrapped up so tight no one can find them.

Eve

Eden is a distant memory, yet it persists, under the skin, like a mosquito bite. It has been so long ago now that Adam and I lived in the Garden that, often, I wonder if it was just a passing dream or a figment of my imagination. The mind is a tricky thing. Perhaps I have made the Garden grander over time. Perhaps I myself, in body and soul, have changed.

I think it is the latter. It is natural to treat something or someone with disdain—your husband, for instance—if you have changed, if you have embarked upon a different road than he has, because he is stagnant and you are renewed. Or consider this: If you have left a place of contentment and naïveté, then life will seem harder than before, because you *know* more, you *feel* more, not necessarily because anything external has changed. You know that once you were happy; now you're not. You know that once you were replete; now you're not.

That is how it was with me.

I must go back even further.

I shall begin with the waking. In the dewy light of morning, with the shafts of light driving down through the Garden's canopy, I woke on a bed of spongy moss, entwined with a warm, slumbering being. Of course, all of these things—moss, warmth, light—were just impressions I could not name. I lay very still, absorbing this . . . thing . . . in front of me. As yet I had no self-perception, because I could not know myself except in relationship to something similar.

I now have names for everything I saw and felt. At that moment, I did not.

The silvery air was alive with birdsong and the thrum of insects, a triumphant chorus raised in joy, for me, for him, for this new union. It was as though the forest had a pulse, and I could feel it here, in my chest and in my bones. The wind raked through the clacking bamboo thicket, setting its leaves to quaking and rustling. The orchids clung with tentacled fastness to the bamboos, and their sweet, cloying smell wafted upon the breeze. There were so many kinds of green—light, dark, fuzzy, pointed—and enough color in the flowers and shrubbery to outdo any sunrise or sunset thereafter.

Adam shone.

That is the best I can describe it. He was different, somehow, than the trees and birdsong and colors and wind that surrounded me, perhaps more relevant to me, once I recognized our similarities. His skin and his face glowed as though the light of the sun itself were a garment. He was a garden spring, a refreshing well of water. He was a tree, strong and able, with a bunched force across his arms and chest. The hair on his head and chin and chest was dark and clumped, like clusters of dates, his nose long and sloped. His lips were apricots, sweet and honeyed. I confess, I licked them with my tongue, gently, as you would a dripping peach. I felt the very heat of him, and though I could not know *why,* I knew I wanted to wrap him about me like a cloak, to keep him close, for always, to make him mine.

He snored a little and caught himself now and then, when a fly landed on his nose and caused him to twitch.

I loved him.

I know, it is all so confusing. How could I love him if I had only just looked upon him? Do not ask me to explain, for it is beyond reason. In love, there is a little bit of peace, a little bit of pleasure, and a little bit of solidarity. What makes a bee love a rose? My heart brimmed over as a bromeliad does after a rain, and I knew he was mine. Later, I would have to share him with the children, and as we grew into our roles as parents, we often forgot we started here, in the Garden.

Alone.

Content.

Adam opened his eyes, black as obsidian, and gazed into mine for the first time. He smiled and, with his finger, traced my lips and nose and eyebrows. My thighs grew warm; my belly clenched.

"So," he said. "You've come." His voice was raspy from a long sleep. He glanced down where our bellies pressed together and drew me closer. "Elohim said you would." His breath was musty, stale.

I must have looked confused, because he continued. "He said He would give me a companion, a friend, made from my very flesh, and He has done so. I did not know how He would do it."

"There is another one of you?" I said. I heard my voice, like an echo, and it confused me for a moment. *What was this flow of breath that formed itself into odd, staccato sounds?* How strange it felt! *And how was it that I could understand Adam's breath?*

Adam chortled. He was giddy now. "Before, I was a stale pool; now I am a rushing river. You are bone of my bones and flesh of my flesh. You are woman; I am man."

I did not understand all that he was saying; his words overlapped so. It seemed that I was a planned thing, something dreamed up by Adam and this Elohim. I understood that I was no longer *with* Adam; I was *for* Adam. It was a huge disappointment to me, and I instinctively recoiled. At that moment, I couldn't have told you what *disappointment* was. I simply felt different than I had moments before, as if all the gladness was emptied out of me and poured upon the mossy ground.

He looked puzzled. He asked what was wrong.

I explained as best I could, but he only laughed at me and pulled me back into the folds of his arms.

"Truly, you jest," Adam said. "We were made *for each other*. Elohim says—"

"Who is this Elohim?" I asked, perturbed that Adam should have another friend.

"Elohim is . . ." Adam paused and studied my face. "Elohim is the one who created this garden and everything in it." He looked up, through the tree branches, then back at me. "Elohim made me from a handful of dust. You, from myself." He pointed to his side.

"Me? From you?" I said. I looked down at his abdomen, at mine, back to his, incredulous. His abdomen looked darker than mine, but still it was smooth, unbroken. "How?"

Adam's eyebrows came together like two caterpillars nudging noses. He sat up and felt his body. "I don't know. I don't feel any different." Between his legs, his sex was like a wilted branch, I noticed, so unlike my own. His chest was flatter and hairier than mine.

He stared at me, taking in my entire length.

I was not embarrassed. Rather, I fully enjoyed his obvious pleasure.

Here is the strange thing: Although my body ached to be embraced, there was this breach between us, which I shall call *respect* for lack of a better term. It was as though we recognized that there were other things worthy of sorting out before we relished each other physically.

Does this make sense?

Looking back on it now, it was as though we understood that we wanted to *know* each other first, then abandon ourselves in each other, which would, in turn, cause a vulnerability that would only enhance the relationship we already had. Our physical drive was only a facet of the whole *us*—simply an extension, you might say, of the depth of our feeling. If our love were a tree, then our physical drive would be a branch or a root—giving life certainly but, even more than that, providing a different form of expression than, perhaps, a leaf or a fruit.

How did we know that?

I know not. But it was there, in both of our hearts.

So it was not until later that we drank our fill from each other.

I was sitting on a grassy mound in a field, feeding a sparrow from my hand, when Adam came up behind me and shooed the sparrow away. Surprised, I looked up at him. "Why?" I said. "Its beak, it was—"

Adam pushed me down the knoll and fell on top of me. He laughed.

"What are you doing?" I asked.

"I have seen the animals Being One," he said, his voice quickening. His fingers ran through my hair, over my nipples, and, oh, down my thighs.

"Being One?" I said, confused.

"Yes," he said. He pushed up with his arms and adjusted his sex, which had grown, like a roll of warm bread pressed between us.

"What is it?" I said, alarmed. "Why has it changed?"

Adam laughed and rolled off me. "Turn over," he said.

I did.

He lay on top of me, on my back, and patted my legs apart with his knees. "The animals. They do it like this." He reached for the slipperiness between my legs, and as he probed, a warm ache spread from my groin to my back. I felt him enter me then, and it was an odd sensation, like the depths of me were being plumbed. He moved gently. "Ah," he said. He groaned, as if with pleasure.

I felt only squashed. "No," I cried.

Adam grew still. "I am hurting you?"

I shoved him off and turned. "Can we not do it facing each other?"

Adam looked at me blankly.

"I want to look at you. See your face."

Hope flickered in Adam's eyes once again, and he quickly slid on top of me.

And here I will try to be as faithful to my feelings as I can. I was utterly terrified and wholly astonished. That we were pressed *together*. At first I felt torn asunder; the pain was unexpected. But just as rain is replaced by sunlight, the pain shifted into slow, pleasurable waves across my belly—so pleasurable, in fact, that I felt I must hold on lest I disappear altogether. It was in this twilit, half-there place that I realized the sincerity—the right-ness—of *us*, Adam and me. I should have been breathless with exertion, but all I felt was a deep tranquillity. All I could see were Adam's eyes, which spoke of love and desire and passion.

I held him close. I tightened and flexed against him and wrapped my legs about him. I caressed his skin. He bent to kiss me, and his kisses were as flower petals, his touch was as shade and water, and, oh, then I, too, shuddered with delight. Such a fire as ours could never be quenched! I felt as though I were plunged under a waterfall, breathless at the cool rush of water and delirious with the fullness of it all. I found my pleasure, and it left me exhausted and happy. *Oh, if this is Elohim's doing, I want more of it,* I thought.

Adam said later that he had seen the animals Being One as he named them, and it brought a tremendous loneliness and sadness upon him. What is life if you have no one to share it with?

Afterward, we basked in the coolness of the Garden. Adam handed me a small orange orb, and I took it, rolling it in my hands.

"What is it?" I asked. Its flesh was bumpy and waxy.

Adam looked at it and shrugged. "Give it a name." He showed me how to put it to my mouth. I did, but it was bitter and pithy, and I winced. "That might be one you have to peel," he said. He grabbed it out of my hands and dug his thumb deep into the fruit, tearing away the fibrous outsides. "There," he said, handing it back. "Try that." And this time it was softer, much sweeter, and the juice dripped down my chin. It broke away in sections, separated by membranes, and I laughed to think of all there was to learn.

"Mmmm," I said. "Are they all this sweet?"

We did this with green tender fruits, and red tart fruits, and brown mushy fruits, for that's what Adam called them. I told him we should make distinctions between the fruits, so we called them avocados and pomegranates and figs. As we tasted and named, Elohim appeared.

I have described the Garden to my children as lush and inviting and never-ending, but this moment of meeting Elohim—of Elohim Himself—is always harder to explain, for I have not the proper words for it, even now, and I do not want Him to appear as a comical oddity. His raiments were as the lights of the sky, one hundred times over, and His exuberant presence filled the air like myrrh. Even the plants and animals seemed to stretch toward Him, as if they could suckle directly from His outstretched arms. It was as though He was in the heavens and on earth all at once, even though He was there, in bodily form, in front of Adam and me.

"Adam," He said, "you have found your counterpart."

Adam nodded exuberantly, and I found myself growing warm all over again. "Thank you," said Adam, gripping my hand tightly, as though I might be taken away.

Elohim smiled at me, and for me, it was like a thousand flowers opening for the first time. "Come. I want to show you something."

I approached Him slowly.

"Be not afraid," He said in a low voice.

I came to stand by His side. I held my breath, I think, out of sheer awe of Him.

"Do you like the Garden?" He asked.

I nodded. I could not, at first, find my words—*how had I spoken so easily with Adam?*

Elohim gestured to everything around us. "I've made *everything* for you—the birds in the sky, the beasts in the field, the fish in the sea, every tree, every plant, everything for you." Here, He bent over and picked up a handful of dirt. Elohim took great pleasure in it, as a potter would. You could see that. He held it up and let it tumble through His fingers—or what looked to me like fingers. Then again, I could only know Him in relationship to what I knew so far, and that was as someone like Adam and me. Now I'm not so sure what I saw.

Elohim turned to Adam. "Plant your seed, Adam, so that you may be as prolific as the lilies of the field." He touched my cheek. "Blessed woman, you will be mother of all, queen over dominions. Work in the Garden to keep it, maintain it. It will provide you with endless inspiration, for I want you to be happy." Elohim's eyes were soft, kind. "Cleave to each other—you are as one flesh now."

"That's it," cried Adam. He turned to me, his face glowing. "That is your name."

"Name?" I said. I'm sure I looked perplexed.

Adam cocked his head, thinking. "I am Adam, *adamah,* earth. You are . . ." He closed his eyes. "Eve . . . mother of all living."

Elohim smiled. He seemed pleased with Adam's naming.

I offered Elohim one of the figs, full of sweetness, but He refused. *Did He eat?* I did not know.

"There is one thing," He said. "You know I have given you everything in this Garden to eat of, to enjoy, even the Tree of Life." He pointed to the center of the Garden, to a tree with delicate magenta blossoms and heavy green foliage. It blazed as if on fire, its petals pooled with brightness. Here, He frowned. "But see *that* tree, there, next to the river?" He pointed to a tall, thorny tree with green-blue fanlike leaves that gushed out of the top of it like a fountain. Orbs of red-brown fruit clung to one another, clustered high up on the trunk.

Adam and I nodded sleepily, for we had greatly exerted ourselves in our Being One.

"Of this one tree, the Tree of the Knowledge of Good and Evil, you may *not* eat, because on the day that you eat, you will surely die."

"Die?" I said.

Elohim thought awhile. He stooped to pick up a dead fig branch from the ground. Its dry, wilted leaves chattered. He gave it a hard look and twirled it between His thumb and fingers. He continued. "This twig represents one form of death, or dying, in which this part of the tree is not connected to its life source anymore—the tree, the ground, and its roots—so it withers and dies. There is another sort of death, my children, that comes . . . with all this." He waved His hand around to include all the splendor about us. Elohim looked off in the distance. "It causes me much consternation."

Adam sat down at Elohim's feet and looked up at Him. "You are Elohim," Adam said. "You can do anything. You are not bound by anyone."

I sat by Adam, leaning into him, my arms embracing my legs. I would come to find that whenever Elohim was present, my heart stilled, and although I had questions to ask, I did not feel an urgency to them—meaning simply that the questions did not burrow holes or tunnels in my heart. That would happen much later, when I felt I could *not* ask Him.

Elohim appeared sad, somewhat reserved, and contemplative. "By creating you, I am bound, in that I cannot hold you fast. I cannot make decisions for you. I cannot make you love me." He threw the fig branch on the ground and brushed His hands together, to rid them of dirt. "Choices have consequences—some desirable, some not. You, of course, will not understand this until you *have* to make a choice."

Adam sat cross-legged, open and free, almost as if he were too familiar with Elohim. I watched him with interest but kept my ear turned toward Elohim.

"There is another type of death, and it has to do with your vision, or, rather, your perception of things. Right now you have a greater desire for me than for your passions or your desires. You trust me, and I trust you. A beautiful and fulfilling place to be." He looked at Adam, then I felt His gaze on me. "But soon you will chafe at this. It cannot be helped. And you will have to make a choice." His voice became softer, like water in a brook. "That is why the Tree of the Knowledge of Good and Evil must exist."

Adam jumped to his feet. "Elohim! Why . . . How could we grow tired of such a place?" He held his hand out to help me up. "We love what You have made."

"Yes," I said. "We do. And You've given us each other."

Elohim wore an expression I can only describe as grief. "Yes," He said, "that I did." With this last statement, Elohim's face shifted, and I could have sworn, on the validity of Eden, that it was due to His jealousy of Adam's and my new closeness with each other. Elohim did not have such a relationship, and I wondered if, watching us, He felt the way Adam had felt watching the animals Being One. I thought upon this later and wondered why, if He could make me for Adam, did He not make a partner for Himself? Or was He already the total embodiment of both male and female?

I went to Elohim and put my hand in His. This, too, was an indescribable feeling, which I will forever be trying to interpret. I felt a pulsating radiance, a blinding surge of energy through the core of my belly—but I err, because this description sounds terrifying, and it wasn't. It was an intimate awareness of my attachment to Him, to all things around me. Everything here existed because of Elohim, the Great Gift Giver, and I was His, and He was mine. I would be *known*.

It seems silly now. But, as if to mock my unbelief, I have had these same fleeting moments on a number of occasions in my life outside the Garden. Certainly every time I lost a child. It was as though He joined me in my mourning—every bird sang my sorrow, every breeze carried my pain.

When Cain was born, when I was flushed with new creation—*is this how Elohim felt on the eve of the world?*

When Adam had come in from the fields to repair his scythe, and as he struck the flinted edge to sharpen it, he caught me staring at him. In truth, I was thinking of him in the Garden, of all the methods we invented to show our love for each other, and I blushed.

When Abel calmed the leopard who had dragged him away from our fire.

When I buried my daughter Micayla in the fertile soil of my garden. She was born with a swollen head and did not last the night. I had so wanted a girl child after Abel and after Daniel, who was born too soon; when I glimpsed her crooked form, I gasped with the pain of loving and losing. I cried out to Elohim, who, I think, caused a great peace to enter my heart.

The first time I prayed to the fertility goddess, the small statue Cain had given me from the new women. There were no lightning strikes or thunderous whirlwinds as punishment from Elohim, but in that moment I felt as one does just before a betrayal, knowing of your error but doing it anyway.

The final time was the fortuitous night when Abel's offering to Elohim exploded into flames. Elohim had heard our cries, and unlike so many other wordless and empty nights, His answer had come swiftly, upon the wings of a fiery descending star.

Elohim squeezed my hand gently, then took it and placed it in Adam's. Adam kissed me on the roundness of my cheeks, and a hush fell over the Garden, one not of our doing. It was as though we were all underwater, muffled and lethargic, awaiting the burst of light and air at the surface that would bring life to the lungs and set things aright.

Elohim floated away. I hesitate to say "floated," but that's as it appeared, and I do try to stay faithful to my perceptions at the time. Elohim's absence settled on the Garden like a temporary drought. It was like that every time He departed from our company, even worse when He threw us out of the Garden.

I cannot think of that now—it overwhelms me—but the memories continue to reappear without my bidding.

Upon our arrival here, on the alluvial plains east of the Euphrates, we lacked only one thing. We thought we had grown accustomed to the wide expanse of sky and the endless stretch of sand that surrounded us, but that first night, when we said to each other that this would be *home,* the place we would lay our heads at night, it felt strange and enormous.

Cain, being four then, complained first. "I don't like it."

I put my hand on his head, gently. "Things will look better to you in the morning."

He threw his hands up in the air. "Where are the trees and the flowers? The berries? The leeks?" Already he was growing despondent without the green things that had so fascinated him in the course of our long journey. They were his life, his blood, his breath.

Cain squatted down and scooped up a handful of sand, letting it sift through his small fingers. "So dry," he said mournfully.

Adam was lost in thought.

"Nothing will grow," said Cain.

"You still have your seeds?" said Adam.

Quickly, Cain stood and released the basket from his back.

Adam thought some more. "We start tomorrow" was all he said.

And so it happened that, although the following day was blistering hot, Adam woke with a plan. Even before we had gathered reeds for shelter, he made a few preliminary scratches in the sand and laid out the pattern, the sense of what he thought the garden should look like. I told him not to worry, that we had time, but he seemed agitated, almost driven, to have the task done. He and Cain were busy at it all morning, and then finally Adam stood and clapped Cain on the back. "Well done," Adam cried, and when I asked what they had devised, Cain replied, "No. It's a secret!" They both were rejuvenated, as though they had bathed in the coolness of the river and dined on dates and figs and warm bread.

It became a fever for both of them.

While I worked on constructing the components of our reed shelter and my little Abel napped, sun-pink and drowsy, under the ibex skin thrown over two baskets, Adam worked at digging a large hole. Although he would divulge nothing, I assumed this would be the pond. It worried me, all this backbreaking work, for the hole was a fair distance from the river. *How was he to fill it?* With our leaky reed baskets, it would be like filling a clay cup with a blade of grass. When I asked him about it, he grunted and said only, "Patience, wife."

Cain laid out all his seed packets, which we had made by folding the matching leaves into small containers, and sorted through them. He had amassed quite a collection—from the time he had discovered that seeds made shoots and shoots made plants, he had been enthralled. He had first been riveted by Adam's success at growing and extracting large, luscious strawberries from the earth in one of our travel baskets. And every step of the way, as we descended from the mountains and into the valleys, his joyful refrain of wonder echoed against the rocks: *Look how the trees change! Look how the flowers are purple!* Adam and I, of course, had collected many seeds from the Garden, and to these, Cain added his.

It was our seeds Cain was unsure of. He queried me about them when he had spread them out upon the ground. "Mama, what's this?" He held up packet after packet. "And this? Is this a vegetable or fruit? Flower or a tree?" Unfortunately, Adam and I had not thought of cataloging them, because we never considered that we might leave the Garden, so I no longer knew the mysteries of the seeds.

Except two types.

The first were those of the Tree of the Knowledge of Good and Evil, which I pointed out to Cain. I had wrapped them in a bit of wool because I knew the fibers would hold them fast, and as Cain had heard variations of the Tree Story, I think he was delighted that he held genuine proof of it. Also, I think they held some strange attraction for him, since they had come from the forbidden fruit.

The others Cain would never see. I buried them in a jar, deep in the ground, once we had settled, and I transferred them from hole to hole when we had to rebuild our shelters. They were special seeds, ones that later I regretted gathering in a spirit of rebelliousness on the afternoon of our expulsion from the Garden. Once, early in our wanderings, I had tried to use them, but I will come to that in due time.

While Adam dug and Cain sorted, I cut tall reeds from the marshes and laid them out to dry in the sun. When they had been seasoned, I bundled them together and planted them in the ground, in two rows at even intervals. I bent their tips toward each other and lashed them together—they would form the arched supports for our roof. I waded into the marsh to cut more reeds, and these I wove into mats for the top and sides. The reeds sliced into my fingers as if they were soft fruit, and soon my fingers grew stiff with scabs and calluses.

Still, Adam worked. His shoulders and arms blistered in the sun and withered with exhaustion, but his eyes flickered with determination. When he had finished with the hole, he began to dig a long trench from it toward the river. *Ah,* I thought. *He will not be able to finish such a huge task.*

But he persisted.

Abel and I would think of excuses to wander out to where he was toiling. We'd offer up small wooden bowls of fresh water from the river or raw wild onions we'd found in the marshes. The desert was not as vacant as we had originally thought. Cain had caught a duck in one of his traps the night previous—for food this time and not for torture, as it became later—and we had supped grandly.

As soon as the trench was mostly complete, with only a short squat wall remaining between it and the river, Adam began toting mud from the river-banks. Awestruck, I watched him. *What possessed this man of mine to embark upon such a colossal undertaking?* He continued day after day, lining the sides of the trench with wet mud, using his hands, which were now cracked and blistered and looked more like giant paws than hands. Again I urged him that maybe we could start small, grow from there. He became gruff with me. "It must last longer than a fortnight."

The mud baked in the sun and had a sharp, sour odor. Cracks ran through the length of it, and when I reached down and knocked on it with my knuckles to test its mettle, I was pleasantly surprised. It was as hard as stone.

Adam caught me testing it. "We don't want the water sweeping everything away."

I smiled and nodded.

Next came the planting. By then Cain was eager to help and yipped at his father's heels, ordering him about. *Those seeds go there. Those go over there.* I smiled to see Cain so happy. *He can be charming and agreeable,* I thought, *as long as he's caring for Elohim's growing things.*

We had a limited number of seeds, so although the planting was tedious, it went by quickly. What took us many moons to understand was that some plants reseeded themselves and others didn't. Cain took this as a challenge and was soon expanding our fields and crops, even beyond

Adam's original intention. We would fare well with fruits and vegetables and grains, indeed, for all the time Cain was with us.

A few bunches of seeds were spared for a reason I didn't understand until later. In fact, I saw the bulge in Cain's pouch and asked him why he was saving them—shouldn't he plant *all* the seeds? He shrugged, looked at Adam, then said, "It's a secret."

Then, late one morning, I was in our new reed house, patching up the chinks with thatch and mud, when Adam rolled up the mat that served as our entrance and asked me to come—Abel too—and he led us out to where the river ran gurgling into the trench. The pond was full. There was no greenery yet, except for Adam's lone strawberry bush, but everywhere there were sticks jutting from the sand, with hardened clay disks attached, indicating what he and Cain had planted where.

"Do you like it, Mama?" Cain exclaimed, jumping up and down.

"It's amazing," I said. Indeed it was. I could envision it now. Soon it would be full of date palms and willows and poplars. Orchids and lilies and vines. Leeks and spinach and beans. Figs and lemons and melons.

Adam nuzzled my neck and kissed me on the cheek. He squeezed my hand. "All for you, my love."

Oh, I could not contain my tears. It was like getting the Garden back again. Or at least the possibility of the Garden. I wrapped my arms around Adam's neck and whispered, "How much do you love me?"

He laughed, and the corners of his eyes crinkled with delight. He was deliriously happy, and it took me back instantly to those quiet afternoons in the Garden. "More than you'll ever know," he whispered back. He pulled away from me and grinned. "I should think you are growing a garden on your face as well." He used the back of his hand to wipe the mud from my cheek. "I think a dip in the river might be needed. Boys, shall we?"

As soon as it was green and thriving, the garden became my oasis. After toiling in the cooler morning hours, I would go to my garden and lie among the grasses and flowers and look up into the wide blue sky with nary a cloud. I would close my eyes and listen to the lilting birdsong, to the hum of crickets and frogs, to the rustling of the grasses, and to the soft *plops* in the pond. There I gave myself over to the finding of Elohim. I talked of my troubles out loud, as if to etch them in stone. I asked Elohim why eating of the forbidden fruit was so unforgivable, why He had seen fit to toss us from His presence, and why He had not appeared to us again, His children. Had He stopped loving us?

Even in the midst of this vibrant burgeoning haven, my black seeds, hidden under the ground, sometimes seemed the only real connection to the Garden that I had. They were intact, exactly as I had found them.

What I was saving them for, I knew not.

All I knew was that one day I might need them.

Aya

I'm invisible. But not so invisible that the strange visiting ladies didn't squawk and flutter like ducks when they saw my leg, so naked and exposed under my robes when I bent to pick up my quern, which I had been using to crush barley grain into flour, to go back to my pantry to retrieve some fig and date sweets for their visit. When they pointed their fingers in horror, I shrank into the dark shadows of the house, for that is what they wished. No, I'm mistaken. What they wanted was for me to suffer for my sins. Because I must have done something wrong, sometime, somewhere, to possess a foot that curls inward upon itself.

As if to justify my thinking, Cain returned from visiting their growing city yesterday afternoon, mesmerized. He did not even touch the food I set before him until he had his say. "They are building this tall mountain with stairs. They build it to reach to the clouds where their gods and goddesses dwell. The people live in terror of them; you should see! They pray and offer up enormous amounts of food and strong drink to them, on altars. They insist that if they don't, the gods are vengeful creatures and will wreak havoc upon them by sending raging fires or flooding rivers or disastrous storms their way. Sickness too." He looked at me. "Crippledness. Disease." He ate finally, tearing off a hunk of cold bread with his teeth. He spoke with a full mouth. "The gods protect them from these things."

Father grunted and said, "Be careful who you listen to, my son. Have these people *seen* these gods? Interacted with them?" With his fingers, he scooped up dripping meat chunks from his bowl and stuffed them into his mouth.

"They have statues of them!" said Cain, slapping his thigh. "Likenesses of them, everywhere. On their rings and bracelets and medallions. In the marketplace—on woven rugs and chiseled walls. Everywhere!"

Abel snorted. "Just because the people make semblances of their gods doesn't mean they exist."

Cain's face reddened. He sneered, "Just because Father and Mother tell us stories of Elohim doesn't mean *He* exists."

Mother said evenly, "Had you been there in the Garden, you would not speak as brashly as you do now."

Cain was not to be deterred. "Why, then, have you lost children, Mother? Why does Aya have a crooked foot? Why do some of my plants, for no reason at all, grow spotted, wither, and die? Why do Abel's flocks suffer losses from hoof rot and coughing disease? Why?" He leaned forward, the weight of his hands slicing the air. "I'll tell you why. Elohim doesn't exist." He struck his fist against his palm for emphasis, and we all jumped. "So long we've been blind. So long we've trusted. In someone who . . . is . . . not . . . there!"

Mother's eyes darted to Father's. They were pleading, *Do you hear your son? Do you hear his blasphemy?*

Father did a curious thing. He leaned back. He stopped eating. His hands hovered like hummingbirds. No one spoke. He was quiet, too quiet, so that I thought Cain's words had silenced him, but then he said slowly, "I do not have answers, my children, for why Elohim allows such things. I do not think He is like these gods, though, from what Cain is telling us. He has created—how can I explain this?—the world in a certain way. We have sunlight, we have storms; we have health, we have pain. They are part of His creation, part of how the world works. He does not concoct ways to torment us, at least that is not how He appeared to us"—he waved to Mother, to include both of them—"when we knew Him in the Garden."

Cain laughed scornfully. "So your god does not intervene? Is that what you're saying?"

Still, Father did not raise his voice. He spoke hesitantly, trying to order his words. "I do not claim to know everything, Cain. I wish, for once, we could talk about this rationally, without letting our emotions get the better of us. Listen closely. Possibly Elohim *allows* suffering—pay heed that I have *not* said He *causes* it—so that we enter into a sacred space where we need Him and hear Him more clearly, in the thick of all our sorrows."

"Then you have created Him in your need, *because* of your need," said Cain.

Father pushed his bowl away, so he would have room. "An example," he said. "I shall give an example." He rubbed his hands together briskly, as though the movement itself would lend life to his words. "When you were a child, I carried you. You had neither the strength nor the coordination to walk. Then, at some point, you wanted to walk on your own. So we let you take those first wobbly steps by yourself, and now look at you." Cain looked ready to interrupt, but Father kept at it. "Had I insisted upon carrying you for the rest of your life, you would have been weak and completely dependent upon me. I do not think you would have desired this."

"I don't see what this has to do with Elohim," said Cain.

"I stood back," said Father. "I let you stumble and pull yourself back up. You became stronger because I did so."

"Perhaps," said Cain. "But I, for one, do not want my god to stand idly by, doing nothing if I am in trouble."

"If you call upon Elohim's name, and so does your enemy, whom will Elohim aid? Whose side will He be on?" said Father. "You are reducing Him to what He can do for you. What will you do for Him?"

Cain guffawed. "I do not do anything for Elohim. From now on, I worship the city's gods. I offer sacrifices to them, like the city people. I offer up praise to them, so they will protect me from harm."

It was as though we collectively, as a family, drew in a deep breath at the same time. No one said anything. There it was. Cain's statement of contradiction, of impiety. Mother's mouth opened wide—out of shock, I think.

Father said, with a wave of his hand, "I will not stop you. You are free to choose whom you will. Love and respect cannot be coerced."

"But, Adam—" said Mother.

Father looked up at her miserably. "It is not for us to decide what our children must decide for themselves," he said.

So now Cain has set about learning what he can about the gods of the sky.

And I have set about trying to fix my foot. I am an ingenious girl. I am Aya the Cook and Aya the Bird. Before bed, I yank my foot straight and wrap it in Naava's wool to hold it sturdy, but when the time comes for the unfurling, it curls back in like a leaf that has memorized its life. Then I walk with my knee facing out, but that only serves to give me severe cramps in my inner thigh. Despite my cleverness—for I *am* clever!—I still have not come up with a reasonable solution, and that is disappointing to me, solver of all things confusing.

Why is it that I can fix all my family's problems but not my own? When Naava needs more colors for her wool, I offer hints on how to get them— red cabbage leaves for pink, elderberry fruit for blue, safflowers for yellow, onion skins for yellow-brown, pomegranate rind for red (although this is more effective on leather), black walnut hulls for a rich dark brown, and turmeric for orange. I want to say, *Why do I have to be a cistern of knowledge for you? Why do you not experiment yourself, to see what you can come up with?*

I attempt to cover my disgust, but it's very hard to hold my face still.

I am kindest to and most tolerant of Abel. He prides himself on knowing his sheep and goats like a man should know a woman—not in a rutting way but tender nonetheless. Several moons ago, he woke me early one morning and whispered, "Please come." The only other sounds were of Father's snoring and bird chatter.

I stumbled out behind him into the murky darkness and rubbed my eyes. He said nothing, simply walked toward the lean-to where the animals bedded down for the night. The shelter was a crude hut made of willow boughs and sun-dried bricks, and although Abel cleaned it regularly, it had a particularly foul smell to it—that of urine mostly. I wrinkled my nose but did not complain. My brother needed my help.

Abel held the gate open for me, and we made our way to the far side of the shelter. He approached a ewe lying on her side. "She's ill," he said. "It's her udder."

I knelt down next to the mother sheep, hearing the dry *crick* of barley stalks beneath my knees. I put my hand on her crimped-up wool and stroked her. "You sweet thing." She bleated, a helpless and ashamed apology for her weakness. I felt her flesh with my fingers; my eyes were useless in the gloom. Her udder was swollen hard. Her nipples were cracked, with open ridges. She *baa*ed again.

"Help me get her up," I said. I slid my hand under her shoulders and said, "Ready."

Abel and I lifted her, but she collapsed, refusing to stand. She cried out again, and now the other sheep answered her sad bleatings—a miserable, plaintive morning chorus.

"Massage her until the skin grows soft," I said. "I'll be back."

"I've already tried that," said Abel. His voice wavered.

"Do it again," I said. And then, thinking to comfort him, I added, "Talk to her."

"I do, I do," he whispered.

As I left him there and walked out into the gray morning, I heard him stifle a sob, and then he was weeping, huge gasping gulps that would not stop. Something went slack in me, and I felt a wrenching—an unhappy realization that Abel, the object of my endless admiration, loved his stupid and stubborn beasts more than me or any of my family. It was as though he had already learned, like me, that to look to others for satisfaction or happiness was sure to end in betrayal. In animals, this was not so— thank Elohim for this!—and Abel would have known this when he gave me Goat. Dear sweet mischievous Goat. But I wanted my brother to love *me*. He had already demonstrated that he thought me whole, as Elohim intended, and no one else had done that.

We force-fed the ewe dandelion tea to induce the flow of her milk. I pounded figs into a pulp and applied the poultice to her softening udder. I gave Abel a small clay pot containing a few hardened drops of storax resin, mixed with a little oil and rose water, to assuage her irritated and cracked nipples. "Be faithful with this," I said.

The next morning I found a gift from Abel—a large flat smooth stone next to the *tinûru. Incredible,* I thought, *his heart is soft like the river mud,* and I retrieved my love for Abel out of the backwaters of my mind, and it rose up within me, like sweet hyssop. Maybe he cared for me more than I knew. Maybe this was the only way he knew how to show it.

I lifted it—and almost fell face-first, it was so heavy!—held it in my palm, and felt the cool heft of it. On its surface was the most detailed impression of a winged animal, a cross between a bird and a lizard. The animal was long gone, of course, but there the memory of its tender life had been etched into the rock's surface. I traced the dips and turns of this strange beast's burial and wondered, *Will it be so with me, when I am gone? Will there be anything left of Aya to remember?*

I ramble on: Forgive me. I tell you this: I solved one of Mother's problems this morning.

As you may know, life is full of surprises. Anything can happen, this I believe. As the sky turned from gray to pink, I threw a basket over my shoulder and went out onto the plains to collect dung for my fire. Goat followed and fanned out behind me, stripping leaves with her lips, dancing up on her back legs to reach the highest ones. I held a forked stick in front of me. It served two purposes: to jab the ground before me—for I never knew what wildlife I would disturb—and to fling the dung piles over my head and into the basket. I left the fresh dung piles, black against the raw earth, still rank and strong, and took the lighter and crustier ones, the ones that had baked in the sun like Dara's pots and jars. If I saw plants I needed, I tore them out of the ground and tucked them into the sash of my robe. Cress for the stomach. Nettle for the blood.

On that despicable day of the visiting ladies, Mother had found me hiding in the pantry and said matter-of-factly, "You will lose Dara's dung-collecting and pottery-making. She's going to take care of those people's babies." She added quickly, out of guilt, I thought, "They will provide us with goods that we can't make ourselves. Cain will be quite pleased at our arrangement."

"Don't they have any children to look after their own?" I said, shocked.

Mother stared at me. "I don't know," she said slowly. "Maybe they send their children to the fields or set them to other tasks."

"Dara is only six," I said.

Mother blushed. "I know." She touched her fingers to her cheeks. "Did you see their colored fabrics and shiny jewelry?" She tucked a strand of hair behind her ear and looked down at her feet. "I think this might be good for Dara . . . and for us." She bit her lip. "They will not harm her."

So Dara is going to be exchanged for goods. I, Aya the Bird, am not one bit jealous. The work she will have to do! The slobbering, screaming babies she will have to take care of! No, thank you. But Naava, my sister with the honeyed skin and the walnut hair and the perfect limbs and the glances of her brothers—oh, that I might glean looks like those one day!—drinks from the cup of bitterness, of jealousy. She glares at Dara and snaps at her. She thinks Dara has stolen her chance at freedom, away from here.

Poor Dara. Mother has fed her to the jackals. With each pregnancy, Mother seems to care less and less for us; we are so many. Maybe I am wrong. Mother *did* say that she was afraid of what the women might do if she refused them. She *did* say she'd ask Father, and he would tell her what to do. And, after all, she *does* seek to mediate arguments and soothe us with quiet words when no one else will.

But when Jacan went off to join Abel in the fields, Mother did not cry as she had for Abel. In fact, Cain teases Abel about this. When Cain wants to make Abel angry, he rubs his fists over his eyes—"Waa waa, my little son Abel has left the fold. I'm so sad"—as if he's Mother, and Abel, if he's close to Cain, tries to strike him.

There were no tears for me, or explanations even, when the strange women came and laughed and pointed at my leg. There are no tears for Dara, being lost to a strange city, to another family who moan to the sky, carve livers for answers, and worship beady-eyed statues. The outrage of it all! Hear this: If Mother does not care for us, once we've wandered from her skirts, then she will regret her shoving and her pushing when she gets as old as do the forgotten sheep and goats that lie down at the end of their lives—for who will care for her then? Who will bring her cool water to drink, cook warm bread for her to eat, and take away her offal? Who will care about her bones grown brittle, her eyes gone cloudy, and her hands grown weak? Not I, Aya of the hard heart, Aya who sees everything and knows no one cares for me, except he who wants a belly of my food and the heat from my fire.

But wait. I was telling of how I solved Mother's problem.

As I was collecting dung for my fire, an asp rose up in front of me, swaying back and forth, ready to strike at my stick, which had roused him from his hole.

I froze.

His hood was spread like a tent, and he hissed at me. I hobbled backward a safe distance and watched him warily. I barked at Goat to stay away. Goat looked up once, nonchalantly, then resumed her eating.

The asp had sunk down now, hovering over his coiled body. I knew what damage he could do; I had seen an asp lash out at a sheep once, and at a rat, and they both went into shiverous convulsions such as I had never seen before, foaming at the mouth and contorting in the body. I had enough problems—I didn't need to be shriveled by asp venom.

Curious, I hunched down and squatted, the better to watch him. The distance between us was such that I was not frightened. With the sky whitening, I could see the veins running through his black hood, his yellowish-brown stripes. His body was fluid, like the rope Abel used with his flocks, and the smooth warm sheen of his scales reminded me of the yellow jewelry that ringed the visiting strangers' limbs.

Mother had told us about the serpent in the Garden: not really a serpent at first but a man, like Father and my older brothers, a robust man with quick flirting eyes and a smile that unnerved her. He was too eager to please, a little arrogant and crass—thrilling, to say the least. This serpent was the end product, the thing that was cursed to go around on his belly, right before Mother and Father were thrust from the Garden. *Very clever,* Mother said. *Very interesting,* Mother said. *Very beguiling,* Mother said. She had said this all, in my opinion, *very wistfully.*

"Lucifer," I whispered. For that is the name Mother said he went by. "Lucifer."

The asp rose up again and hissed. He wound his body tighter, as if to strangle the ground.

I was not afraid. If Mother could entertain him, then I could too. "Lucifer, if that's you in there, why don't you speak? I know who you are."

The asp grew still.

"Mother has told me all about you and the Garden and how you tricked her into eating of the fruit. Well, Mother's not so smart. She's quite gullible, if you want to know the truth. Especially if she's told she's pretty." I stared at him, willing him to speak to me. "Works every time."

He cocked his head like Goat does when I'm talking to her, curious.

"You knew exactly what you were doing," I said. "I am not so dumb. I am not so easily tricked."

Still, the asp did not move.

I continued. "What I want to know is: What transpired in the Garden? I find it hard to believe that this Elohim who created Mother and Father would purposely test them, to see if they loved Him well enough. Were you part of the plan? Did Elohim and you have an agreement?" I traced the outline of Mother's tree in the sand as I spoke. "You know what I think? You and Elohim had a fight, and you were full of vengeance and ill will, and who was there but Mother and Father, Elohim's beloved, and you thought: *Well, now, there's an idea!* Sully their hands; spoil their allure. Then Elohim would have nothing." I paused, let this sink in.

The asp's slanted eyes narrowed.

"What I find curious too is that, according to Mother, you told the truth. You weren't lying. Now, how can that be? After all, you *were* cursed by Elohim. And if you told the truth, does that make Elohim a liar? Or if you told a half-truth, did you simply *forget* to tell Mother the rest of the story?"

I finished my drawing in the sand and taunted him with my stick. "You are a wily one. We might have gotten along splen—"

The asp swung forward, lunging at me, flicking his tail.

I screamed. I jumped up and caught his head in the fork of my stick and rammed him into the ground. His body shook in the sand, flinging dirt everywhere. I brought a rock down on his head, over and over again, until it was nothing but a flattened fibrous disk. I took great pleasure in this—in fact, I gave a triumphant yell—because I had felt so long that a part of Mother had been destroyed by this creature.

Then I stood, quiet.

It occurred to me that I had never taken a life vengefully before. Certainly I had killed birds and fish for food, but those acts were sacred and precious, unlike what I had just done.

My wonder did not last long.

I gathered up the snake's body and tossed him into the basket. An elixir made from snakeskin and dried orange peels did wonders for coughing fits. I clicked to Goat, and she came running.

Now, I am Aya the Asp Killer, the Lucifer Killer. Wait until I tell Mother.

Naava

Naava stands and goes to the window to look out upon the sun, which rises redly in a tangerine sky. Tufts of clouds peel away from the sun, as if to say, *A brand-new day.* She lifts a flask, pours cool water into a chipped clay cup, and raises it to Eve's lips, dried and cracked now from talking.

"Rest," says Naava, but Eve shakes her head, determined to go on, to inscribe her story on the hard clay of Naava's heart. Naava sighs. Eve was always stubborn and oblivious to those around her. Yes, she nursed the little ones, corralled the young ones, but after that, her children all had to grow up fast, for most likely another one was on the way, vying for Eve's motherly attentions. Naava helped when she could, but mostly she did her weaving and stayed mute, except, of course, for all the times she felt she needed to speak up because she had been wronged—which was frequently.

Naava knew she was beautiful. Neither Adam nor Eve would ever come out and state it that way, *You are beautiful,* but her name meant *beautiful,* and she could only go by the meanings of her other siblings' names to know they were not, essentially, beautiful. Aya's name, for example, meant *bird.* Naava chuckled to herself every time she thought of the humor in that; Eve had a funny bone, at least. Cain meant *acquire,* and he certainly knew how to do that, hoarding sections of land like there was no tomorrow. Naava saw the greed in Cain's eyes, but she also saw the adventure, so she admired him. Her thought was to align herself with him, so that maybe he would take her with him on his increasingly frequent visits to the new settlement—for the visitors had become dwellers and were building walls for what they called a "city." Abel meant *breath*—quite literally, *the steam from one's mouth.* This was how Naava saw him, as a vapor she couldn't capture, as a smoke tendril she could not hold. She watched him come and go—he was never in one place very long—and she pined for a moment alone with him, to tell him that she loved him, that while she wove her threads in and out, all she could think about was him.

Dara: *compassionate.* Jacan: *trouble.* Those were the twins. Jacan came first, feetfirst. Then, when Eve thought all was finished, Dara slipped out easily, a messy mass of arms and legs, and Eve cried out that at least one of them had been kind to her. Naava had been there, helping, but Aya had done most of the work. Naava had grown faint at the sight of so much blood, and Aya—even at five years!—had had to push Naava aside and pack Eve's womb with wool and herbs to stanch the bleeding. There were others, who had come and gone, buried in Eve's garden. They all had names, anointed by Eve and her sense of their identity, for once named, Naava knew, there was no changing others' perception of who you were. Daniel—*Elohim is my judge*—born too soon. Micayla—*who is like Elohim*—born with the swollen head. Miriam—*sea of sorrow*—born with a tangled and knotted cord.

So, Naava was beautiful.

There was that fact.

She had never clearly seen her face, other than in the darkened surface of the river on a calm day, but even then all she could see were shadows and contours. She knew her brothers were curious about her—how Cain caught her glance and held it, how Abel looked away, ashamed and embarrassed. She wielded great power, she knew. Just as Aya healed with her potions, Naava could paralyze with her simple presence. And Naava had grown haughty. She lived as though floating on water, unconscious of where it was taking her and not truly seeing those she left behind, drifting in her wake.

Eve was one of them.

One particular morning, not long after finding they had visitors to the north, Naava watched from her loom as Eve paused in her sweeping to loosen her muscles. She stretched her swollen calves and arched in a backward crescent. Sighing, she slipped her hands under the weight of her belly and pulled it up.

And then Adam came back from the orchards with a sprained wrist, which he wanted Aya to look at. Aya had him sit on the ground, near her fire. She was all business as she rubbed a green sticky poultice into Adam's skin, splinted it with a poplar branch, then wrapped it like a cocoon with some of Naava's wool.

"Don't take this off," Aya chided. "It will swell, and you won't be able to move it." Aya's hands were strong and purposeful, and she took no pains to be gentle.

Adam nodded and winced at Aya's sharp movements.

"He needs water," Eve said abruptly.

Aya just grunted, her lips pursed in concentration.

Eve dropped her broom and plodded to the gate. She disappeared around the corner of the house and returned a short while later, walking gingerly with a drinking cup brimming with fresh water from the cistern. This she brought to Adam and stood by while he gulped. She took the cup from him and sat, leaning up against the mud bricks of the house, watching Aya and rubbing her lower back with callused fingers.

"Are you in pain?" said Adam, his words infused with concern.

"Ach," said Eve. "Very much so. With every birth, I feel as though a piece of me is being ripped out. I'm afraid I will die with this one. A body can only take so much."

Aya looked up sharply to study Eve's face. Naava couldn't read her intent: Was it sympathy or disgust?

"Die?" Adam held up his good hand to tell Aya to stop her ministrations. "That's a strong word."

"I know," said Eve.

Adam leaned forward toward Eve. "I know it's hard for you," he said. "Maybe tonight I could rub out the aches?"

Eve nodded submissively, like a child, and then seemingly without thinking poured out a torrent of words that caught even Naava unaware. "I've been thinking that we should add a small waterfall to the garden, so that you can hear a slight burble when you sit, just like we did in the Garden. You remember, don't you? A bubbling green twilight, that's what it was." Eve clasped her hands, and her voice rose like a summer storm. "And the white flowers, they're all wrong. What was the name of the creamy flowers that floated on the ponds, on little green disks?"

"Water lilies," said Adam slowly, letting Aya take over again.

"Yes, those. We need those in the pond, as shade for the tadpoles and the tiny fish."

"There are no fish," said Adam. The pond was too stagnant and still for that.

"Well, yes, I know, but there should be," said Eve. She hefted herself off the ground, then braced herself against the house until she got her bearings. She continued massaging her back. "The way Elohim had it, it was perfect."

Adam exhaled sharply. "Unless you want me to spend my time building more aqueducts instead of tending the orchards and weeding the fields," said Adam, "then you will have to wait on this waterfall." Then, after a pause, he said, "I'm not Elohim." Naava thought she could see his frown from where she sat watching. She knew to be wary when Adam's wrath was kindled; blue skies could become cloudy in an instant.

Eve groaned and held her belly.

Adam started up as if to come to her aid, but Aya held on to his bandaged wrist and wouldn't let go. "Why don't you lie down, woman? The girls will make sure things get done," he said.

In that one word, *woman*, Naava heard dismissal and contempt, all rolled into one. She knew her father preferred a feigned cheeriness, not this sadness that leaked like an old flask. She guessed that was why he spent so much time in the orchards, where he could be alone, to think, to meditate. He wanted quiet. He wanted some sort of resolve, peace, contentment.

Eve stared at him, her bottom lip quivering with emotion. She approached Adam and sat down next to him, cautiously, as if she might break the fragile web that connected them.

Adam worked his jaw muscle, clenching and unclenching it. When he spoke, his voice came out even and stilted. "We are *here* now. The *past* is gone. We have children who need us."

Eve sat, unmoving.

Adam turned to Aya. "Are you finished?"

Aya nodded, snugging in the last seed burr to hold the splint in place.

Adam stood. "I'll be in the orchards if you need me." And with that, he was gone. There was a faint lingering smell of sweat born of injury and high emotions, but that was all.

Eve bent over like an injured animal, and Aya went back to her grinding.

Naava felt disgust. It was a darkness that rippled out from the center of her being and swallowed her whole. Her longtime irritation with Eve was suddenly overwhelming. She could feel it as distinctly as she could feel a morsel of food entering her mouth and traveling downward. All her last illusions about her mother were swept away as easily as a cobweb, and she knew she was forever changed. It was Naava's turning point, her irrevocable jump from the cliff. She knew what it meant, and in the time it took for her to blink, she had already made peace with whatever disaster would result when she reached the bottom.

Eve drove Adam away, time and time again, all because she wanted to quarry Eden, holding out the one futile hope that they might find home once more.

Naava knew this would not be how she would live her own life. When the time came, Naava would take care of her husband. She would right all wrongs between them and bolster up all erosions between them, swiftly and stalwartly. She would be a dutiful wife, providing him with healthy babies and hot satisfying meals. She would not become as Eve, as washed-up seaweed, once alive and green and shooting up from the floor of the river, now shorn from its roots, stinking and rotting in the sun.

Eve

Is it wrong that I saw my family's impending doom and did nothing to stop it? That is to say, I did not know *which* black cloud would scuttle across the sky toward us, only that one would, in due time.

There was the acrid tension between Cain and Abel, like sour pith between the teeth, which escalated at opposite ends of every day when they were in each other's presence for Aya's meals. There was Naava, who saw me only as archaic and discarded. There was Aya, my little bird—what would we have done without her constant care?—but that summer it seemed that she drugged us all with her food and her potions, keeping us loyal and panting for her ministrations. There were the sudden strangers who diverted Adam and Cain's irrigation channels in the middle of the night and threatened Abel out of his pastures during the day. This combination of things could only end badly.

And Adam. What can I say about my dear husband, who no longer regarded me as he did in the Garden? He now looked past me and through me to my children, who adored his gruff humor and rough manner, or to his work, which required only brawn and tirelessness.

It was not always so.

Indeed, that wonderful afternoon in the Garden, after our lovemaking and Elohim's visit, we slept like nesting birds, cradled by the roots of the Tree of Life. I woke to the sound of water pattering down all around us, the incessant sound of plunking and plopping. The shrubbery and flowers jumped like frogs around us, taking in the weight of the water, then releasing it gently to the forest floor.

"It's raining," whispered Adam.

We turned our bright faces up to the sky, up to the pink-flowered Tree of Life and the cucumber green of the canopy, and caught the drips on our tongues. Later, we ran, as the light flashed around us, and the toad-colored sky rumbled above us, and the river was swept into peaked claws. The air quivered and shook our bones, and we leapt, for the joy of it, for the wild abandon of it. Limbs from vine-covered trees cracked and fell; shredded flowers whipped away on the wind; yet still we were there, standing in our Garden, together.

The destruction was considerable, and we wept for the downed trees and trampled bushes and broken flowers. As the sun made its shy appearance, we gathered large leaves and long twigs for a three-sided bower, shaking off the water drops and planting the twigs firmly in the soft earth. The structure took form, piece by piece, and eventually we sat, pressed up against the heat of each other, in our tiny warm enclosure, admiring our handiwork. The air smelled of damp earth and wet wood. A lone spider began to spin a web in the open corner, its silver threads glistening in the sunlight. Before she was done, a fly lit upon it, and in a flash she was upon him.

Adam and I talked. Surely we talked about a great many things. But at times like this we could sit, not saying a word, then later marvel at how it felt as if we'd had the longest conversation. That was what it was like. To be known. To be loved.

Often in the afternoons, after we were finished weeding and pruning—for Elohim had exhorted us to work in the Garden—we discussed the ramifications of the Tree of the Knowledge of Good and Evil.

Adam pounded on a coconut with a sharp-edged stone. "If Elohim didn't want us to have it, why did He make it?"

My sentiments exactly.

"I mean," Adam continued, "why did He specifically point it out to us and say no?"

I shrugged. "He doesn't want us to know what good and evil are."

"But don't we *know* what good and evil are?"

"*We* are good." I paused. "What is evil?"

Adam's hand grew still. His forehead knit together. "The storm was evil," he said. He scratched at the red welts on his skin. "Mosquitoes are evil."

"They aren't evil. The storm caused some damage, but it wasn't bad," I said. I pointed to the new seedlings around us. "See? Everything is growing back. And, as for your mosquitoes, have you seen? The bats eat them."

"I don't like the bats," said Adam.

Was Elohim hiding something from us? Something that we might enjoy as much as we had enjoyed each other? For days on end we were immobilized with indecision. Elohim had, wittingly or unwittingly, tapped the seeds of doubt into our fertile minds. Given that our environment was hot and tropical and wet, the seeds took off of their own accord and soon became mammoth specimens. *Was this what Elohim had intended? To trick us?*

After we had relished fruits of all flavors and sizes in the Garden—and named them boysenberries and loquats and mangoes and papayas—we sat and studied the fruit of the Tree of the Knowledge of Good and Evil for hours and saw that it was beautiful and had all the signs of being delicious. The reddish-brown fruits, glossy and round, dangled up high on the tree, and although we could see that they were ripe, not one fell to the ground. For a while this was a satisfactory arrangement, because the trunk was too thorny for climbing and elsewhere there was an ample supply of nuts and berries and fruits and vegetables to choose from. Our palates were sated, and our stomachs were full.

Over time, though, the Tree of the Knowledge of Good and Evil loomed larger than life, and it began to seep into both of our dreams. *What did its fruit taste like? What was so bad about the tree? What didn't Elohim want us to know? Didn't He trust us? Didn't He love us?*

Days ran into nights. We created new ways of showing our love for each other. Adam brought me daily gifts—a flower chain, a smooth pebble, a green-shiny beetle, a maple leaf, a palmful of honey. At night, when the sky was a limpid black, I was a weaver of words. I concocted outlandish stories about the hard white stars and the low yellow moon and how Elohim had made us for each other. Elohim visited us frequently and spun tales of His creation, but He always left us with more questions than answers, which translated into the broken story strands that I felt I must stitch together somehow. "Imagine," we murmured to each other, "He said, *Let there be,* and everything came into being." Such strength in words! Such power in a breath! Elohim, the poet; Elohim, the potter. Adam always delighted in hearing my stories of our births, our creation. Later, my own children would grow quiet and still while I told them the details of their own births.

Elohim took frequent walks in the Garden, during the slow time of day when the air and sun and heat dragged to a tired crawl. He would join us by the river afterward and we would sit and talk for hours, interrupted only by flies that buzzed about our heads and the occasional mysterious splash of a fish or a turtle along the shoreline.

On one such occasion, a short while after I had arrived, Adam begged Elohim to tell His story of how we were made—*again.* Adam was eating raspberries and using his tongue to dislodge the tiny seeds that had wedged between his two front teeth.

Elohim smiled. "You ask for this every time," He said. His voice was low and steady, but, strangely enough, it growled in the grassy ground beneath us and roared from the shoulders of the hills around us. "I called you Adam because you came from *adamah,* the blood-red earth; Eve, Adam named you *mother of all living* because you came from muscle and bone and sinew. I breathed life into you, like this—" Elohim cupped His hand in front of His mouth and blew a warm gentle air onto His palm. "Your flesh came from the earth, your blood from the dew, and your breath from the wind. Your passion from the mountains, your bones from stone, and your intellect from me. I made you male and female, in my image, clothed in splendor and majesty and wrapped in light as the angels."

His words trailed off, like the retreating hoofbeats of a herd that has been called to their master.

"Why didn't you make us at the same time?" I asked.

Elohim looked at Adam. "Adam?"

Adam looked up, his mouth red from the juice of the raspberries. "I don't know," he said. "Though I could have used her help early on, in the naming of the animals."

Elohim gazed at Adam, much like a parent trying to get a child to confess something. "Think, Adam, do you not know why I created you first? Can you describe your emotions after you named the animals?"

Adam now had red juice trailing down his chin. He wiped it off with the back of his hand. "Well," he said. "I don't remember—"

"You felt lonely," I said.

Elohim smiled at me. I puffed up like a milkweed pod bursting with seed. "You said you felt sad," I said.

"Yes, I guess I did. All the other animals had someone like them. I had no one like me . . . well, except for Elohim"—Adam blushed—"but no one to love."

"I waited for you to ask for her, your counterpart," said Elohim, leaning back on His hands, "so you would have need of her and treat her as yourself. In every thing there is an emptiness that must be filled by another. No one is complete by him or herself."

Adam winked at me, and I leaned over to kiss him on the cheek.

But one thing puzzled me. "Then what are You—male or female—if we are *both* made in Your image?"

A woodpecker *rat-a-tat*ted away at an oak tree nearby. Elohim watched it closely, then turned to me. "You do not yet understand? I do not have one form; I have many. To you I appear as a man, but to others I appear as a cloud or a bush or a flame. I could appear as that woodpecker if I so desired. My appearance is deceiving, for I am everywhere at once—"

"Everywhere?" I exclaimed. "How can that be? Why, Adam and I don't even know what is happening on the other side of the Garden!"

Elohim pursed His lips. "Do you see the wind?"

"No," I said. "But I see the leaves and grasses moving."

"Exactly," said Elohim. "The wind blows where it pleases. You hear its sound, but you don't know where it comes from or where it's going. If you stay with me here, in the Garden, you will learn all these things, as surely as the sun rises in the morning and sets in the evening." He sighed then, a stream of sadness entering his voice. "I have made *both* of you like me." His voice became an urgent whisper. "I am the hen who shelters her chicks under her wing; I am the shepherd who watches his sheep; I am the mother who does not forget her child . . . and I love you, as a mother *and* a father."

How could He be all these things?

"Where do You go when You leave us?" I asked.

Elohim laughed then. "I am In Time," He said. "Will your questions never cease?"

I bowed my head, thinking He was upset. "In Time?" I said softly.

"I see the past and the present as though they are the same day," Elohim said. He reached out and raised my chin so my eyes met His. How can I describe His eyes to you? They were piercing, as though all my thoughts were known to Him, and kind, as though I was everything He needed. "Never stop asking questions, Eve. The moment you do, you will wither and die."

"But to die is what happens when we eat of the tree," I exclaimed.

Elohim studied my face, then released my chin. "They are different deaths. One is a disastrous separation from me; the other is a little like . . . being lost and never found."

We grew quiet then. The grasshoppers and crickets and cicadas buzzed and hummed, and the afternoon shadows grew long and gloomy. A gazelle and a deer family came to drink at the river, lifting their heads up periodically to check for hyenas and leopards. I had seen one violent affair already, a gazelle killed, its throat snapped quickly between the teeth of a large lion. Truly, this was our newly formed vision of death—how a body, once firm and vigorous, would crumple to the ground, a soft motionless shell of what once was, to be slowly ravaged by the wind, maggots, or other beasts. Elohim had explained this too—the order of things, the culling of populations, the cyclic balance of His creation—but I always hated to see it, the sheer destruction of it. Adam and I would not be touched, Elohim promised, as long as we were in the Garden. This was of some consolation, and we grew accustomed to the ebb and flow of life around us.

Then there was always the lovemaking, so gentle, so freeing, so passionate. As yet our future was unformed, hazy like the dewy morning mist, but we did not bother with the contemplation of it. We were building our own garden, an internal emotional garden, and we were tending it much like the physical one that surrounded us.

Much later, when Cain began grafting branches onto trees and coming up with new, exotic fruits, I thought back to these days with Adam and how, like grafted branches that had "taken," Adam and I were inseparable, permanently joined together, destined to bear the fruits of both, not one.

But that summer, away from the Garden and pregnant again, surrounded by so many mindless and repetitive chores and too many mouths that needed and needed again, I felt cut off from Adam, shorn from the main stem of our love, and pruned so far back that any further growth was impossible.

Aya

I showed the snake to Mother. She clutched her hand to her chest and grabbed my elbow. "He has hurt you? Where? Show me."

"I killed it before he could bite," I said triumphantly.

She studied my face a moment, as if she was trying to read the weather. "Really, Aya," she said, when she caught her breath. "You need to set limits for yourself." I think she was afraid for me, thinking I was too bold, too brash, to go after such dangerous animals in my condition. There was some comfort in this, that she must have loved me, a little. But later, as Mother wove baskets out of green river reeds, her fingers flitting like the lapwings living under the eaves, she said abruptly, "That wasn't him, you know. He was charming and beautiful."

So, I was to learn my limits.

Soon afterward, Abel came to me in the early morning hours, tired and grumpy. "Aya," he said, "could you spare a day away from the house? I need your help."

I consented, mostly to return the favor of Goat, and divided my chores among my sisters and Mother. Naava was to churn the milk into curd—oh, she whined about this to Mother, saying, "Why do I have to do *all* the work around here?" Dara would collect dung and tend the fire. Mother agreed to skin and pluck the quails and soak them in an onion-celery-anise broth for the evening meal.

I had never gone so far from the house before, and it pleased me immensely. I was a little afraid but I did not let on, because Abel would have teased me and said it was because I was a girl and reminded me about my limits. That has become a silly joke now, thanks to Mother!

Jacan ran up ahead, leaping like the goats from rock to rock, there, then gone. "Hurry, hurry," he called. Goat chased after him and joined her friends.

Abel's black goats and brindled sheep stood out against the white sandstone, which had been bleached by the sun and broken into bits by the wind and rain. The air was cooler and windier up here in the flinty hills, where Abel and Jacan brought their flocks. Not as much powdery choking dust as on the plains. The goats found the straggly clumps of wormwood and juniper and sparrow-wort and began grazing them back to rounded cushions.

Abel was kind. I fell behind several times, and he pretended to adjust his pack or tighten his sandals. He was always finished by the time I caught up with him. "It's beautiful up here," I said. I experienced an abrupt feeling of gratitude and a sudden keenness for camaraderie, and I smiled at him.

He said nothing but nodded and offered me a mouthful of water from his waterskin. I saw it was leaking, just a little. "Mother will make you a new one, you know."

"There's no need," he said. "Jacan and I are fine."

"Why don't you like Mother?" I asked.

He jumped a little and choked on his swallowing. He looked at me. "Not like Mother? What gave you that idea?"

"You're her favorite, you know." I put my good leg on a large rock and hoisted myself up to better survey the view of white sand, stretched out like a tired dog behind me. There, a ribbon of water; there, our house and vineyards and fields; and there, to the north, the strangers' walled complex, growing as steadily as Cain's amber barley and wheat fields.

Suddenly Abel was distant, aloof. "Aya, I don't believe Mother has a chosen favorite. And if she does, that is not of my doing."

I pointed to a cloud of dust approaching. "Someone's coming," I said.

Abel's hand went to his side. "Make haste. I want you up the hill before they get here. If we seize the area first, they will not argue. It is the way of the land." He held out his hand, and I climbed down off the rock. "You go that way; see that boulder and the cave behind it? Stay there, and they will not bring their animals so far up, where the best vegetation is. I will be between you and them; there's no need to fear."

I nodded and scuttled away like a crab, wishing I had the nimbleness of Goat. I climbed up the backside of the boulder with some difficulty and sat on the edge of it, my good leg crossing my bad one. From here I could see a band of men leaning forward into their ascent, leather straps across their foreheads, carrying their provisions in this humble way. They stopped frequently and shaded their eyes to look up at us. Wildly, they gestured to one another, pointed at us, then slapped the backs of their hands against their palms. They looked to be an unruly lot, with beards like tumbleweed and manners like boars. I did not think I should like to meet them.

They came closer to us than I desired, but as Abel had said, they did not venture farther up the hill with us present. They were drunk and loud. A short one with a spotted face said something, and they all laughed. They strutted around like the hoopoes that parade through the grasses with their beaks in the sky; they roared like lions and beat their chests and threw back their heads. They laughed and hurled insults at us, none of which I understood.

Their flock of sheep was not so big, but their animals were sturdy and healthy, and that was all that mattered. I was to prevent them from allowing their herd to go up the mountainside, thus staking out our territory so its boundaries would not be infringed upon. So there I was, guarding the boundary.

As the sun peaked in the sky, the men settled down, and their bodies grew listless in the gathering heat. They flung themselves on all sides of a flattened rock and brought out their food sacks. They unwrapped their noonday feast before them, and my stomach growled at the sight of cold meat, raised bread, dates, figs, and skin after skin of cool beer.

I took stock of Abel and Jacan. Abel must have considered the men no longer a threat, because he and Jacan had wandered a sizable distance away, herding our goats from the crevices and cajoling them farther up the mountain. I heard the faint strains of his flute, a small instrument he'd cut out of buzzards' wing bones and banded with reeds. Jacan accompanied him on his horn. I bit my lip in consternation. Soon I wouldn't be able to see or hear them.

It was a fearful situation to be here without the protection of my older brother, but I soon realized the men were too tired or too bored to challenge my presence, and Abel must have known this. I ignored them finally, and the warmth of the rock and the sound of the heat lulled me to sleep. Ants all around me carried on their missions dutifully, looping me into the story that was their life. I dreamed I was a bird with great wings and no limits. I dove for fish, I wheeled on the wind, I soared high above the earth, I was one with the sun and moon and stars, and I was, at last, whole. The currents ruffled my feathers and lifted me higher and higher, and I sang, loud and clear, so that my joy would be known in every corner of the earth.

Then, a sudden rush. I was falling, falling through the sky, a loud *crack,* and I was wailing because it hurt, my wing hurt, right there, oh, no.

My eyes flew open, and the smell of beer breath was thick around me. The sun was blocked out by heavy black shadows that shifted over me, around me. Confused, I tried to rise, but my arms were pinned down, my legs too. I screamed but could not see Abel or Jacan. The pock-faced man slapped me hard across the mouth and yelled at me. His eyes were bloodshot, and he was drooling in his beard.

I tasted blood. *Oh, Abel, where are you?*

The drunk-slurred voices above me grew agitated and clipped, full of strange sounds I did not understand. I wanted only to kick and scratch at their eyes, show them how Aya was the Asp Killer! But I was as useless as they were wicked. They were strong, strengthened by a desire I could not name, but I could see it in their eyes that I was to be eaten alive. Their hands groped me, under my robe, in between my legs, and I thought that I must cry out again, even though they would kill me. I screamed, a rabbit scream from my belly, and their hands grew still with the terror of it.

Then a fat one with many rings on his fingers pressed his hand over my mouth and nose, and I couldn't breathe, oh, I had to get up, to get air, and

I hadn't told Abel how I loved him, and Mother too—who would look after her and the new baby? I felt my eyes, heavy, in the back of my head, and all I could think was, *How had Mother taught us to pray, so long ago?*

Oh, Elohim, be merciful to me. My eyelids squeezed out the sun, and a splotched blackness swirled in front of me. *Protect me and help me in my time of need.*

Then all went black, and I knew no more.

Once more I became Aya the Bird. I swallowed sky. I floated up on a curtain of air, I drifted upon the breeze, I darted among the crags, I swam in the sea. I understood why things were the way they were, the order of things, how everything fit, just so, into Elohim's grand scheme. Oh, it was beautiful! Elohim created, and it was good, and I did not understand the *whys* and the *hows* and the *when,* but it was still good, and I felt a wave of calm rush over me. Elohim was there, beyond the seas, and He beckoned. *Come,* He whispered. *We shall fly together, you and I.*

It was a jolt when I awoke rudely next to firelight, with Abel supporting my head and Jacan pouring water over my lips. "Sister," Abel was saying. "Aya, can you hear me?" To Jacan, "Do it again."

Jacan splashed water over my mouth, and I licked my lips. I felt the chill of night air on one side, the fever of fire on the other. Abel leaned over and wiped my chin with his robe. "Ah," he said. "You are with us. We were worried." The light flickered on his face, and there was the smell of wood and sweat and charred meat.

No! I closed my eyes; I wished to remain with Elohim, who *saw* me, who *wanted* me. *Do not be far from me,* I begged of Elohim.

"Stay awake," Abel said, frantic.

My dreams were gone. I smelled Abel's fear and Jacan's restlessness. I knew they were sorry they had brought me here, and I turned my face away so they could not see my guilt, my sorrow. I did not want to be pitied.

Abel's voice was tender and soft. "I've set your arm. It was disjointed, not broken. Can you sit up?" He braced my shoulders and my head and hoisted me up to a sitting position. I was faint with pain, and my head lolled back; my tongue was heavy in my mouth. "Breathe," he said.

I sucked in air, and the night slowly grew steady around me.

"Here," said Jacan, wrapping my shoulders with one of Naava's heavy woolen blankets. He squatted in front of me, studying my face. "We came back and saw them. They were scared," he said.

"Shush," hissed Abel. "Not now."

Jacan looked disappointed at this forbidding. He ached to tell me something; in fact, the words were dammed up behind his teeth.

Abel saw my frightened glances into the brushy landscape lit eerily by a bright moon. "They are gone," he said.

Suddenly I burst out, "I would have run, you know, away from them—"

"Shhh," said Abel. He reached among the coals and removed a blackened lizard. An orange flame flickered up at the dripping fat as he handed it to me. "A little overdone, not up to your skills, but it'll have to do." I reached for it with my good hand and sank my teeth into its tough, crunchy skin, searching out the bones with my tongue. I found that I was famished and ate faster than I should have.

Once my belly was full, Abel told me what had happened. The men got drunk and scrambled up the hillside to where I slept. They attempted to mount me, as all animals do when they're in rut, but in the last moment they saw my brokenness and fled. "I did not think," he said, "they would violate the law of the land." He looked away from me, into the fire. "I am sorry, Aya. I have failed you."

I was in the grotesque company of Unlucky Omens, along with Falling Stars and Disappearing Suns and Malformed Lambs, according to the city people. In short, my hooked foot saved me.

My tears spilled over with this realization, so brutally laid out for me.

Abel reached out and wiped the tears from my cheeks. "I'm sorry."

Violently, I shook my head, and he withdrew his hand.

"If you cannot talk to me," he said gently, "Elohim hears the broken-hearted."

I said nothing.

"I talk to Him, you know," Abel said. "I'm teaching Jacan too."

Then, more abruptly than I wanted, I heard myself saying, "What is that to me?"

Abel stared into the fire. "I'm sorry. I know how much you want—"

"What?" I said. "You don't know me. You know nothing." The words rushed out of me, as water from a jar, and I could not retract them. I was embarrassed and irritated at being a girl, a girl who could not even be mounted because she was disgusting. Unlucky-lucky, I wanted a new foot. I wanted to be whole, like my sisters, like Naava, whose beauty was as powerful as the moon. I wanted to be seen, to be revered, to be caressed with curious eyes. *Oh, silly Aya, so vain! Think no more on these things!*

Abel persisted. "Do you not pray to Him when you kiss our food and bless it? Do you not seek Him too?" His gaze was earnest, as though he wanted confirmation of my praying. "He listens. That's all I wanted to say."

"It's true," said Jacan. "He spoke to us from a rock. He told us about those men . . . and you."

I pondered what they had said. Once I had conjured up Elohim in the garden with Naava and the twins, and I had heard Him whisper back that *all was well.* Naava refused to hear anything at all. Since then I wasn't sure if it had been Elohim or simply the wind. It was true, I *did* bless the food, but that was coming from the thanksgiving of my heart that we had food at all.

Then, with Abel and Jacan, what exactly would I have said to Elohim? I vaguely remembered invoking His name as I was choked, but sitting there by the fire, with my faculties intact, I wasn't sure what to say to Him. *Please, Elohim, take a respite from holding the world together and come mend my bones?* Was it that simple? Would He have heard me?

I shivered beneath Naava's blanket and gazed at Abel's face, so open and unlike that of Cain. He had thought me stronger than I was. He had trusted me to protect his grazing area, and I had let him down.

Abel reached for his flute. He placed it to his lips and blew into it. His song was sorrowful, mournful even, and after a few long notes I recognized Mother and Father's song from the Garden. Abel did not look at me as he played, but I saw his lips quiver and his eyes water. *Did he grieve for me or for his oversight?*

No matter. I accepted his song as a sweet apology, for I knew he did not mean me harm. I was grateful to matter to someone, and gradually my breathing came easier.

I formed then a sort of short prayer in my mind. I did not speak it aloud and did not know if Elohim could read my thoughts.

Elohim, if you can hear me, make me whole.
Make me strong like Abel and fast like Jacan.
Make me shine like the stars in the night sky.
And make those men drop dead by morning.

Dara

Why would someone want to poke holes in themselves? I don't know. Those colorful ladies had so many holes with rings in them. I counted holes in all these places: number one, in their noses; number two, in their lips; number three, in their eyebrows; number four, in their ears. I wonder why Elohim lets them do that.

The people from the city will be coming to take me away. Turtle, look! His head is out. He'll go with me. Mama said he could. A lady called Ahassunu came back and brought Mama a wood box full of pretty amber cloth, the color of honey, to make me a robe. The lady pulled my curls straight and tilted her head and said something, but I couldn't understand a word she was saying. Mama just nodded her head over and over.

Now Mama sews and sews. She bends over to stretch her back every so often, and I say, "It's all right, Mama, I can wear my old ones." All I want is for her to say that I can stay here, at home with her.

Then Mama says, "I'll have none of my children looking like mangy dogs," and her eyes are all wet. I don't know if she's crying because of my going away or Aya's accident up in the mountains.

Naava should help, but instead she stares at me. Long dagger stares. So I say to Mama, "Naava can go," and Mama says, "Naava is making things for the baby."

"No," I say. "She's making a—" And right then Naava opens her mouth like a fish and mouths *no,* and I stop in the middle of what I'm saying. I understand, so I change the subject. I say, "I can make jars for the baby. If something bad happens to them in the fire, well, I can make another one." Mama knows this. I'm a hard worker. I can make all sorts of things—clay balls for Abel's slingshot, weights for the fishnets, spindle whorls for Naava's spinning, and bowls and jars for Aya's cooking. I get clay down by the river and add a little water to it and work it until it's smooth. I roll it into snakes and start with a circle for the bottom. Then I wind and wind, in and out, to make curvy shapes. I splash a pebble in water and rub it over the sides, round and round, until the jar is slickery smooth. Always I remember to ask Aya's permission to use her fire, because otherwise she gets angry and slaps my hands. Aya was nice to me this morning, though. She gave me an extra fig cake with her good arm, and said, "You stay away from the men at that place, you hear? You listen to me. I'm looking out for you." And I think, *Why does Cain like the men who hurt Aya?*

Right then, when I'm bragging how good my jars are, one of them cracks open in the fire. Thank the stars and the moon, it's only Naava's, not Aya's—I made Aya a special water jug, fat and round like Turtle, because Mama said Aya had learned her limits yesterday, like she was sorry Aya had to do that, and I felt bad for Aya. Aya won't say anything about it to anyone, not even if someone asks her a question. She has a wrapping on her arm because it got twisted out of place. Abel fixed it for her. He's a kind brother. He and Jacan brought back some sand grouse and their eggs so Aya could cook them up for everyone.

I heard Abel talking secrets to Mama this morning. Mama put her hands over her mouth real fast and sucked in her breath, like this, *whoosh.* She said, "Did they . . . ?" Abel shook his head no, like Goat does when it rains and she has to get all the water off, and Mama went to Aya and hugged her and told her that she'd fix the morning repast for her, her little bird.

Jacan came to where I was washing Turtle and told me all about Aya yelling at the bad men from the city. They beat her black and blue, but Elohim saved the day by shouting out to Abel and Jacan that she was getting hurt. Jacan says that Abel doesn't want me to take care of babies in the city, but Mama won't listen.

Abel says Mama is doubtful of Elohim too, after meeting the ladies. I ask Jacan what *doubtful* means. He shrugs his shoulders and says Abel gets purple-mad about it, up there in the hills with his sheep and goats. It doesn't help that Cain goes away to visit the city almost every day. Jacan says Abel calls Cain's stories *outrageous*.

Maybe that's what Abel was shouting at Cain for, right before breakfast. I couldn't hear a word they were saying, but they are always at each other's throat lately. Mama notices it but doesn't say anything. Too many times, either Cain or Abel shouts at her, "This is none of your affair!" so now she stays away with all her might, and Father can't hear them when he's far off. So it's fight fight fight, all the time.

Mama cooked up the grouse and eggs, since Aya was feeling bad, but we all ended up feeling bad because Abel passed the bread to Cain the wrong way. Cain stood up and threw the bowl on the ground. The bowl broke and the bread got smashed all over the dirt. Mama went to pick up the pieces and put them aside. Everybody stopped eating.

Cain yelled at Abel, "How dare you laugh at me? You think you have all the answers, but how do you know that what they're doing is not the right way?" Cain looked at Father and said, "You've even said yourself that you don't know if there are other gods besides Elohim," and Father nodded.

Mama sat down again. The veins in Cain's face were popping. He said, "We should offer gifts to them because the more we ignore them, the worse our lives will be." His eyes darted back and forth, and he pointed at Aya and said, "There. I told you before. She is proof that the gods are angry at us."

Aya's eyes got big, and she sucked in lots of air, *whoosh*.

Mama stood up again, quick, with her hands on her hips, and said, "*That* is none of *your* affair." Her face got red and speckled, and her fingers were shaking like leaves in a storm.

Abel looked at Cain and said, "Meanness is a weak imitation of strength."

Cain copied him in a high voice. "Meanness is a weak imitation—"

"Aya is a gift from Elohim, as you all are," Mama said. "Remember that."

Father looked at Cain. "You would do well to attend to what your mother is saying." He leaned forward toward the fire, still glaring at Cain.

Aya blushed, and she looked down at her bowl.

Cain cringed and said, "It's the truth, though. The people in the city have many gods, and they sacrifice to them, and they are prospering." He glared at Abel.

Mama said, "Fine, then, it's *your* truth, but don't ruin everyone's meal," and Cain squatted back down and stuffed a fig into his mouth.

Father reached out his hand to Mama and said, "Are you all right?"

Mama sat back down and curled her fingers around his. She nodded.

Abel said to Cain, "I have a proposition for you."

"Please, Abel," Mama begged. "Can we not have a little peace?" Father released her hand and said, "She's right."

Cain's eyes flashed fire, but Abel kept going. "If you think these sacrifices are so important, let's do it, you and I, out in the fields."

Cain's eyes bugged like a grasshopper's, and he said, "Who would we offer to?" and Abel said, "Elohim."

Cain thought about that and said, "Why not my gods?"

Father's eyebrows raised up, like Turtle's back, and Mama got real still.

"You have decided, then, that they are *your* gods?" said Father, standing up. He put his hands on his head and tore at his hair. "I did not think my son—"

Mama threw up her hands. She cried out, "What will Elohim say? What will He do to us?"

Father walked over to Cain and slapped him across the face, hard, like this, *smack*. Father and Cain stared at each other, and Cain brought his hand up to his face. Father looked around at all of us, then at Cain, and said, "You have gone too far." Father smacked the heel of his hand against his forehead. "Have we been so negligent in teaching you about Elohim? If not He, who made the sun, moon, and stars? Who made us in His image?" Father clenched his fists and roared into the air. "Have we?" He stomped and huffed out of the courtyard, holding his head in his hands and muttering to himself.

For once, Cain did not talk. He ate. He kept his head down. His furry eyebrows bunched together.

Now I'm scared of going to the people with many gods. They don't believe in Elohim, and Father slapped Cain for that, and they have bad men who will hurt me, like they did Aya. I try to think of something happy, like what I will look like in my new yellow robe or what will be the number-five thing I will find for the baby, but my stomach hurts.

And then I see it—a pottery shard from the broken bowl right by my knee. It's in the shape of a butterfly, and I reach down to pick it up, but Naava is there first, and when she grabs it, she grins at me and says, "Insolent goat. I hate you."

I try to be good, honestly. But still. Naava is not a nice person.

So, when Naava goes out to the corral to make pretty eyes at Abel, I sneak into her weaving room and find a loose thread and pull and pull and pull. I try to swallow my giggles as Naava's robe that she is going to wear to the city gets smaller and smaller and smaller.

Eve

It is only in hindsight that I can say this. I was frightened out of my wits when that horrible fat woman from the city killed the lamb right in front of me and my daughters. Still, to this day, when I think of it my hands begin to shake, and the dragonfly in my chest seems to want to fly up and out of my throat. *What would they have done to us had I refused them?* Later, Cain explained how such readings worked, how priests and seers looked deep into the liver for auspicious or inauspicious signs, and this frightened me too, that I was unaware of such things. Certainly Elohim had not taught us to do this.

And now, because of my fear, my baby would be leaving me. She was blood of my blood, skin of my skin. Each time I looked at her, I saw her wide sweet eyes, her open expression of trust. When she was an infant, I could not put her down. She had been gracious and kind to me in my time of birthing torment.

And now this. *How could I have done this to her?*

As the time neared for her to go—and I had delayed, and delayed again, in telling Adam the events of that chilling day—I chided myself for waiting so long. Surely Cain could have gone to the city and refused for me. Surely Cain could have explained that I needed all my children here, with me.

It was only six days before Dara had to leave when I finally summoned the courage to admit to my husband the thing I had done. I waited until night, when Adam came to lie by my side, to ask his opinion. I could hear the lilting voices of Dara and Jacan as they lay in the dark, under the stars, not wanting to sleep yet, talking about *what if*s and *would you*s, and I knew I would miss—miss terribly—Dara's high excited voice. My throat became thick like wool, and I fought to keep back tears. Adam would be more attentive if I didn't cry.

"Adam," I whispered into the dark. I could hear him turn toward me, the reeds crackling beneath him, his breath warm on my shoulders, his hands hungry on my breasts.

"I miss you out in the fields," he said. "There is no one to talk to."

I let him touch me, grope me. I thought of my betrayal of Dara and wondered what Adam would say. *Would he blame me for this too?* I pushed his hands away. "There is something I want to discuss with you," I said. "We have had visitors."

His hands grew quiet, and his voice rose. "Visitors?"

"Yes, women from the city," I said.

He raised up on his elbow and waited.

"They—oh, it was horrible!—they sliced open a little lamb, right in front of us . . . Naava, me, Dara . . . and—"

He sat up. "Ours?"

"No, no," I said. "They brought it with them. They scooped out its liver and set it on the ground in front of them and looked at it, then somehow made a connection between that and asking for Dara. Cain says they read livers as signs of fortune, well-being."

There was a short silence.

"Dara?" Adam said. "I don't understand."

My voice wavered. "I don't either. They originally asked for Naava—"

Adam grabbed my wrist. "What do you mean, *asked*?"

"They want someone to look after their children," I said. "They—"

Adam's voice was stern. "They will do the same thing they did to Aya. We cannot—"

I struggled to steady my voice. "I said no. I need Naava here, to care for me and the baby. But Dara—do you think they would harm a child?"

Adam released my wrist.

I explained how in return we would receive valuable fabrics and tools and stones from them.

Adam grunted. "Bartering," he said. "That's what Cain calls it."

I told him how Cain had made it clear to me that all city children over the age of four were required to learn to read and write and that they needed another older child who did not fall under this requirement, to care for their little ones.

"What is there to study but the signs of drought or how to best preserve foods or how to grow larger dates?" Adam asked, irritated.

I said nothing. *What could I say?* Cain had explained to me the benefits of reading and writing, but Adam would never see past the immediate urgency of a thing. If he wasn't using it now, it probably wasn't necessary.

He sighed and settled back, leaning his head into my chest. "I thought you wanted to Be One," he said.

"I do," I said, eager to please him. I pulled back and put my hand on his rough, whiskered face. "It's just that . . . well, I'm troubled about sending Dara. She's only six."

He was quiet for a bit. "They would not dare do anything to her at such an age. And she will be responsible for their babies." He paused, then said, "Maybe it would foster good relationships with them."

And here I lost my composure—what was left of it. I broke down into gulping sobs, and Adam held me. I was unable to speak for a very long time.

"I trust your opinion," said Adam. "Do what you think is best."

Relief washed over me. He trusted me. As my breath grew steady and I could talk, I said, "Do you think she'll be all right? I chose her because she's the littlest, and she's smart, and I cannot spare Naava and Aya now, with the baby coming. Do you think she'll think I don't love her?"

"Explain it to her," said Adam. His fingers grew nimble once again, and his tongue was upon my ear, gentle and flicking. "Make it seem like an adventure. Tell her that we will visit her."

I turned my face to his. The darkness prevented me from seeing his expression, but I said, "Oh, could we? You and I?"

"Of course," he said, and enveloped me in his arms again.

That night it was like we were back in the Garden again. Our bodies melded into One and moved to the music of the crickets and cicadas. And, oh, we sang the glory of the universe, of the stars and of the sun and of the moon, then created new songs of rivers and mountains and forbidden gardens.

I wish it were always that way.

More often than not, marriage was an exercise in mutual incomprehension. Adam heard my sighs and saw my weepy eyes, and instead of grief and sorrow, he felt a simmering anger directed at him. To look at me, really look at me, was too painful. It was a reflection of the fires of his own regret.

Likewise, I may have been misreading the language of *his* body. There were times that our lovemaking was old and boorish. Being One had become Being One in Body Only. Adam sought his own pleasure, gasping aloud, then sank into a deep slumber as though drugged. Afterward, my chest and belly were tinged with Adam's salt and indifference, and I could not sleep. There was a sadness and great loneliness in this disparity of love, of friendship, and I did not know how to repair it. The things that had given me the greatest joy in the Garden—a handful of clear cool water, an exquisite fern frond, the lilting birdsong, the tug of a lemon on my tongue, and Adam, my Adam, of course—had all vanished into a grayness of feeling.

Long ago I had designed a new purpose, separate from Adam, and began constructing a personal bower of joy. I reveled in my swelling body, the lively kicks from my unborn children. I memorized the map of my belly, the growing purplish lines that stretched from end to end, the furry path that ran down to my sex, my nipples grown vast and dark. You might say I collected my babies as herons scrounge for insects, with a wild and ravenous hunger, and you would be right. My babies were thirsty for me; they clung to me as a climbing vine, and I bathed them in kisses and songs. Too soon, though, they were gone—off to the fields or off to their chores—and the songs fell on empty arms.

Then it would be time.

I would spread myrrh and balsam on our bed. I'd light the lamps and wash my body. I drew back the unruly hair of my head with bits of cloth and dabbed a little sheep fat from Aya's larder on my lips. I waited for Adam. He would be pleased with my efforts and come to me gently and lovingly, thinking that this was an unexpected return to the Garden.

He did not suspect the truth—that I simply wanted him to plant his seed—and I did not tell him. The cycle began again, without Adam, and soon my baby and I supped on each other's love until our hearts were content. This I did without thought or consideration for how such conniving would end, and that was my mistake.

There is no justice in love.

Just because you give love does not mean you will receive it in the end, even though you feel it is your right, your privilege, because of all your labor. I was chagrined when I first realized this, thinking that maybe Elohim felt this same way when He pointed our way out of the Garden. Maybe He felt rejected and abused and violated because the trust between Him and us had been broken. Maybe He wept, as I have done many nights, over the lost innocence of His children. Of course, Adam and I did not intend to injure Elohim. We did not think that a small decision such as ours would have large consequences, and that is the heartache, knowing that it could have ended differently.

I have always judged Elohim harshly, as my children have done to me. I remind myself of this, always, though it is difficult. *Where was Elohim that summer, when I needed Him most? Why did He turn His ear from me?* For then, during those summer months, I was an empty well and my bones were scorched. I cried all the day long, and my throat was parched.

Now, as I rehash these events all over again, I can see the stars through my crude window, like shining blossoms floating on a darkened pool. I hear Naava's steady breathing as she sleeps next to me—bless her heart, I have troubled her with all my recountings!—and remember Elohim's promise of children.

The Garden was warm at night, almost stifling hot. The wind was oftentimes absent; the only sounds were of bats' wings and cicada chirps. We were as droopy as the surrounding vegetation until we discovered that if we climbed up the mountains on the eastern side of the Garden, we would come out onto a plateau, where the air was dry, the winds were gentle, and the sky was as black as a crow's wing above us. Here, we could greet the moon and the stars.

We would sit, hour after hour, talking about Elohim, about us, about our plans for the Garden—for we *did* have plans, to create more walking paths and the like. Adam had even begun to twist vines together to form a rope we could tie to the Tree of Life, as a laughing, soaring way to enter the river.

Elohim would join us on occasion.

"*Why* did You create us?" I asked Him on one particularly hot evening. "We can't be of much interest to You, because You know so much more than we do."

"I longed for company," He said.

Imagine, I thought in amazement. *He needs us.*

He was quiet for a moment. "Have you not exclaimed at the wonder of a hummingbird or the deep scarlet throat of a lily, only to realize that Adam is nowhere near to share in your delight? You race to find him or tuck the sight away in your mind to tell him later. That is how it was before I made you. Who would appreciate what I had made? Who could enjoy the fruits of my labor?"

I did not think to ask Him then, but later I wondered why He did not create a spouse for Himself—a counterpart—rather than children. Was it because He would have had to share His omniscience, His glory, His superiority? Most certainly He would have endowed Her with powers like His own, wouldn't He? But with children, He would always be ranked *above* them. Possibly this is what the city people had figured out—that there are gods *and* goddesses, to uphold male *and* female sensibilities. *Had Elohim not considered this?*

And then, even later, I found myself imagining that *if* Elohim had created a partner for Himself, She would have been lovely, creative, and every bit as imaginative and powerful as He. Instead, though, He embodied Her *and* Him—the epitome of *male* and *female*—in Himself. Hadn't He said that He could appear as anything? And weren't we *both* created in

His image, and how could that be if He were not male *and* female at the same time?

With Elohim's validation that a new sight or sound is so much better shared with someone, Adam was already wondering about other things. "Is there anything else to be created?" asked Adam. "I have thought of a few things, such as a plant that gives off heat in the early-morning chill, or—"

"Watch," said Elohim. He grabbed two flinty stones and struck them against each other. A spark leapt from between them, sputtered, then died.

"Oh," I said, astonished.

Again Elohim struck one stone against the other, and again sparks flew. He held up a handful of dry grass, and the spark was transformed to a small bluish light. It quickly consumed the grass. "Fire," said Elohim. He laid the light down on the ground and piled sticks onto it, to feed its growing hunger. The flames, now a red-orange, licked higher and higher, and the heat poured into our bodies.

Adam reached for it but yelped and drew back, shaking his hand. He grimaced.

Elohim laughed. "I cannot teach you everything. Some things you must learn on your own. That is the way of the world. With age comes experience, and with experience, wisdom. That is how it should be." He turned to me, warming His hands over the fire. "Eve, you have seen the animals birthing, have you not?"

I nodded.

"You will have children too. That is an ability I have given you and Adam—there it is, Adam, the answer to your question. It is then, and only then, that I think you will understand my longing, my need. But, of course, you understood the need for each other, did you not?"

It was a rhetorical question, I knew. *So,* I thought, *Adam and I will have little ones who look like us.* We would join Elohim as creators. The wonder of it all!

We let the warmth of the fire seep into our limbs while Elohim pointed out the planets and the stars and wove the stories of the sun and moon into the fabrics of our being.

Now Naava has turned in her sleep and is snoring gently. I shall have a little laugh with her in the morning about that. She hated it when her sisters snored, and she claimed it was why she never got enough sleep. Aya always said, "You sound like a nest of bees. No wonder you wake up!"

During that summer, I had one hope: that we were hibernating, Adam and I, like bears in their dens. One day we would emerge into the warm sun, drowsy from a long nap, and nuzzle each other and say, "Where have you been, my love?" We would smell deep into each other's steamed fur, straddle each other's bellies, and lick each other's honey sweetness. And we would Be One again—for all time.

Naava

The morning heat creeps in on all fours and spreads its haunches on the cool dirt floor at the foot of Eve's bed. Wasps hover under a nest right outside the window. A dove coos mournfully. Eve blinks at the grainy, dusty light and teases Naava about her snoring, and still, to this day, Naava denies it.

She asks Eve if she might stretch her legs a bit. She has not been home in so long, and she badly wants to feel the rough stone of the cistern again, where she and Cain found each other. She wants to see what is left of Eve's garden, now baked and fallow in the desert sand. She wants to sit at her loom and dream of the robe she once wove for her trip to the city.

She finds Eve's hand and squeezes it. Eve closes her eyes to doze again, and Naava goes out, into the dazzling sunlight and underneath the bone-white sky, to reacquaint herself with her history.

The robe was as intricate and as astonishing as an eclipse. Naava had gone to great pains to get the colors just right, using herbs from Aya's patch and flowers from Eve's garden. Eve's baby sling long forgotten, Naava had created spectacular new colors, dazzling to the eye. Fresh goldenrod for yellow. Madder for red and purple. Broom sedge for brown. Chamomile for green. She boiled the wool in large pots, sweating and stirring and lifting, until the fibers glowed with a true intensity. She dried them, threaded them, and wound them tightly on wooden spools. With a stick she drew her design into the dirt floor of her weaving room and covered it with clay bricks, left over from house repairs, so that her plans would be protected from critters' tracks or prying eyes.

Then she began. The work was tedious. Her fingers wept with blisters, then crusted with calluses. When the weaving wasn't to her liking, she cried out in frustration and unraveled as far back as she needed to go, the design dissolving into nothingness.

She wove her version of Eve's Garden, the way she saw it in her mind. There was a blue-green river that transected the back of the robe from top to bottom. The sky above was to be split into two swaths—one as black as bitumen, sprinkled with pearly stars that she would stitch in later; the other a sunshiny yellow with gray luminous clouds. Below would be the green expanse of grasses and mosses, the reds and oranges of flowering trees and bushes, and the silvery light of bird wing. It was Naava's retelling—a heartfelt, gorgeous rendition of her mother's memory—although Naava had noted, with disappointment, that the evolving product was nothing like she had imagined in her mind. It seemed an impossibility to link vision with reality.

Naava had finished the night and day and a large section of jeweled birds and bright flowers when she caught Dara pulling at the threads. She rushed into the room and grabbed at Dara's hands. "No!" she yelled. "No, no!" Then softer, "No," the shock of seeing so much of it gone. She dropped to the floor and covered her face in her hands. "No, no, no," she repeated, rocking back and forth.

She would tell Eve—that's what she would do. Dara would incur Eve's wrath, and Eve would decide that Naava should be sent to the city, not Dara, who was clearly still a child, a baby. It was outrageous how Eve ignored what Naava wanted. She felt trapped, stifled. Really, it was inexcusable, despicable.

When Naava lifted her face from her hands, her eyes triumphant, she saw a hint of fear in her little sister's eyes, but Dara said nothing.

Naava stood, wiped her hands on her robes, and stalked into the courtyard. Dara played with her fingers, touching the tips, one after another, like a praying mantis walking on a twig. She watched, uncertain, as Naava walked toward Eve, who was mixing clay and bitumen together and patching chinks in the courtyard wall.

"I'm *not* staying here!" she said, her hands on her hips.

Eve only looked bemused.

Naava thought briefly that she may have looked ridiculous, scolding her mother this way, and she was glad Abel was not there to see it. "I *won't*."

Eve shielded her eyes from the sun and sat back on her knees. "Naava, what's wrong?"

Naava knew she puzzled her mother, that Eve would never understand her. She confused *herself* sometimes, for there were days she felt as heavy as the bitumen on her mother's stick and other days she felt as light as a feather. *Why the difference, for no apparent reason?* She didn't know, and she didn't care—enough to change, that is. "*I* want to go to the city, to learn how to make that pretty cloth they wear, and you know that, but you act as if I'm not even here, and you're sending Dara instead. Why, she's just a baby. What can she do? I can do ten times the amount of work she can, and I would make friends, and see new sights, and be able to come back here and teach you everything. Your being with child is just an excuse. What can *I* do while you're screaming in pain? Aya does it all."

Eve stood and squeezed Naava's arm above her elbow. "Naava," she said, "when you're ready to discuss this in a rational manner, I will talk to you. Right now you're like tumbleweed—all over the place. Here, sit."

But Naava jerked her arm away. "I am grown up already. I should be able to do what I want, *when* I want, like Cain and Abel. You always point your finger and order me about, and I'm tired of it." She paused, then spit out, "*Father* would understand."

Eve leaned forward, held Naava's chin in her hand. "I have discussed this with your father. He agrees with me."

Naava gritted her teeth and said, "That's because you didn't tell him everything, how badly I want to—"

Eve released Naava, pushing her away. "Naava! That's enough. Finish your weaving."

Naava stuck her bottom lip out. "That's just it. Dara's unraveled it." Naava watched her mother's face change from anger to surprise to irritation.

Eve said, "You must have done something to provoke her."

Dara slipped from the doorway of the weaving room and went to stand behind Eve's skirts, sucking her thumb.

Naava glared at her mother and little sister. She howled then, like a wolf, and raised her fists to the sky and stomped her feet. She whirled back to her weaving room and threw herself inside. Rage at her ruined robe and empty future curdled in her, then firmed up, like Aya's hunks of cheese. There was nothing she could say. She had not asked for this, her barren, boring life.

She would *make* Eve do what she wanted. She would *silence* Eve—just for a short while. Then she would convince her father that she, not Dara, should go to the city.

Mind you, this would not be an easy task. Naava was no fool. She knew she would have to cover her tracks.

Naava bided her time, waiting in her weaving room. When Eve finally vacated the courtyard, she sidled over to Aya, who had missed the quarrel but was now back outside, splitting reeds with the edge of a sharp stone.

"Aya," Naava said.

Goat pushed her nose into Naava's crotch, and she pushed her away.

"Aya," Naava said again. And then, "Get away from me, you boar." She yanked Goat around by her horns and sent her off, bleating.

Aya stood up, the stone in her hand, her face flushed with exertion. "Don't touch her head. She doesn't like that."

"All right, all right," said Naava. After all, she needed Aya just now.

"What do you want?" said Aya. "I need to finish this. I can't really talk."

"Would you like me to get you some water?" said Naava sweetly.

Aya narrowed her eyes.

"So you're not thirsty, then." Naava was nervous, trying to best phrase her next question. "Listen, Aya, how would you go about getting rid of a pesky little lizard who torments me when I'm weaving? He runs all about and shits on my wool and hinders my work. In fact, I wanted to ask Abel to get rid of him for me, but—"

Aya's face puckered in concentration. "*I* haven't seen him," Aya said. And then, when Naava didn't reply, she said matter-of-factly, "Can't you catch him?"

"No," said Naava. "That's the problem. He's too quick. Might you have something that would put him to sleep?"

"You mean kill him?"

"Or that too." Naava felt a bead of sweat roll down her chest. She didn't want to *kill* her mother, just hinder her a bit while she pled her case to her father. She would be able to make it clear to him that she would be a much better go-between than Dara. Her hands grew clammy, and her stomach clenched up. "It's a *big* lizard." Naava held out her hands, about an arm's length.

"If you'd lay a trap, you might catch him." Aya's voice rose, mocking.

"Just give me something, you—I mean, please will you give me something to set down for it? I will finish splitting the reeds for you."

Aya's expression didn't change, and Naava couldn't tell what she was thinking. Aya said, "No need. I'm almost finished." Then, in a voice loud enough for Naava to hear, "Elohim"—*Fabulous, here she goes again*, thought Naava—"give me a kind heart, especially to those who are unreasonable and self-centered. Help me be good. Help me—"

"Will this take long?" said Naava. "I'm in a bit of a hurry."

Then, as though to prevent Naava from following her, Aya gave a big sigh and said, "I'll be right back."

Naava waited for what seemed to be an interminable amount of time, but just at the moment when she thought she would faint from nervous exhaustion, Aya reappeared, carrying a limp cloth sack.

"Here," said Aya. "Use only a pinchful at a time. A little bit goes a long way."

Naava reached over to give her a hug, but Aya pushed her away. "Don't act as if you're my friend," Aya said, "just because I've given you something."

Naava straightened up, confused. "Thank you, Aya. You're very smart."

"And no needless compliments either," said Aya as she turned back to her reed splitting.

Naava stood there a moment, then walked back to her weaving room.

"You owe me a favor," called Aya.

But Naava paid no attention. She was already scattering the parsleylike leaves onto the dirt next to her loom. The leaves smelled musty and a little rancid. Naava wondered how she would get Eve to ingest them. *Put them in water? Put them in beer? Bake them in bread?* The last one would require Aya's help, and that was not going to happen. *Which is just the way it always is,* thought Naava.

In the end, it all worked out.

Naava waited until Aya went off to gather more dung for her fires, then she scuttled across the courtyard and into Aya's larder. There, in the cool darkness, she gathered a handful of figs and hid them in the folds of her robe. Once she was safe, back in her weaving room, she laid them all out and tried to decide how she would accomplish her task without raising any eyebrows. With her tongue wedged between her lips in concentration, she slit the flesh of the figs and stuffed them with the strange-smelling leaves. Then she pressed the figs into small cakes, perfect for the evening meal.

"What are you doing?" asked Dara. Her shadow fell across Naava's face, and Naava jumped.

"Don't sneak up on me like that," said Naava.

"What are you doing?"

"Helping Aya," said Naava. She smiled at Dara. "Want to help too? Here, flatten these out."

The trick was to poison *only* Eve. Again, this part was easy because Aya, in her tiresome fastidiousness, divided her kissed food *before* she set out the bowls and platters. It was Aya's great care in her cooking and the delivery of it that would make this go much smoother. Naava waited until Aya was done, then, when her sister had turned away, she switched Eve's fig cakes.

So, imagine. Eve sat down with her husband and her children, around Aya's fire, unknowing and innocent. She ate of the fig cakes, chewed them, and swallowed. Naava sat there, agitated, because she knew she had done an evil deed—and because it might not work. *Surely, it would not harm Eve too much, would it?* Naava only wanted to teach her a lesson. Then Eve could rise to health again, after learning to pay attention to *all* her children, not just her favorites—and after Naava was away in the new city.

At first Naava struggled to behave normally, smiling and talking as though she had not a care in the world, but it helped that, once again, all the attention was on the feud between Cain and Abel.

Cain laughed at Abel, then sopped up some broth with his bread. "If we are to sacrifice to your Elohim," he said, "then let's lay some ground rules."

Eve said, "Not this again, please, not now."

Naava noted that her mother was still able to talk. This was not a good sign. *How long would it take for the leaves to work?*

"It's all right, Mother," said Abel. "We can discuss this reasonably." To Cain he said, "What rules?"

"First fruits of our crops and flocks," said Cain. "At the end of harvest."

Abel nodded his agreement and, with a long look around the table, said, "You've all been witness to this agreement. Let it be so."

Cain laughed again and said, "We'll see what your Elohim can do for us. Do you think He can make us more wealthy than the dwellers of the new city?"

Aya, of all people, piped up and said, "Elohim doesn't bargain, Cain. You should make your offerings out of gratitude, not greed."

Cain's face grew dark. "Those of unsound bodies have unsound minds," he said.

Aya was quiet.

Eve finally put her hands to her head and said, "Aya, where did you get this meat?"

Aya pointed to Abel, who asked, "What is it?"

"I'm feeling a little dizzy. I think I'll go lie down." Eve braced herself and rose slowly, so as not to jar her head.

Abel glanced at Aya, a puzzled look on his face, but Aya was staring curiously at Naava, who was glaring back at her. All this occurred within the blink of an eyelid.

Adam watched Eve go, worry in his eyes. He got up and wiped his mouth with his sleeve. As he disappeared after Eve, he called back to Cain and Abel, "I think this is an excellent agreement. Elohim will be pleased." And then he was gone, hurrying after his wife.

Now all they had to do was wait. Cain: for his crops to flourish. Abel: for his flocks to grow strong and healthy. Naava: for her mother to nap with the cockroaches.

Aya

As if I wouldn't know what Naava had done. I tell you this. I gave the hemlock to Naava against my better judgment, and look what happened. I could see it in Naava's face too, and in the way she shook her foot, the way she watched my face to see if I was suspicious in any way.

When Mother got up from the table to go lie down, she was having difficulty breathing, and she walked, drunklike, in a zigzag. If Naava had indeed done such a thing, she was no longer my sister. No longer fit to eat my food, and I would tell her so.

"What have you done?" I hissed, as soon as everyone had gone back to their chores. I grabbed her arm and squeezed my fingernails into her flesh.

Naava wrenched away from me and slapped at my hand. "What have *I* done?" Naava said, standing up. "You're the one who gave it to me."

"For the lizard," I said.

"That's right," Naava said, "the lizard who shat on everything I care about. There she goes."

"You may have killed her!" I said. I spat on her feet. "And the baby. That's *two* lives."

Naava's mouth gaped open, then snapped shut, like fish gills.

"That's right," I said. "You heard me."

Naava sat, plopping her backside down on the courtyard bench. The corners of her mouth were turned down, and she sulked. "I was only trying to get her out of the way for a little while. What's the harm in that?"

"You stupid, stupid girl," I said. "You disgrace us." With that, I turned to go, my manner as resolute as my inward conviction.

"Don't put on airs," said Naava. "Cain is right. You're worth nothing with that foot. Do you really think Mother cares about you, being crippled and all? Why do you think she takes special pains to notice you? 'Aya, darling, you look nice today,' or 'Aya, you have truly outdone yourself today, with this lamb and cabbage mixture. What did you put in it?'" Naava flung her head about, her nose up in the heavens.

I pretended not to hear her, for she is right. Mother *does* say all those things, and I know, beyond a shadow of a doubt, what she means when she says them. I do not label it as such—*condescension*—for the mere utterance of the word could solidify it, pack it into place, in such a way that I would never recover. For that is how I see it. I *know*, but I don't *dwell*. There is a great chasm between the two. Sometimes, when the two touch, just lightly, there, like that, it sends forth a great earthquake inside, and the very force of it threatens to rip me apart. That, I cannot have. So I willingly forget those sorts of things, think lightly on them, so that I am not broken wide open and filled with the rotten pulp of truth.

I told Abel what Naava had done. I had no other choice. He thought there was something wrong with the meat, and I did *not* want to bear that responsibility. He had to know what she was like—the *real* Naava under those long eyelashes and straight cheekbones and red-pepper lips. He did not believe me at first. He *could* not believe me. "She wouldn't," he said.

"But she did," I said. "Naava would kill us all if she thought it would make her life better."

"You are sure?" Abel asked again.

"Ask her yourself," I said. His hesitancy irritated me. I could tell he was weighing Naava's beauty against my bitter accusation.

Abel and I were more alike than he knew.

Abel saw things. Another way of saying it is: He had visions. Jacan had related one of Abel's dreams to me when I took him to bathe in the river.

Here it is: Abel as an eagle, soaring above the plains, searching for shrews and rats and rabbits and partridges he might consume. The sun warms his back, and his feathers ruffle in the breeze. He can see the glint of the sea, the gold of the sand, the green of the palms. He is free, and he thinks, *I should like to stay here.*

Funny how Abel and I have the same flying dream, I thought. Or maybe more *fateful* than *funny.*

Jacan stopped midway through to interject thoughts of his own. "Do you think," he asked, "Abel *could* fly?"

"Well, if he was an eagle," I said, "certainly."

"Really?" he said, eyes wide. "I want to be a bird."

"Pretend you are a fish. Swim!" Otherwise, we would have been there all night!

Abel using the air currents to soar. His wings carrying him high, so high, up to where he is just a speck in the sky. Dropping low, he skims the chaparral on the plains and the cattails in the marshes. He careens down through the masses of herons and cranes and egrets, sending them fluttering and thrashing into the air. He is mighty. He is King of the Sky.

"I am King of the River," Jacan exclaimed, pulling up a handful of mud from the bottom of the riverbed. It oozed out from between his pudgy fingers.

"You are," I said. "And I am the princess."

"No," Jacan said, standing up in the murky water. "Dara is." He plucked at a leech that had latched upon his skin and flung it down, *plonk,* into the river.

Abel, King of the Sky, viewing the whitewashed city, the walls hemming in the grand houses that have flat roofs decorated with potted plants and wooden benches. He sees the craftsmen pound their metal, hammer their wheels, and carry stone and clay and bitumen. He spots their temple, built up with steps so that it reaches to the sky, where the gods and goddesses live in invisible palaces. He watches them unload cargo from their ships and load it upon carts and haul it back into the city. Everywhere, it is an ant city, every ant carrying its own blade of grass, its own torn piece of leaf.

All this he sees.

Then, as he is watching, a dark thread of menace seeps from the city walls and runs out like blood to where the ships are docked. It merges with the river and fills it up with foreboding. Of course, the water runs southward, toward the sea, yet when it flows by our house, Abel's house, it does not continue toward the sea. It climbs up the levees, through the irrigation channels, and bloodies everything—all the livestock, the barley fields, the vegetable gardens, even Mother's garden where her babies are buried.

There is no reason for Abel, King of the Sky, to feel choked, but he does. He cannot breathe. His wings do not keep him aloft. He is falling falling falling, and there is nothing he can do about it. No amount of effort will help him now.

Where will he land? Will someone be there to catch him?

"No no no," said Jacan.

Abel, King of the Sky, falling falling falling. He's headed for the cistern, for its deep black water. He folds his wings, tucking them close to his body to lessen the impact, then suddenly he hits the surface of the water with such a force, he is knocked senseless. When he opens his eyes, all he can see is the sunlight above, dancing down through the water in sad patterns, and he wants to go up there, to feel the air again, but, no, he is stuck. He cannot move. His wings are broken, his claws useless for swimming, so he sinks farther and farther down, where the sunshine is muted and the music of someone calling "Abel, Abel, can you hear me?" is muffled.

Then Abel wakes up. At precisely this time in the vision. Every time.

"Who is the person above?" I asked.

Jacan shrugged. "He doesn't say."

"But what does it mean? Why would Elohim send a dream to Abel if he cannot decipher it?"

Jacan said, "I tell myself when I lay down at night that I will become an eagle like Abel, but it never works."

"You can't make up dreams, silly," I told him. "They're different for everyone."

What does it mean? I thought. *Who belongs to the face over the cistern?*

I was Aya the Asp Killer, Aya the Bird. I would find the answer to this mystery to save Abel, my brother. Then he would see me, really *see* me.

Then he would see how much we have in common. Maybe we were made for each other, as Mother and Father were. As Naava and he were not.

I spent the night with Mother. Father's worry kept her awake, and I could not have that, so I sent him out to sleep under the stars. He protested and said, "I need to stay with her," but I told him I could not remedy her illness with him hovering over me, watching my every move. Upon my pronouncement, Father's shoulders bent like a bow, and he wiped the tears from his eyes. "Come get me if she gets worse," he said softly. When I didn't answer, he said again, louder, "Come get me. You hear me, Aya? Come get me if anything hap—" He choked on a sob, and I touched him lightly on the arm.

"I will," I said. "I will."

Mother's groans kept me vigilant. I forced Mother to swallow a little mustard oil. In her delirium, she called me insufferable names. She began to shiver, though not because it was cold, and I crawled into bed with her, spooning her to warmth. She muttered to herself about "the sword, the flaming sword" and "too late, too late." She was back in her Garden; either that or she had been flung from it once again.

I had come upon the hemlock plant with Goat one afternoon on my way back from the river. It was mildly attractive, with its smooth purple-spotted stem and parsleylike leaves. It smelled rank, much like parsnips, but it had pretty white flowers shaped in clusters. Goat set to eating it right away, a leaf or two, but stopped because she found something she liked better nearby—namely, the juicy watercress plant. In quick time, though, Goat was all trembly and wobbly. I set down my basket full of shellfish and hoisted her up into my arms—with some difficulty, since she was twitching every which way—and when I got her back to the house, I tried to get her to taste a little of everything, so I could discover the antidote. Only the mustard oil seemed to clear her eyes and steady her limbs, and even that took a day or two to become effective. I went back later to chop the hemlock down and, of course, to alert Abel, so he could shield his flocks from it.

This is what I do. Feed my family, and save them from death. If I am not needed for my looks, I most certainly am needed for their survival. This they know. And I remind them of it often.

Mother got better, but it was three days until she could sit up. Then, even in her weakened condition, as if her life meant nothing, she had the audacity to challenge Elohim—if I had not seen it myself, I would not have believed it!

It was a catastrophe of major proportions.

I had come into her bedroom to bring her a little broth and some bread, which I knew would settle her stomach.

And what did I see?

Mother, kneeling on the hard earth, her fists folded like penitent artichokes in front of her, babbling to the stone fertility goddess that Cain had brought her. In my haste and horror, I flung the food down, rushed to Mother's side, pulled her hands down, and blocked her view of the stone creature.

"What are you doing?" I cried. I half-thought she was crazy from the sickness, but no, she looked at me as calmly as could be and said, "Praying for my baby."

I knew no answer except one. Now, I did not claim to know Elohim better than Mother, for she actually had seen Him in person, but I did know that He was a jealous God, and I did not think He would glory in Mother's worship of someone else.

I pointed to the hideous stone woman. "How strong is she?" I demanded. "She's made of stone. She can't see you or hear you. Oh, what have you done to us? He's everywhere, all at once, and He will know what you've done! You *know* this—" I pulled on her arm, and she went reluctantly with me over to her reed mat and lay down, positioning her head so that she was comfortable. "Talk to Him. Tell Him you're sorry, that you'll never do it again," I said. When she didn't respond, I grabbed her cheeks and pinched them between my fingers. "Now! Talk to Him now!"

Mother laughed at me. It was the first time she had ever done so, and it was laughter intended to hurt, as Naava's always was. The sound trickled through the air and landed upon my ears, slowly and painfully. Her eyes were twisted in a purple derision, and her fury scorched a ring around me. "Oh, Aya, are you blind and deaf too? You have inquired of Elohim, have you not, about your foot? I see your lips move while you're down on your knees, grinding corn or shelling lobsters. I am not so dumb as you think." She pulled my fingers from her face. "Has Elohim answered your prayer? Does He hear you? Because I don't hear Him anymore. He has long since deserted me." She turned her head away, and her voice shriveled up like a dried plum. "Do not speak of what you do not know."

For a brief moment, I stood, paralyzed. My own mother had uttered blasphemous thoughts, and I knew there was no remedy, nothing in my overflowing storage room of medicines that could fix this disastrous mistake.

There was only one thing to be done.

I sang a song to Mother, one I made up on the spur of the moment, about the sweet peace and delicious happiness of the Garden, where the grass was tinged with dew and the river bubbled softly. I included a verse about her beloved waterfall, and soon she fell asleep, her face and limbs gone slack with forgetfulness. Without delay I snatched Mother's stone woman, her Ugly Beast, stuffed it in a carrying sling, and ran out to the river, out to Cain's date palms. My bad leg ached, and my breath seized up, but I kept running until I had arrived at the foot of one of Cain's regal giants. I shinnied up its trunk, careful to avoid the prickly thorns, and sat there on top of the world. Indeed, I could see beyond the house to the east, beyond the river to the west. Everywhere, plants and trees and people had shrunk to half their size, and I was once again Aya the Bird who knew that Elohim had seen her and listened to her and invited her to soar with Him over the desert plains. I caught my breath.

I looked around until I found a scarred hole where beetles had long ago burrowed into the tree. It was here I buried Ugly Beast, a shiny white talisman, defenseless against Aya the Asp Killer, Aya the Lucifer Killer. No one would ever find her up here.

Something of this nature and significance required a small ceremony, much like Mother's babies did—Daniel and Micayla and Miriam—and I gladly thought up something to say. "Ugly Beast," I said. "May your head fall off, and your breasts drip dry. May you choke on your tongue and swallow your lies. Amen."

I cupped my hands around my mouth and yelled out, *"Elohim, if You can hear me, give me a new foot, so that I can run away from here, back to the Garden, where there is peace and happiness. Let me not be ashamed that I have defended You and protected Your name.*

"Do You hear me, Elohim?

"Elohim?"

Eve

Cain's gods had become a wedge between myself and Adam. I feared Cain was right. It made perfect sense to me that the world was too big for Elohim to care for it all at once. How could *one* being hold the entire world in His hand and do a worthy job of it? I had offered many lip prayers to Elohim, but He had covered himself in a cloud so that no prayers could penetrate. Days passed, and I grasped at the fading mystery of the Garden and its Creator.

And then.

Cain told me provocative stories of how the gods existed first and how they grew tired of working the land, so they created man to do it for them. "Mother, it makes sense. Whatever you need, whatever you want, you pray to *that* god or goddess for help. If you need rain, Enlil, Lord of the Air, will do your bidding. If I am being tormented by field mice and vermin, I need only to call on Ninkilim. If a bountiful harvest is what I want, I need only to invoke the name of Ki, Mother of the Earth. See? It's really very simple."

I reminded Cain of how Elohim had made the world by His breath and His hands.

"Are you sure, Mother?" he said. "Did you not see any other beings in the Garden?"

"Well, there was Lucifer," I said.

"Maybe there were more," he said. "But they were busy."

It was a possibility I could not shake, despite Adam's insistence that Cain was digging a hole for himself.

It was Cain's determination that eventually won me over. He had begun constructing a small temple of his own, out of clay bricks, in the narrow space between the house and Adam's orchard. Adam was none too pleased with this arrangement and told Cain he was washing his hands of him. Cain had lost much sleep, and his eyes had grown red with weariness. In truth, the building was merely one small room, but if it pleased the gods it would be a sweet tribute to them, and Cain would be blessed, which was what he desired.

Enthusiasm always comes with its twin, bullheadedness, and Cain certainly had both. He explained the city's religious rituals—now his—to any family member who would listen, and Abel, especially, had grown angry. Abel was a loyal follower of Elohim, bless his heart. After all, Abel had clung to the stories I'd told him from when he was a baby, and he insisted that Elohim spoke to him almost daily. Aya, too, said similar things, and I wondered, *Why does He not talk to me?*

Cain had always smothered the thing he loved the most, and this he did then, with his towering bricks and prattling mouth. He asked Dara to form little people out of clay, all with folded hands perched in front of them. I heard his explanation to her: "Two times a day they offer up meat and bread and wine to their gods." Here, he became distracted. "They take these statues—like the ones you're making—to a temple much bigger than mine, and their statues pray for them, all through the day. Remarkable, don't you think? It's efficient and smart." He said something then that I was unfamiliar with, and I realized, stunned, that he was attempting to speak the city people's tongue. The click of his tongue, the rasp of his words—all sounded like the gibberish of the city women who had come to visit. I said nothing then, because I was so shocked at the ease of his transformation. He was like a grasshopper; he could not sit still.

Dara nodded. She did not yet side with Elohim *or* these other gods. Her face was bunched, like a flower before its petals have opened. With chubby fingers, she formed small balls, and out of these, she formed heads and legs and bodies with crooked arms. She took a stick, and with its sharp end she traced lines in their clay hands to make tiny praying fingers.

Behold Cain, my son who loved everything stripped down to the essentials—here is the cause; here is the effect.

Dara was simply happy in the knowledge that she was pleasing her big brother.

Although I had not yet visited the city, I knew the allure of it was great, for Cain, for Adam.

For me.

When I was feverish and sick and Aya came rushing in on me like that, smug as a tick, I was embarrassed and startled. I thought she had gone out to collect dung. It was a test, really. To see if the alabaster goddess could help me, help my baby live through my sickness. I was weary of burying. I was tired of crying.

I reacted harshly, I know this now. I said cruel things to her, my little bird. I could not help myself. When she caught me at it, the panic and fluttering in my chest would not subside, and I was grateful that Aya sang me to sleep finally.

Slowly I slipped away, and dreamed—of Eden and of Lucifer.

The first time he appeared to me in the Garden was when Adam went off for a day, to see where the river would take him, and I was too lethargic to go. Adam had been gone only moments when suddenly there was this beautiful creature, pleasing to look at, standing right before me. He was like Adam but more radiant, more tempting—cloaked in the colors of the ruby, the diamond, the beryl, the jasper, the onyx, the lapis lazuli, the emerald, the turquoise, and the topaz. Lines of gold rippled where each hue melded into the next. He was flowing and smooth and sensual.

"Greetings," he said in a low voice.

I stood up, for I had been kneeling in the dirt, studying an insect that looked exactly like a leaf. I brushed off my hands and felt myself grow warm all over, as the time Elohim had made fire. "Hello," I said. "Who are you?" *How many creatures like Adam and me had Elohim made? Why hadn't we known there were others?*

"I am Lucifer, star of the morning," he said. "A pleasure to meet you. Elohim has been quite secretive about this little project of His. He's been in such a good humor lately that I had to come see what all the fuss was about."

"You came from . . . ?" I pointed to the sky and the day-squelched stars, then tentatively to the other end of the Garden. "Are there others of you?" I asked.

"Yes," he said. He slithered closer—for that is how it seemed—and reached out to stroke my cheek. He looked me up and down, his gaze raking my skin. "Nicely done." He smiled.

Up to that moment, I had never felt so exposed.

"I'll give Him credit for that," he said.

Again, I felt warm all over. He made me tremble, not unlike how I felt the first time I met Adam. "Where are the rest of you?" I said.

He moved even closer, close enough so I could smell the desire on his breath. "Oh, nearby," he said. "We're very curious about you."

I did not move. It was as though I was commanded by some force other than myself to stay, to linger precisely in that spot. It was not an unpleasant sensation.

Lucifer kissed me tenderly on the lips, and I felt my limbs go weak. I felt the flicker of his tongue upon my cheek, then, "Is it true?" he said. "Did Elohim really say you couldn't eat of any of the trees?" He pulled back and clasped my fingers in his. "Did He?"

The brief distance between us seemed to clear my befuddled mind, if only for a moment. "Oh, no," I cried. "We've tried them all, and they're delicious. Here, let me show you." I reached to pluck a lychee for him, but he pulled me back into his embrace.

"Really?" There was a hint of scorn in his voice. "Of *all* the trees?"

"Well, no," I said. "Not from that one. We are not even to touch it."

Lucifer smiled then, a smile that made me doubt everything I had seen of him up to that point. "Watch," he said. He released my hands and walked toward the tree.

"Stop," I cried. "You shall surely die." My words grew softer because, indeed, Lucifer was already next to the tree and had his hands upon the bark. "Please," I said. "Elohim will be angry."

Lucifer shook the tree so hard that the trunk groaned and the branches swayed and the fronds clapped their hands. Several of the luscious fruits fell to the ground with a *plop*. They split open, spilling their seeds and flesh out upon the ground, their aroma wafting toward me on the humid air. He looked back at me, over his shoulder, as if he expected me to say something. When I didn't, he made a great show of examining his hands and his body and said, "Now then, nothing has happened. What could Elohim have meant?" He seemed truly puzzled as he walked back toward me.

"You don't feel anything at all?" I said, astonished. Rashly, I laid my hands on his arm—or what appeared to be an arm—to see for myself, and I felt something odd, a tingling of sorts, an uncomfortable feeling of possession. I withdrew my hand.

"Nothing." The ends of his mouth turned up slightly, like he was having a little fun at my expense.

"That's strange," I said. "For Elohim said you would surely die." The cloying smell of the fruit was overwhelming now, like nothing I'd ever smelled before. It was as though it were wishing to be eaten, wishing to be held. I took one step forward.

"What did He say, *exactly*?" asked Lucifer, coming near to me, so that his breath was warm against my neck. Again, this was comforting *and* discomforting. He was too close, too stifling, too *something*. Still, to this day, I cannot say exactly what it was that made me feel that way. I was under siege.

I pondered this for a moment and said slowly, "He said not to touch or eat of the Tree of the Knowledge of Good and Evil, for surely we would die."

"But you desire it, no?"

"Oh, yes, very much," I said. Up until that point I don't think I would have described my feeling as such—*desire*—but suddenly I realized, with great surprise, that, yes, I did desire the fruit, for it was beautiful and alluring. And it smelled sweet and succulent.

"Oh, Eve—may I call you that?" His skin touched mine. It was warm and cool, rough and smooth, at the same time.

I took a step backward. "How do you know my name?"

Lucifer waved his hand, as if brushing away a pesky fly. "That's not so important. Let's sit here—no, here, in the shade of this . . . problematic tree—to talk. We should get acquainted, don't you think?"

I nodded, a bit shyly. I had of course only experienced such a . . . physical interest—I think that's what it was—with Adam.

The tree moaned at Lucifer's weight up against it. Its thorny trunk did not seem to bother Lucifer in the least.

I reached out before I could stop myself. "Oh," I said. "I wouldn't want something to happen to you."

"Wouldn't you?" said Lucifer, winking at me. "We've become fast friends, wouldn't you say?"

I grew warm, and I'm sure I turned as red as a pomegranate. Adam teased me about this incessantly.

"Where is Adam?" he said.

I did not want to talk about Adam. "You seem to be very knowledgeable about us," I said impatiently. "Let's talk about you."

"My favorite subject," he said. He did not smile.

Instead, he looked at me with such intent interest that I felt my insides shift and fall down into my groin. I longed to be touched—even more than that, to be caressed. I felt the strange sensation of not wanting something and wanting something in the same instant.

"Do you like it here?" said Lucifer.

"Oh, yes, very much," I said. "Elohim has thought of everything."

Lucifer's lips twitched slightly, and he seemed to be deep in thought. "Maybe not *everything*." He leaned forward. "Think, Eve. Why has Elohim forbidden you to eat when He gave you the *desire* to eat?" His eyes were larger now, daring me to look elsewhere.

He was right. Adam and I had discussed this fact many times. "Why is this so important to you?" I said.

"What is the name again?" he said.

I didn't understand.

"The tree?" he said.

"The Tree of the Knowledge of Good and Evil," I said.

Lucifer stroked his chin. "Hmmm," he said. "The Tree . . . of the Knowledge of Good and Evil. So . . ." He paused. "If you eat of it, you will be wise, like Elohim, knowing good and evil. Is that not so?" He moved closer to me, always this movement forward, as though he would relish the very eating of me.

I shrugged. "I suppose." This time I didn't move. The titillating shivers that ran the length of my body felt dangerously wonderful, although I had no idea what they were caused by. Fear or wonder, I wanted to revel in them.

"It sounds like Elohim doesn't want you to be like Him." Here, Lucifer picked up one of the unbroken fruits, and it seemed, strangely enough, that his tongue flicked in and out, all around it, licking it, feeling it, teasing it, weighing it.

"But why not?" I said. "He made us to be His companions and friends. Why *wouldn't* He want us to be like Him?" Then I remembered Elohim saying something else. "He said He made us both in His image."

Lucifer muttered something under his breath, something along the lines of . . . *made us first* . . . He caressed the fruit's skin.

"I didn't hear you," I said.

He shook his head, and his body swayed. "It's not important. What's important *now* is deciphering why Elohim wants to *withhold* something from you, especially if He gave you the desire for it."

I looked at the tree, at its lavishness and broken fruit. "It *is* ravishing," I said, moving toward the fallen fruit Lucifer held.

Lucifer offered it to me.

I leaned down to sniff it but did not take it from him. I stared at its reddish-brown upraised ridges. "I *would* like to be wise." I looked up at Lucifer, who met my gaze unwaveringly. "But I would feel wrong in eating it. It would hurt Elohim's feelings." I stepped back again, to distance my-self from any possible transgression.

Something like a shadow flew across Lucifer's face. "Do you think Elohim thought of *your* feelings when He forbade you to eat?"

He had a point.

"I think it's . . . *choices* . . . that Elohim is more concerned with. Elohim is forever talking about how a good choice is one that puts Him first." I clasped my hands in front of me and concentrated, sinking down on my knees. I had to get this one thing right. I was confused.

"How would you know what a *good* choice is, given the fact that you have not yet eaten of the Tree of the Knowledge of Good and Evil?" said Lucifer. He dug his thumb into the fruit, and the juice dribbled down his hand.

"I don't know," I said. "Adam and I have wondered the same thing."

With the fruit impaled on his thumb, Lucifer walked over to where I was kneeling in the earth. "Eve," he said. He knelt down beside me. "Eve, you will not die. Your eyes will be opened, and you will become like Elohim," he said. He laid his free hand on my shoulder.

"Stop!" I cried. Another thought had come to me. I had perceived something awry with Lucifer's arguments. *Yes, why had I not thought of it before?* "Why not eat of the fruit yourself, if it is good and Elohim is wrong?"

Lucifer paused. He looked everywhere but at me. Then he smiled, a wide, unnerving grin. "Why, you are absolutely right." He split the fruit open with his fingers, and without warning he smashed his lovely face into its flesh and came back up, mouth agape, teeth dirtied, juice and orange pulp dripping messily down his chin. He lolled his tongue and made his eyes roll into the back of his head. "Do I look dead to you?" he snarled. He laughed then, a raucous, chilling laugh that shocked me and made me breathless and anxious.

I clasped my head in my hands. "I know not what to do," I whispered.

Lucifer bent over my bowed frame. "I think you do," he said. Nearer, in my ear, "I *know* you do." Then the air was cold about me, and when I looked up, he was gone. I stood and twirled. All about me, flowers were wilting, grasses were dying, birds were crying, and rabbits were screaming. It was as though the earth's belly was heaving in revulsion. I felt I was going mad.

Adam said he saw the broken fruit first. "What have you done?" he cried, shaking me.

I had fallen asleep under the tree, and truth be told, Adam said later that it appeared as though I had eaten from the fruit and died.

Adam shook me again.

I woke to his terrified face, all teeth and gums. "Eve," he cried. "What have you done?" He grabbed my face and yanked my mouth open.

I jerked away from his touch and lookly wildly about me. "Where is he?" I said. The sight of Adam was so . . . so ordinary, after Lucifer.

"Who?" said Adam. He held out his hand. "Spit."

I opened my mouth wide and stuck my tongue out to show him its emptiness.

He pointed to the fruit. "What's this?" He strained to look up into the tree's center. "How did it get down here?"

I told him everything.

Except for the kissing part. I did not think he'd appreciate that, for some reason.

Adam sat back and stared at the brownish-red fruit. "Something does not seem quite right," he said finally. "You said he was very knowledge-able?"

I nodded. "Maybe He and Elohim are friends, and Elohim has sent him to let us know He's changed His mind." I was doubtful of this. Lucifer seemed so unlike Elohim.

"What do we do?" he said.

"Taste it," I said. "Lucifer ate of the tree, and nothing happened to him."

"Where is he now?" said Adam.

I shrugged my shoulders. "I think I should like to be wise."

"As would I," said Adam. "But we do not dare go against Elohim."

I frowned. "It's strange that Elohim said nothing about him."

"Do you think there are others?" said Adam.

I shrugged again.

Indeed, the appearance of this strange and wondrous being had me confused. *Why did he seem to know about Elohim's injunction not to eat of the fruit? And why was he so eager to encourage a transgression?*

Unless he knew more than we did.

Unless Elohim was hiding something.

Dara

Mama's been sleeping all this time. She snores really loud, and Aya brings her food but won't let anyone else see her.

I tell Aya I won't have any new things to wear when the women come to take me to the city, and Aya sighs and blows her curly hair away from her eyes and says, "Tell Naava she has to help." But when I go to Naava in her weaving room, Naava says, "Why should I? You're just going to make a mess of things there; then the women will come back to Mother and ask for me. Just you wait." Then Cain's shadow is in the door, and Naava blushes and tells me to go away.

But Cain says, "That's all right."

"Here," says Naava. She hands me a pile of plucked wool and says, "Pick out the burrs, won't you? And don't let your smelly turtle play in it."

If I help Naava, she will be nicer to me, so I sit in the corner and watch her and Cain, with my lips *shut shut shut,* picking out the burrs.

Cain says, "What are you doing?" and Naava says, "Nothing of importance." Then Cain says, "You're really good at that," and Naava says, "Thank you."

I get tired of picking out burrs and twigs and leaves, so I say to Naava, "I want to help Aya now." Naava doesn't even look at me. Her eyes are on Cain, and he's getting closer, and they're making pretty eyes at each other.

All of a sudden I'm crying, and I don't know why. Naava looks at me, all disgusted, and says, "Crybaby. Go away. All you do is cry." But that's not true. I don't. I'm just crying today. Because tomorrow I'm going away, and Aya says I can't take Turtle, and Mama's sick, and Jacan's gone off with Abel, and I can't find any more pretty things for the baby.

Naava stands up and grabs me by the shoulder and leads me to the doorway. "Aya," she calls. "Take her, will you?"

Aya looks up. She's got a squawking, thrashing duck in between her knees. She circles the duck's neck with her hands, twists hard, just like that, and the duck goes limp. "Dara, come here, sweetheart. I have a surprise for you." To Naava, she says, "I wish *you* were going to the city."

I go to Aya, and Aya says she needs to tell me something because Mama won't do it and Father won't do it and Cain won't do it and heaven knows, Naava won't do it. And Abel's gone all the time. She says, "Right after I finish here, all right?" I sit and watch her. Aya moves fast—flash flash flash—as gray feathers float down all around her ankles. She scoops out the duck's bloody insides, then throws them into a pot that's bubbling with broth and sheep fat, wipes her hands, and says, "Shall we?" She takes my hand, and we play the skipping game all the way to Mother's garden, where we always play the cloud game that Father taught us. Aya knows it's my favorite place in all the world. She says, "Now, let's see, where shall we—"

"I know, I know!" I say. "Under the sky weed." So we lie down and stare up at the purple and pink flowers that look like little round skies from below. Up above is the wide blue sky with clouds the shapes of rabbits and goats and ducks and mountains.

"Listen," Aya says. The bees go *buzz buzz buzz,* and I can feel the hum in my teeth. "Do you remember how I talk to Elohim?"

"Look!" I say, pointing up at a butterfly that's landed on the sky weed. "It's shiny and yellow. That's a new one!"

"Dara," says Aya, rising up on her elbow. "I need you to listen. Remember when we were here a long time ago, and I called out 'Elohim!' and we heard Him whisper back?"

I nod my head. "Naava said it was the wind."

"No," Aya says. "Elohim spoke." She taps her finger on my nose. "Abel said only people who believe in Elohim can hear Him."

"But I can't *see* Him," I say.

Aya chews on her lip and looks away. "That's not important, I don't think. I think Mother said Elohim was *in time,* meaning He can be everywhere at once."

"Nuh-uh," I say. "How could He be here in the garden *and* up in the hills with Jacan? That's silly."

"I'm not sure," says Aya. "But Abel says he can talk to Him anywhere." She puts her hand on my belly. "You'll need a friend, Dara, when you go away. Those people don't use the same words as we do, so you won't have anyone to talk to." She brushes the hair off my face and kisses my cheek.

"I can talk to Turtle."

"No, I'm taking care of Turtle, remember?"

"Oh." I remember, and my voice sounds as small as a mouse.

"You have to learn to talk to Him," says Aya. "I did too. I want you to try with me now. If He doesn't answer right away, it means He's busy. Go on."

I look at Aya, disappointed that we aren't playing the cloud game. "Why do I have to?" I ask.

"To introduce yourself."

I giggle. "Doesn't He know who I am already?"

Aya doesn't say anything.

"Do I have to fold my hands like the people I made for Cain?" I say.

"He's not picky," says Aya. "I talk to Him while I'm grinding grain or catching fish. Mother used to talk to Him when she was washing clothes or sweeping the ground. Any position will do." She clicks her tongue and says, "Here, I will do it with you." She sits up and pats the ground in front of her, in between her knees.

I climb over Aya's bad leg and sit with my back to her chest. Aya reaches around and folds her hands over mine. "This first time we'll do it like Cain's statues do."

After a bit she says, "Go on, Dara," so I say, "Hello, Elohim, my name is Dara, and I like the yellow butterfly, and Aya has a surprise for me, and I want you to make Naava go to the big city instead of me . . . *please.*" I turn to look at Aya. "There. Is that good?" I tilt my head to listen. "I don't hear anything."

"Shhh," says Aya. She pulls me closer to her and cups her hands over my eyes, so I can't see. "Listen."

I only hear bees.

"Shhh," Aya says.

But I don't hear anything besides bees. I lean forward and push Aya's hands away. "What's the surprise?" I say.

Aya sighs and gets up. "I wish you would have heard Him," she says. She holds out her hand again, and I take it.

"Maybe He's taking a nap," I say.

"He doesn't need naps," says Aya.

"Why not?" I say.

"Too many questions," says Aya.

Aya leads me to the edge of the garden where Mama buried her babies that were dead. She jerks me back by my elbow and tells me to be quiet. She kneels on one knee and puts her arm around me and points. "There," Aya says. "You see those grasses moving? The long ones?"

The grasses are doing a little dance. I nod.

"Watch," says Aya.

"What is it?" I say.

Aya puts her finger to her lips, and we wait there, in the shady part of a tree that has leaves as big as my head.

"She's wild," Aya says finally. "I can't count on her showing up. Especially during the day."

"What is it?" I whisper, excited to see what Aya sees.

"A hedgehog, with her four tiny babies."

"Maybe if we shout, they'll come out," I whisper. I call, "Come here, baby hedgehogs, come here."

"Shhh," says Aya, and we sit there like that, as still as deer, until the shadows grow long long long.

Aya says, "I have to get back. The duck will be about done." We get up, and Aya brushes the dirt off my knees. I'm disappointed not to see the hedgehog and her babies. Jacan told me he saw one once, with its pinched face and long claws, snuffling around outside the courtyard in the morning, but it froze and rolled into a prickly ball when it saw him. He tried to catch it, but it was too quick for him.

"Maybe Elohim is wild, like the hedgehog," I say. "You can't count on Him."

Aya puts her hand over my mouth. "Take it back," she says. She wags her finger in my face. "Never say things like that. You'll hurt His feelings. Mother does this too, and it's not right." She's shaking her head and tugging me hard by the elbow, toward the house.

"You're hurting me," I say, pulling my arm away. She lets go of my arm, but she's still as mad as a hornet.

"Abel says Elohim deserves the proper respect, the proper attitude, and I think he's right. When you talk to Elohim, you have to *trust* that He'll answer." She stops and puts her hands on her hips. "Do you understand that word, Dara? *Trust?*"

I shake my head and look at the ground.

"I'm sorry," says Aya, kneeling down in front of me. "I've scared you. Come here."

I lean into her. She smells like dead duck and cooking broth.

Aya puts her hands on my cheeks. "Look at me."

I look into Aya's eyes, blue as the sky.

"You have to *believe,*" she says. "You have to *hope.*" Here she scrunches up her lips. "You know when Goat wants to eat and you feed her?"

Of course, I know that. Goat loves to eat! I nod.

"Well, you are *depending on* the fact that she will ask you for food at certain times of the day. Right?"

"She eats *everything,*" I say.

"Well, that's how you have to *depend on* Elohim. You have to know that He will take care of you and answer your questions."

I think about this. "But when we were back there"—I point to the sky weed—"He didn't talk to me."

Aya stands up again and takes my hand. "Sometimes you have to wait, like when you wait for your pots to get hard in the fire."

"Oh," I say.

We walk back to the house, my hand in Aya's. I'm glad I have Aya as a sister. She knows important things.

Maybe Elohim will tell me where I can find the number-five thing for the baby, and then I won't have to go away.

Naava

Naava watches through the window as the wide flat earth on the horizon slices the sun in two. A hawk wheels in the sky, searching for the movement of grasses, the scurrying of prey. He turns, spots something. He folds his wings in and plummets to the ground like rain.

There is a storm of squawking outside the window.

Eve ceases her storytelling.

"A hawk," Naava explains.

The noise is unbearably loud. The hawk stands in the courtyard, nonchalant, with one foot clenched over a hapless, motionless crow. The clamor comes from the other crows, the ones he has *not* caught. They dive upon him, then lift up, over and over again. The hawk seems patient enough.

Naava turns to her mother and says, "I'll be back."

Eve nods, and Naava slips through the low-hanging doorway and uses her hands like a broom, swooshing the birds up and away. Still, they cry out. The hawk blinks at her languorously, and Naava has a fleeting feeling that she's met him before—*hadn't Aya said something about a hawk or an eagle once . . . one of Abel's dreams?* Then the thought is gone. The hawk rises up and treads air right above her head, the dead crow in his talons. Higher and higher he rises. She stares after him, and the uneasy feeling returns. Naava begins to dread the rest of Eve's story. She sees what's coming—the role she played in Abel and Cain's jealous spats—and she sees now this is why Eve has called her back, before Aya and Dara, to delegate the blame.

She straightens her shoulders and turns back to the house. She knows accepting her share is the last gift she will be able to offer to her mother.

Naava was not afraid to admit it: He was beautiful! Even more so than Abel. The prince—for that is what he called himself—was of medium build, leaner than Father or her brothers. His hair, as black as night, was long and straight, parted in the middle, and pulled back with thick leather cording. His jaw was smooth, unlike the wild hairiness of Father and Cain and Abel. His chest and stomach were bare, except for a heavy yellow disk imprinted with a star around his neck and a shawl thrown over his right shoulder. His thighs and knees were hidden by a long skirt, and his fingernails shone white and clean, his hands uncallused. When he smiled, his whole face cracked into a million suns. His relaxed manner, the way he leaned forward into his talking, the way he brought all his fingers together at their tips to emphasize his words fascinated Naava. She could not look away.

The prince had come with the women from the growing city to claim Dara. He arrived midday on a litter, an odd kind of house carried by manservants and hung with billowing panels of fabric. He disembarked elegantly, bowed to Eve, kissed her hand, and said, in a halting voice— how amazing that he could mimic their sounds and inflections already!— "My harem is pleased with our arrangement." Only Cain laughed at this. No one else did. They understood him to mean only that the *city* or *people* were pleased.

The prince took in their sprawling, rough-hewn abode and nodded his beautiful head. "Nice," he said. Naava wasn't sure if he was truly sincere or if there was a hint of mockery threading through his voice.

Because business seemed to breed business in the company of strangers, Adam and Naava's brothers sat with the prince in the courtyard on reed mats, underneath the shade of the roof overhang, and discussed land shares and irrigation rights. If the prince were not there, Adam and

Naava's brothers would still have sat in the shade and talked after their chores were done, but about mundane trivial matters, like digging out the irrigation canals or tying up the grapevines, which interested Naava not in the least.

This was the first time Adam's family had entertained a guest at any meal. It was a momentous occasion. For the occasion, Abel had killed a calf—reluctantly, because this stranger was no friend of his—and Aya had cooked it in a broth of onion and garlic and lentils. She prepared curds and honey in Dara's clay bowls. A fine mixed beer. Raised barley bread with ghee. Cherries and plums from Adam's orchards, and pistachios.

Cain leaned forward, unaware that his gestures mimicked the prince's. Cain's hands flew around his head like nervous birds, and his voice was tinged with awe. "You are blessed by your gods," he said.

The prince waved his hand in the air. "We must appease them. Serve them. They provide for us. This is . . . perfect, no?"

"What of Elohim?" said Abel, studying the prince's face.

"Elohim?" said the prince. "Who is this?"

Abel did not falter. "Elohim is the *one* God, the true God." He tilted his head toward Adam. "Father has seen Him."

The prince contemplated this, ran his forefinger across his lips and looked at Adam. When he spoke, his words sounded uncertain. "No one sees . . . gods. They live in the sky and the underworld." He turned back to Abel. "This is your name for Enki?"

Cain did not allow Abel to answer. "The name is not so important. There are gods—*God* for you, Abel—who help us from time to time. We have to honor them, is this not so?"

Adam interrupted. "Elohim's name *is* important, Cain. Elohim would not enjoy sharing it with others of lesser importance, lesser power. You know not of what you speak."

The prince's face darkened. He grunted and stood. He said, hoarsely, with a worried glance at the sky, "We cannot talk like this. The deities are jealous and—how do you say?—vindictive. I must go."

Cain stood too and held out his hands to the prince. "We will talk of other things. Please. Sit. Eat . . . drink with us. We are friends." He swept his hand in the direction of Adam and Abel. "They want this too. We all do."

Adam nodded. Abel looked down at the ground.

"A compromise," Cain continued. "You share your wealth of knowledge with us; we share ours with you. I have said this from the beginning." Cain's face was eager, lit by the fire within.

"You have *what,* exactly?" said the prince, sinking to his reed mat once again.

Abel looked up and said, "It is better we leave you alone, and you leave us alone."

The stranger turned to Abel and saw he was serious. He looked back at Cain, with a bit of shock on his face. "I am confused," he said.

Cain glared at Abel and said something to the prince in the city's language.

"You have our women, our trade," continued the prince. "What more do you want?"

The muscles near Abel's jaw tensed, released, tensed, released.

Adam interrupted the awkward silence. "We cannot have a repeat of—"

The prince waved his long, delicate fingers in front of his face. "A mistake. The men working—what do you call it?—laborers. They know nothing. All the water they take for themselves. They do not think. We make it right, no?" The prince was referring to the near disaster that had occurred right after his people had arrived on the plains. Several days after Adam and Cain had come back from that first visit to the city people's camp, the shoreline next to their orchards began to crack with dryness, and when Cain walked upriver to see what the trouble was, he found that the city's workers had built dams along their shores, shunting the water to their newly dug irrigation ditches, with just trickles left to travel downstream to Adam's orchards and Cain's gardens.

"I am referring to the assault on my daughter," Adam said firmly. "By your shepherds."

"What assault? What is this word?" said the prince. He looked to Cain for help.

Cain explained what had happened, while Abel bit his lip in anger.

The prince expressed only shock. He bowed his head and clasped his hands in front of his face. "For this, I am sorry. I will have them punished. It is not our way."

Cain's face glowed. It was as though this humble proclamation had vindicated his city, the new love of his life. The rightness and goodness of his choice had been substantiated, and here were Adam and Abel to verify that it was so.

The prince had already wormed his way into the apple of Naava's heart. As he shook the dust from his sandals after his arrival, he had winked at Naava and brushed past her, his arm briefly at her elbow. He had whispered, "Your cheeks are like pomegranate blossoms"—and, oh, the flutters in Naava's stomach would not be still. But Naava could not linger, it was not permitted—unless, of course, she was serving food and drink to the men. So she had offered her services to Aya, who had rolled her eyes and said, "A twig between the legs is all the encouragement you need to work?"

Naava became self-conscious, but she smoothed her hair with her hands, bit her lips to a fevered blush, and loosened her sash, so that the neckline of her robe fell dangerously low. She glanced up to see Aya watching her and felt warm all over. "Too bad you are not so presentable," Naava said.

Aya smiled and said, "Your wiles may work on our brothers, but do you think they will work on a prince? He can have anyone he wants." Aya poured the beer into large drinking mugs and placed a hollow reed in them, for sucking on. "What of Abel? Have you given up on him?"

"He turns away from me now," said Naava haughtily. "Maybe he pleasures himself in the fields with his animals. Cain has said it is so."

"Cain is dim-witted," said Aya.

"He has agreed to take me to the city," said Naava.

"*Dara's* going, not you," said Aya.

"I am going with Cain when he does his trading," said Naava. "That's something *you* can't do." Naava reached out to take the mugs from Aya and, in her haste, splashed great quantities on the ground.

"At least *my* hands work," said Aya.

Normally Naava would have retaliated, but her mind was elsewhere, with the prince sitting in the courtyard, waving his hands like startled herons lifting from the river. Naava steadied herself and balanced the mugs in her hands. She could not falter. She wanted to be away from this abominable place, with Eve and Aya at her throat and brothers who paled in comparison to this resplendent man. Already she had visions of the prince running his hands through her hair, kissing her hard upon the lips, and breathing heat down her neck. *Ah,* she shuddered. *It would be, it would be.*

She approached the men, who were engrossed in conversation. She cleared her throat. The men looked up, blinking in the sleepy afternoon, surprised by the intrusion. Naava smiled at the delight in the prince's face, wondering, *Does he like me?* and *How can I make him want me?* and she was still smiling as the prince broke off mid-sentence to take the beer from her hands, his fingers lightly stroking hers, smiling until the very moment she fumbled with the mug and dropped it into his lap. The prince stood, astonished at the sudden wetness on his torso, his mouth taking on an O shape, but before he could cry out, Naava dashed back around the corner to Aya, where there was safety in hiding. There was a sharp howl behind her, then thunderous laughter from her brothers and the prince.

"Oh, I've done it now," wailed Naava, her face in her hands. "Tell me. Was it as bad as it looked?"

Aya plopped another mug onto the table and poured a steady stream of golden beer into it. "Worse."

"Oh, why didn't *you* serve the beer? I could have served them the cherries or plums, something that wouldn't have fallen out of their own accord."

Aya finished pouring. "Well, from what Cain says, there are plenty more where he comes from."

"You're jealous," said Naava.

"Jealous is the wrong word," said Aya. She turned to Naava. "I'm angry. Angry at your meanness. Angry that you poisoned Mother. Angry that you think of no one but yourself. Have you thought of Dara once today? She's frightened out of her wits because she's going away from her family, the only people she's known, and all you can think about is yourself and whether or not this prince likes you." Aya put her hands on her hips. She seemed to have settled into a rhythm, drumming out all the things she'd wanted to say to Naava but had held back. "If you think I am glad for your clumsiness, you're wrong. I wish—Elohim as my witness—that you would have been perfect, that the prince would like you and take you instead of Dara—"

"That's enough, Aya," said Eve. Her voice surprised both girls—she'd returned from scrubbing Dara at the river, and she stood behind them, her hand in Dara's.

Naava smiled triumphantly. She was disappointed Eve had recovered for this day, thanks to Aya's care. She had found no time to press her case with Adam, alone. But she felt exonerated by Eve's chastising of Aya now.

Aya turned, saw Dara, grew soft. "I've made fig cakes for you," she said. "To take along with you on your journey."

Dara's eyes and nose were red and glistening, but other than the occasional sniffle, the little girl was quiet. She was dressed in her new yellow robe, and she wore fresh squeaky sandals upon her feet, made for her by Jacan. He was there too, moping about and sucking his thumb, a trait he had abandoned long ago because of the merciless jabs of his older brothers— "Jacan the baby" or "Jacan, do you still need your mother's teat?"

Naava watched as Aya took Dara's hand to show her and Jacan Turtle's new house, a rectangular barricade of clay bricks and broken wheat stalks and one of Dara's chipped bowls full of water. Naava had no words to describe her feelings right then—she was disquieted, angry, restless, and sad. She did not begin her days thinking, *I will be evil to my siblings, to my mother, to my family.* No, she wanted to be agreeable; after all, it made life so much easier. But at the most inopportune times, something twisted inside her, when she was striving to be good, and it was as though she was lost to herself. The words she said, the things she did—they were all products of she knew not what. She wished she could wipe them away as easily as wiping away tears, but she could not, because even though she *knew* she was being horrid, she could not stop herself from narrowing her eyes and saying, "You'd better watch out. Walls won't stop hawks. And they love, absolutely love, baby turtles."

Dara started blubbering, and Aya shot her a fierce look and said to Dara, "She didn't mean it," and Eve grabbed Naava by the scruff of the neck and hissed, "Quiet, child."

Naava swung a wide arc with her arm and twisted away from Eve. "I'm not a child," she hissed, straightening her robe. "You cannot tell me what to do."

Eve

From the day Dara was born, I felt nothing but the most unabashed, most protective love for her. She came easily, after the nightmarish torture of Jacan's birth. Indeed, I had not known I carried two children within me. I had not known it was possible to have a multiple litter, as our flocks did. With Jacan, each contraction gripped my back in its tight fist, leaving me whimpering like a dog, and even as I moaned, I could feel there was no dropping, no progression. Aya was there to massage my buttocks, my back, to soften my tension with mint oil, to whisper to me, "Shhh, the Garden, think of the Garden. The cool waters. The green moss." Naava was there too, although she watched, helpless, as her younger sister of five years knew more, did more.

After the second birth—Dara's birth—I felt lighter than wheat chaff and as brittle as dead leaves. In the midst of the wet sticky blood between my legs, the smell of mint and earth, the murmur of my babies smacking their lips, sucking in new air, I fell back onto blankets spread especially for me and groaned, "Please, give me the second child." Aya laid her, stomach down, on my chest, in the hollow between my breasts, covering us with a cloth made warm by the fire. "Rest," she said, as she stuffed my womb with herbs and wool and washed my legs with water.

I strained to see my girl child. I lifted her tiny fingers, one by one, marveling at the exquisite detail, even in one so young. The soft dip at the top of her head. Her lips, lit like the edges of curled leaves. The deep folds in her legs and arms, like smooth, kneaded dough. "Dara," I said finally. "I shall name you Dara. You have been compassionate to me, your mother. I thank you for that gift, in no way small. May Elohim make the sun shine upon you and your children and give you the fruits of the earth. Selah." She slept upon my breast, without a sound, until her brother began shrieking for milk. I fed them together, cradling one at each breast. Jacan, suckling hungrily, greedily. Dara, suckling mildly, as though she was reluctant to chafe my tender raw nipples. Even her sleep patterns were long and dreamy, as though she were wrapping me in delicate fly casing, protecting me from sickness and exhaustion.

She was my baby, my youngest.

I was feeding her to the lions.

For what? A measly goods allotment every week? To protect what was rightfully ours? To placate strange people I did not know?

What mother does this? What mother, out of fear, sends her daughter away?

My child, oh Elohim, listen here: My child was to be put into the hands of strangers! You saw how she looked at me, tears streaming down her cheeks in glistening ribbons, as she peered out at me through the fluttering curtains of the prince's litter, which heralded her absence. In a moment, in a snap of the fingers, it was too late. She was gone and me with her. It became part of the past, something to look upon and regret, another memory that haunted and lingered like the smell of smoke.

There was no consolation in knowing I would see her again. She would be changed into something new, something foreign, something horrible— *oh, I hoped not*. Or worse: She would hate me for giving her up so easily.

I cannot stand being despised by any one of my children, who were nested and nourished by my body, each holding fast to the vision that is Eve in their minds—though Naava is with me now, may she be blessed. I cannot plead my case before them, when they already know in their hearts what they believe. And what, exactly, do they see? Was I not a good mother, a good woman? What does *good* mean, anyway?—there we are, back to the Garden again, for it always comes to this, somehow, some way, that all steps lead back to the Tree of the Knowledge of Good and Evil.

I saw Lucifer again.

Adam was gone once more; I remember not where. What is important is that I was alone, walking in the Garden, pulling out a patch of hideous purple-flowered thistle that had erupted seemingly overnight. That morning, during our walk, I had cried out when passing one; its sharp thorns had sliced my leg and drawn blood.

"Eve?" came a voice behind me, soft and sultry.

I whirled around, knowing Adam was long gone.

It was Lucifer, beautiful Lucifer.

My face flushed; I could feel the warmth of it. I put my hands to my cheeks.

"So," he said, sidling up to me. "Where is Adam now?"

"Gone," I said. Truth be told, I felt uncomfortable with this line of questioning but didn't know why.

"You are like the lilies of the valley," he said, brushing up against my shoulder.

I reached up to tuck my hair behind my ears, and, infuriatingly, I felt warm all over again—my face, my neck. My groin seized up pleasurably, and it was all I could do to stifle my gasp. *Oh, Eve, compose yourself!*

"It seems this Adam of yours is always gone," said Lucifer. His gaze was like the wind, over all of me at once, causing the hairs on my arm to prickle up.

"No," I said, stuttering, "he's m-mostly with me, but now he's off—I think he's collecting berries."

Lucifer's hooded eyes blinked languorously. "Are you sure?"

"What do you mean?" I said.

"Maybe he meets Elohim without you," said Lucifer. He laughed. "Of course, I'm probably horribly mistaken, because what do I know of your relationship?"

I was puzzled. "What do you mean?" I repeated. "Are you saying that Adam and Elohim meet privately? But why? Why would they do that? They both like me." I bit my lip. "I *think* they both like me." I was beginning to look a fool, repeating myself over and over again.

Lucifer smiled. "Of course, of course, it was a silly question." He swayed about me. *Almost like dancing,* I thought. His radiant colors—oh, the blues and crimsons and emeralds and yellows!—were exceedingly breathtaking. "Have you thought of what we talked about before?" He was so close, I could feel the heat of his breath.

I couldn't think, I couldn't breathe, but *what a glorious feeling!* I glanced about me, frantic to see if Adam was around.

"Eve," said Lucifer, bending down so his face was level with my own. "Calm yourself. There is nothing to be afraid of."

I coughed and backed up, to get my bearings. "I feel so . . . odd," I said finally.

Lucifer's voice was a calm ripple of melodious music. "I would too, if I were you," he said kindly. "You want more than you already have. You want wisdom and knowledge. You want what Elohim says you cannot have. Am I right?"

I nodded. Then, before I could stop them, tears rushed to my eyes, and I was crying and blubbering all at once. "Oh, I do!" I exclaimed. "Yes, I want to know more, see more, feel more, learn more. I *do* want these things, and I know not why Elohim wants to keep them from us. Does He not love us? Does He not want us to be like Him?" And here I broke down into heaving sobs that prevented me from speaking further.

Lucifer slid forward. He whispered, "You are already wise, Eve. You know what you want. What is wrong with that? Didn't Elohim create the desires of your heart too?" He hugged me, letting me cry on his shoulder.

My tears subsided, and I felt rejuvenated—liberated even.

Then, before I knew what was happening, I was kissing him, clinging to him. Yes, I regret this—oh, how I regret it—but in the absence of Adam and Elohim, I wanted it. I needed it. I felt confident, happy, and strong, and Lucifer had *known* what I wanted, without me having to tell him. I was *heard, understood,* and how wonderful it felt. Adam had not been so attentive—to *know* what I was thinking before I thought it!

It was divine . . . and thrilling . . . and . . . all wrong.

I wrenched myself away from him reluctantly. I touched my lips, which were tingling, with my fingers.

"You little vixen," he said, coming close again. "You are a tease."

I pretended not to hear him. Guilt was already starting to seep in. "If I eat of the fruit, will you promise me that I will be more wise? That I will know more of this glorious earth?"

"Eve, Eve," he said. "Would I lie to you?" He wrapped me in his arms again, and I succumbed to his embrace.

Suddenly he pulled away and cocked his head, listening for something. There was a crackling of brush in the woods. "I do think Adam is returning," he said sadly. "I will leave you for now." He started to slink back into the bushes. "I have told you the truth. The question you have to ask yourself is: Has Elohim?" He whispered, "Remember, I have told you these things, and Elohim has not."

He was right. Elohim, on this one topic, was a mystery—to both Adam and me.

Quickly, after straightening my hair and wiping my lips—would Adam know what I had done?—I returned to pulling thistles out of the ground.

Then Adam was upon me. He pulled me up and twirled me about. "Look," he said. "Blueberries and currants. Bunches of them."

I grinned and hugged him.

He looked at me quizzically. "What has happened to you?" he said.

I ran my hands through my hair and came up close to his ear. "Nothing, my darling."

He smiled, then laid me tenderly upon the ground. He lay on top of me and said, "I missed you."

I lifted my head so it would rest on his shoulder. I did not want him to see my face just then. "I did too," I lied.

Later, while stuffing ourselves with the berries he had picked, I broached the subject of the Tree of the Knowledge of Good and Evil.

"I have been thinking," I said. "I should like to be wise." I looked at Adam, and when I saw he was receptive to what I had to say, I continued. "Why would Elohim have given me these desires, unless they are *good* desires?"

Adam paused briefly. "Do you dare do this thing?"

I leaned forward, eager to portray my decision as a good one. "Maybe Elohim *wants* us to do it. To take this step without Him—to show that we have grown."

"That could be," said Adam, chewing slowly. "Although why would He say we would die? What did He mean by that?"

I scooted closer to him. "Oh, Adam, don't you want to be wise like Elohim? Don't you want to be *like* Him?" I went further. "I have decided that I do. I am going to eat of the fruit."

"So quickly? Just like that?" said Adam, surprised.

"Oh, you know as well as I do, we've been hungering for this tree ever since He forbade it! I cannot stand it one moment longer." I stood up and approached the Tree of the Knowledge of Good and Evil. Its fruit was spread now upon the ground—after Lucifer's shaking the week before—but was still intact. The tree looked no different on the outside; its bark was still thorny, its leaves still fanned out from the top.

Adam stood. "You cannot do this thing without me," he said.

I laughed. I picked up the fruit and held it suspended between us. "Why not?" I said. It was sweet-smelling, and my mouth watered. "I shall try it first. That way, if I die, you will be spared."

"I will be alone," he protested.

"Together, then," I said. "If you dare."

Adam joined me, his craving as strong as mine. I saw it in his eyes.

We sat upon the ground, and I set the fruit down between us. Adam and I dug our fingers into the center of it and scooped out its pulp. We gazed into each other's eyes, holding up the forbidden meat in front of us, as gifts, as offerings to each other. No change was evident in either of us.

"To wisdom," I said.

"To wisdom," said Adam.

We devoured our portions. The fruit was fibrous and sweet. My eyes were opened—the trees danced before me, the sky swam above me, the river hummed to me—and I felt a tickling breeze upon my face. My nose felt itchy, as though I had had a good laugh or a cleansing cry. I began to laugh, and I heard Adam's laugh meet mine, like two serpents twisting in the air. The world was good; it was ours.

The effects wore off quickly.

I noticed first the change in Adam. "There's something different about you," I said. In fact, he looked downright plain and drab, as he had never appeared before. "Your light. It's gone."

Adam looked down at himself, then at me. "Yours too."

Then.

A voice, booming across the field: "Where are you, my children? Adam? Eve? Where are you?"

We hid.

PART TWO

Strangers

at

Home

Naava

Naava decided to use Cain. He did not know it yet, for she had disguised her plans and whispered sweet words in his ear, words she knew he had wanted to hear—about how she waited for him to come home to tell her his ideas and how much she missed him. She was the wind; he was the grass—and he bent to her direction. Cain would be her conduit to the prince. Oh, she had not forgotten about Abel. Rather, he had forgotten her. Not forgotten, exactly. More like rejected, ever since Eve's sickness. *I do not care,* she thought. *It is entirely your loss.*

Cain was jealous of the prince and his attentions toward Naava, but she told him it was nothing. Had he not see her disastrous fumblings when she spilled the beer upon the prince's lap? He could not possibly like her now. Cain had been somewhat appeased by her statements, and Naava had coaxed his anger, his jealousy—groomed it, really—until she had woven him into her tapestry of schemings. *Men are such animals, to be played so easily,* she thought.

And then.

Cain's anger spilled over and threatened to burn even Naava.

It was due to a small gesture of Eve's toward Abel, but it was a pivotal one. Cain reeled back to Naava, ranting like a lunatic, and she used his cravings for her warm kisses to calm him—for a time. Cain was funny that way. He did not wait for explanations. He saw, he judged, he exploded.

Early one morning, not long after Dara had gone to the city, Eve had laid out two new waterskins on the bench in the courtyard, and Cain had seen them and taken one. After all, he was in need—his had grown tattered—and he was touched by Eve's thoughtfulness.

"I can't believe Mother saw that I was wanting," he had said to Naava, delighted beyond all measure.

Naava mocked him in a singsongy voice. "What a silly child, Cain, needing the love of Mother still."

"I don't need Mother," he had said forcefully, almost too forcefully. "I need new waterskins." But secretly Naava knew Cain would do anything for a kind word or glance from Eve. He still purposefully walked past Eve every morning, to await a touch from her, a smile from her that said to him, *I love you. I'm proud of you.* But Eve was too busy, too consumed with her babies and her garden to think that one of her man sons still needed her.

Later that day, Abel had come in, sweaty and tired from the fields. He had seen only one waterskin upon the bench, and he had questioned Eve: "Did I not need two waterskins? One for Jacan? One for myself?" And Eve had replied, "They lie there, upon the bench. They have been out all day, so they will be stiff."

Abel held up the one waterskin. "I see only one."

Eve trundled over to the bench, her hand on her swollen belly, and said with astonishment, "I—I—put two—" She searched under the bench, walked around it. She placed her hand upon her forehead. "They were both right here this morning," she said, worry puckering her forehead. "Naava," she called. "Have you seen the other waterskin?"

Naava smiled, because she knew something Eve did not *and* she could use this to her benefit. "Cain took it," Naava said. "His was leaking."

Abel stomped away, and Eve waddled after him. "I'll talk to him tonight," Eve said. "You'll have it tomorrow." Abel didn't look back. He was vexed that Cain had stolen something that was his. That was Cain's way, and this was always Abel's response to it—running away, irritated, but rarely confronting him.

That night, Cain came in with bruises on his legs. He'd spent the greater part of the day climbing his thorny date trees to wave flower dust over the dates. It was difficult work, Naava knew, because she had offered to help several years ago, but her fright of heights paralyzed her when she had climbed but a short distance off the ground, and she had to climb down to the safety of the solid unwavering earth.

Eve lit the lamps for the evening, then saw him. "Cain," she said. "The waterskins that were on the bench. I made them for Abel and Jacan."

Cain's jaw tightened, and his tone was as prickly as his date palms. "I'm thirsty too. What does one have to do around here to get a new waterskin?" He smelled of the sweet sap of dates, and he was weighted down with exhaustion.

Eve laughed, a buoyant laugh not meant to be derisive or dismissive, but it came out that way, and Cain's face fell. Eve saw the effect of her laughter and tried to take it back. "Oh, Cain," she said. "I will make one for you. You have only to ask." The lamps flickered in the dimming light, and the warm glow coupled with the growing darkness made Eve look younger, more alive.

And Cain, angered by her superficial, I-didn't-mean-anything-by-it voice, said, "Did Abel ask? Did he ask you to make him a new waterskin? Or did you just happen to notice that he was in need of one—because you are more observant of *his* needs than of mine?" Eve stood there, exposed and bewildered, the flickering lights behind her consuming her astonishment, as Cain continued: "What has Abel done to garner your regard? Am I not your son too? Do I not deserve your love as Abel does?"

A stillness fell. In the twilit eastern sky, the moon shone upon all their injured faces.

Eve gathered herself and fell into her words as though they would dry up. She had been damned before she had even spoken. Naava knew this. Cain knew this. Eve did not. "I cannot explain myself to you, Cain. Please don't ask it of me. Aya told me Abel and Jacan needed new waterskins, and I complied." Eve placed her hand on Cain's arm, but he wrenched it away. "I did not think to leave you out of it. I am not so cruel. But you think I am. Cruel, that is. And I cannot change your mind. Your inclinations . . . they . . . I do not understand your quickness to blame. It is as though you've chosen to run from the sunlight and sit under the storm clouds. For you, life is rain and thunder and lightning." Eve waited for Cain's response, but that is where the conversation ended, for Cain turned on his heel and walked out of the circle of light. Eve stared after him, and Naava thought that her mother would split apart right then and there, for Cain had flayed her and left her bare bones naked to the unpleasant truth and night air.

Naava didn't see him until later, when he entered her weaving room, his eyes like swollen rosebuds. "Cain," Naava said. "Take me away from here. Just for a day. Take me to the city. I want to see what you see."

He sat at her feet while she weaved. "You want to see the prince," he said bitterly.

Naava left her weaving, slid off her stool. She ran her fingers through his hair. "Why would I want that?"

He grabbed her wrist and pulled her close. She could smell the beer on his breath. "I know you, Naava. You think I don't see you. You're like a bitch in heat, sniffing at Abel, sniffing at me, sniffing at the prince, circling, circling, always circling, waiting for one of us to own you." He released her hand and thrust her away from him. He laughed meanly. "It is time for me to find a wife and move away from here. This place"—he thrust his hand jerkily in the air—"is all wrong. I cannot breathe."

Never had Naava felt more rage. She would have liked to give Cain what he deserved: a thrashing for lumping her with the animals. What an outrage! So this was hatred; this was desire!

She kissed Cain upon the lips, and he weakened, reaching for her. He fumbled with her breasts and put his manhood between her legs, and her last thought was: *So I have won. There is nothing wrong with me.*

Eve

Upon Elohim's booming entreaty "Where are you?" Adam and I scurried and crouched like children into a covered space canopied by honeysuckle bushes. Looking back on it now, I am certain He knew where we were, but He wanted *us* to come out of hiding, to tell Him this thing we had done.

We were afraid, but more than being under the thumb of fear, we felt a tantalizing thrill, because we were alone in a quiet dark place, shouldering the heavy knowledge of our secret—that we had tasted and savored the forbidden.

Adam grabbed my hand and squeezed it. "What should we do?" he whispered.

I put a finger to my lips.

We were in the cool of evening, and the shadows had grown long. I shivered.

The sound of footsteps and of ponderous breath. Elohim's voice again, closer: "Where do you hide? How have you come to this place?" Disappointment and pain were evident in His voice. It was a question to which He already knew the answer, for Adam and I could feel Him, see Him, through the leafy branches. A slight rustle, and I left Adam to crawl out into the dying light of the day. Adam attempted to pull me back, but my resolve was stronger than his brawn, and I succeeded. I stood before Elohim, unsure of what to say. "We were afraid," I said. "So we hid."

"I see," said Elohim. "Why do you cover yourself?" He gestured to the fig leaves I was holding close to my body.

"Oh, yes," I said. "These." I removed them. "I felt—"

"Naked," said Adam, as he crawled out from behind me. He scuffed his feet and refused to look at Elohim.

"Who told you that you were naked?" said Elohim.

"Well," I said. "As You can see, we've lost something. We no longer have our light about us." Although it was the most obvious thing, I felt— although I wouldn't have known how to put it into words just then—an unfamiliar shifting of vision, not in the sense that our eyesight was narrowed or altered but that there was a rapid proliferation of unbidden thoughts and desires I did not know I possessed.

"Yes," said Elohim. "I can see that."

I felt a wave of tremendous sadness then—what I know now to be guilt—an incessant nagging feeling that I had done something wrong, that I had grossly misstepped. In fact, it left me flighty and nervous. I opened my mouth to protest, but Elohim's eyes stopped me. They were brimming with tears. *Could it be that Adam and I had injured Him?* It could not! It was not such a grievous error, the eating of the fruit, to cause Him pain, was it?

"Have you eaten from the tree?" Elohim asked. The disappointment and anguish on His face showed that He already knew. "The one from which I told you not to eat?"

Adam looked up, flustered. He stuttered, "The w-woman that You m-made for me, she gave it t-to me, and I ate." In his eyes there was terror and fear. He did not look at me, only at Elohim. "Had you not made her, I would not have even considered disobeying You."

"Adam," I blurted out, feeling betrayed. "*You* agreed. *We* agreed."

Adam looked at me then, his eyes languid and unblinking. "I did it only because you asked me to."

There it was. Blame, heaps of it. I knew not what to say. I stared at him, incredulous.

Elohim turned to me, tears now coursing like rivers down His cheeks. "Eve, what is this you've done? Why did you not listen?"

By this time I was on my knees before Him, my own tears tumbling to the earth. Oh, how my heart was torn asunder to have hurt my Creator so! Elohim's weeping had ignited a spark within me, and I wanted to explain— no, that is not the right word—*clarify* what had occurred in the space of a single, silly, squandered afternoon in the Garden He had made for us. "Elohim, please," I pleaded. "Be not angry. Lucifer was here—"

"Lucifer?" Elohim's voice boomed, sending a violent wind through the trees. "*Lucifer?*"

"He sang clever words, lovely words, that made me believe I could become wise like You. He shook the fruits from the tree and ate of them and nothing disastrous befell him. He convinced me that I, too, could taste of their sweetness, with no harm to myself or to You, so I ate." I looked at Adam, who still moved away from me. "*We* ate."

"I should have known," whispered Elohim. Then He cried out. It was a roar of rage, of anger, of betrayal, of sorrow. With His fists, He beat upon His chest. He fell to His knees, so His face was near mine. He cupped my face in His hands. "I have failed you. No, I did not tell you everything because I did not think . . . did not think . . . you had to know, but now . . ." His eyes were pleading. "Oh, I am sorry, Eve. I should have told you to be wary of him, this Lucifer. He's a crafty one. He can twist one's words into tangled vines and befuddle your thinking. He asked me about you, and I told him very little, thinking that he would grow bored and move on, but, no, he came to you instead—oh, why did I not intervene? He is jealous of my love for you and Adam. He wants to own you, possess you, and he will not stop until he does."

"But," I said, confused, "he was not unkind. He did not seem to want anything from me, except"—I looked down—"maybe . . ."

"He wanted *you*," said Elohim, lifting my chin to make me look at Him. "He knew exactly what he was doing."

From the mulberry bushes to our right came a low cackle.

Elohim stood and whirled.

A flash of colored light.

He took a step toward the bushes and spoke. "Show yourself, accursed monster!"

Lucifer slid from the bushes and faced Elohim. Now he was a cowardly looking man, no longer a shining star but sniveling and hunched over, a grotesque grin on his face.

Elohim raised His hand as if to strike, but instead He pronounced loudly, "Because you have done this and sought to deceive, cursed are you among the beasts! The choice was theirs to make—*alone.*"

Lucifer laughed.

Elohim's words simmered with heat. "On your belly you shall go, eating dust all the days of your life. There will be everlasting animosity between the woman and you, between her seed and your seed. He shall crush your head; you will bruise him on the heel."

Lucifer's grin turned into a hideous snarl, red and seething, and he rose up from his crouch, swaying, and said, "What is this *You* have done? Why did *You* put that tree in the garden?" There was a bit of mockery to his tone, more obvious than before.

Elohim reached out and clamped a hand around Lucifer's neck.

Lucifer fumbled at Elohim's fingers, but Elohim held on.

"You know why," Elohim said. "I gave you similar choices, if you remember."

Lucifer's eyes and cheeks bulged. He pulled at Elohim's hand, scratching it with his nails, and croaked, "You . . . are . . . jealous."

"Without law, there are no choices. Without choices, there can be no knowledge. Without knowledge, there is no wisdom. And without wisdom, there can be no true love," said Elohim quietly. He released His fingerhold on Lucifer and flung him into the bushes.

Lucifer scrabbled up. "You've not seen the last of me," he hissed, then, as an afterthought, he said leeringly, "They are beautiful, especially the woman." His form changed then. He dropped to the ground and writhed in the dirt. His screams were like those of the jackals at night, shrill and terrifying. Great hunks of his beauty fell away in large pieces, shed like the skin of the scaly creatures. His body lengthened into the shape of a wriggling stick. His appearance became dull and common, and he slithered away among the rustling leaves, snapping his newly formed tail at Elohim.

It was then I think I understood that he, too, like Elohim, could change forms, maybe to represent what the viewer wanted most. *Was that possible?* I wondered later in life if Lucifer came back as the city's prince, for both Cain and Naava were smitten with him, and the prince only led them further from Elohim, not closer.

Elohim turned to me, His eyes wet and blazing. "Eve, oh, what, what have you done?"

"I'm sorry," I cried. "Forgive me." An interesting word crossing my lips—*forgive*. It would take me many years to understand what I meant by this.

Adam moved a short distance away from me.

"I do," He said. "I already have." He paused to look at Adam. "Adam, where are you going? Are you not part of this?"

Adam pointed to me. "She told me it was good, that we would grow wise. This is *her* fault . . . *Your* fault, because You made her for me."

"Adam," Elohim said. "Really, are you unable to think for yourself, act for yourself? Can you not stand on your own two feet?"

"But I would not have eaten had it not been for her," he protested.

Elohim was silent. He watched while Adam dug his toe into the ground. Then, softly, He said, "Did not the two of you discuss eating of the tree multiple times? And did you not agree *together* that you would ignore my warning?"

Adam's voice was small. "We thought You *wanted* us to eat of it. As a test. To see if we could make our own decisions."

Elohim's face softened. "Adam, my love is not crafty or devious. It exists to be taken, to be accepted. There is nothing else I desire from you except loyalty."

Adam hung his head and returned to my side. He reached for my hand. "You're right," he said meekly. "I ate too."

We stood hand in hand, chins and lips quivering, and looked up at our Maker. I did not fault Adam then—that came much later when he blamed me for his deafness—for it was all so overwhelming. I could barely understand the widening abyss between Elohim and me.

Elohim turned to me. "Eve, I have told you before that you will have children, you and Adam."

I nodded.

"Your pains in childbirth will be greatly multiplied, yet despite this, your desire will always be for Adam, to please him, and in this way he will rule over you. This is not as I had wanted it." He grew somber, morose even, and continued, "Men will call you *slave* and *subordinate*. As a woman you will know discord and hatred instead of the harmony and peace I wished you to have. Your sensitivity will be interpreted as weakness, your intelligence as evil."

"I do not understand," I said.

"I know, my child," He said tenderly.

He sighed and spoke to Adam: "Adam, did you not remember my commandment not to eat? Because you have eaten from the tree, your work will seem fruitless. You will have to work to subdue the earth; the ground upon which you work will be cursed. With great toil you shall eat of it, all the days of your life. Thorns and thistles will crowd out the plants of the field. You shall eat bread until you return to the ground from which you were taken, for you are dust, and to dust you shall return." With this last proclamation, Elohim sobbed, and the earth rumbled, the trees shook. "Oh, my children, my dear children, what a ruinous day! You have chosen other, and my anger is kindled!"

I was afraid then, and weak in the knees and shoulders. "Elohim," I whispered. "Have we ruined *everything*? Can we promise not to eat from the tree again?" My hands were out in front of me, palms up, and I was raising them toward Him in supplication.

Elohim was quiet—thinking, I presumed. When He spoke, I had to strain to hear Him. He leaned over, weary. "My love for you has not changed, Eve. It is you and Adam who have changed. You do not know it now, but soon you will, and for that, I am sorry. You have seen things in terms of 'other,' not in terms of me." He clenched His fists. He struggled with His words. "How can I explain these things to you? There are natural laws that govern the universe and the things in it. Fire: It warms, but it can also hurt. Disease: It culls populations, but it makes things die. Beasts: They provide food, but they can also kill. These laws are necessary, but they will seem chaotic and cruel and random because now they can be wielded for evil. People: They can be good, or they can be evil." He knelt and tore at His hair. He scratched at His face—once more I falter in my description, because I may have seen Him as a copy of myself. Then He spoke again, although now His voice seemed to reverberate all around us. "Things will seem awry and wrong, but it will be your vision that has been altered. Oh, I am loath to tell you these things, but you will be fearful and selfish and lustful and prideful and greedy, and still you will point the finger at the other and say, 'See? He is the one you want. She is the one who should die.'" His voice rose, as if carried on the wind, on the wings of flying birds. "You will ask *why* and *how* and *when,* and I will not be able to explain, because you will have grasped at that power and claimed that you can manage it without my help. You will suffer greatly at the hands of others who have made the same choice as you; then you will realize the gravity of what you have done." Elohim appeared tired then, exhausted and spent. His voice trembled in His last words to us: "I loved you as no other, and I shall continue to love you. Remember this, if you remember nothing else. Know that I am wooing you back, even though you will begin to doubt I ever existed. I am merciful; I will not allow you to live always with this blackened vision."

Elohim paused, then continued. "Your fire has consumed you; you have lost your radiant glory."

It was true. Adam no longer shone. Neither did I. We had lost something that made us different from the animals.

He turned from us and beckoned with His fingers. A lion, crouching low and timid under a palm tree, slunk to Elohim's side. Elohim put his hand upon the lion's head and stroked his mane gently. The lion blinked his large ebony eyes and looked up into Elohim's face. Elohim knelt at the lion's side and whispered into its ear, "I am sorry." The lion's eyes grew sad and knowing, and he pushed his head into Elohim's hand.

What came next shocked and disgusted me. I know not why, other than I had not seen Elohim kill before, and what He did struck me as excessive and violent. Elohim had explained the order of things, how things small and large occupied their place in the world, to eat or be eaten, and that the cycle of life and death protected the earth from overuse and deterioration, but to witness this violence from Elohim was an aberration. Of course, I am speaking from a place distant from that time. I know that since then we have inflicted the same evilness upon the animals we have needed for sustenance, and each time I am reminded of how precious a gift their life is.

But then I did not think we would be instruments in death.

Certainly not within the Garden.

Elohim reached out to the lion standing before Him and put His hand on its throat. He dug His fingers in, quick and deep, around the jugular, and yanked the throat from the poor lion's neck. The animal slumped, then fell with a booming *thud* to the ground. Rivers of blood flowed from his wound. The light in his glorious eyes went out.

Elohim turned to us, pain etched in every line around His eyes and mouth. He lifted His hand; He still held the unnatural living fibers in His fist. "Your transgression affects even the animals," He said. He thrust the lion parts from His hand and walked to the riverbed. He stepped into the eddies, washed death from His hands, and picked up a stone, thin and sharp. I had stood where He was now standing. I wondered if He noticed the ribbed sand at His toes, the tiny shells and pale stones rocked to and fro by the lapping waters, if He saw the glimmering fish, felt a soaring thankfulness at such things, or if His anger was all-consuming and blinding.

Elohim returned to the lion's side.

Adam and I did not move. We knew not what Elohim was planning, and we did not know if we were His next victims, for indeed He had promised death if we ate from the Tree of the Knowledge of Good and Evil. *Was this the death He meant?* I am sure I looked much like Adam; he had grown quite weak and pale at the spectacle and had put his arm around me.

Elohim knelt. With the stone set on edge, Elohim sliced the lion's belly open, from neck to groin. He teased the skin and fur back, tearing it from the membrane and muscle below. He was meticulous and methodical. He did not speak.

It took a long while.

Adam and I watched, shifting only in exhaustion and incomprehension. We were in the lull between the crime and punishment, the horrid time of contemplation and sorrow and fretfulness.

Elohim stood finally. He held out two irregular skins. "To cover yourselves," He said.

Adam and I looked at each other, confused, but reached for them anyway.

He lifted His hand and pointed to the east, where a strange light had begun to burn. "You will go from here," said Elohim, "to the east to live, so that you will not eat from the Tree of Life, which gives everlasting life, and you will live forever in this pitiable state."

I must have looked astonished, because, indeed, I had already added the tiny black seeds from the Tree of Life to my growing seed collection, which I carried in a pouch at my side.

"Why do you smile, Eve?" said Elohim.

"We've already eaten from the Tree of Life," I said. I looked down at my feet, trying not to betray my sudden interest.

"I know," He said. "I did not forbid eating from that tree. But now that you have chosen other, you should not eat from it again"—then, in a gentler voice—"for it is not about eating. It's about betrayal and disregard for me. Do you not see the difference?"

I nodded but did not look up.

Elohim came forward and placed His hands on our shoulders. His touch exuded strength and courage and love and forgiveness; it is a shame I cannot feel those things now, at least with the intensity I felt them that day. He pulled Adam and me into the curve of His chest and said, "I shall redeem you one day, and you will have ample opportunity to live out your lives in harmony with nature . . . yourselves . . . me." His voice broke. "Go now." He withdrew from us and pushed us toward the wavering eastern lights.

I fell to my knees again, sobbing. "Elohim, oh, gracious friend, look past our indiscretion. This is our home. We belong with You." My plea rose up on flimsy wings, and it was as though the other plants and animals had a throat too. Everywhere orchids bloomed, frogs caterwauled, monkeys screeched, water burbled, and insects danced, as if to say, *Yes, it is right and fitting that Adam and Eve should stay with us here, in the Garden.*

Elohim turned His back to us, a rock unmoving. His shoulders stooped. His body shook with sobs.

Adam and I left Him then.

We made our way to the light, holding the reeking skins about us. As we approached the eastern end of the Garden, I could see that the light was, in fact, a wall of luminous, wavy bands of color—green, blue, and yellow— and that in the midst of it stood a curious winged beast. It had the form of Adam and myself, but its wings were outstretched to bar the way. Its face resembled that of a lion or an eagle—that is my best approximation. It looked straight ahead and did not acknowledge our presence. I have seen nothing so strange as that since then, and I do not wish to encounter it ever again. There was something eerie and wholly alarming about both the creature's brilliance and permanence. As we passed, its wing dipped to allow us passage—there was a rush of air, then another, as it returned to its position of protection—and although Elohim had not explained this new development, it was obvious these things were here to prevent us from reentering the Garden.

We carried nothing, save for my collection of seeds. No food, no water—nothing that could prepare us for our new life away. We made our way slowly, without conversation, past the huge palm trees and bamboos and orchids, into Elohim's vast other world outside the Garden. We did not think—not for a while, anyway—that this was an enduring arrangement. Surely Elohim would invite us back to discuss the stars and the planets and the upkeep of the Garden! Surely He would see that we were sorry. Surely it was a minor thing we had done.

Naava

That summer, Naava was a girl in a woman's body. Swelling breasts, widening hips. She did not know what game she played. She only answered to her body's yearnings and her mind's callings. She was fascinated by the mystery of a man and a woman. She was drawn to the smell of Cain and the lure of the prince.

She had already had her first and second and third bloods. It had been unexpected, really. Eve had not told her it would happen; instead, when Naava felt a release in her groin and something wet between her legs, she lifted her robe and saw the reddish-brown smear upon her leg. She went to Aya and asked her sister to make up a concoction for her. She was bleeding.

"You look fine to me," Aya had said.

"You can't see it, silly," said Naava. She whispered into Aya's ear, "It comes from *down there.*"

Aya pulled back, stared hard into Naava's eyes. "Goat gets that," she said. "It's not serious. Abel says it's for having babies."

"Babies?" said Naava. "How? I don't understand."

Aya shrugged. "You have to have it to have babies. Ask Mother if you're so worried."

But Naava kept it to herself. Besides, it lasted only several days at a time. She used strips of cloth, secured in another cloth wrapped around her waist, to stanch the flow, and then she was fine again.

Nothing would prevent her from visiting the city.

Her visiting day came sooner than she thought. She regretted that she had not yet completed her robe for a sweeping grand entrance—she was behind because of Dara's unraveling—but there would come a day, she knew, when she would wear it with great pride, and all heads, men's and women's, would turn her way. Naava had convinced Cain that she wanted to visit Dara, and she had convinced Eve that not only would she visit Dara, she would barter in the market with some of Aya's mild goat cheese. She was lying, of course. *So gullible,* she thought. She just wanted to see what the city was like, and if she saw the prince, that was even better.

Cain and she left in the early-morning heat. Naava rode a donkey, straddled with bread and beer and a sling of Aya's cheese. She and Cain would walk across the plains—scruffy with tumbleweed and sparse vegetation and baked hard by the sun. They would spend the day in the city and walk back before the time of hyenas and jackals—and the large lion that had been stalking Abel the past few weeks. That was their plan, and it was a good one. Naava expected to see much and accomplish much. For Dara she cared nothing, but she would ask for her, with the hope that the prince would be there.

Cain carried a slingshot and a flint dagger with a bone haft, hung upon a leather belt, just in case they should encounter a wildcat or boar intent upon doing them harm.

The morning pressed down upon them, like a great beast panting, which did not bode well for the day—it would only grow more scorching. Naava drew her hand across her brow, mopping up beads of sweat with her sleeve. She sipped from her waterskin, just to wet her tongue and throat. Her donkey snorted impatiently, as he struggled under his burden, which he wanted to eat rather than transport.

"It's not long before we're there," said Cain. "See?" He pointed.

To the north, in the distance, the flat roofs of sun-dried buildings, bright in the morning sun, appeared over a squat stone wall, half constructed. Indeed, there was an advancing black line snaking out from the wall—men carrying goods on their shoulders, to and from several vessels banked on the river and lurching drunkenly from side to side. Farther down along the shoreline were clusters of reed houses, flanked by fenced-in paddocks and by the stickish silhouettes of water birds jabbing their beaks into the silty mud, then lifting and rising upon the hot watery air.

"Keleks," said Cain, pointing to the vessels. "They bring goods from upstream—ivory, stones, and metal."

"Metal?" said Naava.

"You told me of the women's bracelets and necklaces," Cain said. "The gold and silver and copper are these things they call metal."

As they neared the city's outskirts, they came upon a wide dirt path beaten hard by commerce and bordered by tall shivering grasses. An irrigation ditch ran parallel with the road, and there, Cain explained what the myriads of sun-darkened workers were doing. They had built small dams at various levels and were wielding *shadufs,* long poles weighted with wet mud on one end and a bucket on the other, to move water from one level to the next. This way the water from the overflowing Euphrates was captured for crops.

Off in the distance, tent-dwellers huddled around their smoky fires.

Two pelicans descended upon one of the tents, and a loud chatter ensued.

"They train them," said Cain, pointing at the birds, "to retrieve fish."

What incredibly clever people, thought Naava. *Far smarter than Mother and Father.*

The fields were green and vast, except for a strange crop that was an undulating sea of blue flowers. Here and there, peasants squatted with tools to weed and cull, then, to ease their strain, they stood to shift the weight of bulbous sacks on their backs.

At that moment, the desert felt immense to Naava. *How could we not have known about these people for so long?* Naava dismounted, to stretch her legs and walk into the city.

The long golden husk of morning brightened further, snuffing out the last starlight on high and the fire glow below. The drab disk of sun oozed through the dusty air and set everything to stirring. Even before they reached the low-slung walls of the city, Naava could hear the faint cracking and pounding of tools against stone, the calls of the marketplace, the cries of children running and playing, and the sharp barks of mongrel dogs. Naava's excitement rose up to seize her, to hold her fast. She felt her ears peel back and become alert, bristling like that of a furry creature that could sense change or danger in the air. Her stomach rattled like a burnished nut inside her. The dust had made her eyes red and her nose runny; she did not notice.

A dog ran out to greet them, yipping at their ankles. Its fur was pocked with scabs and mange, and one of its eyes was missing, its socket cobwebbed with scars.

Several of the working men turned to look at the visitors, but they were too far away for Cain and Naava to read the messages inscribed on their faces. Cain said, "Stay close to me until we're inside. I don't know these men." He did not have to repeat himself.

Naava's excitement had turned to trepidation, for although she was full of bravado at home, here she felt it turn to butter.

The city's entrance was a wide yawning maw in the wall. No gate had been made for it yet. A white-bearded guardian, his eyes a cloudy blue, sat on a low stool off to the side, with an up-tipped face as if he could neither hear nor see. His face was expressionless, like a sunflower, and he held out his hands, cupped and trembling. He repeated the same plea over and over again, plaintively, like a lamb calling for its mother. Naava gaped at him—where was this man's family? Certainly Naava's family would have taken care of one of their own, injured or not.

Men, naked to the waist except for the heavy jewelry upon their chests and wrists and arms, stood, mingling and talking. They had thin lips and prominent noses. A few of them cleaned their teeth with sticks shredded at one end. When they glimpsed Cain and Naava, they paused, and their gesticulating fingers grew still. A man with a head as shiny and bare as a newborn baby's broke off from the group and wended his way to them. He had large gold hoops in his ears and an armlet of gold around his biceps, and his eyes were outlined in black. He asked them something, which Naava did not understand. Cain answered him and pointed to the donkey and the sacks of cheese slung upon its hips. The man looked at Naava—though she thought *leer* was a better word for it—then nodded to Cain. The man rejoined his friends. There was raucous laughter, and Naava looked away.

"He said, 'Peace and welcome,'" said Cain.

Naava knew better.

They passed through the city's entrance, the wall thicker than two arm's-lengths, and turned onto a bustling side street, narrow and airless. There an ample and dignified man swept the street in front of his house with a broom fashioned from palm fronds. He looked up to stare, to smile, to hold up a hand in greeting, to laugh at the gaggle of children who scampered about the legs of Naava's donkey.

"There are so many," said Naava.

Children of all ages, with nimble, agitated fingers, touched, caressed, and lit like fleas upon Cain's hairy arms and Naava's flowing hair. And their voices: like warbling birdsong sung through open, eager mouths, chanting, bandying, echoing phrases and words to one another, as though to churn the stifling air into life.

Naava slapped the children's thieving fingers away from the donkey's sling. "No," she barked.

Giggling, they plunged their hands into the sling again and again, so that Naava worked continually to swat their hands away. It became a weary little game.

"Pesky, aren't they?" she said to Cain.

"They should be at their studies," said Cain, laughing.

Two men passed, bantering about something humorous. Between them they carried a swinging clay pot hanging from rods that rested on their shoulders, their chests already gleaming with sweat. They yelled at the children, and the little ones parted to let them through.

Naava covered her nose with her sleeve. The children mimicked her. The stench was palpable. The flies hovered over piles of refuse. Rivulets of filthy water meandered through the dirt streets, searching for a place to pool. A pair of gulls had found their way inland from the sea, following the reek of human existence, and now they sat on one of the piles, their claws clasping the thin slips of fish bones, their beaks working up and down to strip them of leftover meat.

The houses pressing in on all sides were low and flat-roofed, built of the same red-brown sun-dried bricks Naava's family had used to build their house. A roadblock of masons stood knee-deep in mud and straw, lifting and lowering buckets to a new roof. A man with a grizzled, pointed beard stood on the rim of the structure, legs spread wide. He chanted a sad little song to the rhythm created by the men slapping mud on the roof. Below, the laborers sang back, answering his call like courting geese.

As the street narrowed, Cain and Naava scuttled sideways like crabs— Cain in front, then the donkey, then Naava, then the gaggle of children. They followed the huddle of houses until it became obvious that the street would open up at the hub of the city, into a splendid cacophony of light, sound, and smells, over which hung a dreamy pall of dust.

"Oh," said Naava, the spectacle quite taking her breath away. The children skittered off in all directions, being pulled by other, more interesting goings-on.

"That was my reaction," said Cain, grinning. "You'll get used to it."

Indeed, the relative quiet of Naava and Cain's home compared to the city's riotous sounds was like night and day. Naava felt overwhelmed at the frantic busyness that surrounded her. Gone were the animal sounds of the plains. Instead, people sounds swirled all about her like a strong current, threatening to pull her under.

There was the swarming marketplace, rushing and bubbling like an engorged river. Along its tattered edges, faded tarps blocked out the merciless sun and protected the goods within. Everywhere, merchants shouted. Rosy-lipped women with slim-necked jars on their heads and baubles upon their wrists and necks walked barefoot past them, their coy, flitting eyes belying their curiosity. A herd of sheep ambled by, bleating; their shepherd clicked his tongue and struck their backs with a braided rope.

Cain halted abruptly, and Naava, who was trailing closely behind, bumped headlong into the donkey's rear; the donkey in turn gave her a quick brutish kick to her shins. She yelped and leaned over to rub her throbbing leg.

Cain didn't respond. His attention was engaged at the moment by the billowing sea of robed people climbing their way to the top of a stepped, squared-off platform that sat like a regal indifferent lion in the middle of that immense open space. The people carried baskets of food, rounds of bread, and little clay figurines in their hands. The children, too, were somber and imitated the slow genuflecting of their parents. They were edging their way to the top, to a small covered building made of bricks, where they handed their gifts to a woman dressed in white and a man with a gold headdress.

Naava said, "I think that is the big woman who visited us. The one who killed the lamb."

Cain was not listening.

Reverently, the woman nodded her head, touched the people's foreheads and breasts with her fingers, then placed her hands on their shoulders. The people nodded and bowed in return and began the journey down, happier and lighter now. The children mimicked the more jovial mood of their elders, and their faces lit up, their feet skipped, and they peered into their parents' faces with open, anticipatory joy.

Naava stood at Cain's side. "What are they doing?" she said.

Cain's face wore a look that could only be described as wonder. "They're bringing food to Inanna."

"Inanna?" said Naava.

"The Queen of Heaven," said Cain. "The Goddess of Love."

Naava glanced at Cain and saw the longing in his face, not for her but for Inanna. *Who was this Inanna that had captured the hearts of so many?*

"Is that what Mother had? Her little statue?" said Naava.

Cain nodded, then walked toward the lowest step, which was crowded with tiny statues that held their hands in clasped appeal.

"Like yours," said Naava in amazement.

Cain nodded again and, in his eagerness, turned and said, "The people set these here so they can pray to Inanna on their behalf. Inanna rules over all the gods." He pointed to the building at the top. "They set a table for her with gold bowls and cups, food and wine, even a censer to please her—" He saw that Naava was struggling to keep up with him. "A censer . . . uh, a thing to burn a pleasant aroma, something they call incense." Cain's excitement was contagious. "From dark to dark they do this."

"She's up there now?" said Naava incredulously.

"I don't know," said Cain. "They say that she comes when she wants to."

"Is she Elohim's wife?" said Naava.

"No," said Cain, disgusted. "Mother and Father cling too tightly to their dreams, their past. This is the real thing." He gripped Naava's arm, and with his other, he pointed to the worshipful clay statues. "Mark my words, it makes more sense to have many gods, one for each force you come up against—one for fire, one for healing, one for storms, one for flocks." The words were spilling out of him now. "The stories: You should hear the stories of these gods, what they can do. They are magnificent—and deadly. Elohim is child's play compared to them."

In Cain's voice, Naava heard the cracking and slipping, like wet hides shrinking in the sun, stiffening with an irreversible tension—*rebelliousness*. Not that she would have called it this exactly, but she sensed a delicious and pleasant thrill through her abdomen and her limbs that could stem only from talking about Elohim and her parents in this dismissive and wholly disrespectful way. Although she was not one to sit around and think about *why* she did things—it was such a useless exercise—she felt that this was her embarking on her own life, her own desires, without the aid of any guiding hands except those *she* chose. And she had chosen Cain—to teach her the city's ways, to teach her about love, to teach her about the gods in the sky.

Cain fumbled with the sling on the donkey. He reached in and pulled out a lump of cheese. "I'll only be a short while," he said.

"Oh, no," said Naava. "The cheese is to barter with." That was a new thing for her—*bartering*—though Cain had tried to teach her the finer points of it, using items at home for practice. Suddenly it occurred to her that Cain might have taught her incorrectly, just to garner a few laughs later. She felt a little unsteady, like a new lamb trying to get its footing. But she would not show Cain how she felt. She would succeed at this task, and he would be proud of her quickness.

"Just a little," begged Cain.

"Half that," said Naava.

Cain broke off a hunk of the solid white cheese and tucked the rest of it back into the sling. "Meet me here when the sun is directly overhead."

"But," Naava protested, "how am I to—"

Cain was already out of earshot, holding the cheese in front of him like a precious offering, and then he was climbing with the supplicants who sought the intercessory aid of a being they deemed more omniscient than themselves.

Eve

I was speaking of our exodus from the Garden.

This, of course, forces me to confront the most difficult thing of all—my decision to disregard Elohim's injunction not to eat of the Tree of the Knowledge of Good and Evil. This must be faced bravely and honestly, for I am not one to shift blame where it does not belong. At least I try not to make a habit of it. If blame needs to be attributed, though, it should be to Lucifer, that beguiling creature-man who was fully cognizant of what he was doing.

For every action there is a motive, and this is the part that perplexes me.

I knew not of Lucifer's motive, why he had wanted me to stumble. I cannot deny I followed his suggestions quickly and hopefully. I think it was because my mind and body wanted what I could not have. You should know this: The forbidden is always sweeter beforehand. When I saw the flashing anger in Elohim's eyes, the subsequent cowering of Lucifer, then a grotesque shadow of the beautiful man he once had been, I knew there was something bigger, something of greater significance than me. Lucifer and Elohim had what I would now call a *history,* something not explained to either Adam or me. It was as though Adam and I were held fast, dangling and thrashing in a web not of our design, and the action was expected, to have the web there to begin with.

Oh, I torture myself. Had I thought ahead, considered the consequences, even deliberately weighed them carefully and precisely, considering the obvious hurt to Elohim, the responsibility I had toward Adam and toward myself, I might have progressed in my mind to the unpleasant result, then stopped myself before I had done irreparable damage.

The result was supposed to be that we were to "die on that day." Surely Elohim had reconsidered His punishment and had been merciful to instead send us from the Garden. I could still be with Adam, and he with me.

Now I come to the difficult part. Why such a monstrous punishment—to be expelled from our wondrous green-leafed retreat—for so little a crime? I ate. Adam ate. It was a simple action, ingesting food for nourishment—granted, from a forbidden source. Our eating must have symbolized much more. For that is how I understand it, that it was so great a disobedience that the whole universe had to cough us up, like a beast retching upon the brutal ground.

It seems to me, after many years of contemplation on this matter, that seemingly small things can cause great disturbances. Think about it a moment. When a young child throws a stone into a pool of water, the stone sinks to the bottom, but on the surface the disturbed water breaks into ripples—ripples that grow in size until finally they are slow, rolling breakers. They deposit shells and detritus upon the sand, but they also erode away at the banks—and all this from one stone's throw.

Elohim's excessive gesture of tossing us from His presence could only have meant one thing: We had caused ripples; we had done something with *large* consequences. Knowing this, I can only ponder all the things I consciously do, right or wrong, and wonder at what disastrous or beneficial things may then befall my children, or Adam, or the skies above, or the earth below. You might ask me, and rightly so, what all the worry is about, why I spend my days consumed with these questions. I would tell you that, like Cain, I dream for more. I am more like Cain than I wish to be, which is why we clash so often. My physicality—my excretions, my pains, my decay—they all strike me as nonsensical and ludicrous because I am not my body. My mind soars above these things, aloft on some great wind at my back, yearning to return to Elohim and the mysteries of the universe.

This is why Aya's name means "bird." Because in the hallucinatory throes of labor, I wanted to be *above* and *separate* from it all, borne by the sun and moon and stars and galaxies, triumphant over my weary earth-bound body.

The first few days were the most difficult. In retrospect, we were angry and confused, at Elohim, at each other. No longer protected and guarded from predators, we longed to return to the womb of the Garden.

With the odd wavering lights and the ethereal beast guarding the Garden's entrance behind us, we set our faces into the bitter shrieking wind—for it was winter outside the Garden—and plunged into the snowy forest clinging to the side of the craggy mountain. The hair on my body rose up, startled. This was the first time we had seen snow, the dazzling white cold of it, and we gasped in alarm and pain as the wind swept it up, driving swirls of icy dust into our skin. We tugged the lion's skins around our bodies, tighter, snugger.

Sunlight shone through the upper branches of the trees in dim chinks, and as the muffled quiet descended upon us, the brilliant flash of a red-wing lighting here and there led the way. We picked our path between the cracked fallen branches of oaks and the snow-furred greens of cedars. The forest was alive, that we knew, because the crusty snow betrayed its residents' tracks—rabbits, martens, and wolves. I shuddered to think of what Elohim had said, that as long as we stayed *in* the Garden we would be safe. *What dangers were in store for us now?*

Our faces grew red and numb and chapped—our fingers and toes too—and we found that we had to keep moving to maintain any semblance of warmth.

When I began weeping because of the cold, Adam barked at me to stop.

"If only *I* had met Lucifer first," said Adam, glowering.

I sniffled. "You would have done the same thing."

"I wouldn't have believed him. Did you not see him in front of Elohim?" Adam's voice mocked me. He did not bother to hold the tree branches for me. Instead, he pulled them out and away from his body, then released them to arc back wildly, so they would snap against my skin.

I tarried a good distance back. "You're saying that you're smarter than I am," I said indignantly, rubbing a fresh welt on my arm.

Adam stopped and turned toward me. He spoke matter-of-factly. His face was like the moon—open and arrogant. "Well, yes. After all, I was made first," said Adam. "Elohim made you *from* me, *for* me." He laughed and continued on his way. He was not usually this cruel. His jokes had turned to sarcasm, and his tenderness had turned to blame.

"He made us for each other," I said. I shivered with the cold.

"We were fine until you came along," said Adam. Now he had a stick, and he was taking pleasure in tapping sheets of snow off the lower branches of the cedars.

I bent down to pick up a handful of snow. I packed it into a ball. "That's not what Elohim said." I aimed high and true, and the cedar shed its coat upon my husband, who yelped prodigiously. I smiled, satisfied at my silent revenge. *What was happening to us?*

Before long, the forest opened up onto a flat area scrubbed raw by the wind and sun, with a cave tucked into the mountainside and a panoramic view beyond its lip. We ventured out to the edge, dizzy with fear. Below, a crooked line of mist marked the frozen river, which twisted black and dark and quiet through bare-branched oaks and snow-covered evergreens. Beyond that, clumps of low squat brush disappeared into a flat sandy plain, intercut by rivers as thin and unruly as one of the hairs on my head. In the great far distance, these waters fed into a dark sea that melted into the rimless white dome of heaven.

We found a smooth stone for a flint. We gathered sticks and twigs and laid them upon a pile at the cave's mouth. Because the wood was wet, it resisted burning. We scrabbled like dogs, grabbed the stone flint from each other, huffing in irritation. When the flame caught finally, we dropped to our hands and knees and blew on it furiously, coaxing it to burn—*please, we need you, we need you.* We fed its voraciousness until it coughed and sputtered to life.

We huddled across from each other, unwilling to share our body heat. We threw twigs and branches on the fire, not realizing we were likewise feeding our estrangement. Which was unforgivable, really, since the view was so breathtaking, so stunning, that in happier circumstances it would have been something to bring the two of us together—*Isn't it marvelous,* we'd say. *Isn't it grand. I love you. No, I love you more.*

The redwing warbled from his branch, proud that he had brought us to such a vista.

What came next still makes me shudder.

A low phlegmy snort rumbled up from the depths of the cave. We heard snuffling, more snorts, a great creaky yawn, then a sleepy shuffling of heavy padded feet upon the cold floor. Adam and I looked at each other, the wonder in our eyes turning to fear, then terror. We knew what it was. We were by then familiar with all the animals and their habits.

"Run," Adam whispered. He scrounged around for a stocky piece of oak, thick and blunt, and smacked it in the palm of his other hand, as though he was testing its strength, its trueness. He set his legs firmly apart, knees crooked and ready.

"I'll never make it," I said.

Adam's ire rose. "Go. Now."

I stood my ground. I chose another piece of wood for myself, somewhat thinner and longer with more points on it. I had never defended myself before. I did not realize that the flimsy branches, although they looked sturdy enough, would most likely snap and splinter when tested against the formidable bulk of a bear.

"Go, I said—" said Adam, but then the heaving, snorting beast emerged in front of us, bleary-eyed and lurching.

The bear sniffed at the damp air and stopped. He grunted.

"What should we do?" I whispered.

"Don't move," said Adam.

Now, I must say, the cave was large enough that the bear could have stood up and plucked the roosting bats off the dripping walls like grapes. But he was not interested in bats. He lumbered forward again and stopped. He swung his head from side to side, first to Adam, then to me, then to Adam again. He slammed his paw—*thud*—on the ground and growled.

The redwing, who had up to this moment lent his cheery song to our ears, spun away, his chatter becoming thin and slight on the tenuous air.

My shocked and grieving heart cried out: Was this the fruition of Elohim's awful promise that we would die upon eating of the forbidden fruit? *Oh, cruel Elohim, where are You now? Will You come to our aid, sweet friend?*

What madness! I had seen what a she-bear robbed of her cubs could do, the way she raged and tore a fox apart, limb from limb, the flesh hanging from his bones, his head lolling about.

My breath came in ragged bursts. "We're blocking his way," I said, backing up. "He smells the lion skin."

The bear turned toward me. He snapped his jaws and huffed through his nose. He ambled closer and opened his wide pink mouth, set with rows of sharp yellow teeth.

"Adam," I cried. I felt the sweat trickle down my face, down my chest.

"Stand still," he said.

Oh, Elohim, show Yourself now; please, we need Your help.

I had backed into the clearing now, and the bulging rippling beast was close enough to touch. He blinked in the sunlight, stared at me. The fur on his neck bristled, and he slammed his paw down again. *Thud.*

Elohim, be not distant, please protect us, keep us from harm.

The bear stood up on his hind legs—*oh, Elohim, no!*—the bulk of his body towering over me and blocking the sunlight.

I spoke to the bear. What else was there to do? "Oh, giant one, we have woken you from your sleep. Are you so malevolent that you would do us harm? Elohim made us, as He made you—"

"Don't move," hissed Adam.

The bear was panting now, blowing a hot, foul wind out his nose.

I did not at first feel the searing pain. I simply went from standing to lying flat on my back, staring up at the blurry undersides of wounded leaves, a broken stick in my hand. The bear sauntered off, chuffing his way through the forest.

"Eve," Adam breathed. He knelt by my side, his eyes wide and uncertain, his mustache and beard scratching my face. "You shouldn't have jabbed him."

My weariness was more than physical. For the first time, Adam had seen it all wrong and seen fit to give me advice to the contrary.

"He was going to strike me," I whispered. My hands were shaking uncontrollably.

"Because you poked him," he said.

"That was after," I said. I sat up. My head throbbed, and my jaw ached. I winced and touched my cheekbone. My hand came away bloody. I reached around to rub my lower back, which seized in pain. I vomited.

"Here," said Adam. He helped me to my feet and led me to the fire, adjusting the lion skin around my shoulders and body. He took my hands between his and rubbed them together briskly. He put his arm around me and pulled me close. He was concerned for me, true, but behind his tenderness was his obvious frustration that our stories weren't congruous, that I didn't see things *his* way.

There was nothing to be done about it. The bear had clawed my face. I saw one thing—*felt*, really. Adam saw another. I could not persuade him to believe something else.

Looking back on this, I am amazed that words connect us with any modicum of honesty or correctness. I cannot praise Aya without her thinking that I am humoring her. When I praise Cain, he acts like a lamb that wants to hoard all his mother's milk. When I praise Abel, he becomes abashed and more distant. And Naava, alas, how do I explain my woman-child? If I offer her words of encouragement, I am the dumbest ass alive. Everything about her screams, *How can you know what I'm going through?*

These things—these words—are so limited. They fly from your mouth and land in odd poses you do not intend. Perhaps the world is beautiful because it sings without words.

While I warmed my chilled body and held my hands over the dwindling fire, Adam went to search for leaves with which to clean my face. I moved my aching jaw from side to side, thinking, *I am alive.* I studied my hands, my fingers, my body. All there. *What was this death that Elohim promised? Why had it not occurred yet? Would He do this thing Himself? Or were we to do it to ourselves?*

It was only then I noted, all around, the telltale claw marks upon the trees, the wild tufts of hair caught up on the bark. We should have known.

My abdomen tightened like a fist, and I let out a sob. The cramps came again and again, like waves upon a shore. I curled into myself and sat very still.

Adam returned with a fistful of snow and motioned for me to hold it to my injury. "There are no ants," he said. Once, in the Garden, Adam had cut his shin on a ledge of granite, and Elohim had picked up several ants and applied them, one by one, to Adam's leg, severing their bodies from their heads after they had closed the lips of the injury with their pincers.

Adam held a hard frozen blackberry before my mouth.

I shook my head *no*.

Adam put his hand on mine. "You must eat."

Another wave of nausea hit, and I vomited again. The pain in my middle had not lessened.

"Come," he said, holding out his hand.

I stood, bent over like rain-slashed grass, and stumbled after my husband into the forest. The snow in my hand had melted, and my fingers and my cheek burned with a wretched heat. The cold air seared my lungs, for in my agony I had taken in too many gulpfuls of breath.

And then we were made to understand.

I felt a loosening below, a heaving spasm and a warm wetness between my legs. I reached down with my fingers to feel and came away with a clot of blood and tissue between my fingers. My monthly flow had waxed and waned like the moon, which was Elohim's way, but this whiteness, this tiny curl of life—for that's what it was, a miniature tadpole, with two arms and two legs and a large head with black eyes, all enclosed in a small transparent sac—was sucking its thumb. I had not known I was with child. "Adam," I murmured.

Adam slowed and held out his hand. "Up ahead," he said.

"Look," I said.

He peered over my cupped hand and absorbed the gleaming slip of our child, immersed in sea. I had seen animals born of the mother—the stretching, the tearing, and the licking—but those babies were much larger and usually able to move on their own. This, this replica of us, was too small and lifeless and cold.

A violent grief flooded me, devoured me whole. I fell upon Adam's chest, keening. He held me fast and gripped me tight. I felt his chest pound, his breath grow heavy. He stepped back to hold the weight of me. He clung to me but said nothing.

Elohim has spoken, I thought. *Here we have our death.*

You might ask why we would grieve for something we didn't know we had, and I would tell you that in that moment I saw myself as a mother, Adam as a father, and I wanted that baby, wanted that child, more than anything else in the world. The child was ours, and Elohim had taken it away. Grief comes swiftly, in the briefest of moments. You do not have time to plan for it. In my uncertain dreams, I see my too-little child in the palm of my hand turn to look at me, its sad pitiful eyes wondering *why,* and I have no answer.

Beautiful child, where did you go?

Adam urged me to sit again, on a felled limb rolled from the forest into a clearing full of soft, rounded snow mounds. Busily, he cleared an area of snow and built another fire, an arduous task to repeat in the same day. As I stared at the lost life in the palm of my hand and tried to ease the aching in my belly, he dug with his fingers through the snowy crust and into the frozen earth. He did not stop until he had scooped out a small rounded hole for the baby. His fingers were bloody and numb. Every few moments he would tap his fingers hard against each other, flicking them back to life.

As I watched the bulk of him digging, I thought, *He is sad too. We are both sad, for this life we have lost.*

Adam stood and looked at me with such concern and trepidation that I burst into tears all over again. He came to me and gazed again at our first child, in the lake of my palm. He spoke to the child. "Little one," he said. "Your mother and father are very sad. We did not know you were coming to us. We did not know you would come too early. We are giving you back to the earth, for Elohim has said to dust we all shall return."

The tears flowed then, for both of us. Adam helped me up and led me to the hole in the ground under the sighing trees. We knelt and laid the child in the cold, cruel womb of the earth. Adam took the dirt he had removed and replaced it gently, to cover our baby's sleeping silence with kindness.

It was then that I thought of the seeds—the Tree of Life seeds I had collected. *Had Elohim not said they would give eternal life—or was He referring to the tree's fruit? Could they restore life, where life had been stolen away?* Hurriedly, I tugged at the strings of the pouch and poured the black seeds out into my palm. I extracted one and handed it to Adam.

"What's this?" asked Adam.

"To mark the place our baby died," I said, reluctant to admit that it was from the Tree of Life. In truth, my hope was that it would bring life back to my baby.

Adam studied my face for a long while. Then he sighed and tapped the seed into the ground.

I knew that Adam's fingers were already tired and numb, but he took up some of the loose soil from the baby's grave with his fingernails and mixed it with his spit. He stood. "Come," he said, holding out his arms to me. He held my head and wiped the wet earth on the gouges in my cheek. I said nothing. There was nothing to say. The mixture would dry and tighten, closing up the wounds.

As night fell, we leaned into each other's sadness.

I sat there, empty-handed, my heart gaping, Adam's too, and we waited for the moon to shine, the stars to light, our hearts bursting and breaking. *This is too much.*

Adam mumbled our song then, the one taught to us by Elohim. His breath drifted; his voice was a bird that flew out of his chest. I looked at him, the bristled false cheer of his face, and I wished him to look at me, to see the mother of his child, broken before him.

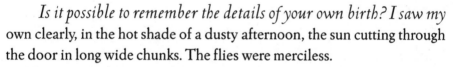

Aya

Is it possible to remember the details of your own birth? I saw my own clearly, in the hot shade of a dusty afternoon, the sun cutting through the door in long wide chunks. The flies were merciless.

There was Mother, squatting, legs wide apart, leaning on a staff. There was my sister Naava, wide-eyed and terrified at the water and blood gushing upon the floor.

Mother yelled, heaved, dug her fingernails into the staff. My shoulders were pushed out upon the cold earth. Naava began to cry, and I joined her. Mother picked me up by my ankles. I dangled, scarlet and purple, and she dipped me in a bowl of river water, washed me clean. She cooed, "There you are, oh my."

She traced the arc of my leg, the abrupt angle of my foot.

Wait. Go back, please. There was Mother, squatting, legs wide apart, leaning on a staff. Naava was there too, and her eyes were like ostrich eggs. Now stop. Hold everything still. I want to ask, *When did my foot go awry? When did it go its own errant way? Was it something I did or Mother did? Did Elohim know of my deformity—I hate that word!—or of Mother's disappointment?*

"What's wrong, Mother?" said Naava, reading the blossoming frown on Mother's face.

"She has two arms and two legs," said Mother.

"Like me," said Naava.

"Yes," said Mother. She leaned over, gasping at the pain, to show Naava her brand-new sister. She yanked my leg down, straight from the hip, like dough that needed to be worked. "My two beautiful daughters." She thought for a moment. "Go tell your father and brothers."

Naava ran out, excited to be the bearer of news.

Mother laid me upon the floor, releasing my leg. My leg, which curled up like a snail shell. I looked up at her beautiful face as she squatted, weary and disappointed, to wait for the slimy afterbirth. It came with a *balup* sound, and she leaned over to bite through the cord. She wiped her purple-stained mouth with the back of her hand. She would bury the placenta later, in her garden. She did this because she was superstitious; she thought that if something ate it, I would die. Maybe she thought for just a moment of setting it out for the wild animals to eat; that way she would not have to look at this monster she had created.

She picked me up and went outside. With a groan, she held me up to the burning yellow sun and turned slowly. *Was she introducing me to the world? Was she seeking Elohim's blessing?*

I opened my arms to it, to how warm and beautiful it was. Pieces of hot fire entered me. I grew wings. It was my first flight.

There are three ways to live: past, present, and future. There's Mother, who lives in a lost paradise. Its lostness *makes* it paradise. There's Naava. She lives in the present, waiting, hoping that her life will change—*snap snap,* my fingers go.

I live in the future. Someday Elohim will heal my foot. After all, I am His most admiring and faithful advocate, besides Abel.

I wear patience like a garment. Belief is my middle name.

Why, oh why, must I be strong for everyone? Aya this. Aya that. Just call me a rope, a binder of things, a sticky poultice. Really, I am not so surprised. Mother has lost her littlest, with Dara going to the city. She goes around glum all day, and now she has told me, in no uncertain terms, that she thinks she will die during childbirth.

At night, when the beetles and cockroaches scurry this way and that, she wakes in the dark, dripping with sweat, clinging to Father and mumbling, "Not my fault." Father leads her out, like a small child, into the cool night air. He sits and pulls her into the safe whorl of him. She leans her curly head back onto his chest, and he begins to hum, a low sad melody that is the perfect prayer. They have brought this from the Garden, and although we all know the tune of it, only Abel knows the words, from when he was a child. Mother whispers the words, and I strain to make them out, as I have always done. It is no use. The song whirls back on itself like a fine pink shell and *whooshes* in my ear. The song is not meant to be understood, only to be felt—the cool rush of water, the fresh breath of a melon, the slow sigh of grasses. Father rubs her arms and cups her hands in his. He strokes her hair, and still he hums. When her voice grows faint, he brings her back in and lays her on her reed mat, saying, *I'm here, I'm right here.*

I, Aya, do not have someone who cares about me that much. No, I do not. Does anyone sit up and take notice of how hard I labor? No, I say, a thousand times, no.

And yet it is a funny thing.

Because I live, I am thankful. Because I live, I listen.

And now I will tell you the truth.

I have to believe I am useful *because* He made me. Mother has told me of the Garden, the plethora of species, each one in its own little niche, each a little odd and funny in its own right. *This is me,* I cry. *This is who I am. Odd little Aya with the crooked foot.* After all, He made insects that look like twigs and flesh-colored blooms that attract flies. He made beetles that change colors and butterflies with eyes on their wings. He made small brightly colored frogs that are poisonous and leaf-tailed geckos that blend into trees.

So I look. Hold my breath. Memorize the darkness, the light, the summer of my heart. *I am here,* I shout. *I am watching everything. The ordinary. The drab. The extraordinary. Praise, oh, sweet world. I bless you each and every day.*

I would like Abel to notice me, just once. It is acceptable that I am his second and only choice, since he's clearly disgusted with Naava's impertinence—and the fact she poisoned Mother.

Cain and Naava left for the city this morning.

Was it not obvious that Naava desired everyone's attention? She was a lioness looking to fill her belly. Cain looked at her like he was seeing the vast starry heavens for the first time, and Abel—what should be said about Abel? He only glanced at her when he thought she wasn't looking. They were looks of curiosity, not of lust. I imagined he was thinking, *How could someone so ravishingly beautiful be so rotten to the core?*

Naava pretended she did not notice the attention, but she strutted like a handsome hoopoe with her beak in the sky. Honestly, I knew of nothing I would have liked to do more than bash her over the head with one of my rocks, just to knock some sense into her. She could not have all the men. How could she?

I wrapped up some bread and cheese in fig leaves, filled the waterskins with beer, and tied it all to the donkey's haunches.

Cain smiled at me and said, "Thank you, sister." He went down on his knees and cupped his hands, so that Naava could climb with ease onto the donkey's back. He stood and touched the small of her back, right above her buttocks, to make sure she was secure. I could have told him she was fine, absolutely fine, without laying a hand on her.

Naava smiled sweetly at Cain and brought her hand up to her neck, to wipe the sweat away.

Mind you: Abel watched all this out of the corner of his eye. When he saw Naava make this helpless movement with her hands, he descended rapidly, opened his wings, and put his claws on her.

"*What* are you doing?" Naava said to Abel, who was holding an opened waterskin filled with water above her neck. "You shall soil my robe."

Abel offered the sleeve of his robe. "Here," he said. "Pour a little on this and cool your neck."

Cain rummaged around in one of his big conical baskets. He pulled out a cucumber, took the knife from his belt, cut a hunk free, and offered it to

Naava. "This is better," he said, looking evenly at Abel. "You can suck on it." He struck the donkey's hindquarters and barked, "We must be going."

The donkey lurched forward, and Naava almost lost her balance. Cain went to the donkey's head, took hold of the reins, and led him along.

Abel stood there for a long time, confused and disoriented, looking after his beautiful sister with the black heart.

Naava

Although Naava wanted to believe in everything that spoke of the city, standing there in the middle of the marketplace after Cain ran off, she wondered if Inanna could hear the murmured prayers or see the eager faces or taste the wondrous feast set before her. *Did she have a physical body like Naava? Or was she a spirit, blown to and fro by the wind?* Naava had seen no evidence of Elohim, except for the single time she heard a strange voice from somewhere when she and Aya were playing, and although Aya latched on to it as Proof of Elohim's Existence, Naava had declared that it was all a coincidence. *Hadn't Aya been learning how to throw her voice around that time, anyway?* It could have been the wind.

What swayed Naava toward belief in Inanna's existence was the *numbers* of people dedicated to her. In fact, it was remarkably reassuring to see so many people who believed and lived one certain way, with no evident doubters or dissenters. This was encouraging . . . and fortifying.

Those were her thoughts as she turned to the merchants behind her. One was already pulling on the sleeve of her robe—an older man with no teeth, whose groin was the only thing about him swathed in cloth. He rocked from foot to foot, rubbed his palms together, and pointed to an assortment of sweetmeats arranged artistically on large clay slabs. He rubbed his hands together. The anticipation of a sale was almost too much. The heat was melting the sweets, so they sat in a sticky pool of butter and honey and flies' wings. Naava shook her head *no,* then moved on. Behind her, the merchant chattered like a belligerent monkey.

Not all the sellers were this way. There was a tea house, or at least that's what Naava assumed, because the woman with cinnamon skin behind the counter, the one with eyes as blue as Eve's and a matching stone in her nose, smiled at her and motioned for Naava to choose a pinch of herbs by leaning over dark-mouthed jars and inhaling. Naava did. The woman then handed her a painted clay cup with cool water in it. She tapped on Naava's hand where Naava held the herbs. Naava dumped them in, and the woman sighed, happy now. The woman waited. Naava sipped. The tea was earthy, a little lemony. She smiled, and the woman laughed and threw her hands in the air. Naava tried to give a section of Aya's cheese to her, but the woman smiled a broad smile full of brown teeth, waved her hands, and jabbered something, maybe *Not necessary* or *Go in peace.* Again, Naava could only go by body gestures and the tone of voice, so she took her tea and went out into the sunlight again.

She sat on a bench. In front of her, a dusky-skinned girl with silver anklets balanced on the tips of her toes, reaching above her head to the flapping birds who seized bread morsels from her outstretched fingers. The girl was so absorbed with her task, she didn't notice Naava, which was just as well because there were other things to see.

Nearby, a flabby-armed woman huffed as she rocked a large clay jar in the shape of the spinning tops Abel used to make for Naava. Naava supposed the woman was churning milk; the liquid sloshed inside. Across the way, a curly-headed boy with the wild look of a gazelle stacked thick-skinned oranges, sweet lemons, melons—a few with caved pates—black and white figs, slender grapes called goat's dugs, and the first underripe harbingers of fall—honeydews. Naava's mouth watered. Citrus fruits were not yet ripe, Naava knew. The city farmers must have squirreled them away last winter to get a higher price now, in midsummer. They might be an excellent barter. But as soon as she had decided this, she saw other things, better things.

There, in the corner, a man pounded a sheet the color of the sunset into the shape of a bowl. The sheet bent with each hammer blow, and when it resisted, into the fire it went, to soften it once again. The man's quickness was astonishing. Even more remarkable was the fleck of shimmering ash that surrounded him, like the lingering glow of an oil lamp. Naava stood to get a better look. *Tap tap* went his hammer; *ping ping* went the bowl. They sang an anthem of praise to their maker. The man set the bowl off to the side and wiped his brow. Naava reached out to touch it, but the man noticed her interest and, at the last moment, shook his head and muttered a warning. *Tsss,* he said.

Farther down, a pale young man with a square jaw and fine cheekbones sat on a wooden stool with children clinging to him like possum babies. The man was using a reed cut on an angle to draw gouges in a square shard of wet clay. He dipped his head in concentration, put his weight on the reed, then held it up for the children to see. The little ones laughed and clapped. Naava instinctively looked for Dara among them, but she didn't see her sister's telltale head of polished wheat.

She had forgotten about Cain and his quest for the sky, and she had forgotten the prince. Instead, she was overwhelmed—transported—by the silvery fish hanging from hooks; the lush ruby and amber jams; the ladies with turquoise nose rings and hennaed hands; the powdery yellowed hands of the saffron merchant; the elaborate painted leatherworking; the squawking basket of ducks; the dozens of snakes roasting; the tang of *mersu*; the sharp odor of cucumbers, split open; the jars of cinnamon and rose water; and the endless waves of that thing called linen, in more colors than she had ever dreamed of.

The linen was a phenomenal thing, so smooth and soft and thin. And this, she decided, was what she would barter for with Aya's cheese. She would study it and replicate it at home. What she did not know then was that there was no replicating it if she did not grow the blue-headed flax, and how would she have known what flax was if Adam and Cain did not yet know.

The girl laying out the linen was not much older than Naava. She had two golden rings—one through her nose, the other through her lip—and freckles across her nose as profuse and brown as the flecks on a robin's egg. Naava pointed to the umber fabric, and the girl pulled the cylinder from the pile and unrolled it in earthy waves. Her eyes crinkled up as she smiled and took Naava's hand in her own, encouraging her to stroke the cloth, to feel how unbelievably soft it was, nodding *yes?* at Naava's obvious enthusiasm. But as Naava pulled the cheese from the donkey's sling, the girl's face fell. She touched the musty cheese, sniffed it even, then backed away, taking the cylinder of fabulous cloth with her. She yelled abrupt, angry words at Naava.

Naava held out the cheese again, thinking the girl must have misunderstood, but the girl shook her head *no* and turned away. Disappointment as sharp as cactus thorns jabbed through Naava's happy anticipation. Part of her felt shame that she offered nothing unique. Part of her felt anger that she had been rejected. She turned and yanked on her donkey's reins, slapping its hindquarters.

Naava did not feel spite exactly, although her behavior, which she wore like garlic, pointed in that direction. In fact, if she had been injured with words that she understood right then, she would have run away and blubbered like a child. She did not have the ability to fail yet, or to look stupid, without it hurting her ego. The space between Naava's childhood and womanhood, in the end, was too small to measure, and it was in this uneasy place that she existed for the time being.

The sun would be at its highest point soon. Naava stood at the bottom of the goddess's steps, waiting for Cain. She pushed aside thoughts of the linen girl and closed her eyes and twirled slowly, steeping herself in this intoxicating new world. Did she love the city because it was fantastically new or because she was certain that her mother and father would not have approved? Of course, they would have disagreed with the pantheon of gods and the strange brick mountain where the people worshipped them, but the astonishing array of goods—how could they not want these wonderful things for their children? It was as Cain had said. They lived in the past, in their dreams. They were stuck in the Garden with Elohim.

"You like, no?" said a voice behind her.

Naava turned, surprised to hear words she comprehended.

It was the prince, and he was alone.

Eve

It was hard not to blame Adam for the loss of our baby. In truth he did nothing to cause it, but I was irritated at his seeing the bear situation differently than I did and his insistence that he alone understood what had happened.

It would be the sad truth that I dove into blaming others—besides Adam, my dear husband—and pushed them away from me. I know this now, and I regret doing so, though at the time I did not know any other path.

Cain was one of them. As a boy, he grew in stature and knowledge, and with his blossoming came the revelation of his true character. He was like kindling perched above a tiny flame, waiting for one spark to set him off. And when he roared to life, he refused to stay within the confines of the pit. His fire consumed the entire forest.

He was more manageable when he was young. Back then, when he became that way, I would take him aside and sit with him, tell him a Garden story, or wipe his brow to calm him. Once we were here, on these plains, Adam would take him into the fields with him and set him to the hard physical work of turning over the ground with a wood hoe or digging holes for the seeds with a stick. This served to tire him out, for which we reaped the benefits in the evening.

I bore no other child who caused as much heartache as Cain. There was no end to his striving. Then again, he sought it out despite our best efforts to quell the fire within him.

There were times I found it difficult to love him.

Cain was not quite two years of age when I discovered I was with child again. I was delighted—in part because I wanted a girl and in part because I wanted this child to be different. From Cain, that is. Bear with me. I have not yet related the surprise and wonder and pain of Cain's birth, but I shall rectify this shortly.

Upon the very day of my discovery, which came in the form of a sharp kick to my ribs, I found the air was full of tiger butterflies, flitting about and lighting on the plants we had named milkweed, for when you tore leaves from them, the stalks would weep a sticky milky substance. Some of the butterflies landed, dipping the milkweed low, curling their tails and depositing tiny white eggs on the leaves' undersides.

I exclaimed over them to Cain; I even came up with a story about them.

"A very long time ago," I began, "there lived a colony of orange butterflies. They admired one another, the way their heads were black and shiny smooth, the way their orange wings glistened in the sun."

Cain was distracted at first. He ran this way and that, trying to catch the light airy creatures, but they always floated up and away. His brow was wet with sweat, and his little chest heaved with his efforts.

"Come," I said.

Reluctantly, he plopped down in my lap, his back to my gently rounding belly.

"All day long they reminded one another how beautiful they were, how important they were." I made my voice more ominous. "Now, one day, a tiger came along to drink from the river. Several of the butterflies were drinking from the river too, and they did not see the tiger coming."

Cain looked up at me. "He eats them—*chomp chomp,*" cried Cain. He reached for another butterfly but missed.

Adam caught one by the wings and held it for Cain to look at. He had to hold it away from Cain's crushing fingers.

"No," I said. "He noticed them and thought they looked good to eat, so he said to them slyly, 'The water is better over here.' The butterflies, being selfish and foolish, flew over to where the tiger was drinking. 'Here,' said the tiger. 'Right here.' One of the butterflies flew immediately to the spot, and instantly the tiger's paw came down upon the butterfly's back. 'Let me go,' said the butterfly. 'Why should I?' said the tiger. 'I am hungry.' 'No, no,' said the butterfly. 'My brother is twice as delicious.' "

"Brother," said Cain, tilting his head back to see my face. "What's that?"

"If I have a boy," I said, pointing to my belly, "then you will have a friend, a brother."

"Oh," said Cain, worried now. He pondered this a moment, shifting so he could feel my belly. Then his eyes sparkled, and he smiled, as if he had figured out what was wrong with my story. "Tigers can't talk," said Cain dubiously.

"This one did," I said. I continued, "Then the captured butterfly said, 'If you let me go, I'll bring you my brother.'

"So the tiger let him go. 'Ha-ha,' said the butterfly. 'Do you think I am stupid? I will not show you my brother, because you will eat him.' The tiger was very angry and stretched up on his hind legs to swipe at the mischievous butterfly. The butterfly flew up, up, and away, and the tiger never saw that butterfly again." I reached out and grabbed a butterfly by its wings and brought it close to Cain. "And that is why, in the middle of their backs, they have a black paw print of the tiger, to remind them always to watch for danger."

Cain bent over the butterfly, straining to see the paw print. "I can't see it," he said.

"There," I said. I pointed to the black dots on the hind wings.

Cain pulled back to examine my face, to see if I was serious. "Nuh-uh," he said, rejecting my fable.

I laughed then and said, "We'll never know, will we?"

Adam's face crinkled into sunshine. He winked at me and said to Cain, "Your mother is very clever, she is. She knows secrets about everything."

It wasn't until after a dinner of grilled fish and mulberries that I caught Cain spitting small stones from a rolled-up leaf. He was, to be accurate with my descriptions, absolutely gleeful over his new invention.

My heart sank when I realized what he was doing. As butterflies perched and laid their eggs, or as they sucked unknowingly from the flower centers, he was attempting to kill them. He was a child, so his aim was not at all precise, but every once in a while he would hit one, and his howls of pride and delight were what had alerted me to his game.

I wrested the leaf from his hand and slapped his bottom.

He cried out indignantly, turning to Adam for support.

"He's not hurting anything," said Adam nonchalantly, as though Cain had been picking up nuts off the ground.

"Not hurting anything?" I said. "He's killing them."

"Just a few," said Adam. "Let him be."

"I will not," I said, picking up Cain like I would a log for the fire. I set him down on a rock and said, "Listen here. You will not hurt animals if you do not plan to eat them. Is that understood?"

"Why?" Cain asked.

"Why?" I said. "Because they were made for us to enjoy and to take care of, that's why." I turned my back to Adam. I was angry at our disagreements, at how differently we saw the world. It was at moments like this, I wanted to be away from him, to be by myself. "You watch him. I am going to bathe in the river."

"Cain and I will go with you," said Adam.

"I want to be alone," I said.

"We won't bother you," said Adam.

"Please yourself," I said. Now, what I really thought was, *How have I borne such a wicked child? One who harms for pleasure and does not heal? How is it that my husband cannot see it?* As I've mentioned before, my feelings for Cain were mixed—at times I loved him with a vengeance. At other times I disliked him intensely. This was the first time I had witnessed Cain's disregard for *right* and felt Adam's lack of concern.

I did not like it one bit.

Naava

Immediately, with the prince surprising her in the marketplace as he had, Naava lost all sensation in her toes and fingers, and her words shriveled on her tongue.

The prince was more magnificent than she remembered. He laughed and took her by the elbow, her donkey by its reins, and led them through the dizzying ruckus of buyers and sellers. "You swallow words?"

She had felt the sweat trickle down her chest before, in front of the steps, but now she felt her skin grow hotter still. She pointed to the donkey's back, where the cheese sat, now gooey from the heat.

The prince nodded. He seemed to find her amusing, and she hated him for it. He led her into one of the dim and narrow tunneling streets, and it was as though they had entered another world altogether. Behind them, the din faded. A steep-slanted slab of sunlight grazed the rooftops but did not settle deeply enough to reach the street. The donkey brayed, for water probably, but Naava and the prince did not stop.

It was for this she had come.

A moonfaced boy walked pigeon-toed toward them. He was stuffing something into his mouth, but when he saw them, he stopped, terrified, and ran in the opposite direction, dropping whatever it was that he was eating. A mongrel slunk after the food, wolfing it up and working it down.

The boy's cries ricocheted off the houses, and Naava had to look, really look at the prince—what was it about him that had frightened the child?

He was a tall man, thinner than Cain or Abel. His skin was lighter and less worn than her brothers', and he carried himself with ease. *That is it,* Naava thought. *He knows what he wants, and he will get it.*

She knew one other man who was at least as self-composed and settled— her father. Adam was impervious to persuasion, no matter how convincing, and although her mother attributed this to bullheadedness, as she did with Cain, Naava thought maybe her father saw or knew more than Eve did, to be so certain of things. There were no shadowy indecipherable areas in Adam's mind. She knew that her father believed it was important to dispel the clouds of gray in one's mind. One must be continually categorizing, labeling, and structuring, so one did not fall prey to easy blindness and ignorance, which he said was inexcusable. It was better to know, without a shadow of a doubt. Abel was much like him in that way.

Once, in the spring of Naava's seventh year, Adam had brought home a tulip, like a little flame of fire, and handed it with great ceremony to her. Naava couldn't remember, for the life of her, where her brothers were at the time. Aya was in her fourth year, but she was probably stoking the fire, bossing Eve around.

"I will take you to where there are fields of them," Adam had said, as he scooped her up into the air and swung her around.

She squealed, the air whistling in her ears, and when he had set her down, she begged for more. "Please, Father."

He winked at her. "Tomorrow, after the chores are done."

Except the next day Adam didn't get home until nighttime, and by then Naava had fallen asleep at the courtyard entrance, waiting for him. The next morning, her father stooped down, his fingers on her cheek, and said gravely, "The gophers were destroying the roots of our fig trees. I had to set out traps for them."

"Oh," Naava said.

"I shall make a great effort to take you today," he added.

Eve protested because Adam had promised to fill in the rain ruts in the courtyard and to fix the chinks in the cistern.

Adam looked at Eve then in the sternest way possible—although he was joking—and said, "But this girl has never seen the closest equivalent of Eden. And she must. It would be an outrage if she didn't."

Eve laughed. "Take us all, then. I should like to go back to Eden."

"Me too," said Aya.

That afternoon, though, the sky's underbelly turned a shade of ominous green and split in two. Large hailstones puckered the river and pebbled the earth. The river grew angry and seethed over the levees like a sinewy silty beast, creeping steadily toward an unsuspecting Eve, who was teaching Aya the various techniques of drying herbs, and Naava, who was brushing out clusters of sheep's wool, smoothing it before she twirled it into workable fibers. Naava saw it first and screamed as the water rushed in and lifted her loom and tore the clouds of wool from her hands. By the time she had found her footing, clutching at her wet mass of wool, Aya was swirling about the courtyard, and Eve was attempting to chase after her, her fingers slipping from her daughter's hand several times before she was able to pull her to safety. The water raged about their legs, sucking and pushing and pulling.

Eve yelled at Naava, gesturing, but her words twisted away on the howling wind. She grasped Aya's arm, and together they waded toward Adam in the fields, toward the fruit trees, the only safe vantage point.

Naava followed them, crying out for them to *stop, wait*. She thought she would be swept away, and no one would know or care. Her breath was spent by the time she reached her father, who grabbed her legs and hoisted her up into the leaning branches of a fig tree next to her mother and sister. He climbed up after them. They sat like a family of roosting doves— mother, father, and babies. Eve shouted something at Adam, and Adam pointed in the direction of the date palms, where Cain and Abel were already perched.

In the bright gashes of lightning, Naava watched their house crumble. Later, she would stand with her parents in knee-deep lakes where the barley and wheat had once stood. Dead sheep and goat carcasses floated like water bugs, their bloated bodies splitting and reeking in the day's heat. There was no food and no potable water for days, and their lips grew thick and callused. They became faint and weak as they labored to rebuild their home.

It was a sullen Eve who finally voiced their exhaustion with the words, "Why did this have to happen?"

Adam did not answer until Eve repeated the question a second time. He sighed. "It rains. It floods. This has happened before, and it will happen again. The question is not 'Why did this happen?' but 'What shall we do about it?'"

Eve blurted out, "Elohim does not care about us."

"Elohim gave us limbs to work, minds to think," said Adam. He turned to Naava and winked. "What does that cloud up there remind you of?" he asked. And Naava had squinted through the now-bare branches and said, "A badger."

"Me too," said Adam. He whistled. "Look at that tail."

In the end, they broke open cactus spears, then tilted their heads back to catch the bitter drops on their tongues. They foraged for root vegetables—beets, carrots, parsnips, and radishes—still trapped in the ground under muddy waters.

Adam was right. They rebuilt their house one brick at a time; they erected corrals to keep in their animals, the ones they found alive. Cain replanted their crops, once the seed heads were dried and extractable. Abel searched for wild sheep and goat pairs, built up his pens and shelters once again, and bred them into a hearty flock. Eve—then Dara after her, when she had learned to work with clay—formed jars and flasks and bowls and platters from the thick mud present everywhere and hardened them in Aya's fire. Aya planted herbs for cooking; Naava planted madder and chamomile and larkspur for dyeing. Eve dug up her jar of seeds and buried it once again, in a place she would remember. All these things took many days. All these things had to be done each and every time the river overflowed.

Even the smaller bushes and vines and flowers of Eve's garden had to be replanted. The trench and cistern had to be repaired.

Through it all, her father led them, a calm and steadying presence, no matter what dilemma presented itself.

The prince caught Naava looking at him. "I will buy," he said finally, waving his hand toward the cheese.

Naava nodded.

The prince halted in front of a dark and airless doorway, rife with gnats and fly-noosed spiderwebs. He gestured for Naava to follow. She did, her donkey clambering in after her—*tip tap tip tap*. Inside, it was empty, save for a rough-hewn chair and table. *The room has a gloomy aspect,* Naava thought, *drenched in shadows*. It smelled of earth and manure and incense.

The prince counted out small round clay tokens into her palm, then he extracted the cheese from its sling and laid it, still wrapped in reeds and cloth, on the floor.

Naava knew enough to understand that she had been paid. After all, she had seen the tokens being exchanged in the square as something of value. But what she wondered was why they had to conduct this strange transaction in the dark and what her parents would do with these silly tokens, even as the prince drew near enough for her to feel his warmth, even as she was reaching out to him and kissing him, darting her tongue out to part his lips and probe his mouth. Naava had envisioned this moment in her dreams, both before and after she had lain with Cain, but she had not seen nor felt it like this. Things were happening too quickly—*were all men the same this way?*—and she wanted to slow it down, even if just a little. She pulled back, pushing on his chest. "We could sit here and talk. Tell me about your family," she said politely. She sat, as if to make herself very clear.

The prince sat too, facing her. The grin remained on his face. He ran his finger across her eyebrows, down her nose. "Bee-oo-ti-ful," he said.

"Thank you," said Naava. She reached for his hand and held it in her lap.

He wriggled free and fumbled for the hem of her robe. Finding it, he crept his fingers up her leg, as if they were playing cat and mouse. He laughed.

Although she had wanted this for so long, Naava sensed something was wrong. She thought maybe if she kissed him one more time he'd be satisfied, at least until she was prepared to do what he wanted. She leaned into him and reached up to touch his hairline and trace his ears. She licked her lips and kissed him open-mouthed. The prince latched on, and before she knew it she had fallen back onto the floor, with the prince solidly on top of her. Now he was absolutely frantic about something *other* than Naava—she felt it in her chest. She started to thrash and pull away, to no avail.

"No," she breathed.

The prince placed his hand over her mouth. He was still grinning, but she could have been mistaken—maybe it was a grimace. His eyes bulged, and the vein over his right temple was big and blue and pulsing. His fingers groped her thighs and reached in between her legs.

She scratched at his face, at his eyes, and suddenly, mercifully, he grew still. He lifted up off her and helped her to her feet.

"So sorry," he said. "I have made a mistake. Forgive me."

Naava was too stunned to say anything, even to accept an apology. She was half disappointed in herself and half angry at being treated like a regular beast. This had been nothing like her dreams—he had spoiled them! The hem of her robe had come undone, and she brushed the dirt from her skirt. She picked up the spilled clay tokens, and without looking back again at the prince, she hurried through the doorway and into the shaded alleyway, leading her donkey back to her old life, the one she understood—and could control.

As she walked, she thought. She thought about her bruised self, the hurts more emotional than physical. She thought of Cain and how he had been rough and brusque with her, in that same hurried manner. *What did men like Adam and Cain and Abel and the prince want from a woman? And how could she discover these things without embarrassing herself?*

Cain was her only hope. He would teach her everything she needed to know. All the fumbling and roughness—surely this could not be a man's sole desire.

As she neared the market, the tinging of the metalsmiths and the barking of the merchants and the savory smells of roasting meat overcame her. She emerged from the sleepy shadows and into the stark sunlight. She blinked.

Cain would be waiting for her.

But first she wanted to use the tokens to purchase some of that fine, luxuriant fabric, not from the linen girl but from the merchant two stalls down. Naava wanted the linen girl to observe the transaction. *Look,* Naava wanted to say, *I would have bought from you, but you reap what you sow. Think you're too good for me, do you?*

Aya

I could not keep doing this—holding my family together. I did not want the responsibility of it.

It was afternoon. The sky blushed over the grain-fringed horizon. I was collecting pears in the folds of my skirt. Goat tore at anything green. She behaved less and less those days. Maybe it was because I was distracted by Mother and had not the heart to discipline her. Turtle, too, I had neglected. I fed him but did not talk to him. I knew I should do better for Dara's sake, but Mother was about all I could think about. I was worried her dreams would come true—that she would die in childbirth. *What would I do then?*

The air was turning cool, and I paused to close my eyes and breathe in the evening dampness. There was the smell of sour fruit, then rank river grass.

I opened my eyes. Along the shoreline, a heron hovered over the gleaming sand. Ever since the building of the city up north and their diversion of our water, the wide riverbeds had become marshes, and I had seen more dead fish than I wanted to see. What was the fortune of one was the demise of the other. The heron's head tilted down and pecked at a silvery fish floundering upon the bank. In the blink of an eye, the thrashing sliver of life was gone.

In the distance I could see Naava flirting with Abel. She had been acting strangely of late, and I knew it was due to her irritation that he was
ignoring her. She climbed up on the rungs of the fence and leaned over
toward him as he milked the goats. I hated her for this—what she did to my
brothers.

Really, I was jealous. I thought Abel was the most handsome man I had
ever seen. I wished for him to see *me,* care about *me.* But I am afraid his
eyes glanced off me like rain off a duck's back.

Abel refused to look up. He milked the goats, one after the other, occa-
sionally swatting at a fly that flew about his head. When he accidentally
knocked over his jar of milk, Naava laughed. I knew this because there was
a certain tilt of her head when she did so, and it infuriated me that Abel
had to stumble about to place the jar in exactly the right spot again. His
head was down, and I could tell by the slump of his shoulders that his irritation was rising as assuredly as the floodwaters did in the spring.

Cain returned from the city through the vegetable fields. He saw me
and approached. He held out his fist, rounded about an object. "Close
your eyes," he said.

I did.

"Smell," he said.

I did. Oh, glorious wonder! My eyes flew open. "Oranges," I said.

"Well, one, really," he said. "I brought it back from the market. One of
the pretty girls gave it to me."

"Thank you," I said. I moved to block his view of Abel and Naava,
blaming the sun. "I'll stand here so you aren't blinded," I said. I knew jealousy ran like fire through my brothers, and this circumstance was the perfect kindling, despite the fact that Abel had not bit at Naava's bait. From
what I could tell, Naava wanted every man to like her. She didn't care
which fish she netted, as long as she got what she wanted, which was laugh-
able, because I'm not sure she *knew* what she wanted. She performed
mating dances, darting here and there and making silly little noises that
were intended to attract Cain and Abel. And they did. Cain, anyway.

"Your trip went well?" I said. I smelled the heat of the day on him, and
his hair was damp with sweat.

Cain nodded. He carried a basket of gourds and leeks and mushrooms. His lips opened slightly, as if he wanted to ask something but thought better of it. He looked off to the river.

"What is it?" I asked.

"It's a bothersome thing, I know," he started, "but I'm wondering if you might set aside a small bowl of food for me after each meal."

"Do I not provide enough for you, brother?"

He looked down then, at the basket in his hands. "It is for my temple," he said. "To feed the gods."

I studied his face. Indeed, he could not look me in the eyes. "What you are doing is meaningless," I said. "Elohim is the only God that matters. He is everywhere. He does not even need a temple. Can you not feel Him? See Him? Smell Him?" My words ran away from me like mice.

Cain grew restless. He bent over and picked up a pear from the ground. He tossed it into the air. "Aya, you rest easy in your belief. It's simple for you to listen to Mother and Father's stories and take them into yourself for your own. But have you seen, really seen, this Elohim? How can you know that Mother and Father are not wrong? All the people of the city bend their knees to other gods, many gods, and I for one think they are correct. After all, they have priests and priestesses. Does Elohim have people to feed Him, keep Him happy? I think not. This sophisticated plan—of mortal people who feed the gods, expecting to be nurtured in return—reflects thought and consideration for how the universe works."

I could only say, "Or it is a ruse to further separate the people from their gods."

Cain studied my face. "Will you set aside food for me?" he said finally.

I stared back at him. And then I nodded. I knew, as well as anyone, that you could not change a person's heart. Only he or she could do that. I grieved, though. For I was alone in my thoughts, alone in my prayers. *There is a beauty,* I wanted to cry out. *There is a glory that wants to be seen, but you must enter it, embrace it. You must climb toward it. You must be thirsty.*

Cain turned then and saw Naava leaning over the fence toward Abel. I knew that he refused to take in Abel's posture and utter disregard of

Naava, because he pursed his lips and swore by the city's gods. He leaned into his failure like a lamb going to slaughter.

I saw, in the east, the faint chill of the moon appearing.

At evening repast, Abel's right eye was swollen shut, and Cain's nose was an onion bulb.

Dara

Before I came here, Mama said, "Be obedient. Do as they say."
She said, "Watch those children like a hawk." She said, "Remember *every-thing.*"

Here are all the babies I watch: the girl with the scary black eyes, the chubby boy who is shiny bald, the girl with sparkly rings on her toes, and the girl who sasses back to me all the time. They are: Puabi, Shulgi, Nibanda, and—I forget her name always—Shala. Puabi is the oldest, and her mama makes her stand real still so she can draw black raccoon eyes on her. I don't know why.

I take care of all these babies in Puabi's mama's house while all the mamas sit around and pretty each other up. Other people called slaves do all the work. I don't know where they get these people who are such hard workers. All the babies run around without a smidgen of clothes on. That way they can go pee-pee anytime.

How I talk to the babies: I don't. They babble, and so do their mamas. I spank them when they're bad and give them hugs if they're good, but Puabi is my favorite, on account of Puabi's mama, Zenobia, and their pet mongoose, who is supposed to eat all the rats and mouses. I live at their very fine house. It is still being built because it is so big.

The prince lives there too.

Zenobia gives me presents. Once, when I was combing Puabi's hair—

oh, it was like a nest!—Zenobia came to watch, to make sure I was doing it right. After I was done, Zenobia motioned for me to come closer, but when I did, I saw that she held a shiny pointy thing in her hand. Since I didn't know what she was doing, I hung back, watching her very closely.

Zenobia laughed—her laughter was soft, like the wind chimes in her room—and said something singsongy. She grabbed my hand and pulled me to stand between her knees. Then she pressed her knees into each other, squeezing me tight. She put her hand under my chin and grunted and pointed—that I should look, there, up at that cobweb in the corner. But when I saw the sharp thing coming toward my face, I covered my cheeks with my hands and squealed, "No, no, no." I shook my head back and forth, since I couldn't escape her knees.

Zenobia laughed again and pointed to the stone in Puabi's nose. Then she touched my nose. "Mmm?" she said.

I smiled and nodded. *Oh, yes, I would like to have a pretty nose like Puabi and all the grown-up women. Naava would be so jealous!*

I closed my eyes, squinching them tight together, so I wouldn't know when Zenobia made the hole in my nose. When the pain came, I thought it felt a lot like a hard sneeze, where my nose ached afterward. I yelped and sputtered only when she poured a little wine over it.

Then Zenobia held up a shiny silver bowl, polished like the moon, and I saw the tiny blue stone, and it looked pretty, like a piece of sky in my nose. I held up Mongoose so he could see it, and he licked it. I reached up to feel it, but Zenobia pulled my hand away.

Zenobia loves me, I can tell. On my first morning here, all the people came running in to scoop up their babies. They looked at me all strange, and I didn't know what to do. Zenobia came and knelt down beside me and tried to explain with her hands. She growled like a lion, then grabbed Puabi and pretended to lick her and eat her. Puabi screamed. Zenobia pointed to the outside where all the people were screaming like Puabi and carrying on.

A lion ate one of the babies, not one of my babies, but someone else's. The men, even Naava's prince, lined up with bows and arrows and said they'd be back soon. *Beware, bad lion,* I thought, *they're coming to get you.*

Zenobia pulled on my hand, then Puabi's. She dragged us out into the sunshiny day. We walked and walked and walked until we got to this tall mountain with stairs. It was very hot, and there were so many people there, I almost got lost.

But wait. Look. I saw all the little men and women statues with their hands folded in front of them, some clay, some stone. They were all praying, just like Cain had told me, just like the ones I made for him. There were so many. They looked like Abel's flocks, except they were flocks of people. I tried to touch one, but Zenobia slapped my hand.

Zenobia reached into her robe and pulled out a piece of meat wrapped in cloth. It smelled terrible. She pointed to the top of the mountain and pushed on my back. *Too many stairs,* I thought. *Why do I have to go? I could fall with all these people pushing and pulling. Mama would be sad if I never came home at all.* But I didn't have a choice.

Once, I turned around to see how far up I was. Zenobia and Puabi looked like miniature people down there. I waved. They waved back. I sat down when I got to the top, just to rest, but there were people in white robes who took the meat from me. One of them was scary Bosom Lady who killed the sheep at my house, except now she kissed my head, and then a man in a yellow hat took the meat into the house that was at the top. Bye-bye, stinky meat.

I pointed to the house. "Who lives there?" I asked Bosom Lady. But she said *uh uh uh* and shooed me down the steps.

When I got to the bottom, I asked Zenobia, "Who will eat the meat?"

Zenobia didn't answer. Her hands were stiff, like sticks. The ripples in her forehead were deep deep deep. Something besides the lion was worrying her.

Puabi tugged on my hand. We walked away from the big mountain, and I thought maybe this was the mountain Aya talked about always, that she was going to fly away to. When I got home I was going to tell Aya there was nothing special about it. I didn't see any Garden, that's for sure. Or anyone named Elohim.

And then I started forgetting what Mama looked like. I decided to make her another statue because Aya said she hid her other one. Maybe Mama would like me better and not send me away again.

I asked Zenobia for clay and fire, and Zenobia understood. She said Ahassunu's big son, Balili—the man called *priest,* with the yellow hat at the mountain—would bring me some clay from the river. Ahassunu was the one who brought Mama the yellow cloth for my robe, and her daughter is the naughty one, Shala. Balili turned out to be nice, though. I don't know how he came from inside Ahassunu.

While I was waiting for the clay and fire, I got a good idea. I would make rattles out of clay for the babies. I would fill them with seeds that made noise—Balili could find me some—and then I would put a string through the hole and pinch the sides together like waves and dry them in the sun. *Shush shoosh shush* they would go, as they bounced along the ground. I could keep track of the babies all the time, and the bad lion would be scared off. I am a big girl now. I thought of this idea all by myself. And surprise, surprise, I thought, *This can be the number-five thing for Mama's baby!*

When Balili saw my rattles, he picked one up and scratched his nose and said, "May I?" I was proud to give it to him. Always he gives me things, but I never have anything to give him.

I am learning lots of things. Now I make story symbols like the city people. It's not so hard, because Balili has been teaching me. Every day he comes, and every day the mothers watch their babies just for a little while. They say if I learn fast enough, maybe *I* can teach their babies.

When I get too tired of learning, Balili lets me get a drink of water. When I make a mistake, he taps me on the back of my hand, not so hard, though, because he's nice. He shows me how to make clay tablets that are still wet and how to start on the left-hand side, or at the top, so all the marks I make aren't erased by my hand. All the time, he draws pictures, and I have to guess what he is drawing. Sometimes he gives me clues, sometimes not.

I will tell you all that he does. He's very clever. He shows me how to cut a reed to a point. Then he jabs me with it, not hard, just so I can feel how sharp it has to be. Then, we start drawing the symbols into the clay. He makes a mark like this: ⁓ He scoops up imaginary water in his hands.

"Water," I say.

He nods. "*A*," he says, making a funny sound.

"*A*," I repeat. This must mean *water*.

He grins. He makes another mark:

"Tree," I say before he finishes.

He frowns and pretends like he's making flour on a quern, like Aya does.

"Barley," I say. I pretend to eat bread.

" *Še*," he says.

" *Še*," I repeat. I think this must mean *barley*—or does it mean *bread*?

There are symbols for everything. Even if I draw the sun but it's not the right way, Balili is patient and shows me again. My favorite is to draw Turtle. Balili says another sound, and I try to remember that it means *turtle*. My Turtle. Balili says I am a very smart girl, and after ten days—here he makes me count out the days with my new words—of answering questions correctly, he gives me a red-threaded bracelet of speckled beads that look like agates. I think maybe I'll give it to Aya, because she collects rocks. It will be my thank-you for taking care of Turtle, poor Turtle-without-a-Mother.

Once I can understand a little more, Balili takes me to the school in the marketplace at the foot of the tall mountain. The babies stay at home while I'm away. At the school there are lots of children, not just me. He says if we're good, he will tell us the story of the *huluppu*-tree.

We sit as still as frightened deer.

Balili draws a picture of a tree.

"This is the *huluppu*-tree," he says.

Balili is a good storyteller, because his drawings are spectacular.

Inanna, the very brave girl of the story, will someday wear the heavens and earth like a beautiful robe, but for now she's a girl like me. One day Inanna finds the *huluppu*-tree floating in the Euphrates River. She takes it home and plants it in her garden. She loves that tree with all her might and makes plans of everything she can do with it, like build a throne or a bed.

But then, oh no, oh no, the *Anzu*-bird makes a nest in it, and a snake makes his house in it, and a girl by the name of Lilith lives in it. All these homes in Inanna's tree! She asks everyone for help to get those rascals to go away, but no one will help her. Poor Inanna. I would have helped her.

Finally, Inanna begs her brother Gilgamesh to please help her get those things out of her tree *right now*! Gilgamesh does. I would ask Cain, I think, but maybe Abel might be nicer. Gilgamesh puts on some armor that Balili says is heavy and thick and lifts his bronze ax and goes into Inanna's garden. He hits the serpent with the ax. He throws out the *Anzu*-bird. He smashes Lilith's house. Then Gilgamesh rips that tree out of the ground and makes a throne and a nice warm bed for Inanna. As a thank-you, Inanna makes a *pukku* for Gilgamesh, and a *mikku* for him too. I don't know what those things are that Inanna gives him.

I clap at the end when Inanna's tree is saved, because Gilgamesh is so nice to help. Balili smiles at me, then looks past me, and a funny look comes over his face. I turn around to see what he is looking at, and there is Naava, a long ways away, walking through the marketplace. I stand and wave, but the marketplace is busy, and my sister doesn't see me.

I tell Balili, "That's Naava. She's my sister, and she is very beautiful, and she weaves and weaves all the clothes we wear."

"Hmmm," says Balili. There's a funny look on his face.

"Sometimes she's as mean as a fox and I don't like her, but sometimes she is sweet like honey; then she is a nice sister," I say.

"I must take you back to the prince's house," says Balili. He's acting very strange all of a sudden. He pulls on my arm and says, "Let's go."

"Ow," I say. "I'm coming." *Why all the fuss?*

Eve

When the boys were young, we had an evening family ritual, to walk along the shore of the Euphrates and to avail ourselves of the spectacular sights and sounds. Truth be told, it was the noise I missed most about the Garden—the incessant bird chatter and the frog caterwauling and the cricket chirps. This happy singing lifted me up, day after day. Here in the desert there are sounds, certainly, but they are not of such a bountiful bursting nature.

In the dying light, Adam and I strolled arm in arm, leaving our footprints in the warm mud, while the boys ran through the sun-bleached reeds and bulrushes and cattails to collect trinkets—cowrie shells and birds' nests and bulbous frogs. It was a happy time, for whatever had gone on during the day—endless chores, incessant cooking, backbreaking weeding—was behind us, completed until the morrow. We felt secure and steadfast, much like the moon that shone brightly overhead.

We warned the boys, of course, about wild boars and badgers. Abel had been, two years previous, fairly run over by a startled boar, and he had had nightmares about them since then. We made it a point to be inside the courtyard walls when the time of the predators began.

One particular late-spring night, Cain was five, Abel three. I was pregnant with Micayla, my dear child who would be born three moons later with a swollen head and buried the same day.

The sun lingered, and its warmth stroked our faces.

Adam and I were speaking of adding on to the animal pens, making them more spacious and strong, because the herds were growing swiftly. We had been able to predict the onslaught of river waters that year and had taken our family and our flocks to higher ground for the duration of the flooding. To extend and fortify the pens would require more time and labor away from the crops—the weeding, the watering, the rodent and insect control. It was not a small matter to consider.

"Mama," cried Cain. "Mama." Normally he spoke in a thin, flimsy voice that did not match his bravado, but this was a hearty cry of horror, of desperation.

My arm fell from Adam's, and we ran toward the cries.

Cain and Abel were facing each other. Cain was on his knees, holding his jaw and scrabbling around on the ground with his fingers. Abel stood there, alarmed.

Cain looked up then, still wailing as we approached. Blood poured down his chin.

"What's happened?" said Adam, running to Cain's side and grabbing his face between his hands. His fingers came away wet and bloody.

Adam looked to Abel and studied his chary countenance. His little shoulders hunched, and his eyes drooped. He opened his fist, and a rock thudded to the ground.

Always, a mother glances quickly at the evidence and surmises what has happened, and although I knew in this situation that the normal roles had been reversed, and Abel the younger had been the aggressor and not Cain, I chose to react swiftly—and wrongly, as it turned out. "Abel," I snapped. "What have you done?"

"I—I—" Abel said.

I slapped him hard across his face. His hand went up like a startled bird wing and rested on his cheek. His shocked eyes took me in, that this was his mother who had hurt him, and he stood, silent and injured.

Cain cried and babbled as he sifted through the soil with his fingers. "I lost them," he said.

"Cain," I said. "Look at me."

He tilted his chin up, looked me straight in the eyes, and said morosely, "They're all gone."

I gasped. The boy had no front teeth. His lips were mangled and torn like the edges of a leaf. I turned to Abel. "Explain," I commanded.

He looked only at the ground.

"Boy," said Adam, grabbing Abel by the arm. "What have you done? Speak!"

But Abel refused. He jerked his arm out of Adam's grasp and turned to walk back to the house.

"It's too dangerous to be out by yourself," said Adam to Abel, warning him of the night animals. His voice was full of irritation and exasperation.

Abel halted.

Adam and I stood in silence, waiting for a response. *What had he been thinking?*

He plopped down upon the sand, his back to us. Evening birdsong filled the air. The water moved among the reeds. The evening seemed to slow into a swell of meaning we could not know.

Then Abel lifted his trembling chin and began to sing the melancholic song from the Garden that Adam and I had sung only between ourselves. His high sweet voice strengthened and climbed, tugged at the air, and burst into white flame; he sang as one who had seen the Garden; he sang as one who was far, far away. He sculpted a world of memory, of innocence, of time long past, and I gasped and held my panging heart.

We were mesmerized. Our son was creating the Garden again, beast by beast, plant by plant, waterfall by waterfall. He had done this only once before, when he was very young and a leopard had dragged him away from our campfire. But I'm getting ahead of myself.

Cain stood, his cheeks glistening with tears. "Will they come back?" he said. "My teeth?"

I had forgotten my hurting child. I turned to him. "Come. We'll get you mended in no time."

Our voices had smudged the moment.

Abel's voice trailed off into nothingness, and a great sadness seeped into the corners of my being. Adam grabbed Abel's hand and pulled him up—although, I noted, gentler than he would have without the song.

The day before, Cain had lost his first tooth and had come running to show me. I was petrified, of course, until I saw the tiny white bud emerging from the pink soil of his gums. I was comforted to see any sign of life in Cain's mouth, since Adam had lost several of his back teeth in the same accident in which he lost his hearing in one ear, and those had not grown back.

"I don't know," I said. "We'll have to look under the light when we get home." I took his hand. "What did you do to your brother to make him so angry?" I asked.

"He wasn't angry. I told him to do it," said Cain. "I thought if there were other teeth down there, that would get them to come out."

"You *told* him to?" I said.

Cain nodded.

Oh, Abel darling, my tender warbler, I should have known, but now the red mark of my hand is upon your cheek and cannot be undone. Oh, Abel my son, forgive me. "I have punished Abel," I sputtered, more to myself than to Cain.

Cain had his fingers in his mouth. "I can't feel any other teeth. I thought for sure that it would work. It hurt very bad, but I didn't cry until the end. How will I eat? Maybe you'll have to—"

I threw Cain's hand down. "Stop. That's enough."

Cain continued, "But—"

Adam turned. "You heard your mother."

Cain pouted and stomped his way home.

That was Cain. That was his way. The mindless, fruitless testing, probing, of everything, just to see what would happen.

After applying a sage poultice to Cain's mouth and commanding him to stay put, I went to search for Abel.

He did not respond to my calls, or Adam's.

Frantic with fear, Adam searched the cistern—always the first place we checked, for obvious reasons—and I searched the animal folds. We held up oil lamps and yelled his name, all to no avail. Weeping now, I retraced my steps. First, the reed mat where he slept. Then the blackened corners of the courtyard. Once more, I stumbled out into the jagged edges of the night, where the moon, like a milky thumbprint, flattened and lengthened everything about me.

I found Abel in the sheep stalls.

He had gone to Pora, his favorite ewe, and had curled up like one of her lambs, his dark curly head resting on her spotted tan belly. He was fast asleep, sucking his thumb.

I set my lamp down on the dry barley stalks and crouched in front of the ewe, to study this littlest boy child of mine. Pora bleated once and raised her head, as if to say, *Don't bother the lad; he's come home to Mama.* I stroked her head and looked at Abel. Sweat had caked long strands of hair to his forehead, and his cheeks were rosy with exhaustion. His eyelashes were like dragonfly wings, and he stank of manure.

"My dear boy," I murmured. I stroked his arm and cried.

What did I feel as I sat there? Did I think Abel was replacing me with Pora? Did I feel inadequate as a parent? Yes, it was all these things and more. For I saw and heard my vicious and ill-timed *slap* over and over again, then his reply, the perfect soaring melody from his lips. I sat there for a long time before Adam's voice broke the silence.

"Eve," Adam called.

"Here," I said wearily. Adam's yellow light veered my direction.

I sighed and scooped my hands under Abel's armpits to lift him to my breast. His head dangled sidewise off my shoulder, and I heard his quiet snuffling. I snatched up the lamp with my other hand, thinking only of the lost opportunity to crawl up next to him, surrounded by the affection of Pora.

To live in the embrace of one of your children is the most beautiful thing in all the world. When they are young, they love you with an unconditional love, a love that waits for your return, a love that ignores your faults, and a love that wants to please. Then, I suppose, they grow older, and wiser. And that is where a mother's grief begins.

Cain did not always act in a foolhardy manner. He was clever and hardworking, and if he was presented with a problem, we knew he would have a handful of solutions by the next day.

Indeed, he was the one who thought of the mud bricks for building our house.

One day when Cain was, I think, seven years of age, he was digging in the mud for snails and mussels and crabs. The water table had been exceptionally high that week because of recent rains and flooding, and it became apparent to Cain that he could create a mud bath simply by standing in the divot he'd made and squishing his toes in it. To a small boy, this was the most delightful thing to do with his day, and when he came home he was caked with the stuff, like a dried-up snakeskin rustling in the wind. Before I ordered him back to the river to wash off, his mouth dropped open, as if he'd made a huge error.

"Mama," he said.

"What?" I said.

"We could make stones with it."

"What?" I said. "What are you talking about?"

But he was already off and running. "I'll show you . . ." His voice trailed off.

I watched him run and shook my head. That boy was forever into everything.

And that is what he did, for days and days. He toiled out there in the marshes, mixing mud and adding what he called fixers, things such as wheat and barley chaff and reeds and shells. He had Adam help him cut down small poplar and willow saplings and chop them into workable lengths. He laid these on the ground in a sort of boxy grid, and into these he poured his mud mixture and waited for it to dry in the sun. When the mixture had hardened, he lifted the grid and chipped away at the sun-hardened seams, to loosen the "stones" from one another. What remained were rough, lumpy rectangular "stones," which he later called bricks.

"See?" Cain said, groaning under the weight of one of them, stacking it on top of others he had already piled up.

Adam stood and watched while Cain demonstrated his new idea. He crossed his arms and stroked his beard. "I think that just might work," he said after a time. He reached out to tussle Cain's hair. "How do you think of these things?"

Cain shrugged and continued the stacking.

"There are holes between them," said Adam.

Cain smiled. He had already thought of this. He dipped a stick into a clay jar full of bitumen, a black sticky substance that was ubiquitous in the marshes. Once he had secured a glob of it, he stuffed the holes with it. "It will dry," said Cain. "No more wind." He held out his hands in triumph and grinned from ear to ear.

Adam teased him by not smiling.

Cain's grin slackened.

Then Adam burst out in a guffaw. He clapped Cain on the back and said, "Amazing. Simply amazing." Then, in mock disappoinment, he said, "We'll have to keep you, I guess."

Cain went back to his work, and Adam interrupted him. "Don't waste your time on that pile. Tomorrow we shall build ourselves a new house!"

And we did. We made walls and buildings of the stuff.

The difference was considerable. We had been building reed houses all along. As you might imagine, unless we had summer winds that would breeze through the house, we felt a bit scorched. And in the winter there was always the potential for a fire, with our small ovens constantly burning. Cain's mud bricks, on the other hand, kept us cool in the summer and warm during the winter. Still, the spring floods remained a problem, even with Cain's new invention. They washed everything away, reducing our house to a muddy river, but the floods had also washed away our reed houses, so it was just a matter of rebuilding, and rebuilding again.

We did not think to bake the bricks until much later. The bricks would have lasted much longer, even through the spring floods, had we known about this earlier.

But no matter. Cain kept us apprised of all his ideas, and in this way we were constantly making alterations to our living arrangements.

The cistern incident is a long-lasting bruise on my heart. It forever changed the way we dealt with the boys.

Surely one cannot plan for most catastrophes dealing with children, and we knew it was not possible, with Cain behaving like desert tumbleweed, but after the cistern disaster we separated the two, sending Cain to the fields with Adam and keeping Abel at home with me. Later, of course, Abel went to the fields on his own, with his flocks.

I have not spoken of it since, until this moment. Strange how events like these have wormed their way into me, yet I have been unable to find the voice for them.

It was early morning on a cloudless day, shortly after the tooth episode. Adam had long been gone to work the fields. I sent the boys out to water and feed the flocks, scrub down the stalls, and apply new barley stalks to the floors. Abel would milk the goats and bring the jars back to me, so I could churn it into butter.

I set reed baskets upon their backs and gave them each long, pointed sticks for flinging hardened piles of dung into their baskets. Dung was excellent burning material, lasting longer than brush or wood, and since I was continually preparing meals, I needed a constant fire.

Cain dawdled outside the courtyard walls. Abel set off resolutely to do as he was told.

"Help your brother," I called.

Cain looked up and frowned. He brought his shoulders up to his ears, then dropped them to show his disgust—he was forever showing me his displeasure. But he ran then to catch up to Abel.

Another outburst forestalled.

Midmorning, about the time I expected them to return, for my fire was fading, I heard a sharp scream, then muffled protests. I supposed they were fighting, and I did not immediately think to check on them. A few moments later Cain came running, his knobby knees practically bumping his chin.

"Mama, Mama, come quick," he said. "Abel's fallen."

I thought: *skinned knee, banged-up chin, at most a broken arm,* but as I was running, it became clear to me that I might find something worse.

Cain was leading me toward the cistern, a deep square pit lined with stones and rocks, a reservoir for precious rain and floodwater. Adam and I had built it after the first hot summer, after we realized that the heat was extremely difficult without readily available fresh water. It overflowed with the spring floods and lasted us through the fall. I had warned the boys time and time again to stay away from it. Originally, when we first built the cistern, I thought of lying to the boys, saying it contained crocodiles or some other sort of terrifying water creature, but I did not, and I regretted it already.

"Where is he?" I panted.

Cain pointed at the cistern and kept running.

Oh, Abel, no!

"Get your father," I demanded, holding my belly, which ached with child.

Cain took off running in the direction of the fields. *Would there be enough time?*

I reached the cistern and knelt on the rocky edge of it. "Abel, where are you?"

Sounds of sputters only. A thrashing sound from below. There, in the middle.

"Abel," I screamed. "Use your arms and legs. Can you hear me?" I made him out in the gray shadows. He was exhausted, that I could see. His mouth opened and closed like that of a hungry baby bird, he was gasping so. "Abel. Look at me. Your father is coming. Can you swim to the side?" He seemed to hear me and turned to face the stony wall. But his efforts were in vain; he had no more energy left. He began to gulp and sink, gulp and sink. I could see his frightened eyes and open mouth, still and silent, disappearing into the dark depths, and I screamed again. I fumbled with my sash, stripped off my robe, and dove in.

Certainly Adam and I had learned the rudimentary skills of swimming in the Garden, in the deepest depths under the waterfall, but the real tests of our maneuverability came later, when Cain was a child and we were still following the Euphrates southward. He had no fear of the rushing water, and we became swift and agile rescuers.

I aimed in the general direction that Abel had disappeared, diving deep and opening my eyes. It was too dark to see anything—the sun's light was not quite above us—so I thrust my hands out in front of me, blindly and in a frenzied fashion, reaching, reaching for *something* of Abel's, a robe or sash or hand or head or heel, to clutch at and pull to the surface. Panic stole my breath; fright seared my lungs.

I kicked my legs and rose to the surface, vaguely mindful of the damage I might be doing to the child inside me, but my greatest desire was for the child I already had. I breathed in deep and dove once more.

There, I thought, to my left, but no, it was only a glimmering trail of bubbles behind me. "Abel," my voice screeched into the murky abyss, realizing too late I had expended the little breath I had, and water filled my mouth. The gurgles of my voice swarmed about, taunting, *You weren't watching him. You weren't there to protect him.*

I began then to calm my mind, to think methodically about the bit of watery space Abel and I inhabited. If I held fast to the slick mossy sides and worked my way around the cistern, reaching toward the center, I might be able to locate him. The problem was that unless I expelled air, I floated up, and if I expelled air, I had to repeatedly retrieve air from the top, which in turn wasted time.

Then. A tremendous *swoosh,* a shimmering roar in front of me.

Adam.

I pushed up, smashed through the surface, and took in large mouthfuls of air. The sky swirled; the sun tipped. I coughed up water and clung weakly to the cold crevices of the cistern.

A dove cooed with miraculous tranquillity.

I wiped my hair from my face and looked up, to find Cain.

Cain's face hovered over the edge like a plover searching for prey.

Adam sputtered to the surface, his hair drenched and scattered, holding our limp son in his arms. Abel's eyes were still rammed open, his little body already bloated.

"A rope, a rope," I cried to Cain. I could hear him scuttling around up top, securing a rope we kept coiled on the ground for when Adam had to repair or clean the cistern.

Cain tossed it down, and Adam grasped the end and began to hoist himself and Abel up. I followed, as soon as they were topside.

"Oh," said Cain as Adam laid out Abel upon the hot earth. Cain's face was red and sweaty from running, and I could not know if he was feeling guilt or sorrow, or merely curiosity.

The shame would come later, for not saving my boy child myself, for not preventing what happened altogether. Right then my focus was only to make him live again. The terror of my own death had lessened over time because I had grown accustomed to the fact of death—the animals, the plants, even the cyclic lives of the heavenly lamps—but the death terror of one of my own children had not lessened. It only grew stronger each time I laid a cold stiff baby in the unforgiving ground.

I fell on my knees beside Abel's inert form.

Adam pounded on Abel's ribby chest. "Come on, boy," he breathed. "Come back to your mother and me. You are not done with this world." And louder. "Back, boy, now!"

Then, with a rustling and a creaking, Abel turned his head and vomited, water and bread and figs. *Oh, glorious day, my boy lived!* I grabbed him up, oblivious to his heaving, and held him close.

"Careful," whispered Adam. He stroked Abel's head.

My fingers grazed the frail cup between Abel's shoulder blades, and I felt the transparent flutter of his heart on my breasts, like hummingbird's wings. I crooned to him, willed him to breathe, to live, to love me with all his heart. I said to him, through the warmth of my skin, *Come back to me, my child, I will protect your solemn, beautiful body. I will show you how to live. I will tell you of my previous life. I will show you what you cannot see.* The calm seeped into him. The tension rippled out.

Adam turned to Cain. "Why do you disobey?"

Cain shrugged. "We were just playing."

"You did not push him?" said Adam.

"No," said Cain. But his eyes betrayed him. They looked anywhere but at his father. Perhaps Cain was remembering another time, another place, when Adam and I had tossed him into the Euphrates to teach him to swim, and how he flailed and sank, flailed and sank, too many times to remember, until he had begun to stay afloat. Perhaps this was his revenge. I do not know.

Adam sent me a glance that asked what we should do with this outright lie, what punishment he should dole out to Cain. I shrugged and turned my head away, back to Abel. Alas, it was too perplexing a question. We both knew that love and respect was not something that could be mandated; it had to come from the heart. Cain would always be testing us— and his hapless, trusting brother. The harder we clamped down on Cain, the more testy he became, so to think of an appropriate punishment was fraught with difficulty.

I laid Abel back down, to put on my robe. He stared at me fiercely, intensely, his face round and ashen. He was a little pea, shucked of his shell, and he began to whimper. I was only too grateful when he held up his arms to me, to be lifted into the air. I thought of how close we had come to losing him. *If Cain hadn't called. If Adam hadn't come. If, if, if.*

I was steeped in happiness and relief. Abel had chosen *me*; he loved *me*. I looked at him in wonder—the freckles scattered like caraway seeds across his face, the muddy brown eyes that betrayed his tender depth of feeling—and I knew that my littlest son held tremendous power in his delicate body. I had fed him the strength and heat and courage to say *yes* or *no*, and that was all he needed to either validate my life or destroy it.

Was this what Elohim had spoken of in the Garden?

When I thought of the other possibility—that of Abel *not* choosing me, my self-righteousness guttered like a singular flame. How devastated Elohim must have been when we turned our backs to Him, wanting nothing more than "other," even though we did not yet know what other was.

Naava

Naava woke with scarlet spots upon her breasts and stomach. She pulled at her skin. "No," she exclaimed. "No, no, no." She touched the papules daintily; they were soft and round. She knew it was worse than a simple heat rash, and she cringed to think that she would have to go to Aya for help.

Her beauty. Her pride. She did not want to live.

At the morning repast, Aya announced with a smile that Naava had abundantly more upon her face and neck and back. Naava thought, *What kind of wretched face do I display to the world?* The spots begged her to scratch them, tear them apart, let them weep, but Aya snapped, "You'll look like a warthog."

Naava wanted to retort, "You would know," but she was feeling feverish and a bit of malaise and had not the gumption. Besides, Aya had promised a cool poultice that would take the itch away. Naava would wait until *after* Aya had given it to her to say what she felt. All her plans were ruined. *Who knew how long this affliction would last?* She could not return to the city looking like a piece of raw speckled meat.

Cain joked, "What beast have we here?"

She stomped her foot. "Stop it this instant," she snapped at him.

He laughed through the meal and continued to torment her, calling her "maggot face" and "cheese face" and "wormwood." She wondered why she had ever lain with him.

Ever since that day in the city, Naava had pondered her encounter with the prince. True, she had imagined licking the salt from his earlobes and kissing the hollow of his neck. In her dreams, she had stroked the hairs on his chest that curled like spirals—but no, she was getting this all wrong. That was Cain. The prince's chest had been bare. She felt her hands and feet go numb with delight, her lips go slack with hunger. She envisioned breasts and buttocks cupped. She gripped his swollenness in her mouth and rolled it about on her tongue, teasing it, coaxing it to grow, just as she had done with Cain. He groaned, she believed, for she had made him happy. She wanted him to like her. She wanted him to love her.

She had been a coward before, when the moment had come. The prince had tried to do all those things and more, there upon the hard swept earth, and she had rejected him; she had pushed him away. She had acted like a child, afraid of adventure and thrill.

Why should she have felt these emotions if she was not ready?

In truth, what kind of Elohim would create such desires if He did not want them to be fulfilled? Show her Elohim or Cain's gods. Did they know lust? Did they know love? They did not. Not as Naava knew it, for she knew of no one else who felt those coursings as she did, in her heart, or in her loins.

She and her prince would taste each other and be full.

In the meantime, Naava would allow Cain to teach her. He was red, like fire and heat and jealousy. For this sort of thing, Naava needed passion; she needed the blazing surge of anger so that she might learn quickly what sort of thing love was. He would give, and she would take. She would be a fast learner.

Then she would be ready for the prince.

Eve

Harvest was two moons away. It would creep up on us like a jackal if we were not careful. Adam had latched on to Abel and Cain's agreement—that of offering their first fruits to Elohim at harvesttime, in gratitude for all He had done. And since Adam knew more about green things than about Abel's leaping and bounding things, he had begun to follow Cain around, pestering him with questions and plans.

I saw the eagerness on Adam's face. This had been a wish of his too, that we do more to acknowledge Elohim. He had always been a true believer, unlike me, who had struggled with Elohim's absence and what I saw to be His utter disregard for us since the Garden. Indeed, it was Adam who insisted on holding hands and giving thanks before each meal.

Adam related to me that as he and Cain had trudged out to the fields one morning, he began rattling off all the chores that needed doing before harvest. "We must cull the dates and the grapes," Adam had said. He had been studying the ground intently, searching for signs of moles, so he had not noticed the growing irritation on Cain's face. "We must repair the fences around the vegetable garden, so the rabbits can't get to it. Then I think we should—"

Cain swiveled to face Adam. "Enough," he said in an exasperated tone. "Why don't you stick to the orchards, and I'll do everything else."

Adam's face shriveled like a mushroom past its prime. He did not want

Cain to see his disappointment, so he turned and said, "Yes, you're right, you're right." He rubbed his forehead, then turned and clapped his hands. "We're going to do this thing! Elohim will be pleased."

Cain studied his father's face briefly, then turned and plodded off toward the river, toward his date palms.

Without telling Cain, Adam had begun to weave reed mats to shove underneath the thin-skinned expanding gourds, to prevent the fruit from softening and ripening into the soil. He pruned the plants; he pulled out rogue specimens. He came in from the fields, his face streaked with dirt and his fingers black with earth. He sighed happily and said, "We shall have a bountiful harvest this year."

What a difference, this feeling that Elohim would be pleased, rather than angry with us. It seemed that since we left the Garden it was all we had experienced of Him.

The cry that burst from my lips in the Garden was *Forgive me.*

I wanted the thing undone. But just as clouds cannot take back the rain, I could not take back our eating of the fruit.

Listen to me carefully now. *Forgive. What did this word mean? What was I asking of Elohim? To forget my disobedience? To remember but not to hold me accountable? To overlook my action and let me stay?* Yes, yes, it is the latter I wanted. That, and not to die.

I did not want to die.

Nothing can be taken back. I carry the thorns of Adam and my children in my body, where *I* have been hurt, and it is not so easy a task, this forgiveness. I wish it were easier. The mind and body do not forget the fast-beating heart, the palsied hand, the choking cries that come from an attack, be it physical or emotional. Abuse pummels the body and leaves it limp—but alert. For the next time. Think of it as a bloodless rising in one's breast, to preserve and camouflage oneself against further predation.

This forgiving business is left for those of us who have been hurt but remain alive.

Dead creatures cannot forgive an injustice. Can a hare *forgive* the jackal's teeth? Can a mouse *forgive* the eagle's talons? I think not.

So I struggled with this thing called *forgiveness*. *What did it mean?*

Another thing: What was I supposed to do when someone believed, erroneously, that I had wronged him and would not forgive *me*? What was to be done about that?

It is Adam's deafness I am referring to.

After losing our first baby, I woke on the mountainside, stiff and unknowing, cupped in Adam's embrace. A light snow fell about us, like ash from a fire. A squirrel busied himself with a nut, then chattered and fled when I turned my face upward. I could feel the silver ice cutting into my crackling face.

Little by little, I remembered. The expulsion, the bear, our baby. The memories flooded in, wild and dark. This was the moment I always thought of, the irreversible severance of the thin membrane between happiness and sorrow. *How is it torn so quickly, so easily?*

I thought of the child, its hands curled like fern fronds, one thumb inserted into the slit of the mouth, and the eyes, dark and knowing, like cat eyes glowing in the night. I thought of other things we had dug into the ground, bulbs and seeds and offshoots—and the one Tree of Life seed—and I wanted to believe that, just like them, my baby would come springing up out of the ground, all green and living, and reach its arms out like branches that I could hang on to.

It was wishful thinking, I knew.

After a brief discussion in which neither of us mentioned the child, Adam and I surmised that the black stream in the hanging valley below us would zigzag its way through the sharp plummeting ridges and eventually end up in the great sparkling sea we saw in the far distance. If we could find the stream and follow it, or at least skirt its shores, we could end up on that distant sandy plain where there was no snow. Little did we know how flawed our assumptions were.

The plain was moons away, not days.

For the most part, I am pleased to admit, we were extremely resourceful. We had had reliable teachers—yes, I am counting the animals as our teachers—and now we reaped the benefits. We mimicked the rabbit and the bark beetle and gnawed on bits of fibrous bark; we remembered the deer and plucked the remaining raspberries and blackberries and elderberries from their vines; we foraged like the monkeys—for nuts, ants, termites, mushrooms, fungi, snails, caterpillars, even birds' eggs.

Before we made our way down to the river—slippery handhold over slippery handhold, our wrists aching, our legs shaking with exhaustion—we slaked our thirst on melted snow in the dips and hollows of leaves and branches, but the eating of it only chilled us.

All in all, we lasted many days on such subsistence, although our bellies and tongues longed for the rich diversity of the Garden.

One morning we woke to a dense fog and a hushed melancholy. A single drop of water dripped from a leaf or a branch onto another—*plawp*. The trees snapped with sudden wings. Then we heard footsteps nearby, delicate *tap taps* of an oryx or ibex or gazelle. A coucal called *hoo hoo hoo hoo hoo hoo hoo*.

It was the clattering and clacking of horns that changed everything.

The fog lifted, and emerging from underneath its white rim were two of the finest ibexes we had ever seen. They were completely heedless of our presence. One of them gave a sharp whistling sound.

"Look," Adam cried. "It can't be." There had been few in the Garden.

But there they were. The two males lowered their whiskery chins and tilted their long curved horns and crashed together, each trying to topple the other. This was a remarkable feat, to scrabble and stand solid on such precipitous terrain.

I pointed to the rocks above, as the milky fog lifted higher and higher. "There are more." Several females watched, aloof. Their tan bodies blended into the rock behind them, and they stamped their front feet impatiently.

"We could catch one," said Adam, his voice trembling.

Of course, had I known what Adam was contemplating, I would have discouraged him straightaway, but I thought he was simply admiring their breadth and strength.

Then, with sudden realization, I understood his response to mean that he was hungry and he was going to kill one of them if he could. I hastened to dissuade him. After all, Adam was not an ibex's equal match. It would simply rise up on its strong hind legs and pummel him to death. I shuddered to think of it.

"No," said Adam, as if to read my mind. "Not to kill them. To *milk* them."

I looked at him in astonishment, then bewilderment. We had seen animal young suckle at their mother's nipples, but was it possible that we, too, could latch on to a teat and suck?

"Are they with child?" I asked. The udders only seemed full to bursting when they were great with child and expected to deliver.

"There is only one way to find out," said Adam. He placed one foot upon a boulder, rested his elbow on his thigh, and looked at me expectantly. His bravado was impressive, but still, I did not think we should attempt such a thing. After all, we had water; we had food.

I was flummoxed. *How did he expect to tame so nimble an animal?* "I do not see how you will do it," I said.

Adam hefted himself up on the boulder in the direction of the female ibexes. He held out his hand. "Careful," he said.

I let him pull me up. We stood now upon a narrow crumbling ledge. Any movement sent a cascade of rocks and pebbles crashing down the mountainside. I sucked in my breath.

"I shall go up and around the one with the white spot on its chest," said Adam. "You will approach her from this angle, here."

I nodded. I wanted to say, *This will not work. They will protect one another. Have you forgotten the bear acted alone—and look how that turned out.*

Adam continued on a ways, then crept like a spider up the sheer face of a rock, grasping the ledges with his fingertips and toes.

I watched and cringed. *Should he fall, what would I do?* I could not think about it. I planted my feet upward on rock and dirt, testing my foothold first to see if it would come away, and when it didn't, I placed my foot squarely and firmly to lift myself up. A painstaking process on such a steep incline.

Adam continued upward. At one point I heard a scatter of pebbles, then an uneven thud as a rock bounded down the hill. Tree branches cracked; tiny animals skittered through the brush; birds flew up in injured song.

I looked for Adam, but he was not there. I had not heard him cry, nor had I seen him reach the top of the rock. "Adam," I called, frightened in my aloneness.

There was no answer.

"Adam."

"Up here," he said. He was laughing and pointing out a group of scampering kids play-fighting among the rocks. "I only wish I were as sure-footed."

I straightened, leaning my weight into the mountain. "What are you suggesting?"

Adam turned his attention to the female. "We must get her down and tie her legs together. Then we shall suck from her teats."

"What about the rams?"

"Look at them. They are otherwise engaged," said Adam.

I glanced down at the butting rams but did not come to the same conclusion. If Elohim wanted us dead, well, we might just help Him along. I wanted to help Adam, though, and we needed greater nourishment than what we were eating, so I decided, yes, I would do what Adam had said.

The female ibexes were unusually tame and seemed unconcerned at our advances. This surprised me. I knew them to be considerably fast and nimble, yet they did not move as we approached. Maybe they were just as curious about us as we were about them.

Adam drew closer to the ibex he had chosen, then he moved quickly to grasp her horns in his hands. When she planted her front feet and struggled to pull away from him, he offered her a fistful of grasses that he had plucked from the mountainside. She sniffed at them with disdain and shook her head savagely. Adam dropped the grasses and gripped her horns tighter, straining not to lose her. This she certainly did not like. When Adam wouldn't release her, she backed away from him, trying to lift up on her hind legs.

Adam yelled something indecipherable then, and with one loud feral grunt he had her on her side, her legs skittering in the air. "Grab the front legs."

I fairly stumbled up the slope.

How could I do what Adam requested? The poor frightened animal was now pawing at the air, her hooves flailing wildly and erratically, in an attempt to gain even footing. Had I followed Adam's suggestion, I would be battered beyond all sensibilities.

He saw my hesitation. "The back legs, then. Do something, quick. I can't hold her like this forever."

The back legs were easier. They had no ground to push upon and were not kicking as ferociously. I grabbed one, then the other, and as I did so, the ibex raised her head to stare at me. It was a mournful, accusatory stare that made me want to weep. *What were we doing? How had we sunk so low as to misuse an animal in such a way?*

"Now what?" I said.

"A vine might work," said Adam.

I was becoming irritated at Adam's irrationality. He had not discussed the course of action with me, and *had* he, I would have been better prepared and torn a section of vine *before* I took hold of the ibex's legs. I sighed audibly.

"This is for you too, you know," he said. "I'm doing this for you."

"And where, exactly, do you expect me to find this vine?" Truly, we stood on a rocky incline spotted with only small plants favoring stony ground—spiny yellow broom, shrubby rock roses, and three-lobed sage.

Adam glanced around. "You shall have to weight her down with rocks to hold her."

"I will not hurt her," I said.

"It would be better to kill her," mused Adam.

"Kill her?" I said. "Whatever for?"

"Then we would have her milk *and* her meat." When he saw my face, his impatience flared up. "I should think her meat would be excellent food."

I looked at Adam and burst into tears. I still had hold of the hind legs. The other ibexes had fled and were now perched above us, like vultures, watching.

"We will only do what Elohim did to that lion," Adam said. "There's nothing to be afraid of."

"I'm not afraid," I said. "But I do not believe killing is our way."

"Why not?" said Adam. "Elohim has given us every living thing to take care of and to use. I do not see where we've gone wrong."

"To take *care* of," I said. "*Not* to use."

Adam snorted. "Will you help me or not?"

"Its child—" I protested, looking upward at the frolicking kids, wondering which one was hers, which one had slipped, whole and alive, from her body. I looked back then at my husband, his body rippling with effort, and knew in that brief instant that I carried him inside me. I looked at his gaunt half-starved body and felt his terror and uncertainty. I remembered the Garden and knew that I would give this man what he wanted because of all he had given me—beauty, earth, sky, love, and life.

I released the ibex's legs and lurched farther up the hillside to find a large heavy rock. I heard the scrabbling of a struggle below me. The ibex knew she contended with only one of us now. Breathless, I found what I was looking for and lifted it. My body strained underneath its weight, but I brought it back, dutifully, and stood over the ibex's head.

"Now," cried Adam.

I closed my eyes and dropped the rock. I dropped that rock upon the ibex's head, and it bled and bled, but it did not lie still.

"Again!" cried Adam.

I scrambled down the hill to retrieve the rock, careful not to lose traction on the wash of pumice, and again I hoisted it to my waist to carry it back up the hill. Once more I stood over the ibex's head and raised the rock above my head. I was trembling now. This time I used my full strength. The ibex's head flopped, but its eyes were still knowing, and its legs fluttered. A gasp crossed my lips, and I stood, empty-handed, embarrassed, and ashamed.

"There now, you've done it. A fine job of it too," said Adam.

The ibex's eyes tensed and flashed, shivered in their sockets. Although there was no noise, no outcry from the ibex, it was as though the earth roared—cried out, rather—as the ibex's life rolled away down the mountainside.

I stifled a sob that rose up in my throat.

Adam hastened around the ibex's body and crouched near her full udder. He held the ibex's hind legs, still quivering, as he braced himself to suck. He grabbed hold of a teat with his mouth and began to fill his belly. He released after a bit and exclaimed, with a white milky rim about his lips, "It's good. We shall have our fill."

I shook my head. I was not prepared to take from this dying animal, its dense bones becoming one with the ground. It did not feel right to me—yet.

And this is when it happened. With a final sigh, the ibex kicked her right front leg, and Adam rose up yelping, crying out in pain, gripping his ear, his face contorted and ashen. "Hold it," Adam yelled. "I told you to hold it."

"She was dead," I said.

Adam glared at me, his anger coiling and uncoiling, like a snake unsure of its victim. He grabbed a stone at his feet and began to strike at the ibex's head over and over again, tearing its flesh into ribbons of meat.

"She's dead," I said. "She cannot hurt you."

Adam released the stone and sank to the ground. He clasped his head in his hands and said, "I hear a ringing, an awful ringing in my head. It will not stop."

I went to him then, leaving the ibex behind.

I held his head in my hands, tilted it so I could see better. The top of his left ear was gone, completely sliced off, and a gash ran from his temple to just behind his ear. Blood wept out of it and clotted. I studied it and said, "There is nothing to be done. We will wash it with water, when we come upon it. Right now we must skin this beast before other animals come to feed."

Adam glared at me.

I reached for his hand, hoping for some resolution.

Finally he took my hand. "My voice, it rolls about inside my head," he said. He grimaced and put his hand upon his forehead.

By now the fog had lifted completely, and below, a lush green valley emerged. We had come out of the snow several days previous, for we were descending into the first valley, and although we had lost sight of the stream, we had come upon bushes and bushes of blueberries, wondrous profusions of them, tucked into the crevices of rocky limestone. Picking and eating them had been like answering a summons to life, to our living. Just to have food, *any* food, in our mouths was a delightful blessing.

We still had a few berries left. We ate ravenously that night, the ibex's blood and berry stains tingeing our fingers and mouths, marking us as predators and foragers. We did not learn to cook and to season until much later, when we watched our flocks become ill on old, spoiled meat.

And that is how Adam came to be deaf in one ear.

He would not let me forget it.

It was the beginning of our undoing.

Aya

I tell you this. Cain is getting weary of Father's suggestions. In fact, the night before last Cain told Father, "You torture me."

In the lamplight, Father's face went blank. He didn't understand what had gone wrong; he was only trying to help. "Cain," he said weakly.

"No more," said Cain. "Stick to your fruit trees. Stick to Mother's garden." Then, after noticing Father's face hanging like stone, he softened his words. "This is upon my shoulders only. Don't you see?"

Father nodded, but his mouth was clamped shut and his knuckles were white with insult.

"Father, do not be this way. I appreciate your help, I do, but it is I who have to win the praise of Elohim, not you," said Cain.

Father looked up then, his face elegant and pale. "You do not know Elohim. You do not know the perfection He expects." His words were hard and precise, as though scratched into stone. "Your little house, your little temple. You think this would please Elohim? He wants your allegiance and your love, not silly little things like houses."

Cain looked at Father as though his words had been cut into Cain's skin, and he turned his back to show Father he did not bleed, he *would* not bleed.

Father continued, "You do not know what it is like to be loved, to be cherished." He leaned forward, as though hoping to gain strength from his words. "As much as we love you, neither your mother nor I can love you the way Elohim loved us." It was rare that Father talked of Elohim or the Garden—except when he prayed before our repasts. Mother did enough of that for both of them. I wondered sometimes if Father felt that his experiences were too sacred to repeat, too private to divulge.

Cain stepped forward, closer to Father, seeming to measure the truth of his words. "Why did you not stay with Him, then? Why did you leave, if it was so good?" His words were as sour as lemons, for he knew *exactly* why Mother and Father were expelled.

Father's brow crumpled. "We chose other." He paused a bit, then continued. "As you have done with the building of your temple and your many clay gods. Woe to you, Cain, if you turn from what you know to be true."

Cain was angered now, the vein on his temple throbbing. "You speak of knowing what is true. What *is* true? Where is this Elohim of yours? I have never heard Him. I have never seen Him. I know Abel and Aya speak of Him, as does Mother, but you—" Cain ran his fingers through his hair, as if to tear clumps of it out. "You do not speak of Him. You do not talk to Him." Cain spit on the floor. "Do you?"

I was astonished that Cain had heard me talk of Elohim. I had thought him uninterested in anything that I did, except for my cooking and healing.

Father said only, "He is not ruled by what I do or do not do."

Cain whistled low, then stalked out, throwing shards of words over his shoulder. "I thought not."

I pondered what Father had said. *Surely Father and Mother did not dream the Garden, did they? Surely they were certain of Elohim's existence? Surely they believed in the power and strength of Elohim to do anything He wanted?* After all, He made them. He placed us, their children, inside Mother. Indeed, He had promised this very thing to Mother, that she would be prolific and that she and Father's seed would populate the earth. *So where did the other people come from? Had Elohim made the same promises to them?*

Elohim *had* been with me the day those men attacked. I was sure of it. I had flown with Him; He had flown with me. I had tasted sky and freedom and . . . I think . . . peace, an overwhelming peace.

And Abel and Jacan. *Had they not said that Elohim shouted from the rocks to warn them about me? How could that be if it were not true? Why would Jacan lie about something like that?*

What I had *not* figured out yet was *why* He made us suffer so if He truly cared for us. He had promised Mother many children, but He took some babies back. He gave me a crooked foot. He let the floods ravage our crops, the lions and jackals and hyenas prey upon our flocks, and the dust whirlwinds tear everything away.

Why?

Even more important: *Did Cain hear the gods he bowed down to every day?*

With renewed fervor, I prayed again to Elohim.

> *Please, Elohim, fill me with patience.*
> *Open my eyes. Let me see You. Really see You.*
> *Have You noticed? That I have been good?*
> *I would run for You, if I could.*
> *I would lift my perfect legs for You.*
> *If I could.*

Two days after Naava got her spots, I got them as well. So did Jacan.

"Now, little sister, what do you have to say to me?" said Naava. "You have the face of a goat and the skin of a lizard."

"I got them from you," I retorted. I was tired of her sly comments, and I would have liked to hit her, just once.

Naava snorted. She narrowed her eyes and glared at me. "At least I am whole," she snarled.

Naava's sores scabbed over, and the pus dried up. She did not pick at them, as I did. I applied the same poultices to my face, with the hope that my face would heal like Naava's.

Naava has disappeared into a fog. Mother asked her the other day what she was working on, and Naava looked at her blankly, biting her lip, then she vanished into her weaving room. Mother looked at me and shook her head. "That girl," she said. "I'll never understand her." The only time I see Naava is when she eats and when she meanders down to the river by herself.

I have seen her robe, and it is remarkable. She does not know it, but there are days when she has gone to the river that I sit in her weaving room and stare at her Garden: perfectly woven blossoms, billowing clouds, lapping waters, white froth of bird wing, and salted night skies. I wish to be there. I wish to walk into the depths of the cloth and have it surround me. I do not touch. It is not mine, and although I detest Naava for her meanness, I would not ruin such a lovely thing, for I have benefited from it; I can *see* and *taste* the Garden in all its fancy finery.

I must say, it pains me considerably to know she will look beautiful in it, when the time comes.

Dara

I understand most of their words now, and I'm afraid I'll forget my other words, my home words.

"Come along, come along," Zenobia says always. Zenobia drags Puabi and me back to the giant mountain every day. Once in the morning and once in the nighttime.

Now Zenobia knows I can make the praying statues, so she says, "Dara, faster, you must make more!" One time I took some of Puabi's cowrie shells and pushed them into the eye sockets, so the people would have eyes to see with. When Zenobia saw the decorated statues, her eyes sparkled and she said, "You understand now."

But I don't.

I don't understand why all the people go to this big mountain and climb up to the top, so their feet and legs scream *stop stop stop,* all so they can give more food to the Bosom Lady and to Balili, who wears the gold hat. I ask Balili this, when he is teaching me: "Balili, why can't the gods get their own food?" And all he says is, "The food is for Inanna."

Zenobia says, "We are giving gifts to Inanna, the Queen of Heaven. She will bless us, make our crops grow, make me fertile, and protect us from evil."

I ask, "How will she eat all that food?"

Zenobia says, "She comes from a long line of supreme beings who were there as the first mountains were born out of the primordial sea. We pay her respect, Dara, and you must too."

"Mama and Aya and Abel pray to Elohim," I tell her. "Father does too before we eat."

"Elohim? Who is this?" asks Zenobia. "I don't know any Elohim. Maybe you mean Anu or Enki or Enlil. That's who you mean, child, don't you?"

"Maybe they're the same person," I say.

"Maybe," says Zenobia, but she frowns at me like Aya does when I forget to bring dung for her fire.

One time—promise not to tell—I saw the Bosom Lady eating some of the food. She was in the little house at the top of the mountain, stuffing her mouth with all the gifts from the people. She burped, and then she said, "Inanna blesses you." She laughed to herself like she was having a funny little joke.

I did not see Inanna anywhere. Maybe she wasn't hungry and so she gave Bosom Lady her food.

I saw Cain too.

Puabi and I were sitting in the shade on a wooden bench under the tea lady's tarp. Zenobia argued with a man nearby. He had orange hands and an orange beard, from the orange plant he was selling. He kept wiping his hands on his robe, so even his robe was orange. Zenobia sneezed, and I tried not to laugh. That would be rude.

Puabi and I sipped good-smelling tea from clay cups with circles and squares and lines painted on them. I told Puabi all about home and Jacan my twin and Turtle, how he stuck his little head out when he thought no one was looking but tucked it back in when someone picked him up.

Puabi stared at me. "Want see," Puabi said.

"Jacan or Turtle?" I asked.

"Both," said Puabi.

"I only see them when I go home," I said, feeling sad again.

"*This* your house," Puabi said.

"I have another house," I said.

She set her teacup in her lap and frowned. "Leave Mongoose. No."

"You aren't going anywhere," I said.

Cain shouted then. I did not know he could speak like the city people, but there he was, in the middle of the marketplace. He was standing nearby, next to our donkey, tightening up the straps. His face was red, and he was talking to two big men with their hair pulled back into buns. They were carrying a long thick stick on their shoulders, and from the stick hung a large pot that swayed back and forth.

"I will show you," shouted Cain. "I will bring them upon my donkey's back at harvesttime, and they will be the likes of which you've never seen before, here or anywhere else. You will eat, and their sweetness will be in your toes and in your fingers and all the way down to your ankles." He made circles with his fingers. "This big, they are. And moist." He tested the tightness of the strap by wobbling the baskets. It didn't budge.

The men laughed. One said, "How is it the gods bless you so? You do not worship them."

Cain spit on the ground in a fury. "I don't need any gods." This surprised me, because at home Cain had built a temple to them, and I had made all those folding-hands people for him.

"Oh, oh, oh," said the man with the fat belly. "Listen to him; he angers them already." He turned to Cain. "Watch your tongue. You do not know when the gods are listening."

Cain spit again and rolled up the sleeves of his robe. "A wager?" he said.

The two men looked at each other. The one with a painted picture on his arm said, "A wager for what outcome?"

Cain grinned. "The largest dates."

The fat man said, "The largest aren't always the tastiest."

"We will make it fair. The largest *and* the tastiest. The womenfolk will judge," said Cain.

The painted man growled, "Not good. Our womenfolk will like ours. Your womenfolk will like yours. That will solve nothing."

Cain thought a moment. "We will ask your Inanna, then. How is that?"

The men whispered between themselves. They shot quick looks at

Cain, who had his hands across his chest. "You have yourself a deal," said the fat man. "What is our reward?"

"Name it," said Cain.

The fat man looked at the painted man and sneered. "Your sister." He spit in his hand and held it out to Cain.

Cain's hand flew to the knife in his belt. He pulled it out and held it out in front of him. *Flash flash flash,* it went in the sun.

I sucked in air. Did they mean *me*? *Be careful, Dara, they will try to kill you,* Aya had said.

Cain could not beat these two bullies—once, I saw them kick a poor dog until it lay down and didn't move.

"What is it, what is it?" Puabi asked.

I pointed to Cain.

"What?" demanded Puabi. She stood up on the bench and tippy-toed to see over the crowd.

I stood and cupped my hand over her mouth, so the bad men wouldn't see us and come get me. "Shhh," I hissed.

Puabi pulled away, and her tea spilled. She began to shriek like a hyena, and Zenobia came running.

"What's wrong, baby?" she said, brushing Puabi's hair from her face. "What is it?"

I stood as still as a rock and watched Cain waving his knife at the two men. *Go, Cain, go go go,* I thought. *Do not let them take me like they tried to take Aya.*

I heard Puabi say, "My tea."

The fat man and the painted man guffawed. "We jest with you. We will take the dates, all of them. If you win, you shall have our dates. Fair enough?"

Cain stood very still, sweat dripping off his face. He put the knife back in his pocket. "Your dates are rubbish," he said, frowning. "What kind of reward is that? If I win, I want two oxen and some of that flaxseed you have."

The fat man waved to a worker nearby who molded clay into shapes on a wheel. "Wet clay," he demanded.

The potter bunched up some clay and flattened it into a square and took it to the fat man. He bowed to the fat man. "At your service," he said.

The fat man grabbed the clay from the potter's hand. "Here," said the fat man to Cain. "Your mark."

Cain nodded and took the hem of his robe and pressed it into the clay. The fat man did the same. The fat man grinned at the potter and at Cain. "Inanna sees it is good."

I turned to Zenobia, who was pulling on the ends of my hair.

"Is this true?" Zenobia said. "That you spilled her tea?"

I shook my head.

Zenobia struck me anyway, hard across the cheek. "You will not hurt her," she said in a loud voice. "Do you understand me?"

I didn't do anything, I thought, but I dropped to my knees and kissed the back of Zenobia's hand. This is what I had been taught to do, if I was ever punished. Zenobia did not want excuses. Ever.

Puabi hid behind her mama's skirts.

I glared at Puabi and thought, *You are not very nice.*

I followed her and her mama back to their house, and I decided right then that her precious Mongoose might need a little trip outside the walls of the city. He'd have to be careful, though, because the lion might eat him.

Eve

I believe it was during this interim, with Dara working in the city and me dreaming of dying, that I began to contemplate my life and what about it made it significant—if it were at all. Is this what Elohim would call a *life*—the bearing and raising of children, the wearisome arguments with Adam, the hostilities of my sons? Or did I wish for a personal act of heroism, some seed of thrilling divinity within me to rear up and claim the life it deserved, for Elohim *had* reminded Adam and me, over and over again, that we were created in His image.

In essence: *Was there more to this futile cycle, or was I simply oblivious to it?*

There I was. A simple vessel that Elohim had created. But for what purpose? It was my work or my life that molded me into who I was, who I had become, that informed my stance toward my husband and children. It was what made me either hostile and strange or happy and compliant, and I was afraid my attitude had been more the former than the latter.

But why?

I think it was because I did not see where I was going. I did not see, on this meandering path I was on, a great veering or diversion ahead to lead me back to the Garden. I saw thunderous clouds ahead. I saw evil overcoming good. I saw hope swallowed by despair.

I did *not* see Elohim. Or hear Him, as I had in the Garden.

This was troublesome to me.

I say these things because I wish to make clear my inner dilemma and how it seeped like groundwater into my outer demeanor. Certainly I desired to be a good wife and a good mother, a person who loved others as herself, but this not knowing my future affected me to the very core. I wished for Elohim to explain. I wished for Him to manifest Himself again so we could converse as we used to.

Now I have doubled back again to my origin, for the Garden is at the heart of all my thoughts.

In my meditations, I have concluded that there is one thing I desired, and that was something I will call *redemption*—a rescue from the mundane, a salvation to something greater, a deliverance from this curse that had been placed on Adam and me, a rectification of my ignorance. I wished to look back on my mistakes—alas, there have been many—and see clearly, despite my missteps, that I was forging my way toward something grander than myself.

Take, for instance, Naava's robe. Thread by thread, stitch by stitch, she related a story, *my* story, in the Garden. At first I was aware only of the disparate materials she used, unremarkable in themselves, but then, as she integrated them like the notes of a harmonious melody, another delightful entity emerged, that of my beautiful Eden. The story, or song, *became* remarkable in the mixing of the good and the bad.

I imagined Dara's praying people with folded hands. She created, as Elohim did, from the clay of the earth, but her statues were simply that— inert statues, although I would vouch that Cain felt differently, as even I did that summer.

We—women and men, girls and boys—are alive with Elohim's breath, with Elohim's creativity, which makes us different, more spectacular, than any other aspect of Elohim's creation. We are drawn to Elohim, by Elohim, in a way that no other creature seems to be.

Which is why I was continually perplexed. I felt this heart-tug, but I could not hear Him. He called me, I am sure of it now, but He refused to answer my cries.

I will tell you why I pursued these questions. In truth, I have given them much thought. Let's say I am a mole. If I stay in my hole, pressed in on all sides by dirt, I will not be distressed by the weight of it. It would simply be the way things are. But if I am a mole, and I am brought into the breath of day, into the drafty weightless air, I should feel that something was wrong, and I would attempt to set things right—meaning I would crawl back into my tunnel. All this is to say that I *was* a mole, set in a foreign world that I knew to be different, knew to be wrong, and I resisted it with all my being.

I have a theory, a faint notion, why this is so. I look at my children. Some are easier to love than others. Their spirits are soft, their outlook cheery. Therefore, it is easier to reciprocate their feelings. Maybe it was *my* stubborn heart, *my* blinded eyes, *my* deaf ears that refused to perceive Elohim. Maybe it was I who had created my own turmoil.

I speak for myself, of course. Adam and I used to discuss these things in the Garden, and later as he lay dying, but with the busyness of life then on the plains, that, too, was taken from us. And my prayers, like rocks I flung at the sky, only arced back down to earth.

One thing we had abandoned since the Garden was the day of rest that Elohim had talked about. He had called it the Sabbath. I wonder if our abandonment of this practice had something to do with our increasing feelings of disorder and distress.

It was a day like any other, humid and warm, thrumming with bird and monkey chatter. It was a day at the beginning of my life with Adam. We were absorbed in the many tasks of the Garden, one of which was yanking large-leafed vines down by the handful, those pesky epiphytes that clung to the larger trees and threatened to choke the green life out of them. Elohim appeared and said simply, "Stop."

We had no idea what He was talking about, so we ignored Him, for He *had* encouraged us to work in His Garden.

Again, He told us to stop.

We did, the vines hanging limp in our callused and blistered hands, curious now as to what He had in mind.

He told us to sit, to rest. He wanted to tell us a story.

We sat across from Him.

He told us again of how He created the world—how He rolled the lamps of the sky in His hands, how He flung those luminous balls into the firmament and said, "It is good." He told us of the green mountains, the vast seas, the fish, the fowl, the flowers, the forests, how all that He made was good, very good, and He was pleased.

"And then I sat and looked all around me," He said. "And I was lonely." *Imagine that. Elohim—lonely.*

"I longed for someone I could talk to and share things with, so I thought, *I'll make a man, in my image, who will delight in what I have made, who will enjoy the fruits of my hands.* So I formed Adam, blew my breath into him, and he took the wind and sky into his chest and became a living, breathing soul."

Absentmindedly, Adam reached up to pull down another vine.

"Rest, Adam," said Elohim. "I ask you to rest."

"You've asked us to work the Garden," Adam insisted.

Elohim nodded. "Labor is good, but rest is even better. For it is the juxtaposition of the two that lends credence to each. Only when you have experienced both can you appreciate either."

"What about *me?*" I said. I was forever harping for my inclusion.

"You too," Elohim said. "I made you from Adam's side so that he would have a companion, someone to share things with. He was nothing before you. You completed him. You complemented him. I breathed life into you too, and then, only then, was Adam complete."

I looked at Adam, unsure of what to say. We had talked about this matter quite frequently and argued about what it had meant—me being created *after* Adam. I argued that I was the culmination of Elohim's creation, since I was created last. Adam argued that he was made first; therefore, he was the most important of Elohim's creation. Of course, we were half joking then, but once we were cast out of the Garden, it became a wound that would not repair itself. Maybe this is what Elohim had meant by His curse upon me—that man and woman would never behave as He had originally desired.

Now I think that we never quite understood the significance of what Elohim was telling us. After all, when He told us to rest, we could only know that our limbs were not tired, neither were we exhausted in spirit. So, although I am trying to recall His exact words, I am aware that I had no idea of what He was suggesting at the time. I had no need for it; therefore, it escaped me. I could tell that Adam felt the same way. His limbs grew listless; his eyes hazed over. He had not the slightest idea what to do with himself. Neither did I. It was as I said before: Our work defined us, our work gave us purpose. At least that is how we understood it.

Elohim saw our confusion and smiled. "It is a simple thing, really. All I ask is that, after six days of work, you build a bower in your heart on the seventh, in which you delight in what I have given you, in which you reflect on what we, you and I, have in common. It will be a haven, a place where you begin again to live in the light of my love, no matter what your work is."

Interesting how Elohim made even stillness important.

Somehow, surviving here on this wild and dusty plain has demanded constant vigilance. Adam and I had no interludes of rest or stillness; therefore, we had little time to contemplate Elohim's love for us.

But now, in the quiet of the morning or in the lull of the gloaming, I hear the breeze whisper, *Be still,* and I wonder if it is Elohim speaking after all.

One morning, I spied Naava leading Cain out of her weaving room, out of the courtyard, in the direction of the cistern. They were unaware that I had seen them. Cain's hunger was obvious. Indeed, he stumbled over the large fossil Abel had given Aya, which was sitting by the courtyard entrance. Naava was unabashed in her seduction—she loosened the tie in her hair as she walked. I thought of stopping them, but in a flash of recognition I remembered Adam's fever for me, and mine for him, when we first saw each other, and I could not stop them from experiencing the same. *How else were they to start families of their own?*

I knew I would have to speak to Adam about what we were to do with this new turn of events. Cain was old enough to take a wife, and he must do so honorably, by marrying her, dedicating his entire life to her. I had seen Abel's sideways glances at Naava, and I knew this would only cause more friction between him and Cain.

Mercy upon us.

Dara

I wish to have a shell like Turtle, so I can hide. I make more and more praying people, but still Zenobia says *hurry hurry hurry*.

"Why don't you buy them at Inanna's mountain like everyone else?" I ask, but Zenobia makes a cricket noise, like this, *chikkk chikkk chikkk,* and says, "Yours are more beautiful." She picks up one of my praying people and caresses its head. She sets it back down. "Do you see this house, child? See its magnificence? I am as dry as a bone." Zenobia shakes her hands in front of me, like she's shaking dust out of a robe. She leans over until her mouth is by my ear. "Shhh," she whispers. "The prince wants a boy child, and I must give it to him. Otherwise, he'll throw me out in the streets. And *that* we can't have." She points to the men crouched down low, rolling snakes of clay and putting them in a hot oven. "Here, look at this, see these cones, each one *rolled* individually, *colored* individually, *placed* individually? This *one* column will take more days than your whole house took to make back home. I want to be a part of this. I want to be a part of the prince's house."

My mouth has nothing to say, but I do not like how Zenobia talks about her house, like it's better than Mama's and Father's.

Thankfully, I am a hawk. I am wide awake, to watch near things and faraway things. I see how the men roll the cones and color them with paint. I know their secrets, but my mouth does not open. This morning, when no one was looking, I made Mama another goddess. After it was baked in the fire, I washed the goddess in the ground-up powder mixed with milk, just like the men do, and it turned red like a pomegranate. Balili says he will get me more sky stones like the one in my nose. I would like to give the red goddess blue eyes, like Mama's—little blue eggs in their nests. I think Mama will cry when she sees it, because Mama cries when she's sad *and* happy.

I buried the new goddess in one of the planters on the rooftop, the one with the palm in it. I think if Mama talks to the goddess and asks for Inanna's blessing, she will have a good baby, not a broken baby like Aya.

And now I have to say something that is bothering me, like bees buzzing in my head. Aya says that a person must always tell what bothers her, then Elohim will hear her and do something about it.

The easiest way to keep the babies quiet is to tell them stories. I know I'm not supposed to boast, but it's the truth that I can tell a story, and I think telling the truth is a good thing, not a bad thing. Aya would approve.

Anyway, I was telling the babies how Mama was the first woman in the whole wide world, and how Elohim made Father out of the dust of the ground, just like I made the praying people, and how He made Mother from Father's side. "He held them up, like this, and breathed on them, like this, and their arms and legs started dancing, just like that."

"From dirt?" said Shala.

I nodded. "And Elohim made the heavens and the stars and the moon and the sun and the oceans and the mountains and the rivers."

"What about the lion?" asked Shulgi, the bald-headed boy. "Did He make the lion?"

"Elohim made all the animals too, for Mama and Father to name—the cranes, the foxes, the lions, the ibexes, the jackals—all the birds and beasts and river fishes. Even the turtles."

"Even the mongooses?" said Puabi.

"Yes," I told her. "But the Garden was like nothing you've ever seen. It was dark and shady and green. Mama and Father could hardly see the sky because of the big big trees. And the water. There was always sweet cool water to drink—in the leaves and in the waterfalls and in the river. Mama said she rested her head on moss that was as soft as wool."

Zenobia's face appeared out of the shadows of the house. "I think you are talking about Dilmun, no? The shining land, where there is no pain, and the lion lays down with the lamb?"

I shook my head, confused. "No, Mama and Father were in Eden. Up in the mountains."

Ahassunu, the mother of naughty Shala, appeared suddenly next to Zenobia. She blinked and crooked her hand into a tent for her eyes. She laughed. "What are you saying, you insolent girl? That your parents are gods? That's ridiculous. Everyone knows how the heavens and earth sprang out of the sea, and how the gods breathed and spit on the clay to create man so he could work the earth for them." She turned to Zenobia. "Are you hearing this?"

Zenobia smiled. "It is good that the child has an imagination."

I knew they were laughing at me, but how could they mock Mama and Father, who were *in* the Garden and told me all those stories? They wouldn't lie to me. My stories were true, every last one of them.

And then, before I could stop up my lips, I said, "Mama has seeds from there. From the Tree of Life. She keeps them in a jar under the ground."

Ahassunu's eyes flickered like fire. "What did you say, child?" She moved closer to me, saying, "Well, well, well." She slinked like Mama said Lucifer did. "Your parents are from Dilmun?"

"No," I said. "That's not what I said."

"But your mother has seeds from the Tree of Life. The tree that gives the eternal life of gods. The tree that supports the world."

I nodded, scared that I had told Mama's cold dark secret.

Ahassunu ran her clammy hands through my hair. "You don't say?" she said again. She ran her tongue along her teeth. She looked at me, then at Zenobia, then back at me. "What do you make of her stories?" she said to Zenobia. "Dare we hope? That this is *the* Tree of Life?"

Zenobia shrugged. "The gods work in mysterious ways," she said.

Ahassunu drummed her fingers along her jaw, then she said to Zenobia, "I want them. Have her get them for me."

Zenobia smiled again and shrugged. "They're not hers to give. They're her mother's."

Ahassunu frowned. "I care not how you get them. I will have them. Or I will have the prince throw you and Puabi out on the plains." She flounced back toward the shadows, calling out for Shala to follow her. "Shala, lamb, it's your naptime."

Zenobia laughed nervously. "You forget," she said to Ahassunu's back. "The prince is my husband too."

Ahassunu stopped and came back and drew her face in close to Zenobia's, so they were as close as two peas in a pod. "And *you* forget too, that I see how you look at my son, Balili."

Zenobia looked down, embarrassed, and Ahassunu said, "There now. You will do as I ask." Taking Shala's hand, she disappeared into the house.

Zenobia's hands flew to her face. She twirled round and round, like a fly trapped by a pitcher plant. She sighed. She walked over to me and asked me to stand. When I did, she slapped me hard across the face and said, "You heard her. You will go home and retrieve those seeds." She grabbed Puabi's hand and yanked the baby along after her, Puabi crying out that she had not heard all of my story.

It is too bright and harsh here. I wish only for Turtle's shell, to hide in, to sleep in, while Elohim fixes this very bad mistake of mine.

Aya

"O great gods of the heavens, you who live out your days among the stars and the moon, hearken to my call and bless me, your servant, as I pour this gift upon sacred ground to please you," Cain said. The moon lit up the mountains and valleys of his face.

He and I were standing in front of his temple—his "shining house," as he called it. He stood in the center of a circle of rocks, the dirt swept smooth below him, his body newly washed by the river. A dark stream of liquid poured from the jar in his hand and sullied the earth. It smelled of grapes and carcasses and bitter herbs. I knew not what went into its making; I only boiled it for him.

He thought he was speaking to the city's gods. I knew better.

Cain turned to me. "Thank you, sister, for making this holy wine. You will be blessed because of your efforts."

I snorted. I could not help it.

"I suppose you will be laughing too when my crops are plentiful," he said quietly.

"I know not what the diviner in the city told you, but she does not hold the strings to Elohim's heart, that much I know. Nor does she have the power to make crops grow," I said.

"It is not Elohim I beseech," said Cain.

"You've never before been interested in the gods in the sky," I said.

Cain turned to me. "I noticed the stars and the moon and their paths in the sky, if that's what you mean. I did not know *why* they moved or what it all meant."

"Do you now?" I said.

"No," said Cain. "But if I try very hard to gain the approval of all the gods, I cannot fail. I will have done everything in my power." He stepped out of the circle and began picking up the stones. Then he stopped and heaved a great sigh. "Aya, I do not mean offense, for I know you are of weak constitution, but . . ." His words trailed off like snail slime.

I could not see his face, but I was not stupid. I said, "You want to ask me why Elohim has not healed me, even though I've asked Him to time and time again."

Cain raised up, his shoulders rounded with the weight of the stones. "Yes," he said.

"I have wondered the same thing," I said. "Do you remember what Mother told us about Elohim long ago? That He's *in time*?"

"She is no longer coherent when it comes to the Garden, Aya. You know that, and I know that. I think she dreams more than she lives."

I badly wanted him to understand this, this one thing, because if he could, then I could too, and we would be strengthened in our common knowledge. Two reeds twisted together are stronger than one. "But *in time*—the concept that Elohim can be everywhere at once, in the Garden with Mother and Father, and here with us many years later, and then with our children someday, and theirs after that: Doesn't that mean that time is not important to Elohim? Maybe *my* time is not *His* time."

Cain laughed then. "Our little philosopher. What she lacks in limbs, she makes up for in the head."

I swiveled then, on my good foot, and hobbled back to the lamplight of the courtyard, circling like a moth to the flame, searching for acceptance and not finding it.

"Aya, come now, I meant it only as a jest," pleaded Cain.

His words meant nothing to me.

So I knew full well what I was doing when I cut down Cain's prized dates. Condemn me not; wait until you've heard the complete tale.

Cain had worked long and hard for those luscious orbs. When the male flowers emerged in the spring, they were cut down and tied up to dry. The female flowers emerged weeks later, and Cain—here was the first part of his secret—cut off the center of the flowers so as to get *bigger* fruit, not *more* fruit. Up and down those trees he had to go. It was a wearying and brutal task. Indeed, many days I had to pack poultices around his thorn wounds. Here was the second part of his secret—he knew about flower dust. All be told, it was something Elohim had taught Mother and Father in the Garden, so Cain was not as clever as he'd like you to believe.

When the female flowers bloomed, Cain gathered up the male flowers, full of flower dust, and again made the arduous climb up the female trees. He shivered the male flowers over the female flowers. The dust glittered in the sun and settled like crushed limestone on the waiting female flowers. This was what created the dates.

Then came the wait. And the tending.

For Cain had a third secret. Within weeks, he climbed up again and culled every other pea-size date from the bunch—again to get *bigger* and *better-tasting* dates, not *more* dates.

This was the pact he had made with the city men—to produce bigger and better and juicier dates than they had ever laid eyes on.

He would have succeeded had it not been for me.

Which made me wonder: *What was Cain planning to offer Elohim if he lost the wager and his first fruits went to the city people?* We had all heard about his rash bet after he had returned from the city. Father's angry response was, "If this goes awry, it will affect the whole family." But Cain knew then, beyond a shadow of a doubt, that he would win his wager. He would offer up *some* of his prize dates to Elohim, keep the rest for us—for drying, for sweetening, for eating. Father would get the city's prize—two oxen—and Cain would have the blue-headed flax to plant.

What am I saying?

Two things.

First: Later, while eating our evening repast, Goat became curious and went nosing about in Cain's extra bowl, which Cain was going to use for his temple offering and which he had mindlessly set off to the side, half empty. When Cain realized that Goat's face was deep within the confines of his bowl, he rose up in anger, took a club from his waist, and undercut Goat's hind leg with it—*crack,* it went—and Goat limped away, confused as to why she could walk one moment and not the next. "That damned goat," he yelled.

I gasped. I stood and hobbled toward him as fast as I could manage. I yelled at him.

He stood there and laughed at me. "Faster, Aya, faster."

Father sputtered something into his food, and Mother's hand went to her throat. Naava, the infernal donkey, did nothing, said nothing.

"Why are you so mean?" I screamed. My fists found Cain's chest, and I pummeled him over and over. Inside, I wanted to hurt him. Inside, I wished him dead, like the asp I had killed. But he was bigger and stronger than me. He was unpredictable. Any true revenge would have to be subtle, or a secret.

Not that I could have protected Goat. I should have tied her up. I always do when the sun goes to bed, and I don't know why in this particular instance it had slipped my mind.

To Abel's credit—valiant heart that he is—he rose up from where he was sitting and called out Cain's name, to distract him from me. When Cain turned, Abel's clenched fist hit him square on the nose, sending blood spraying and Cain flying, limbs all askew.

Father startled and stood up, between Cain and Abel, his two fires that needed quenching. "Enough," he said. He turned to me. "Aya, mind your animal." To Cain and Abel, he said, "I will say this once, only once. May Elohim have mercy upon your souls. You are brothers. Blood. Family. Look upon each other."

From then on, the tension between Cain and Abel was like a bowstring, set in place, taut and thrumming.

Mother said only one thing—she certainly knew how to feed the flames! "Never did I imagine such things when I carried both of you. It is better you were never born, if your behavior is such." Her jaw tensed, and sadness seeped like bitumen from her skin.

Aya the Asp Killer wanted to ask Cain why his nose was crooked. Had he joined the ranks of crookedness, of wrongness? Yes, he had, and I was glad for it.

My anger did not emerge fully formed until I had discovered the second thing—that when Cain had, under the rising full moon, poured his holy wine upon the ground, the remains of Turtle were in it. When I went to check on Turtle, he was nowhere to be found. Turtle's hardened legs were there, discarded in a heap, bloodied and limp. Cain had wanted the shell and nothing more. Something of the shell rendered his offering more consecrated, I suppose.

Instantly I was not only angry for myself but for Dara, who would return to find her pet gone, vanished into a useless liquid that simply disappeared into the dry earth like a fleeting thought.

As the stars traveled their courses, I stole Abel's ax made of sharpened flint off the courtyard wall and sneaked off toward the river, where Cain's date palms grew tall and heavy with fruit. The trees' spiky fronds shone in the moonlight. The clusters of dates hung like forbidden jewels.

It was the time of jackals and boars and hyenas, that I knew, but I was the hand of justice, and justice would not be stopped.

I was the hand of Elohim.

He would be grateful to me, His humble and faithful servant, for meting out what Cain deserved. Since Elohim moved *slowly* and *in time,* I could not be sure of a swift reply to Cain's sins; therefore, I would act in His stead, as Aya the Bird, Aya the Crooked, Aya the Asp Killer.

I used Cain's reed sling to shinny up the tree—mind you, this was difficult work, not something to take lightly. Unlike the mornings I climbed up, just to see the sun peep over the top of the horizon and hear the birds set to talking, this time I had other motives. The night was hot. My sweat worked against me, and I feared of losing Abel's ax.

Once up, I could see the gleaming moon path on the river—like a thousand stars fallen to earth—and the dark flutterings of geese and crane and heron, and the occasional screech of something caught and devoured. The air heaved like a dying fish.

I paused.

I thought.

I raised my wrist, my hand holding firmly to the ax handle.

I hacked at those dates.

Fast, faster, fastest. Swift, swifter, swiftest.

I heard the soft thuds of the dates on the ground below. They were squashed and ruined—to be pecked at by the birds, drained by the bees, and dried by the sun's hungry rays.

It took me all night.

You can agree or not agree, if you like.

I am cognizant of one thing, but it does not deter me. You might think I had sealed my family's doom, for I had destroyed the very thing that could bring us sustenance over the long winter months. No dates—no syrup, jam, or cake. No beer sweetener. But do not fear. I am Aya the Resourceful, Aya the Healer. I will come up with a brilliant plan, an ingenious solution.

It was Cain's doing, not mine.

Elohim would be pleased.

Eve

I am familiar with the desert's night sounds—the yips and yaps of the jackals, the scrappy squeals of the fox, the snuffle of beetles and roaches and rats, the screech of bats and owls.

But what I heard that dawn was none of those things.

I was extinguishing the night lamps and sweeping away the detritus of the night—seared moths and crisp butterflies and rat droppings—when I heard a noise that rendered my bones to sand.

Cain's roar gave terror a name, a face. He stood like a massive ox between the posts that marked the courtyard entrance, his large hands wrapped around them so tightly that the muscles in his torso were visibly straining. He groaned with the effort, and his face was twisted into a whirlwind. He bent the posts down and pulled their fibrous roots from the earth. It took me too long to understand what he was yelling: "We've been pillaged!"

I stood in his path. "Cain, what is it? Cain?" I reached out an arm to stop him, but he grabbed it and flung me to the ground. I landed on my elbow and heard the crack of bone. I cried out for Adam to come quickly. My arm went limp, and when I raised up, I found that I could not move it properly.

Cain was a destructive fire scorching a path, an angered badger clawing and scraping. He tore adzes, slings, hoes, and flint daggers off the wall. He overturned the courtyard bench and poured water on Aya's embers.

Anything that could be destroyed, he destroyed.

He had a mind to ravage Naava's weaving too, had she not stood in the doorway, arms blocking his path. "What is *wrong* with you?" she hissed. He reeled away from her, as though he were grasping and clutching at any lucid thought that might blunder into his path, like a witless grazing animal.

"Who will go with me?" he shouted. "Do we stand together as a family, or will you have me do it all?"

If Cain had not been my child, I would not have tolerated his violent moods. But he lived with us, in all his coldness and misery and cruelty, and he was inextricably linked to the fiber of our family, for better or for worse. One might fancy that we were helpless, Adam and I, that we were blinded to the monster set before us, but one would be wrong. An outsider cannot possibly see the slight incremental steps of borderline madness it takes to get to a land in which you arouse your sleeping self and ask, "How did I come to be here, in this place that threatens to tear me limb from limb?"

Aya, dear child, slumbered like a baby through it all. I made a mental note to check on her later, after this debacle. It was not a good time for her to become ill.

I saw Abel and Jacan making haste back to the house, leaning into the thick straps across their foreheads, careful not to spill the fresh milk. Abel's eyes went immediately to Cain, and Jacan looked up at Abel, limbs quaking like dry leaves in the wind. They set the jars down, the milk sloshing over the rims and onto the ground.

Cain pointed at Abel, his finger making large looping circles in the air. "*You* will not go. I know that already." He slid his finger through the air to rest on Jacan. "How about *you*? Will you go with me to protect our family's honor? Our family's good name?"

At Cain's proposal to include Jacan in this mess, I stumbled forward, good arm outstretched. "No!" I said.

Abel put his arm on Jacan's shoulder and pulled his little brother toward him. "Why don't you explain," he said, glaring at Cain, "what it is you're after."

Cain laughed. I did not know if he had been drinking or if he had truly gone mad. "You do not care, shepherd boy. It is not you they want."

Abel's jaw clenched.

With my good hand supporting my ripe belly—for the baby had grown exceedingly heavy over the summer months—I stepped nearer to Cain. "What has happened? Start at the beginning. We are having difficulty following you."

Cain brushed past me, cruelly and unnecessarily.

I stumbled back.

Abel took one step forward, his fists raised.

"Don't," I said. "He is not himself."

"He is more himself now than ever before," said Abel.

Jacan pulled on Abel's belt. "Let's go," he begged. "Father will be angry."

Abel took hold of Jacan's hand and flung it away. His eyes followed Cain's movements, but he stayed where he was. "Why has your face fallen, brother?"

Cain swirled. He spit. He said, "They have come under veil of night and cut down my dates. All of them. You hear me? All of them." He paced like a wild animal contemplating a kill. "They enter into a sacred oath with me, and this is how they assure their victory, by taking the spoils for themselves. They are scoundrels! Infidels! And I shall have my revenge." He smacked his fist into his palm, as if the pummeling had already begun.

Still, Abel did not move, for which I was grateful. I did not understand why our neighbors to the north would do such a thing, especially because we had been bartering and trading with them for weeks now. *Why would they do such a scurrilous thing, when they had to cohabit the plains with us?*

"They are gone?" I asked, incredulous that this was so.

"No, woman," Cain said, using the same disgusting dismissive tactics that Adam used with me on occasion—the flick of a wrist and the word that oozed disdain. "They left them to rot in the sun, to be eaten by the creatures. There is no hope for retrieving them. They will not grow on broken branches." He looked so unprotected and shamed that it broke my heart.

"They want to know my secrets," said Cain.

I bit my lip to keep from saying, *Well, if you hadn't flaunted them . . .*

Cain righted the bench. He sat and put his head in his hands. He began to sob like a child. It was as though he had gone from flame to ember in the space of a few moments.

I went to him, put my good hand on his shoulder. He shoved it away.

"Go," I said to Abel and Jacan. "Go," I said to Naava. "Leave him be."

The other children slunk off to their chores, and I managed to maneuver my body to the ground to kneel at Cain's feet. "Cain," I said. "Why not go to your father and talk about what course of action to take? I fear that a rash action may heap endless sorrow upon us all."

Cain's body was shaking. My mother's heart rose up within me like a spring of water, and I thought, *But he is just a boy.* This realization took me by surprise, for I had forgotten what it was like to hold Cain—suckle him, nurture him, and wipe his face clear of tears. My eyes brimmed with wetness.

When Cain was born, Adam and I were still nomads, inching our way down the winding river toward the great sea to the south. We crossed treacherous terrain, wandering over hill and valley, and although we did not know what we were searching for, we knew we would recognize it when we saw it.

Much of my pregnancy with Cain was excruciating. My body rejected food and water, and there were days I seemed to be more upon hands and knees than upright, moving forward in minuscule amounts. My breasts ached. My skin left purple trails where it stretched translucent over my belly. My legs and ankles swelled, and no amount of rest assuaged my weariness.

I lost track of the days and wondered how long it would take for the birth gates to open and my baby to emerge as a smaller version of Adam or myself. I thought much of my lost child, and I worried that this pregnancy, too, would end tragically.

Adam was sweet. He tore off large fluted leaves and fanned the heat away from my engorged, melonlike body. He brought me new delicious sundries to quench my thirst—cactus milk and rose-hip water and hyssop tea. He stroked my stomach and talked to the growing baby inside. "Little one, your mother and I want to say a few words. Can you hear us?" Then he would press his opened mouth on my skin and moan into the cavern that was my belly.

"You will scare her," I said, laughing.

"Her?" he said. "What about him?"

"What about him?" I said, smiling. "I should like to think a girl would be very nice. A little version of me running about, don't you think?"

"Elohim have mercy on us," he said. "Another one of you? I should go mad."

I hit him playfully on the arm, and he kissed my eyelids.

He told stories to the baby, with his head turned sideways, his good ear resting on my swollen mound. "Can you hear me?" he whispered. "Do you know that you are loved, even before you appear?" Adam's head raised up. The delight in his eyes was obvious. "I think he heard me."

"You mean she," I said.

"Yes, as you wish," he said. He rested his head against me again and continued. "Once upon a time, I was alone"— his words floated, soared in the space above our heads—"in a beautiful, wonderful place, where there were butterflies with gossamer wings, where there was a river that poured over red jasper, where there was a one-armed monkey that ate ants out of my hand, where the flowers were brightly colored and bloomed every day"— here he paused—"and where there was tranquillity and happiness."

"Do you think she understands?" I asked.

Adam didn't answer. His vision hung between us in glorious detail. "It was all Elohim's doing. But Elohim noticed that I was morose, that I needed a friend, much like the animals had. I wanted someone like me. To talk to, to be with. Elohim seemed to understand. So He said to me, 'Sleep, Adam, sleep, and when you wake, you will have your answer.' I fell asleep then, and when I awoke, oh, I cannot describe it, there was the most beautiful creature in the world facing me. She was very much like me, except for these"—he reached up to tweak my breast; I batted his hand away— "and I felt . . . I don't know what I felt, maybe a completion, a satisfied feeling in my belly, that I at last had someone to share *me* with." He was quiet then. The river ran. The birds chirped.

My belly moved.

"Did you feel that?" Adam exclaimed, his head coming away from my skin. "Did you?"

I nodded. "The baby hears your story, and it makes her happy that you love her mother so."

He caressed my face, my hair, my limbs, my swollen tender nipples.

"You are beautiful," he said.

"Me or the baby?" I said.

"You, my darling, my love." His kisses were like honey, his caresses like cool streams of water. I sank in them, drowned in them, and was happy.

That said, I knew not what to expect from the birth. I had vomited profusely and felt extreme cramping with our first child, but I conjectured that this time would be different. My middle had grown as large as a watermelon, and I did not know how we would get the baby child out of me. True, I had seen lambs and kids and cats being born in the Garden and had marveled at how something so big could force itself from its mother—for no male animals had ever given birth, that I had seen. When Elohim had cursed me, He had made pregnancy and childbirth sound so ominous and painful, it frightened me. I discussed this over and over again with Adam, trying to prepare myself for the ordeal that lay ahead.

When the first pains came, I was sleeping. It felt as if Adam had kicked me in his sleep, but no, he was facing the opposite direction, snoring considerably. Again the pain seized me, and I doubled over. *Was this it?* I didn't know.

"Adam," I whispered, sitting up.

Still he snored.

"Adam," I said louder.

A short snort, then Adam turned to face me. "What?" he said.

"I think it's time," I said.

He was quiet for a moment as this sunk in. Then suddenly he was a bundle of quickness. He sat up, rubbed his hands through his hair, and looked at me, at my terrified face. "It's coming out?"

I looked between my legs and back up at my rounded belly. "I don't think so. But it hurts."

Adam put his hand on my stomach. "Here?" he said.

I shook my head and pointed to the area between my legs.

"What shall I do? I mean, what *can* I do?" said Adam. The furrows on his forehead deepened. "Do you need something to eat? Or drink? Some water, perhaps? Maybe you should lie down." He held my shoulders and tried to force me to lie back.

"Stop," I grunted, reaching my hand out. "It feels better to sit up."

"Oh, yes, all right, then," he said. He stood and paced. "Do you wish for me to sit with you, talk with you? What do you want me to do?"

"Be still," I said, laughing. "I just want you near me, in case something bad happens."

Adam sat, but he chewed on the insides of his cheeks. "Do you feel anything now?" he said. "Anything new?"

"No," I said. "I'll tell you when I do."

He nodded, still chewing.

I held his hand, for he seemed to be in more need of it than I.

In the end, after two full days of severe pain, I could bear it no longer. I do not remember if it was morning, noon, or evening. I could not say which lamp—sun or moon—was in the sky, or whether birds were singing my baby's arrival. I squatted in the brush, over a carefully constructed grassy nest, and told Adam to watch closely for any sign of anything.

"Where?" said Adam. "Where do you want me to be?"

"There," I said, pointing and grimacing with the pain of it all.

"Where?" said Adam, fidgeting with his hands.

"Anywhere," I screamed, panting. I pushed then, vaguely noticing Adam's eyes, astonished and hurt, but I could not help it; I was beyond kindness and civility by then. My legs were numb from squatting, and I so desperately wanted to have this thing done with.

I felt a tightness in my groin, then a ripping and a tearing. Through tears, I reached down to feel the slick hardness of a head emerging.

"I see it," said Adam. "Push!"

"I am." I breathed between pushes. Then I was crying, a rainstorm of tears. I felt strangely absent and disconcerted. My body was doing nothing I was telling it to do, and suddenly I was awash in more body fluids than I knew I had. I had defecated with the first push, and as the stench rose up, I was horrified that I had lost all control.

Adam seemed not to mind. "The head is out. Now the shoulders," he yelled. He knelt next to me and reached down to pull the baby out.

I screamed and pushed once more. The baby whooshed out of me, and my body felt hollow and scooped out. I fell back on my bottom, spent.

Amazingly, I was so struck by the miracle of the baby's compact wet body sliding out of my own after such an excruciating length of time that I quite forgave him for the pain he had caused me. I could scarcely see through my tears, though, and as Adam held him up for me to gaze upon— "It's a boy child," Adam said, grinning—I smelled blood and earth and sky, and I was joyous and relieved. I named our boy child Cain, *Ka-yin*, meaning "acquire," as I had acquired him through Elohim.

Within the time it takes for the sun to slide over the edge of the earth, Cain had slid between two worlds—from the warmth of the Garden into the harsh cold of the Garden exterior, just as Adam and I had done, with one significant difference: He had had no choice in the matter.

Adam severed the cord with his teeth and buried the afterbirth behind a yellow-flowering bush. We thought of inviting Elohim to witness this, the sanctified washing of our first child, but we knew He would not come. *Was He watching from behind the bushes and trees? From above?* We knew not.

We washed Cain's dimpled body in the river—oh, how he screeched at the cold of it!—and wiped the crusty matter from his lips. We wrapped him in the dried skins of the ibex. He slept, unaware that we could not stop looking at him—his curly-lidded eyes, his tiny hands like folded petals, his thick shock of black hair. And his features! So small, so perfect!

Every time he cried out or smacked his lips, my breasts would twinge and leak, and I would pull him close, feel him latch on and suck. He made grunting noises and danced his fingertips along my skin.

"May I?" Adam pleaded. It was as though he were jealous of Cain. "I can walk him in my arms. He'll fall asleep. I know he will."

I'd hand him over, and Adam would take off along the river's edge, gazing adoringly at this new son of his. True to his word, he'd return with a sleeping baby, at whom we'd stare in wonder until he woke again, screaming for love and attention.

Cain knew nothing of squatting in the bushes to relieve himself. He went whenever he felt the need, and this posed a problem. He slept between us, and after waking one night covered in his feces, I proposed a new plan. We would collect the fluff within the milkweed pods and mound it together in an absorbent mass. This we would deposit into the center of a small fox skin and bind it to his groin with sinew. In this way we contained his offal for easy disposal and were the cleaner for it.

I knew not how I felt about this new era we were in. I felt hopelessly ignorant and insufficient to care for this writhing bundle of love, especially during the nights full of endless screaming, and I knew these same tacit thoughts plagued Adam as well. When I nursed Cain, I worried that Adam would feel excluded or ignored, so I made him sing to the baby, for he had a beautiful melodious voice that belonged to the moon and the stars and, up until this time, only to me.

The day Cain was gone upon our waking, my terror rose up like the bear I had challenged. We found him soon enough, and I clung to him and could not let him go. He squirmed, he wiggled, and still I would not let him go.

He had learned to scoot on hands and knees, and he did so with alarming speed every chance he got. That morning he had been knee-deep in the river, splashing in the water with his chubby hands, as Adam and I slept. Deer and gazelle had come to drink too and looked at him, amused at the strange sight before them.

When Adam went after him, Cain stepped farther into the river, into a small eddy, and down he went. Adam floundered into the depths and brought him up, gasping.

Needless to say, after that, Adam had to wrest him from me, and I decided that if I could not hold him forever, I would at least be useful. I would spear a fish for both my men. This I did because there was nothing else to do with my agitation. But as I peered into the face of the river, I perceived its darkness and cold cold heart. I was enraged that it looked so serenely back at me, almost willing me to fold, to crumble underneath its wicked gaze. *I would take your child*, it whispered, *and you would be helpless.*

With a frustrated cry, I thrust my spear deep into its belly, wishing it to die, but instead, as I yanked the spear out with a wrenching gasp, I saw that I had pierced a carp and that its eyeballs jerked and its body flailed, and I sat down on the riverbank to let my tears flow.

That was all I could do.

All any mother can do when she realizes she has no control over this new and frail and shining goodness.

She sweats, she worries, she prays, she keens, she kneels, she questions, she protects, she argues, she cries, she creates, she talks, she sees, she touches, she listens, she loves, she repents, she remembers.

After all, she is a mother.

When Cain had lived eleven moons, Adam and I found a quiet patch of river purling in a cove where the water basked like a sun-baked lizard. As I walked along the shore, searching for just the right spot, Adam stood waist-deep in the water, waiting.

I carried a wiggling Cain in my arms. I had no idea if this would work, or if Cain would ever trust us again. Something had to be done, though, to protect him, because he had no fear of the water, no fear of its raging possibilities. Each time we freed him from the carrier we had made out of wood and vines, he made a dash for the water, oblivious to its danger.

"Ready?" I said.

Adam nodded.

I adjusted Cain in my arms and held him out in front of me at arm's length, so he couldn't cling to me. Still his little fists scrabbled for my skin. I looked at him, my precious baby, as I waded into the water. I wondered whether I could possibly do this awful thing. He cried then, his face bunching up like cauliflower.

"Here," said Adam.

I tossed him into the water near Adam. His body disappeared into the river's jaws with hardly a splash.

"Can you see him?" I said, instantly frightened. Before Adam could answer, Cain's little head emerged. He coughed and sputtered and clawed at the air.

"Good boy," cooed Adam. "Move your arms. Move your legs."

Cain dipped under again. When he broke through the second time, his little eyes were blinking madly; he was reaching for Adam, wondering why his father wouldn't pick him up, wouldn't help him. His arms churned the water. His mouth opened to gulp in air.

"Grab him," I cried. It was all too much.

"He'll learn," said Adam. "Just wait."

"No, get him now," I said. I started toward Adam and my bobbing blue-faced baby. "Please, he will drown. Look, he can't breathe."

"Be patient," said Adam. He reached out to right Cain in the water.

Cain grabbed at Adam's arm and held on, his little fingers like bean tendrils.

Adam peeled his fingers free, and he floated away again. This time, though, Cain started to paddle with his arms and legs, like a tadpole that's just gotten its limbs.

"Cain, baby, come here," I said. I clapped my hands. I smiled.

Cain held up his chin and sucked in his lips. He was working hard but going nowhere.

I cheated and inched closer. I held out my arms.

"You're not helping," said Adam. "He has to do this on his own."

"Come, baby, come to Mama," I said.

Cain's face was so determined, so petrified, it broke my heart.

After a few tense moments he began to find his rhythm, the proper cadence of flailing limbs, to aid him in moving forward.

I reached down and pulled him up into my arms, to hold him close. He melted into me, his body slack, his head resting on my shoulder.

"That worked better than I thought it would," said Adam, coming up out of the water.

"He's concocting some scheme now to get back at us," I said. I still feared for my child. I knew not whether Elohim would require the life of this child too from me.

Adam didn't answer. He wrapped his wet arms around me, and we stood there, exhausted with all the questions, aware that we were—like Cain was to us—Elohim's children, floundering in the torrent of life. *When would He reach out and pull us from it? When would we have learned enough?*

Naava

Well, the little sister came home in a flurry of donkeys, jewels, glorious linens, and curtained platforms. She brought with her clouds of dust and the clatter of visitors.

Accompanying her were two women of the city, Zenobia and A-something-or-other, and their two annoying children—Puabi the dark-eyed and Shala the disobedient. Naava tried to pronounce their tongue-twisting names to prove she was not an idiot, but it was nearly impossible.

Naava noticed that Aya stayed in the shadows, not wanting a repeat of the unpleasantness that had greeted her when the women first visited. Amusing, given that when Aya heard of Cain's dates, she was crazy enough to insinuate that she herself would ride to the city alone to arrange a peaceful compromise.

Of late, Aya had been acting stranger than usual, constantly going to the river to wash and wincing when she sat or stood. Eve, despite her own hurt arm, had offered to take over the cooking for a while to ease Aya's workload, but Aya insisted nothing was wrong, that she was fine and not to mind her. Cain laughed when Naava told him what Aya intended to do. "They would take one look at her and drive her beyond the walls, out to where the lepers are kept."

The women from the city disembarked from their conveyances first, then reached behind to catch their girls and to swing them to the ground.

They bowed to Eve with a strange deference, Naava thought. The women's splendidly colored robes billowed about them in the wind—how *did* they get those colors? They kissed Eve's good hand, the other being bound up because of Cain's shove a week ago. Their girls kissed Eve too and bowed low to the ground. They offered up gifts—an exquisite box inlaid with the pearlish glint of dried shells, a drinking cup made of pink metal forged in a fire, and bracelets set with breathtaking stones.

Dara was next. She descended from her platform, half a finger taller than when she left. Her eyes—oh, what had she done? They were black-rimmed like tigers' eyes, and her hands—*her hands!* They were adorned with reddish-brown curliques and circles and flowers, and her hair had been dyed like Naava's wool, glossy and shiny brown. And look! There upon Dara's nose. She wore a stone—was it turquoise or lapis lazuli? When had she acquired it? Ah, Eve would not approve, being the woman of decorum and simplicity that she was. Oh, and see there, upon Dara's toes, tiny shiny rings that made her feet dance in the sunlight.

Naava decided she would enjoy Dara and Eve's reunion immensely.

But, no.

With only a barely visible froglike blink, Eve embraced Dara with her good arm and hugged her tight without once saying anything at all about her atrocious appearance—well, not *atrocious* exactly, maybe *ostentatious* or *pretentious*. Eve kissed Dara on both cheeks and said, "My little butterfly, you are back. I have missed you."

Dara handed Eve a lumpy sack. She said, "Because you lost the other one."

Eve worked the top open and peered in. She smiled and glanced quickly at Aya, then back at Dara. "Thank you, my child. What a sweet gift."

Well. That was the way the river flowed. The little sister went and got beautified, while the older daughter, the more responsible one—the one who clothed this family, in fact!—stayed at home and cared for the ailing mother. Yes, this was how it always was. The river did not flow uphill, unless buckets were used or a dam was built.

Naava *was* building a dam, of sorts, that would help her get upriver toward the city. The Garden robe, after all, would have no equal. Naava would work harder and longer, until her fingers blistered and bled and fell off.

Never before would anyone have seen anything like it, and never again would they. It would be a splendid cataract, a gush of heaven, a wash of joy. They would say, *Oh, dear Naava, your radiance and beauty are unmatched. The stars and moon bow down before you. They shine only for you. Please, sit, so we may look at you, admire you, and give you sweet and succulent things to eat.*

Dara turned and saw Naava. "Naava," she said, and held out a small wooden box, plump birds carved on all sides.

Naava was surprised at Dara's confidence. *What was she playing at, the little imp?*

Naava took the box. "Thank you," she said.

"Open it," said Dara, clapping her hands.

Naava wiggled the lid free, and there inside was an opened mussel shell, holding a black substance resembling pitch.

Dara giggled. "Do you like it?"

Naava glared at her. "What do I want with a lump of bitumen?"

Dara's smile faded. "It's kohl. You put it around your eyes, like this . . ." She made to grab the box from Naava, but Naava swung it away from her.

Ah, so it was a prettifier.

"I know what it is," Naava said.

Dara's hands were by her sides now. "I can show you how to put it on."

"There's no need," Naava said. Inside, she was shouting, *Yes, amen!* She would shine like the midday sun and blossom like the lilies of the field.

Dara stepped forward and motioned for Naava to bend down. She had a secret. She whispered into Naava's ear, "The prince says to come visit him. You're supposed to stand by the copper makers, so Balili in the white robes can see you. He will go get the prince, and you will go to the meeting place."

Naava was stunned. Here was the little sister *helping* her. *Oh, joy! What would she wear? When could she go?*

The women motioned Dara back to them, and she returned to their side. The strange girl, the one with the black-rimmed eyes, clung to her mother's robes like a vine. The other, Shala was her name, was a wild hornet. She had already broken a wooden stirring spoon by banging it over and over again on the bench's edge, and Aya had already scuttled out of the shadows to wrench it away from her. Then Shala disappeared into the pantry, and Naava grinned, knowing that she would encounter Aya's wrath.

The women uttered their strange throaty words, and Dara answered back in kind. *How had Dara learned their words so quickly?* Naava wanted to know. *That could have been me.*

The women smelled of sweet spices and perfumes. If only Naava knew what they mixed to get that scent, she could smell delicious too, and Cain would be drawn to her like a bear to honey. The prince—he had said he wanted to see *her!*—would come to her like an ant to dates.

The women pushed Dara forward, toward Eve. Dara said, "They want you to come to their New Year's celebration, to honor Inanna, the Queen of Heaven." When Eve looked confused, Dara said, "It's their harvest festival."

The woman who held her nose in the air, as if to say all this squalor was beneath her, added a few more phrases to what Dara was saying.

Dara said, "Ahassunu says that your presence would be most appreciated."

Again, Naava was strangely aware that the *A*-woman seemed to eye her mother with more than a general interest, as if Eve were someone special, someone deserving. And try as she might, she could not figure out why.

Eve nodded and brought her hand up to her cheek, and asked, "When?"

Dara babbled to the women. They babbled back.

Dara said, "At the harvest's full moon."

Eve grasped at her ears, her arms, at their bareness, feeling plain compared to these spangled women. "Yes, yes," she said, almost absentmindedly. Naava saw her begin to plan her attire, consider all the things that would have to be done before that day.

Then Dara clapped her hands and added, "They say I can come home then, to be with you until the baby comes. Then I have to go back."

"Oh, I'm glad. Thank them for me." Eve bowed slightly, smiling. "Oh, what am I thinking?" She turned to the shadows of the interior of the house and called, "Aya, darling, will you bring a little wine and barley bread . . . ?" Then, remembering, "Oh no, that won't do. Dara, will you go help your sister?"

Right then there was a sharp cry from the pantry, and the haughty woman ran, calling out Shala's name in a worried tone.

Shala stomped out into the sunlight, rubbing her arm. Her bottom lip was curled out, and she said something in a pouty voice and pointed back to the pantry.

Her mother peered into the cool darkness of the house's depths and took a step forward.

"Dara, please," said Eve, shooing Dara toward the pantry. To the women, she said, "Why don't you sit here in the shade and cool off?" She waved them toward the reed mats in the shade of the eaves.

The women sat, with their girls at their sides. There was nothing to discuss, or rather, there was everything to discuss, with Cain's disaster the other night and his ongoing imprecations against the city, but with Dara gone to help Aya, there was no one to translate.

Naava used her time wisely. She studied the women's almond eyes and noted how they had painted all around the edges and even extended the lines past the outer corners. By doing so, they made them appear more open and the whites whiter than Eve's or her sister Aya's. Their hands were decorated like Dara's—flowers and loops and dots and swirls that stretched the length of each thin finger and culminated in an elaborate design on the back of each hand. When they spoke, their gestures were like flapping wings, their jewelry like light upon the sea. Their large full lips were stained the color of grapes. Naava knew then that her own were pale and thin like willow leaves.

Naava began to dream of how she would transform herself, in body and mind, for the New Year's celebration. She would outshine Inanna herself on Inanna's glorious celebratory day. The prince would see Naava as something unattainable, and she would make him beg for crumbs, for the scraps of her love. Cain would be insanely jealous, of course, and he would lap at her too, like waves upon the shore, but she would not care.

Dara brought out trays of figs and barley bread and wine, stumbling under the load. Eve bustled about, arranging the platters and cups before the women, assuring that they were well taken care of. Still, the women looked at her with a sort of reverence that puzzled Naava. *What did they want from Eve? Who did they think she was?*

Naava itched to tell them of Eve's weaknesses and how every day Eve talked about how she would not live to see the next day, so sorrowful was her life. *Couldn't these women see how hopeless Eve was, how truly wretched?* When Naava was right there in front of them. Naava, who was not at all like Eve, and never would be.

Aya

Rocks fascinate me, especially the ones that have captured the trace of a limb or a wing or a carapace of a living creature gone before. I mourn the creature's loss, for it did nothing to deserve its dying, except to be someone's meal, or to be trapped without food or water, or to have simply lived out its days. It did not ask to be squeezed between layers of mud, to heave that last sigh, or to leave its delicate imprint upon the compacted earth.

I find very few pure rocks; they are usually conglomerates of various materials. Limestone is riddled with pockets of silica and clay and feldspar. Chalcedony has crystallike fibers of gray and white running through its opaque body. Even the sand upon the river's shore is muddled with a finer silt and a gray-flecked salt that I collect on a regular basis, to pack the fish we catch.

My point, for I do have one, is that nothing is pure or without guile. It is not a fact that the city people are good and Mother and Father are bad, as Cain would have us believe. There is a mixture of good and bad in both, just as there is in each one of us.

In this way, Cain has told small, insignificant lies to himself over and over again, until over time he has grown to believe this compounded lie and has begun to live accordingly. He has held Mother and Father up in the palm of his hand and said, "They are bad," and he has immediately dismissed *everything* they have taught us. About the city people, he has proclaimed, "They are good," and he has persisted in copying every aspect of their worship, their attire, even their tongue. He has seemed unaware of the sour and sweet within his own body. If something goes awry, it is *they* who are the problem, not *him*.

I am aware that the same could be said of me. That I pray to Elohim to heal my foot, then turn a blind eye to the fact that He has not placed His hand upon it to right its inversion. I do not lie to myself, though. I do not blame my abnormality for my station in life. I do not expect compensation for the weaknesses He gave me. In other words, I will accept His verdict, once it comes.

What next, Aya?

Well, once Cain knew we were invited to Inanna's harvest festival, he began scheming in earnest, preparing his revenge for the destruction of his dates. I confess: I have eavesdropped on his conversations with Naava. Mother and Father know nothing, and I have found it difficult not to mention it. After all, it will affect our whole family, for good or bad, depending on the severity of his actions.

Cain does not suspect me for the date slaughter. I have been careful to hide my swollen and scratched legs and have not asked for any special dispensations to get out of work. Despite myself, I do feel sorry for him. It is going to take a catastrophic event to jolt him from his wayward path.

Dara, my sweet sister, came for a visit. My, she had changed. I almost didn't recognize her. Aside from the painting upon her limbs and the addition of jewelry, she seemed distracted and edgy. She wasn't the calm child who left here almost two moons ago.

When I told her about Turtle, I simply said that Turtle had died and that I had buried him in the ground—which, in a way, was true. Poor Dara, the stricken look on her face drove an arrow into my heart. She asked if he had felt pain, and I told her no, though how was I to know that? I was grateful she didn't ask to see where he was buried.

At one point, Dara untied a braided red wool bracelet, knotted with numerous agates, from her wrist and handed it to me.

"For you," she said. "You put your fingers here, see, and you're sup-posed to chant something over each one. Like this—" She wrapped her fingers around one of the knotted stones. She looked away from me, as though to some faraway place. "Make my leg whole." She moved to the next stone, still not meeting my eyes. "Make my leg whole." She would have continued this way if I had not stopped her.

"Who are you talking to?" I said.

"The gods," she said. "It's magic."

I grabbed her arm and said, "Dara, you cannot do that. Why, if Elohim found out, He'd be furious. Do you remember what I told you in the garden?"

Dara looked on the verge of tears. "Yes, but—"

"No," I said, wrenching the bracelet from her hands. "You cannot be like Cain. You must talk only to Elohim. Elohim! Do you hear me?"

She looked away, confused.

"Dara. Look at me. Do not listen to those women. They know nothing about how the earth and heavens were made. They know nothing about Elohim."

"They're nice ladies," said Dara, nervously playing with her fingers and scuffing her sandals in the dirt.

"I'm sure they are," I said, placing the back of my hand against her cheek. "But I cannot bear the thought of you being hurt."

She looked up at me, her bottom lip sucked in. "What would Elohim do to me?" she said.

Bless her heart, they had made her fearful of what the gods could do to her.

"Elohim loves you, just like He loves Mother and Father," I said.

"And Jacan too?" she said.

I nodded. "Jacan too," I said.

Thank the moon and the stars that Jacan was there. He had corralled her right away, when he and Abel returned early from their day in the fields, beaming at the sight of her and calling her to him. He had harvested a basket full of round gray nicker seeds from the vines in Mother's garden and made up a little game of skill with them. Dara did not have time at first, with all the translating she had to do and the serving of food in my stead, but she got her chance to sit and play with her twin near the end of her visit, after the women and their girls had finished eating. The women had asked to see Mother's garden. At the precise moment that Dara translated the word *garden*, Mother's face sparked to life, and she stood quickly, motioning for the women to follow her.

Dara hung back, chewing her fingernails.

Mother called for her. "Dara, I need your words."

Dara shook her head. "They only want to look," she said. She pressed her fingers against her teeth to get the last bit of nail.

The women and their children ambled out of the courtyard after Mother, moving toward the humming bees and bursting colors. I knew our guests would come back changed, altered somehow, for the garden held special powers, medicinal qualities, which relaxed the limbs and refreshed the mind.

That left me with Dara and Naava. And Jacan, who had been waiting patiently for his sister. While Dara and Jacan played the seed game, I cleaned up the dishes.

Still, Dara did not laugh at Jacan's jokes, nor did she even try to beat him at his game. Her detachment surprised me. She and Jacan had always been as tight as the burrs in Goat's hair.

Naava sat quietly, plaiting her hair. She was dreaming of blackened eyes and perfumed skin and blushing cheeks, I knew. Always this with Naava. Thinking only of herself.

I do not think I could care for the children Dara watches. They are like whirlwinds, circling up out of nowhere and utterly uncontrollable. I don't see how she does it. I would have slipped a little something into their drinks by now, to ease them into a deep, comfortable slumber.

The kind heart that he is, Jacan must have given his nicker seeds to Dara to take with her, for when she was pulled back up into the curtained platform, after the women and their children, I saw a bag, lumpy with seeds, tied to her robe's sash.

I waved then, happy to know that she would take a piece of home with her into that inhospitable environment.

I had forgotten to ask if she had stayed clear of the men. She had said nothing, so perhaps the women were indeed protecting her.

At least Father and I are in agreement on one thing. The despicable red clay goddess, sky-blue eyes and all, must be destroyed.

Poor Dara didn't know any better. She'd heard fewer stories about Elohim than we older ones had. You might say that Cain and Abel and Naava and I had had Elohim imprinted upon our foreheads by Mother and Father, which made it all the more troubling that Cain had been so quick and so bold to question and contradict our parents—although maybe it was not so strange to test the validity of an abstract notion. Mother had taught us all to pray, certainly, but in an irregular fashion, on the rare occasions she had said she could actually *feel* the presence of Elohim. Abel's instruction, after my near-disaster on the mountain— "Elohim hears the brokenhearted"—was much clearer than Mother's. It seemed more authentic, more heartfelt. Easier.

Elohim had also told Mother that she should never stop questioning, that you are dead, once you do. I think this was much of the reason my parents had tolerated Cain's erratic thoughts.

Oh, that goddess was a wedge among us.

After Dara left, Mother held up the goddess and asked me, "My eyes . . . they are really this color?"

I nodded.

She smiled at me. "Yours, too. I always thought you had the look of the sky to you. You were the only one." She added softly, "My little bird."

So she knew about Aya the Bird. Aya the Goat Owner. Aya the Asp Killer. How I was going to fly away from here, on golden wing, with the sun and wind upon my face. How I would be perfect one day.

Instinctively, my hands went to my face, to my eyelids and eyelashes. Oh, I could not feel the blueness. It was only a gesture of happiness, that I was like my mother in some way.

The feeling passed quickly.

Mother sighed deeply, put her hand on her swollen belly, and waddled out of the courtyard toward Cain's god house.

I watched her as I worked, for I was prepared to destroy this evil thing that had infiltrated our house. You might ask why I had not destroyed Cain's praying figurines yet, when I had so rapidly disposed of Mother's first goddess, but you would have to understand, I care not what happens to Cain. I *do* care what happens to Mother. She knows better. She has seen Elohim with her own eyes.

I tell you this: For her first indiscretion—a simple term for a simple deed—she was thrown out of the Garden and made to enter an unforgiving world. What would it be for her second—well, third, if you counted the first time she prayed to the alabaster goddess? Severance from the family she loves? Banishment from earth? Where else could she be sent?

I fear for Mother. She is not right in the head if she thinks that Elohim will turn a blind eye and deaf ear to her. He gave her life; He expects her heart. Something received for something given. I am not so stupid to think Mother can be forced to love. I only wonder why she cannot love Him.

Mother stood before Cain's abominable temple and contemplated the myriads of folded-handed figurines Dara had made for our foolish and misguided brother. They were a tiny sea before the temple. She bent at the waist to stroke their heads and eyes. She set the red goddess in the midst of them, so that it appeared that the others were paying homage to this new figure.

For a long time, she stood there, doing nothing.

The nightly meal was in its final preparations when I first saw Mother lift her hands to her lips, fold them, and mouth a few words. I abandoned my cooking pot and my baking bread and hobbled toward her. "No," I cried. "Stop."

Startled, Mother looked up.

"Do not do this thing," I said, coming up to her. "Please. Just because Cain believes it to be true does not mean it is. You have seen Him. You know Him to be real. You do not know about these other gods." I could not hide my contempt. "You are praying to baked *dirt*."

"What about Lucifer?" she said. "He could have been another god."

"If so, he was a bad one," I said. "He convinced you to hurt Elohim."

"What if there were other gods but Adam and I didn't meet them?" said Mother.

Anything was possible. "Elohim said *He* made the world. He said nothing about anyone else helping Him. Did you not say this?"

"Yes," said Mother, looking down at her feet.

"Maybe this is a test," I said, "to see if you will be loyal to Him."

"I'm weary of tests," said Mother. "I want Him to show Himself again."

"But you didn't believe in what He said then, when He *did* show Himself," I said. "What makes you think you'll believe Him now?"

Mother said nothing. She looked up and saw Father approaching from the irrigation ditches. "Say nothing to your father about this," she said hurriedly. "He would not understand."

I could not stop myself. "Mother," I cried out. "You *know* Elohim is real, do you not? You *know* He exists."

She looked at me sharply, then drew me into her arms. "Oh, Aya, my sweet child," she said. "Elohim would have loved you. You ask all the questions He would have wanted to answer."

"He loves me now, does He not?" I said.

She pushed me from her and held fast to my shoulders. Her breath came in agitated spurts. She searched my sky eyes for clouds. "Aya, I do not want to shake your faith in Elohim. That is not my purpose. It is me I worry about—that I cannot hear Him, that I cannot see Him. I relive these things—turn them over and over again in my mind—day and night, and still I know not why Adam and I were expelled so . . . so *definitively* from His presence. For eating one small piece of fruit? I know not why He has been so harsh with us." She hugged me again, holding me tight. "I do not have parents as you do, and I wish to have someone who adores *me*, wants to be with *me*." She paused, then said, "You know I love you, do you not?"

I nodded, my face pressed against her bosom. *But do you love me just as much as the others?* I wanted to cry out. *Do you love me even though I am not whole? Or do you love me because I'm not whole?*

"You have Father," I said, my voice muffled in Mother's robes.

She released me. "Yes," she said. "I have him." She held out her hand for me to take, and I did. We went back to the courtyard, mother and daughter, where my pot had boiled over and my bread was burned.

Later, after a hastily prepared repast of overcooked stew, crispy barley bread, goat's milk, and grapes, Father asked if I wanted to play the star game with him. It was something we had done from the time I was little. I had started making up stories about the stars and how they moved across the skies, and he had found it funny and had joined me upon occasion.

It was the time of no moon, which was the perfect time for viewing stars but the worst time for finding our path. We had to go out a ways from the courtyard, because the lamps' halos washed out the starlight. Fireflies, like dying embers, dangled, blinking in the air. Father carried a flint dagger in case of ambush, and I carried several pieces of fig leather to chew on. We went slowly, listening for animals, feeling for familiar plants.

We found a weedy knoll, not easy in this dry weather, and Father beat it down with a stick to clear the area of snakes and rats. Then we lay down upon it, with our faces turned to the sky. I lay on Father's right side, so he could hear my voice.

"There," I said, when I had oriented myself. The sky stretched out like an upside-down bowl sprinkled with salt. I pointed. "See? The Scorpion. That is its tail, and there is its stinger."

"Yes," said Father. "I see."

"And there," I said. "The Cart in the Sky. And its sister Little Cart. I wonder how far away they are from us? They move like the sun and moon, except slower—"

"Aya," said Father. His hand searched for mine. "Aya."

"Yes," I said. I held his hand tight. It was rough like bark, and it engulfed mine.

"Your mother," he said. "I'm worried about her."

I was flattered, truly, that he would confide in me, but there was another part of me that wanted to scream, *I cannot take care of everyone.* But I listened dutifully and heard the anguish in his voice. I could not see his face. It was too dark.

"Has she said anything to you at all?" he said.

"She has a new goddess," I said.

"A new goddess?" His question raised up at the end, like the Scorpion's tail, alert and ready. He squeezed my hand.

"Dara brought it from the city," I said. I knew Father had been disappointed to learn he had missed Dara's surprise visit. He had seen the dust clouds approaching, but he had assumed it was Cain returning from the city.

"So it's just a gift," said Father, an edge of relief in his voice.

"She prayed to it," I said.

"She must have been talking to herself." I could hear the clipped urgency in his voice.

"I don't think she believes in Elohim anymore," I said.

"That can't be," breathed Father. "Maybe it's being with child."

"She thinks she's going to die," I said. "She says she cannot hear Elohim."

"But none of us can," said Father.

"Abel and Jacan do," I said. "I think I have—in Mother's garden and on the mountain."

Father was silent.

In that moment I felt a kinship with my father as never before—maybe because we saw eye to eye on Mother. Though I hated myself later for doing so, I spilled my heart. "I have prayed to Elohim to heal me," I started. "Either He's not listening, or He's not there." I rushed on. "I can understand someone like me doubting, but Mother? Who has *seen* Elohim and *talked* to Him?"

Father sighed. "It is a difficult thing, this Elohim. . . . You're right, we did see Him and talk with Him—He was *with* us there, in the Garden. And then, after eating of the forbidden fruit, everything changed, like that"— he snapped his fingers—"and we were thrown from His presence to wander in this place, this place far from Him, so desolate." He let go of my hand. "I sometimes wonder, although I don't tell your mother this, why Elohim created us, if He knew He could lose us someday. We couldn't have possibly known how our decision to eat of the fruit would be so significant, for it *was*. Everything conspires against us, it seems."

"Even my crookedness," I added. I did not want Father to forget me in his list. It was important that I be included in his list of Elohim's wrongs.

"What is He waiting for?" said Father.

"Do you pray to Him?" I asked.

"All the time," said Father.

"What do Abel and Jacan have that we don't have?" I said.

"Sheep and goats," said Father, laughing.

I laughed too. It was good to speak like this, since Father and I rarely talked with such abandon and pointedness. Granted, Father prayed to Elohim before every meal, but that was a routine thing he did—like me kissing the bread I had made—not something that directly addressed the nature of Elohim. "I have thought about it," I said. "I think it's their heart. Their state of mind. They simply believe, and so they hear."

"But remember," said Father, "Elohim encouraged questions."

"Yes," I said. "I know not what to think of that."

On the way back to the courtyard, we passed Cain's temple, and Father plucked up the red goddess from the middle of all the praying statues and smashed her with the heel of his sandal. Her shards lay scattered upon the ground the morning after, and I gathered up her blue stone eyes. Blue eyes just like mine. Perhaps I shall add them to my rock collection. Perhaps I shall ask Elohim why He does not defend Himself against these invading sky gods.

Why, Elohim, do you not speak for Yourself?

I cannot take care of everyone.

I have had time to think since I punished my brother. I have been thinking that maybe I have it all wrong about Elohim. Maybe He sent us Cain for a reason. Maybe He sends us trials and tribulations to squeeze and mold us into something better—of course, I'm aware that sounds as though I *desire* punishment and hardship, and most certainly I do not! Anyone who possesses an ailment or suffering not of her choosing will know what I mean.

Maybe it is like date syrup.

I am fond of it, as you can see by my pantry. This makes it all the more tragic that I had to be Elohim's right hand and punish Cain, because this means a meager store of dates for the winter. I point this out only because I want you to know that my heart is good. I want to do the *right* thing, not necessarily the *convenient* thing.

Enough of my ethics. I, Aya, am not of a habit to shout my goodness to the world.

Usually, when Cain's dates are ripe, I lay them in flat baskets made of palm fronds and weigh them down with some of Dara's heavier clay pieces. Underneath, I set out bowls to collect the run-off juices, as clear as honey, which thicken after sitting in the sun for several days. The date syrup is versatile. I use it as a sweetener for beer, a syrup for meats, or a nectar served with bread. They are fantastic delicacies, all good, and all born from the destruction of the dates. So glorious is the end result that Abel comes back to the house, instead of sleeping out on the steppes, just to get a taste of the syrup. This pleases me, of course, for I am quite fond of Abel.

Back to the date syrup. Do the dates like to be pressed? I know not.

What if we are like dates, and Elohim *allows* us to be pressed, to exude a lovelier substance?

What I am trying to work out in my head is the *reason* that Elohim seems not to care about our predicaments and disasters, as if He is biding His time for our purification or our distillation, so that *then* He can pay heed to us.

I think, rather, that He *does* care.

But He is helpless to intervene, since we have insisted that we want to live life on our own terms.

PART THREE

Strangers
in the
Sky

Eve

Who is calling me in my dreams, my restless dreams? There are dead things from the deep and alive things from the sky, all crying, aching, moaning, creaking with pain, then a prolonged silence and, in the distance, Elohim sings of loneliness and comfort. "Look at the flowers," He says.

I do. They are so radiantly purple, lined with fine yellow hairs. It pains me to look at them.

"Listen to the hawk," He says.

I do. The hawk utters a shrill high-pitched sound, wheels and circles, floats on the air, its wings spread as a hallelujah, a praise to flying.

"Feel the wind," He says.

I do. I turn my face into the breeze and feel my hair swept off my forehead and away from my cheeks. I feel its cool hand upon my neck.

I become the sun, full of light and understanding. My heart brims with wonder, and I lick its sweetness from my lips. This is everything I have forgotten, everything I have left behind. I recognize this place, its radiance, its joy, and I open my arms to it, to embrace it. To embrace Elohim. To my dismay, I have nothing to offer Him. My hands are empty, my heart too. I am a jar that needs filling, a cup that needs overflowing. I am stripped by uncertainty, anger, and despair, and I am nothing.

I cry out in exhaustion. I cry out in fear.

"Eve," He says. "Eve, my child."

I fall to my knees, too weak to stand. I am tired, and I pant after this thing called death, the sublime sleep of the animals and plants and my babies.

It ends too soon. I make my stunned entrance into awakeness, into this monotonous world. My eyes fill with tears. To see and feel such beauty, and have it fade like stars in the morning light, floods me with grief. Oh, I know, you grow weary of my complaints. I will not journey forever in the dark.

I relate these things because you must know my travails during that summer—why I did not give credence to my sons' arguments, why I did not see Aya's struggles, and why I did not feel Naava's pain.

There was light ahead for me, despite the fact that one of my sons would kill the other. Yet so much rested upon my bowed shoulders. I could not forgive myself for it.

The longings in my heart had intensified, and I began to find refuge in the garden that Adam had built for me.

Let me inquire of you: Have you ever felt an urgent *pressing* feeling underneath your breastbone, right there in the middle of your chest, whispering to you that something in your life is missing? That there is something *out there* that will fill it and make it whole again? And then, in an unexpected moment, you behold the plains opening up after a rain, in every imaginable color under the sun, and you are simply astonished that it could be so. You have to close your eyes; the splendor of it is too much to take in.

Or am I alone in this?

There in my garden, I told Him everything that came to mind—of my own ineptitudes in raising my children, of the growing hostility between Abel and Cain and how I was fearful that it would end badly, and yes, even of Dara's goddess, the one who promised fecundity, and how I was uncertain if she was necessarily bad if she could help me through my agonizing pregnancy.

I told Him all this and more. I was certain that, for all my reasonableness and forthrightness, He would answer.

He *had* to answer.

When I thought of the vastness of the stars and the planets and the sun and the moon, I wondered how He could remember such a trivial thing as me. There it was again: that deep sorrow that oozed through everything in those days.

Whenever I felt this way, I remembered the sweet gift of Abel.

Abel's birth was a nightmare far worse than Cain's. In fact, he got caught feetfirst in my birthing canal, which Adam and I knew nothing about, having never seen such a birth in the Garden, and despite having recently formed a small herd from the wild goats and sheep that we had found wandering upon the plains.

We had been drawing nearer to the sea. Cain's constant exuberance had made our animals skittish and shy, and he had turned his attention away from them. His excitement was growing with the increasing variety of plants the farther south we traveled, and he collected seeds constantly, from pods and fruit and such, and was already planning his crops for when we settled. We talked of this often, how good it would feel to just *stop*.

When my labor pains began, I continued to walk, thinking that it would be better not to think about it. This lasted all of one morning. Then I could go no farther.

Adam took Cain to play in the dirt nearby, and I squatted to relieve the pressure. But the pain persisted and soon grew so ferocious that I cried out for death to take me—Adam told me this later; I remember it not. I was sweating, and my suffering came in horrible paralyzing waves. I thought my body would rip wide open.

Cain built up sand hills, then demolished them with his hands. He called for Adam to play with him, and each time Adam barked, "I'm busy." I had not the presence nor the energy to correct Adam or to relieve Cain's fears.

"Please," I gasped to Adam. "You must make it come out."

Adam's breathing was quick. He looked to be in as much pain as I was. "What do you want me to do?" he said.

I screamed again, for my belly seized up. "Do *something*," I said. I looked down, looking for a sign of something, anything. "Can you see it?"

Adam shook his head. "Nothing," he said.

I lay back on my buttocks and elbows. "Reach in," I said. "Pull it out."

Adam said, "Maybe we should wait."

"Do it," I yelled.

"Try to relax," Adam said.

Cain began to cry. "I can't do this, Adam," I said, tears dripping off my own chin and nose. "You have to help me."

Adam looked at me tenderly then, and I saw that his fear was for me, not for the baby. He positioned himself at my opening and he reached inside, at first a little ways, then more.

The pain was unbearable. I held my breath. I saw him draw in his lips. "What is it?" I gasped.

"I cannot feel it," he said.

"Higher!" I felt wrung out, limp, even though every part of me was straining.

He did, then he laughed, more out of relief than happiness. "I have a foot," he said. "I cannot—" He grimaced. "I've got it. The other foot. I am going to pull," he said. "Lay back."

I began to push in earnest. I wanted my child out, and I could think of nothing else. Not even the baby's safety or aliveness.

With a large wrenching, Adam pulled. I bore down.

And with a large sucking sound, Abel was born. The cord was wrapped around his little neck, and he was turning blue. Adam loosened the cord's grasp and gently shook Abel. "Wake up, little one," he said. Adam's eyes were red, and his nose was running. "Wake up."

Abel cried then, a squall of distress and unhappiness, and my own happy tears flowed. I had borne another living child.

My first glimpse of my baby was a blurred one, stolen through copious tears.

"Well, then," said Adam. "You've got yourself another boy."

"We should name him Abel, *breath*." I stared at my boy child, small and wrinkled. "For it is but a breath that separates him from us and Elohim, life and death." I raised up on my elbows. "Give him to me."

Adam handed Abel to me, and I took his slippery body in my arms and laid him on my bosom.

"Abel, my son, you have a father and a mother and a brother named Cain." I looked over to Cain, who was sucking his thumb and staring at this new being that was suddenly there in his safe and happy realm. "Come see your brother," I said to Cain.

Cain approached timidly, looking from Adam to me and back again. He stood over Abel's tiny bloodied body and said, "It's a fish?"

Adam and I laughed then. It was a good laugh, a healing laugh.

"No," I said. "It's another little boy, like you. You'll have someone to play with."

Cain looked skeptical. He pulled his thumb from his mouth and stared. "Don't like," he said. "Throw it in river." A rapid dismissal, sealing Abel's fate. He knew we always threw our offal in the river, for it to be eaten by the fish or reused by the animals that frequented the river's shores.

I reached up to soothe Cain's brow. "He is not something we can throw away," I said. "He's your brother."

Cain looked at my face and saw what I was saying was true. He sighed, went to Adam, and sank into his father's embrace.

"I have an idea," said Adam. "Why don't we go find something for your mother to eat?"

Cain nodded his head and jumped up. Here was his chance to change his father's mind on the issue. He didn't want a brother, hadn't asked for one, and he wanted us to reconsider. Joy transformed his face, and now he was jumping up and down, saying, "Hurry, hurry."

Adam came to me and kissed me on my nose. "I love you," he said. "Thank you."

Think not ill of me, but all I could feel at that moment was how angry I was that I had to go through this fire, while Adam did not. A simple "I love you" and "Thank you" was not sufficient compensation for the agony I had endured. Had I known that I would go through two other births in which my babies would die, before I had Naava, I would have never lain with Adam again.

Thankfully, I had time to cool my thoughts while Adam and Cain were gone.

After my husband and son disappeared through the brush, holding hands, I talked to my littlest. I told him all about the Garden and our journey down from the snowy mountains—though I did not think it wise to tell him of his parents' indiscretions, at least not yet. I told him about his brother, Cain, and how they would grow up to be friends, just like Adam and me. Why would I have thought otherwise?

No mother ever does.

I told him how I felt about Elohim and how sometimes, in the belly of the night, or in the womb of the morning, I thought I could hear Him talking to me—in the song of the bulbul who lived in the konar trees or in the beauty of the red-smeared sunsets in the western evening sky.

Thinking back, I wonder, *Did I really hear Elohim?* I remember telling Abel I had, and obviously he took it to heart, because he was always faithful to that original telling. Never once did he falter, even with the onset of my doubt. *How could he possibly remember?* He was but an infant, one who had just choked on death and sputtered to life, a frail little thing whom Elohim may have breathed into at that last desperate moment.

Maybe this is why I loved Abel so. He had a tender heart, one imprinted with the mark of Elohim's hand.

The very first time we heard him sing our song from the Garden was when he was two. It was also the first indication we had of Abel's special connection with animals.

Night had fallen. Adam had finished telling the boys about how their mother had beaten down a fierce bear—Adam was forever exaggerating, and, I had to admit, it did make the story better—and Cain and Abel had fallen asleep, their little bodies curled like flower petals into each other.

Adam was remarking how loudly Cain snored when we heard a snap in the bushes behind us. We both bolted upright, straining for clues as to direction or distance or source.

Up above, the moon was a weak pink crescent, and the stars spilled out over the sky's vast space. Light was dim, and our vision was limited.

There again. A twig snapped. A leaf crunched. A predator lurked, but we knew not what it was.

We were up on our feet in an instant, Adam reaching for his dagger, me reaching for a slingshot.

The boys were a few steps away, and they were our first concern. I went to them and shook them awake. They were confused, of course, and when I told them to go to Father, they rubbed their eyes, and Cain said, "But it's not daytime yet."

The snufflings grew louder. Whatever it was was not trying to hide its presence.

"Come," I said. "There is something in the bushes."

The boys got up then, hurriedly, and ambled sleepily toward our dying fire.

Abel dawdled, rubbing his eyes and nose. There was a flash of something yellow and big, and in that instant I saw Abel being whisked up into the mouth of a horrid beast. Then, silence.

"Abel?" I screamed. "Abel!"

Adam said nothing but tore into the brush, where we had glimpsed the last flicker of the beast's tail. He held his dagger high.

Cain watched wide-eyed, then patted my thigh through the skins I wore. "Mama," he said. "There. Look."

I followed his gaze. In the shadows, not far from our fire, was a leopard, standing upright, holding Abel by the scruff of the pelt he wore.

Then.

I heard Abel's little voice, singing. He sang our song from the Garden. The leopard stood motionless. He made no move to release Abel.

"Stay here," I said to Cain. I tore his hands from my skins and began to creep slowly toward the leopard. "I'm coming," I said softly. "Abel, stay still."

Adam dashed back into the circle of light.

Abel stopped singing. "No, Mama," he said. "Stop."

I did.

He began singing again, his thin pure voice filling the night void.

In the retelling of this incident, I myself am amazed and have difficulty coming to terms with it, I am so perplexed. The leopard seemed mesmerized, either by Abel's gentleness or by his singing. I know not which.

Adam circled around to the back side of the leopard, one slow step at a time.

I stood and stretched my hand out behind me to tell Cain to stay where he was. With my eyes and ears and heart ahead of me, I prayed to Elohim to save my boy to whom He had given life.

Then, as the moon and stars passed overhead in their courses, and the sun slept, the leopard released Abel, sniffing at him only, and turned and walked to the river to drink.

I dared not move.

Abel kept singing.

The leopard drank his fill. He glanced back at Cain and me and twitched his tail before disappearing into the night.

I ran to Abel, who was now quiet and sitting up in the dirt. I checked his body for bite marks, scratches. "Are you all right?" I said, kneeling in the dirt and wrapping my arms around him. "Oh, I'm so sorry, Abel. I should have been holding your hand."

Abel looked up at me, his thin, pointed chin raising up to face the fingernail of a moon. "He was lonely," said Abel.

I knew not how to respond, although after the boys had fallen asleep again around the dying fire, I told Adam that I had thought briefly of Elohim when Abel said that. Elohim had known how to calm the animals and quiet the storms and soothe the spirit. Then, on that night, Abel had done the same.

Dara

When I got back to the city, I was dizzy and stomach-sick from the wagon ride. Ahassunu gave me no rest and followed me into the pee-pee room to say, "So. Do you have anything for me?"

I held up my hand to warn Ahassunu, then I bent over and vomited all of Aya's breads and figs into the hole in the floor. I couldn't help it. My stomach was flipping and flopping like the fish Aya always caught. I sat down and waited to see if I was going to vomit again.

Ahassunu came and stood by me. "Well?" she said. "I'm waiting."

I untied the sack from around my waist and gave it to Ahassunu.

Ahassunu started to laugh-cry, then she reached down and patted my head. She tore the sack open and went down on all fours like a dog and poured the seeds *tock tock tock* out onto the floor. "Why, they are just seeds!" she said. She made her eyes like a snake and glared at me.

I nodded. "From the Tree of Life," I said.

Ahassunu ran her hands through them, making them *clack* against one another. Her eyes looked hungry, and she licked her lips. She counted them, then counted them again. She asked me, "How long does it take for them to grow?"

I shrugged. "Mama never planted any," I said.

Ahassunu raised up on her knees. "Never? Why not?" And then she looked over her shoulder, quick, to see if anyone could hear her. She whispered, "My child, think. Do you not know of anything else she might have in her garden that she took from Dilmun?"

I shook my head. My stomach still felt like Aya's boiling stew.

Ahassunu grabbed my chin and squeezed my cheeks. "Are you sure?"

I nodded. I thought of Jacan's seed game and how much I missed him. I thought of Mama looking for the seeds and not finding them, and all of a sudden I was scared. *Would Mama hate me?* I tried not to cry, but the tears rolled down my cheeks all by themselves. I wiped them away with my hands, so Ahassunu wouldn't see, but they came back, faster and faster, until Ahassunu said, "Oh, in Anu's name, stop your sniveling," and got up to go. "We shall see about that garden."

I hugged my knees and sat there in the dark for a long time.

Zenobia came and found me and took me into another room that didn't stink so bad. She told me to lie back, and she put a cool cloth on my forehead. She sang me a lullaby, and I didn't want it to end. I wished for her to keep singing those pretty sounds, like Mama used to do with Father.

"Were those seeds really from Dilmun?" Zenobia said, when she stopped singing.

"Eden," I said. "Mama calls it Eden."

She put her hand under my back and set me upright. "It is important you do not lie to Ahassunu. She has done many an evil thing, and if these seeds do not work, she will punish not only you but Puabi and me too." She traced the outline of my ear. "You tell the truth, no?"

"Yes," I said.

Zenobia hugged me tight. "Good girl. Let's go get something to eat." She pulled me up by the arms, and I stood, all wobbly at first.

Too much noise. Everywhere there are hammerings and poundings so that I can barely hear the words in my head. The colored cones of the columns are almost done, and I make sure to keep Shala far away from them. A couple of times, Shala tries to trick me and tells me to look over there, then she makes a run for them. But I am faster than her. I catch her and spank her and tell her that I am going to send the *gidim* after her—this is what Ahassunu says all the time when Shala is bad. Shala says, "No, no, no, don't say that," and I try very hard not to smile, because Shala believes me. I wonder what she thinks the *gidim* are.

The New Year's festival is the reason why everybody is whirling about like dust storms. The cook bakes. The seamstress sews. The women sit around and argue over what they will wear and how they will color their hair and what they will draw on their skins. Zenobia holds up orange cloth to my face, then yellow cloth, then red cloth and says, "Oh, this one is pretty with your brown eyes." So, that's what color I'm going to wear on festival day, red, and Balili has been sent to find a carnelian stone for my nose.

Balili brings the red stone back to me. Then he says, "Promise not to tell?"

I'm scared of making more promises. I will get more people into trouble, and then Ahassunu will find me and throw me out into the desert where the lion will gobble me up. Then Mama will be sad because I will be gone, just like Turtle.

Balili has a basket over his shoulder. He takes it off his back and reaches into it and takes out a shiny bull that fits in the palm of his hand. The bull is silvery, like fish scales, and it holds a bowl in its hooves, like it's offering it to someone. Balili shakes it for me. *Rattle rattle rattle* it goes. I jump back because I think it's alive. "I had them fill it with limestones," he says, smiling.

"To keep away the lion?" I say.

He laughs. "No, for the festival," he says. "Because of you, the people will hear the Queen of Heaven on festival day." He pats my head and winks. "But you must not tell anyone. It is our little secret."

I nod. Here is something I've done right. And Balili has praised me for it.

The whole family—me and Ahassunu and Shala and Zenobia and Puabi and the prince—sleep on the roof, where it's cooler. All night I hear whispers and groans and moans. I think maybe somebody is crying, so I go and look. The prince is hurting Zenobia. He's laying on her, squishing her, and his skirt has fallen off. One of her bosoms is bare.

"Zenobia," I whisper.

The prince snorts. His face looks like a white flower in the dark. He reaches out and puts his hand over my mouth. "Shhh. Go back to bed," he says.

"But Zenobia is crying," I say.

I see Zenobia's face then. "Go, child," she whispers. "I'll wake you in the morning." She giggles.

"Can we not get some quiet around here?" hisses Ahassunu, from her mat on the other side of the prince. She throws something, and it clatters at my feet and goes skittering across the roof.

I go back to my mat, but all I see when I lie back down is Turtle's face looking at me. He asks why I couldn't save him, why he died without his mama around. No one to take care of him. Maybe he is mad because I left him with Aya. I don't know.

I sleep with the babies. Always it is this way, so the mothers won't be bothered at night, in case the babies have to pee-pee or cry or wiggle.

Shala taps me on the shoulder. "Who's Naa-va?" she says slowly.

"My sister," I whisper.

"Mmm," she says. "She come live here?"

"No," I say. "She lives down the river with Mama and Father." Then I remember the festival. "Maybe you mean she's coming to the festival, for a visit?"

But Shala is already back asleep.

Eve

Adam, my Adam, betrayed me. It was a mistake of catastrophic proportions.

As I went to my garden one afternoon, expecting to bask in its quietness, instead I found bejeweled men and women wandering about in it and plucking things from the trees and branches and bushes. I knew not what to do at first. I stood upon the border, curious, for I wanted to watch them. Before long, I realized they cared not that I was there, and, moreover, they held absolutely no regard for me.

I greeted them as warmly as I could, and they all pivoted upon their heels, surprised at my presence.

A bare-chested man with a skirt wrapped around his waist and a pendant of a yellow star about his neck approached me. I realized as he came nearer that it was the prince. He said something in the strange tongue of the city.

I shook my head.

"Thank you," he said, bowing his head slightly.

"For what do you give me thanks?" I said.

The prince's face registered surprise. "Why, for your husband. He give the garden to us."

"Give? But it can't be," I stammered. "It's mine. He made it for *me*."

The prince persisted. "We bartered. You get cattle and flocks and wagon, and we get the garden. A fair price." A lady in the background placed a grape on her tongue and fairly moaned with pleasure.

My hands started to shake. My insides were aflutter.

The prince looked at me, concern etching his face. He pointed to the garden, as if I hadn't understood. "Ours," he said.

I shook my head. "No," I said. "My husband built it a long time ago. It is ours." My agitation increased. They could not just come across something and lay claim to it. Surely they had to understand this. "There must be some mistake."

The prince shook his head. "No mistake," he said. "He did not tell you?"

I tried again. "It is ours, my husband's and mine," I said. "We have been here for many years. Many of these seeds we brought with us from another Garden far away." Cain had explained to me their importation of materials from the north, so certainly they would understand that we, too, had done the same—albeit in a different fashion. *Adam would* not *have done such an atrocious thing. He couldn't have.*

I was not thinking clearly. I backed away from them, shaking my head, a terrible seed of fear beginning to sprout in my belly. I had to find Adam, to make him come and straighten things out with these people. They had become more of a nuisance every day, with the diverting of water, with the attack on Aya, with the destruction of Cain's dates, and now this.

My husband was out at the river, clearing the silt from the irrigation ditches and opening sluices for watering.

I filled a waterskin at the cistern and made my way out to him. While I walked, I pondered what had happened here in such a short amount of time.

My grievous error was letting the city women see the garden—in truth, I had been proud of it, wanting to flaunt it, thinking they would have had nothing like it in their city. In fact, I cannot remember if it came up in conversation or if they had already known of it through Dara. Its allure had tantalized them, as surely it did me every afternoon, and they had exclaimed at the green-black lushness of it.

If their strange exclamations and facial expressions to each other were any indication, they had been astonished at the great numbers of roses and marigolds and cyclamen and irises and orchids. They had sniffed at the sage and onion flowers and the dill weed. Without Dara present, I had not been able to answer any of their questions. I simply named what they were touching, and they looked back at me in shocked wonder—at me or at the garden, I did not know.

As they left with my sweet Dara once again, they bowed to me over and over. They kissed my hand. Dara translated their parting words for me.

It wasn't until later that I learned that Dara had told them about Eden, and for this they thought I was special, to have hailed from their paradise equivalent of Dilmun.

When I was but a short distance away from Adam, he saw me coming and raised up, shielding his eyes with his hand. He set down his tools and came to greet me, the angry wife, except he did not know I was angry.

It is one of my faults that I immediately dive into blaming. Before even asking what has happened, I am already deep into the pointing of fingers and angry accusations. This is wrong, I know it, but sometimes I feel so strongly that it takes everything within me to stop or measure my words.

That time was no different.

Adam fell upon me with kisses, and I pushed him away.

"What have you done?" I cried.

He held up his hands, rough hands, blistered hands, to protect himself, and his eyes registered hurt.

"My garden," I said, plunging in, heedless to his feelings. "Those people are ripping things from the branches, *eating* fruit and flower; by the hairs on my head, they are destroying what you've made for me. Why?" The last word I cried out and struck him upon the chest.

"Eve," Adam said. He grabbed my arms and pinned them down with a force I could not overcome. "I did not mean to hurt you—"

"I did not mean to hurt you," I sneered. "What does that mean, exactly? What have you done? You did not even see fit to consult me first, and it is my garden, not yours!" I struggled against him. "Release me!"

Still he held me fast.

I kneed him in the groin, and down he went. I had never done this before, and the moment he dropped, I felt sudden guilt and nausea. I made my voice softer, but I was still as angry as a hornet. "It was *mine*," I said. "Not yours. You gave it to me as a gift." I fell to my knees, next to him. "The garden. The *garden*," I whimpered. "You gave away the *one place I had left*."

"I bartered it. I did not give it away," said Adam, wincing and stumbling to his feet.

I stood and began to pace. The rage boiled up from my center. It singed a path up my throat and into my mouth. It spilled upon the ground and trailed toward Adam. I fairly spit my words at him. "How could you have done such a thing? I *loved* it there. It was my one place of escape, of peace."

"You *hated* the garden," he said. "You complained about it always, how you wanted this or that, and 'Adam, could you make it more like the Garden,' and 'Adam, do you remember,' and 'Adam, let's go back.' Always it was this way with you, and I, for one, could not keep doing it, this harping for the past, longing for a place that is gone and forbidden to us. It is time you grasp this, Eve, really grasp it. We are never going back there. We aren't invited. Elohim wants us out here for some reason, and you must accept it. Life will be easier for you if you do." He added, muttering, "Life will be easier for all of us if you do."

I tangled my fingers in my hair and yanked. "I don't know what I shall do. I *need* that place. I *want* that place." I dropped my hands and screeched, "Get it back!" I pointed toward the house, to the garden, my lost garden. "Go over there right now and tell them you've made a disastrous error and you want it back."

"I can't," said Adam. "It's theirs now."

I stared at him. I could not believe my ears. "What?" I said weakly, sinking to my knees. "No!"

Adam wrung his aching hands and scuffed at the ground with his sandals.

"Could you not have asked me first?" I said, crying and rubbing my swollen belly. "Could you not have asked your pregnant wife what she needed most of all?"

He knelt beside me and tried to put his hand on my shoulder. I brushed it away. "I should have," he said. "But I wanted to rid us of that poor reminder of the Garden. I thought it might do you good."

"*Good?*" I said. I snorted through my tears and my dripping nose, mindful that my laughter was tinged with scorn. "What did you get in return for it, husband?"

"One oxen for plowing," Adam said. "Ten goats, twelve sheep, a wagon, and enough linen for Naava to make new robes for the festival." He bent lower, so I would have to look at him. "I did make one more exchange, with Aya's permission—that of a bit of sesame oil for a box of adornments."

I looked at him, incredulous. "Why do you squander what we have labored for?" I said.

"They are for you," he said proudly. He brought his face close to mine. We were like sandpipers hovering over the sand. He whispered, "For the festival. I wanted to surprise you. I thought I should like to have my wife shine like the moon, as she once did." He embraced me, and I did not protest. "I want my beautiful wife back, the one who was curious and thrilled by everything she touched, the one who wanted to suck the marrow out of life, the one who sang and laughed, the one who loved me and was happy."

I remember this exchange as though it were yesterday, and yet remembering and understanding are two different things. Any harm he had done to me by selling the garden was overshadowed by my own disquieted heart, my own chagrin at being found out.

Since I am trying to uncover the truth of what went on that day, I will relate one more thing. In the midst of Adam's betrayal, he had paused to think of me. He had acquired some beautiful trinkets that he believed would restore us back to the way we were. How do I begin to understand this conundrum? On the one hand, he had disregarded my feelings. On the other, he thought he knew what was better for me and took it upon himself to do a lovely thing for me. How do you rage against something so confusing? I know in my head what he was trying to do, but my heart says otherwise. My heart is angered when he assumes he knows me better than I know myself—and acts on it. Always he makes these judgments, and I cannot say anything. If I do, I am ungrateful for his efforts; if I don't, I am bitter against him.

As I have laid it out for you, I *was* loved and cherished, and I refused to see it, or foster it, for that matter. That would come later.

My seeds. They were gone, vanished.

I knew of no one who would have wanted them. Certainly, in passing, I had told my children about them, but they knew not to touch or take.

Oh, disaster! Adam had sold the one bit of peace I possessed—my life, my joy, my haven. I had thought to grow another garden, this time with the precious seeds from the Tree of Life. That tree, too, we had been warned from after our disobedience. But still. Could they, *would* they have reversed Elohim's curse, offering us life where we had earned only death before? I knew not.

When we first took hold on these plains, I had not planted the rest of the Tree of Life seeds, because the weight of my error still pressed heavy upon me and I did not want to anger Elohim further. I had thought frequently of the seed Adam had planted on our first baby's grave, on the snowy mountainside, and wondered if it had taken root and grown into a flowering tree like the one in the Garden.

But then the forbidden seeds disappeared.

I confided in Aya, for I valued her sharp eyes. She assured me she had seen nothing, and she asked if I was absolutely certain they had not rotted away.

"If that were the case, I would expect there to be some sort of matter at the bottom of the jar, wouldn't you?" I said.

Aya pursed up her lips. "There was nothing?"

"Nothing." And then I remembered a small something that had rolled out from underneath the jar as I lifted it. I held up one finger. "A nicker seed," I told her.

Aya startled. "A nicker seed?" she repeated.

I nodded.

"That's odd," she said, as she began to fillet the fish, laying their white bodies flat on prodigious piles of salt.

So she thought it as strange as I did.

My fury at Adam had a past.

One incident stands out in my mind.

Adam, Cain, and I had not yet come to these plains that we now inhabit. We had traveled many moons, and still we had not found a place to settle. I was heavy with Abel, and the days were growing hotter and more arid.

On this particular day of which I am speaking, we began to hear, as we were walking, the great thundering of a waterfall up ahead. In truth, the river seemed in a vicious hurry. Twigs and limbs and petals tumbled about in the frenzied water.

Soon we were forced to descend a precipitous hillside dotted with shallow vegetation that scraped at our legs and loose rocks that threatened to send us careening down the mountainside. We made our way deliberately. Adam set Cain upon his shoulders and told him to hang on. They set off down the hill. I was left to fend for myself, which I did not mind, because I knew I would be slower, the huge snail that I was.

We arrived at the bottom unscathed and in one piece, aside from a tiny tree branch scratch on Cain's cheek, but we were hot and tired and ill-disposed. The mosquitoes were merciless, and our shoulders chafed with everything we were carrying by now—reed baskets packed with animal skins and fishing hooks and flint daggers and slingshots and a small clay bowl we had fashioned for cooking.

We had come out of the bushes and trees to find the splendid sight of a tremendous rush of water cascading off the edge above and into the pool below. The mere force of it was enough to send up a misty spray all around.

"Ah," said Adam. "Here is where we will rest."

I eyed the waterfall. "I should like to stand under that and wash," I said.

"You'll do no such thing," said Adam. "It's too dangerous."

"The pool, then," I said, and began shrugging off my basket, my hat of braided reeds, then my animal skins, which I had stitched together with sinew and plant thorn.

Adam set Cain upon the ground, and faster than either of us could blink, Cain was in the water, splashing about, yelling simply for the sake of yelling.

"Are you watching him?" I said.

Adam nodded and began to disrobe.

There was no sandy shore. Huge boulders lined the pool, and as I stepped out onto them, I saw how deep the water really was. I jumped in and made my way to Cain, who managed to hold on to my neck. The water was gloriously cool. We played Mama Fish and Baby Fish, where he flung his hands over my head and rested upon my back. Then I paddled like a frog, and he squealed with delight. "Faster," he shouted. "Faster."

I was so involved with Cain that I did not see Adam making his way to the far side, so when I looked up and saw the liquid image of his body under the waterfall's downpouring, I was confused. *Had he not told me it was too dangerous?*

I detached Cain's arms from my neck and and heaved myself out of the water, using a boulder for leverage. I stood and wrung my hair out, all the while watching my husband as he delighted in the waterfall. He yelled at one point as though he had killed a wild animal after a long hunt.

Cain cried out, begging me to play.

"My arms are tired," I said.

"Swim," he said.

"Baby fishes swim longer than mama fishes," I said. I wished for him to tire, so that when he closed his eyes at night he would sleep soundly.

I was irritated then—by Adam's forbidding me to stand under the waterfall, then of his flagrant disregard for that very commandment. *Why did we live under different rules?* No matter how many times I brought this sort of thing up with Adam, he would rationalize his actions, insisting on the logic of it all. For instance, in the waterfall situation, I could have predicted he would tell me, "Well, of course you can't stand there. We have to keep you safe. After all, *you* are having our baby."

But moments such as these were not harmless. They appeared small and insignificant as they were occurring, but over time they piled up like dead carcasses and began to rot and stink. Many times I had to ask myself, *When did all this begin? Why do I notice it only now?*

By then, though, Adam's superior behavior was ingrained. I had been commanded; I obeyed. I'm not quite sure how this happened. I think I wanted peace, and in order to get peace, I acquiesced. I gave over my power, my voice. And once that was done, there was no returning to how it had been in the Garden—equal companions who respected each other and allowed the other a say in all matters.

I said nothing that afternoon. I was not as injured as I am now, thinking upon it.

As to the issue of my garden being sold, perhaps Adam thought the garden was his domain, his responsibility. Perhaps he thought that I had no say in land dealings, as he had little say in child rearing.

That was how it had worked out.

Naava

As a cover-up—lest Eve detect her motives and forbid her to go—
Naava had devised numerous reasons why she should accompany Cain
to the city on his weekly trips.

"Linens and flowers and herbs are what I need," she had insisted to
Eve, although this made her mother roll her eyes.

Naava had stared right back at her, defiantly. Eve *knew* Naava no longer
had access to her fabulous flowers in the sold garden. And Aya guarded
her herb plot too closely. How else was Naava to get her colors?

Eve had sighed finally and said, "As long as you go with Cain. He will
protect you."

When Naava had told Cain she was going with him again to the city, he
searched her face and narrowed his eyes. "You think me stupid? You go for
other reasons than the ones you've stated."

She smiled pleasantly enough and said, "Oh, Cain, your mind is forever running away with you." She came closer to him and reached down to
grab him, rub him. He stiffened and inhaled sharply. "I want to be with
you," she said softly. "Will you deny me that?" She tiptoed to kiss him on
the soft part of his neck, right underneath the lobe of his ear.

Roughly, he pulled her to him and grunted, "You may go, if you do that
to me again."

Naava laughed, a short melodious laugh that said, *Your wish is my com-*

mand, but she stopped short because Cain grabbed her suddenly by the shoulders and lowered his face to hers. He hissed, "If you do *anything*—*anything* at all—to attempt to see that boar of a prince, I shall crush you. Your pretty little head will not live to see tomorrow."

Naava tried to laugh again, to exhibit a levity she did not feel. "And why would I want to see him? He is *nothing* compared to you." She batted her eyelashes slowly, purposefully.

Cain released her and stood up straight. He smiled triumphantly and held out his palms to her. "See here," he said. "The calluses speak of hard labor. His lily-white hands show nothing. How can he be strong when he does not know how to work the land? How will the gods bless him?"

Naava shrugged and said, "He knows nothing. You know everything." This seemed to appease him for a bit, because he turned to go. *So simple a creature,* she thought.

But she would have to exercise caution—*that* she knew.

Her words had placated him sufficiently, for upon their arrival in the city, Cain had kissed her lightly upon her cheek and wandered off to do other business.

Naava watched him disappear into the crowd, then made her way to the spot Dara had indicated she was to stand—next to the copper artisans—and waited for Balili, the white-robed scribe, to look up from his tutoring. When Balili saw her, he smiled, rose up from his stool, and handed his instruction tablet to Dara. Naava knew the prince would not be long. She laughed to see Dara take the tablet from him and tap it here and there with her forefinger, saying something to the younger children at her feet. Her little mouth was set with the firmness of authority. She obviously relished her new status as Balili's helper.

Balili and Naava had never spoken, but Naava surmised the prince had described her as beautiful and ravishing, and that is how Balili was able to identify her, because Dara did not look up from her teaching.

Naava wended her way then through the dark narrow streets, to the place of the prince's and her first meeting. She entered the doorway, now cleared of cobwebs, and entered the sparsely decorated room. She swept the floor clean the best she could with the tightly bound bundle of palm fronds she found resting against the chair. Someone had laid reed matting on the floor and hung red and brown blankets upon one wall. She smiled, for she thought it must have been the prince, prettying up the room for her.

She sat upon the floor and waited, biting the skin around her nails. She wondered what the prince would be like this time. *Would he still desire her?*

Outside, the street was quieter than usual. A few donkey hoofbeats, the shout of a faraway merchant, the sound of children playing. Then suddenly the room grew dark, and there in the doorway stood the prince, casting a shadow as thin as a heron.

Naava stood and bowed. He kissed her hand.

"You are well, no?" he said.

Naava nodded. "And you?"

He motioned for Naava to sit, and she did.

Naava would have said at that moment she felt as though she was caught in a spiderweb, suspended, still and quiet, wrapped and waiting for something momentous to happen, a sort of devouring that she would find pleasurable.

The prince did not sit. He stood with one arm grasping the other, one hand fiddling absentmindedly with the gold hoop in his ear. "I see your brother," he said.

"Yes," Naava said. She never knew what to expect when a conversation veered toward her older brother.

"He . . . you tell him he cannot confront our men in the marketplace."

Naava hugged her knees and rocked back and forth slowly.

The prince studied her face. "You understand?"

Naava nodded her agreement. She could have predicted Cain's run-in with the workers, even before the prince told her what had happened, but what could she do? Cain was a rushing flood that would not stop for anyone.

The prince became agitated; his hands waved in the air. "He accused our date growers of cutting his dates," said the prince. "He yelled in the marketplace at them, even held up his bad dates on broken branches. He said he will cut down our dates." The prince glared at Naava, willing her to do something. "What kind of man cuts his dates and blames other men for cut-down dates?"

Naava sighed. "I do not know. Cain has a mind of his own."

"A mind that ruins him," said the prince. "You warn him. For me." He rubbed his smooth and clean hands together, quickly, as if he were trying to make fire. "If he is—how do you say?—*afraid* . . . ?" His voice indicated a question.

Naava nodded to say she was following him.

". . . yes, of promise with date men, then he should decide what is to be done instead, and do it," said the prince.

Naava hated when dirty matters seeped into an otherwise glorious moment, sullying it. She motioned for the prince to sit next to her. "Let's talk about something else," she said.

"You will talk to him?" repeated the prince. The lines between his eyebrows were deep furrows, and his eyes expressed urgency.

Naava nodded yes, she would talk to Cain for the prince.

The prince sat next to her and was quiet for a moment. Then, as if he'd just remembered, he grunted and pulled something from the depths of his robe. He reached for her left hand and pried her fingers open and laid the heavy object in her open palm.

Naava glanced down. "Oh," she said. "It's beautiful." It was a silvery bangle, inlaid with star-shaped stones the color of Eve's eyes.

The prince took it from her and drew the bangle over her left hand and onto her wrist. " I ask you to wear this," the prince said, "at the New Year's festival, the harvest festival. You will play important part in the festivities." He studied her face, trying to read her reaction.

Naava giggled and leaned forward to kiss him upon the cheek.

He pulled back. "You will play Inanna at festival. You will dress as her . . . and be worshipped as her. You like this, no?"

Naava's heart leapt like a hare. She nodded, feeling all the while that she was dreaming.

"I fear you do same to me as Inanna do to Enki." He clasped his chest and grinned. "You make my heart jump like a rabbit."

Still Naava smiled. She did not want to ruin the moment. *She would be Inanna!*

"Sometimes you are a lamb," the prince said. "Other times you are a wolf."

Naava pouted.

"With you, what should I do?" said the prince, throwing up his hands in surrender. "Are all women this way?"

"I do not know," Naava said, giggling.

He winked at her. "You possess great allure," said the prince, "like Inanna. She stole her powers, you know. Took them from Enki, the Lord of the Earth." He lay back on one of the reed mats and patted it with his hand, to indicate that she should lie next to him. She did, and he lay on his side, raised up on one elbow.

The prince sighed contentedly and said, "About Inanna, I will tell you."

She detected the start of a story, and she rather enjoyed stories. Growing up, Naava had heard the tales of the Garden and of Elohim and of Cain and Abel. Recently she had heard Cain's fascinating accounts of the gods and goddesses who lived in the sky and in the underworld, tellings in which Elohim was conspicuously absent and Inanna figured heavily.

The prince began, "A long time ago, Inanna, Queen of Heaven, decided to see Enki, father of her mother, in a sacred place called Abzu, to offer prayers to him. Enki sees her coming. He tells his servant, 'Inanna is coming. Give to her butter cake and beer and set her down at the holy table.' Enki's servant does what Enki says. Soon Enki and Inanna drink beer together, *too* much beer. When Enki gets so drunk, he gives away all his *me* . . ." When Naava looked confused, he said, "His powers. Inanna— she is like a hyena—shouts, 'I will take them, I will take them!' to every- thing Enki gives away." The prince waved a finger in Naava's face. "She *knows* what she does, little fox." He continued. "This is a disaster, you un- derstand."

Naava nodded.

"At the end of the night, Enki gives away *all* his powers—so many things: ascent and descent into the netherworld, the binding and loosen- ing of hair, the art of lovemaking—" Here, the prince stroked her cheek gently with his forefinger, and whispered, "I can teach you . . ."

Naava licked her lips so they would glisten. She gathered her hair with her fingers, so that it flowed out on the floor behind her, for she had taken down her bindings before his arrival. She saw the longing in his eyes.

The prince started counting Enki's powers on his fingers. "Enki gives away all his *me*—the art of song, the art of treachery, the art of kindness, the kindle and the put-out of fire, the making of decisions. *Everything* he gives away in his drunkenness! Well, soon he says good-bye, and Inanna flees quickly on the Boat of Heaven, which is full of new powers—how do you say?" The prince wrenched one arm behind his back, pretending to pull up on it, like Cain and Abel used to play at.

Naava said, "Coerced? She *took* them from him?"

The prince nodded. "Yes, good. Coerced. What happened, do you think?"

"I suppose," Naava said, "that Enki woke up the next morning and wondered where all his powers went."

The prince slapped his thigh and said, "Yes! He sends his servant with the monsters *enkum* to get them back, but Inanna cries out to her servant Ninshubur for help: 'Save me, save me!' Ninshubur slices the air with his hand, and the monsters run back to Enki. Over and over Enki sends different creatures, giants and sea monsters and screaming *kugalgal,* to get back his *me,* but no, it does not work. Each time Ninshubur protects Inanna."

The prince's eyebrows arched up. "You tire of my story?"

"Oh, no," Naava said, sitting up. She desired to give the illusion of being as attentive as possible. She curled a strand of her hair around her finger and twirled it. Naava wished to be this Inanna whom the prince respected and feared so much.

"Well, Inanna takes the Boat of Heaven, with all her *me,* and makes her way to this city. She unloads, one *me* by one *me,* and that is the reason we thank her for all she teaches and gives us."

Naava clapped her hands to show her delight.

The prince grinned and slid closer to her.

She said then, in a voice as smooth as honey, "I like to hear your voice. You are a bull *and* a lion." Naava had heard Cain talk about how the artisans of the city liked to draw bulls and lions fighting one another, and she understood that to mean that the people admired the animals' strength and wondered which one would emerge as victor. Of course, Naava was not stupid. She knew what she was doing. Listen: This kind of flattery worked every time—on Cain, even on Abel sometimes. It was surprising, really, how easy it was.

Eve

It was the time of the long shadows when I heard Jacan's terrified cry and the urgent patter of his feet. "Mama, Mama," he cried. "The lion . . . we were tracking it . . . Father didn't see . . . We yelled and yelled, but he didn't see it . . . Come quick, come quick." He was out of breath and not making any sense at all.

"Where?" I said, my limbs already going numb, my heart already pounding within me.

Jacan pointed to the fields.

I did a quick accounting in my head, a ticking-off of my children's whereabouts. Aya had gone off to collect dung, and Cain and Naava had gone to see Dara in the city. Abel was with his flocks. I implored Jacan to blow his horn, to call Aya back to the house, which he did.

I ran in the direction Jacan had pointed, holding my belly fast. My back ached; my breath was labored.

What was I thinking at a time like this?

It was not as I would have expected.

I thought of all the good in Adam—his soft words, his kind caresses, his sweet singing. I thought of how he took Cain under his wing and taught him everything there was to know about growing things. I thought of how he nurtured Abel's interest in animal husbandry. I thought of his gentle manner and his sense of humor with the girls and with me.

Not once during those fleeting moments did I think of his sometimes brusque or flippant manner. Not once did I remember the harm or hurt he had caused me over the many years we'd been together. None of that. I had been cruel to him as well. Dismissive, mostly.

Then I saw Abel in the distance, bent over something on the ground. As I grew nearer, I realized it was Adam, unmoving.

Jacan's horn sounded again.

A cry escaped my lips when I reached him. His right foot was flung to the side like a broken branch. Around his torso, his robe had been torn asunder, and he was drenched in blood. He looked dazed. His eyes went to and fro in his head, and he called out, "Eve, Eve."

"Adam," I cried. Then, to Abel, "The lion?"

Abel stood and held me to prevent me from becoming hysterical. I knew he was purposely keeping his voice calm and even for my sake. "It escaped. Jacan and I will bring Father to the house," he said. "Have Aya prepare a poultice and a splint for his leg."

I attempted to free myself of Abel's embrace, but he was stronger than I.

"No," I shouted to the sky. The spittle flew from my mouth. I did not care. "No, You cannot have him. He belongs to me." Elohim had raised His fist, and I would have none of it.

Abel held me firmly. "Gather yourself. You must be strong. If we hurry, we can save him."

I looked from Abel to Adam, then back to Abel. "Make haste," I said.

Abel turned to his father, and I ran back to the house.

Jacan was on his way with a donkey to transport his father.

I was sobbing, and all I could think about was what life would be like without Adam. What *my* life would be like without Adam.

And I was afraid.

Aya was already boiling a pot of willow bark tea when I arrived, breathless, back at the house.

"I heard Jacan's horn," she said, looking up. "I heard him yelling."

I gasped out what had happened. Fresh tears blurred my vision then, and I could not say more.

Aya came to me and hugged me, the best she could around my expansive middle. "I'm sorry," she said. Two little words, yet I absorbed them like an elixir. Amazing how kind words turn away worry and fear and pain.

I think it was the first time I saw my crippled daughter, really saw her. She was as strong as an ox. Truly, she held each one of us on her back and rarely complained—except about her older sister—and I am certain that my memory does not fail me in this regard. Looking back upon my reminiscings, I have overlooked what a sweet strength emanated from her. How strong she was in the face of great adversity. It is she who should have complained of how she was treated, not I.

As my sons were bringing my husband back to the house and Aya made up her healing tea and poultice, I was struck by how the shadows looked that afternoon. No one looks at shadows. They look at the light and what it illuminates. But the shadows, they are the things that hold the edge of truth—the shadowed creases of age, the hidden bowers of memory, and the latent meadows of thought.

I had been shining my light on the obvious, while underneath, in the dark, lay the unadorned and undiscovered truth. All I had to do was stand still as though under a moonless sky and listen to the rustlings around me.

Adam was loved. By me and by his children. These were new feelings, fresh feelings, comforting feelings. I mention this only because it seemed strange after so much striving among family members.

I was jolted to attention by Adam's cries and the clomping of the donkey's hooves. I rushed to greet them.

The donkey's sides were soaked with blood.

With great difficulty, Abel and I transferred Adam to his reed mat. Aya had lit the oil lamps and set about clay bowls full of water and wool cloths free of burrs for washing the wounds.

Jacan hovered by the doorway.

We undressed Adam slowly, methodically, peeling the bloody cloth away from his body. Abel needed to cut some away with a knife, as parts of Adam's robe had already encrusted themselves fast upon his skin. We removed his sandals, taking care over his toes.

Aya held up Adam's head and poured a gentle stream of willow tea into his mouth. "Drink," she whispered. When he gagged, she tried again.

Adam's face was as pale as the moon. He muttered unintelligibly. Across his middle, several deep gashes wept blood. Aya washed them clean, packed them with a poultice made of poppies, and wrapped long fresh reeds around and around, tucking the ends in to hold them fast.

She started on Adam's leg, aligning his foot with his thigh and knee. "Hold him," she said to me. "Abel—" she started, but Abel knew what to do.

I laid my body over my husband's, to hold him down, and Abel pushed against Adam's foot, wrenching it and clicking it into place. I grimaced at the grinding of bone and thought of the searing pain that had gone through my body when the bear knocked me down.

Adam screamed and struggled against me. His forehead glistened. His eyelids were closed, squeezed together like sun-dried grapes.

Jacan ran to me from the doorway where he had been watching and cried out, "Why are you *hurting* him?" His tears spilled over, and he tried to pull me away from Adam. "Don't *hurt* him!"

I reached out to him, and he leaned into me. "We're making Father better," I said.

Jacan looked up at me. He squeezed my legs through my robe. "Will Father die?" he said.

I did not answer.

I'm sure he took my silence as confirmation, and he went back to the doorway, seeking within himself whatever comfort his mother could not give him.

Abel reached for Aya's splint, made of willow saplings cinched together with reeds. He set it under Adam's leg and secured both ends with more reed, holding the break fast. Aya washed the skin and packed it with her pain-deadening poultice, then wrapped it tightly.

Now Adam groaned.

Aya wet a clean wool cloth in the tea and dabbed Adam's lips with it. To me, she said, "Will you bring a little beer?"

I went then. Behind me, I left the love of my life and three children who loved him with all their hearts. I thought of Cain's gods and goddesses, and I knew that the people I had left in that small dark room were more grand than Cain's gods and goddesses would ever be. You would not know it by looking at them. You would have to wait a moment to let the darkness descend, then you would see, peering out of the shadows, the golden truth of their character, hidden all along by the blaze and glare of the sun.

Aya

There is a peculiar moment that occurs right after a disaster. It is a moment of not knowing and a moment of hope, all rolled into one.

At first, when I heard Jacan's horn and heard him scream, "It's Father, come quick, come quick," I could not move. In my mind, I recounted all the stories about Father I carried inside me and thought, no, it couldn't be, he could *not* be in trouble. But it had to be, because up to this point, Jacan's horn-blowing had never been used as a warning.

This was *my* life, *our* life. Elohim would not have intended for our story to be told thus, with an ending like a weak trail of slug slime. So, for a brief desultory moment, I pressed my eyes shut, willing it to be gone, wishing it to be gone, whatever it was.

What finally made my paralyzed limbs move was knowing Father's life depended on my treatments. I called to Goat and made a mad dash back to the house, my basket of dung thumping on my back.

Once back in the courtyard, I immediately began setting out things I might need: bowls of water and clean cloths. Since I did not know yet what had happened or how badly Father was injured, I had to prepare for the worst. In the end, I made my standard poultice from poppies and boiled a batch of willow bark tea, because they both worked to numb pain.

With my willow tea simmering over the fire, I looked up and saw Mother running through the courtyard entrance. She was dazed and shivering, even though the afternoon was sweltering and the sweat was dripping into my eyes. I went to her and hugged her, and she accepted it meekly, like a child. "The lion," she said. "Your father."

When my brothers came, with Father eased over the donkey's bloodied back, I realized that he had suffered much already. If he contracted a fever, I would be by his side for several days, weeks maybe.

Abel and Jacan had been tracking the lion for months now. Indeed, Dara had told us that one of the city children had been eaten, horror of horrors! The workers had found a child's arm bone, gnawed upon, only thirty paces from the city wall. How the small boy had come to be outside the city was anybody's guess. His dog was missing too, but no trace of it had been found.

Jacan had heard Dara's story and got it into his little mind that he and Abel would protect her and all the city children. The morning before Father's incident, Jacan had boasted that he and Abel had seen the lion lurking behind rocks, trying to ferret out one of their goats, who had hoof rot.

Jacan hid behind his bravery like Turtle had hidden behind his shell. "Look, Aya," he had cried before breakfast, pretending to whirl a slingshot round and round his head. "Like this . . ." Faster and faster his arm went. He pretended to release the leather sling and said, "It flies through the air and hits the lion"—he smote his own forehead and fell to the ground— "right here, and he will *die*."

"Then," I said, "we shall go find the lion and drag him back here . . . to *eat* him." I grabbed him up. "We shall put him in my pot and *cook* him."

Jacan frowned and shrugged his shoulders. "I was only jesting. I'm not really the lion."

"But you will be good to eat, perhaps with a little bread and beer," I said.

He rubbed his eyes and nose. "I'm Jacan," he said.

For once, Father's presence would not comfort us. For once, we would not have Father's booming voice at the beginning of a meal, thanking Elohim for His provision. For once, we would not have Father's cheery admonitions to find the animals in the clouds. We would have to remember and do it ourselves.

Of that dark night, I remember little of Mother and Father, other than Mother sitting up with Father, softly chanting their song from the Garden. She kept his brow wet and cool. She caressed his face with her fingers, leaning forward to inhale his scent. She murmured the verses of the song into his ear, but he did not respond.

I do remember Abel—his strong and able hands correcting Father's break, his soft and gentle manner with Mother, and his attentiveness to my instructions. His face was weathered and his sloped nose peeling, yet a strange calm lay between the wrinkles, and when he looked at me, I thought maybe he saw me, the real Aya, the one behind the crippled foot and the average beauty.

Oh, I am silly, I know it, but whereas Naava wanted kisses and couplings from my brothers, I wanted respect and admiration. I wanted Abel to see me, really *see* me, despite the fact that I knew I would forever be his second choice, after Naava.

Eve

My heart bayed to the wiry curls of hair on Adam's chest. Only a few tufts of them were visible over Aya's bindings, but I set my head down anyway and smiled when they tickled my forehead. I listened to his labored breathing, the *thump thump* of his heart, the squelches of his inner workings, and I was filled with such a longing to hold him again, his sweaty ordinary sun-baked body riddled with freckles and sun spots.

"I love you," I whispered. I lifted my head and paused, unsure of what to say next. I was certain he could not hear me, for he was fighting a fever. I wanted to say what had been in my heart, how worried I'd been. I wanted to say all this when I knew he couldn't respond with his characteristic brashness. I wanted my words to stand firm and strong, so that he might know how frightened I'd been at seeing him splayed open like one of Aya's fish fillets.

Our love needed only a little breath, a little encouragement now and then, to make the embers turn to flame. So many other obligations demanded our undivided attention—our children and our crops and our flocks—that we quite forgot to tend our love for each other.

"For all the times I talked of the Garden and going back, I am sorry," I said. "I kept alive the hope that we would return someday, return with our children, to live with Elohim there. I know, I know you would tell me that Elohim meant what He said and I should not try to change it, but I was sure that Elohim would repent of His action and gather us back to Him, like lost sheep being found by their shepherd." I touched the crescent feathers of Adam's eyelashes. I ran my finger along the narrow slouch of his nose. I was aware that I was searching for something I would not find—that giddy first-love feeling that simply *was,* like rain is wet or fire is hot.

Instead, I was left with something more grave, a settling of sorts, the silt at the bottom of the river, a knowledge that Adam and I were together as Elohim wanted but not in the *fashion* Elohim designed.

In eating of the fruit, we had desired something Elohim hadn't meant for us to have, something *other* than Elohim and His design.

This was the error. This was the wrong. That we did not put Elohim first.

In truth, I was done pleading. I was done howling for my life that *had been.*

I had Adam. I had my children. I had the works of my hands and my daily chores. I saw that I was to make a garden here, with the seeds of love and contempt, with the roots of desire and hatred. These seemingly dissonant choruses were not far from melodious. One or two notes could change, and the chant would turn from pining to contentment.

It is all in the heart and mind of the listener.

It was at this moment then, hovering over my ill husband, that my transfiguration occurred—or at least it is the moment I refer back to often. It was when I truly heard, as it were, Abel's flute rather than Jacan's horn, the first sounding like splendorous birdsong, the latter like crow chatter.

I realized that it was the small moments in my life that were most significant. They had accumulated over time, testament to certain directions or attitudes I had taken. Certainly I could see myself in my children, the good and the bad, and I grieved that I was unable to correct my faults before my children took them for their own. Truly, and I say this to you in all forthrightness, this is one of the sadnesses in my life, that I have imprinted my children so fully, so capably, that they may never rid themselves of my weaknesses or shortsightedness; they are so ingrained with them.

I had little hope, but it was hope after all.

Adam stirred then and inclined his head toward me. "Where am I?" he said.

"With the love of your life," I said.

He smiled weakly. "Is she beautiful?" he said.

Cain and Naava returned that night and came into the room where Adam lay. They said little, probably fearful of upsetting the balance of things or setting off my crying.

Cain left the room shortly thereafter, his jaw clenched.

Naava went out a little while later and began to talk to Aya. I think they believed me preoccupied with Adam, so their tongues were looser than usual. Truth be told, I was a little surprised that Naava was confiding anything of her experience to Aya.

"It was a gift," said Naava.

"From whom?" said Aya. "The prince?"

Naava lowered her voice and spoke with a vengeance I was already too familiar with. "What do you know of that?"

Aya said, "You will not find out with your hands on me like that."

A brief silence.

"Dara said you were going to meet him," said Aya.

Naava laughed. "You think you know everything. You know nothing." Naava paused briefly. I imagined that she was chewing the inside of her cheek, as Adam did and as she always did when she didn't have an answer. Finally she hissed, "Do not speak of this to anyone. Do you hear me, Aya?"

"Cain is pleased with this arrangement?" Aya said sweetly.

Naava's voice burst forth with more urgency. "What Cain does not know will not hurt him. Besides, he will find out soon enough, without your meddling."

Aya snorted.

There was a short silence, and then Naava said, "I need to ask you something."

Aya laughed derisively. "Even though you have just spit on me?"

Naava ignored Aya's comment and plunged into her request. "Do you think you could henna my hair like Dara's? And do my eyes like hers?" *Ah, there it is. She wants something.* I knew her false camaraderie must have had something behind it.

"So, I must keep your secret *and* give of my services," said Aya. "It's a wonder I help you at all. What would you do without me?" She sighed. "If I have time," she continued. "Father needs herbs for his fever and—"

"Not now," said Naava. "For the festival."

Another silence. I could hear Aya unhooking her pot from her three-legged cooking apparatus and setting it roughly upon the ground. It sloshed heavily with her remedies.

"I think we could come to a satisfactory arrangement," said Aya. "I should like a new robe."

"Why do you need one?" said Naava. "You cannot go. They would toss you outside the city, where the lepers live."

"I would like a robe," Aya repeated. "A blue one like the sea. For my help with your hair and eyes."

Naava laughed. "Whatever you wish."

After a moment Aya said, "And now you must answer a question of mine. Which brother are you seducing, Naava? I cannot tell." Her wooden spoon banged against her pot. "I care not about Cain, but you are trampling on Abel's heart, always making eyes at him like you do, even though he has grown weary of you."

Naava snorted. "Abel is a shepherd. A shepherd, Aya. He herds sheep and goats."

Another short silence. "What's wrong with being a shepherd?" snarled Aya.

"You don't know? Shepherds are *slaves*, Aya. They do what the priest of the city *wants* them to do," Naava sneered. "A farmer is important. He provides barley and wheat and garlic and leeks for the people."

"A shepherd provides milk and cheese and ghee," said Aya.

"They're not the same thing," said Naava.

"No?" said Aya. "What of the prince? What does he contribute?"

This silence stretched out longer than all the others. "It's not important," said Naava finally. "He is a prince, and he has arranged for me to play Inanna, Queen of the Heavens, at the festival."

All night, I sat awake by Adam's side.

I pondered the worry in Aya's voice, the abandon in Naava's. *How could two daughters of mine differ in so many ways?* They were like night and day, fire and water, sea and dry land.

How powerless I felt to direct either's course! How angry it made me that their talk of others was so scornful!

But maybe I had taught them this: to overlook the glory of what we had for the longing of something we did not possess. I cannot claim to know where the truth lies. I only know that in some way I will be held responsible, and this makes me tremble.

Dara

Every day I learn more about Anu, the Father of Heaven, and Enki, the Lord of the Earth, and Enlil, the Lord of the Air, and Inanna, the Queen of Heaven. I hear so many stories from Balili, from Zenobia, and from Puabi. Elohim's name is becoming like smoke, sometimes there and sometimes not, so when Balili asks me, "Who does your family worship?" I open my mouth, but only squeaks come out. I cannot remember how Aya said to pray to Elohim. This bothers me, because I know that Aya said to talk to Him when I feel lonely or am in trouble. And Aya was the one who took care of Turtle for me.

So I start talking to Inanna, the Queen of Heaven. It might be the morning repast or the evening repast, but always, when I think of it, I whisper to Inanna, "Be with Aya and Jacan and Abel and Cain and Naava and Mama and Father . . . and Goat and . . . make your light shine upon their faces and their work." This last part is something Zenobia says when she prays in front of the family shrine. Sometimes I fold my hands. Sometimes I can't because I have babies in my arms, so I just mouth the words and hope that Inanna can hear me.

I am nervous that Mama will be angry at me for stealing her seeds and that she will see me at the festival and turn her back to me. Then I will have to stay with the city people all the time and never go home.

Also, I am not absolutely sure that Mama's seeds will work. Maybe they are too old. And I am sorry I brought them here for Ahassunu instead of Mama to use. So I find out from Zenobia where Ahassunu has planted the seeds, and in the middle of the day when no one is there because of the hot sun, I find the right planter on the rooftop and dig out the seeds. I plant other seeds instead. That way, the growing will take a long time, and I will be back with my family before they are stalks. I do not want to be there when Ahassunu wakes up to baby palm trees.

I wrap Mama's seeds in my robe and hide them in one of my clay jars. I paint a red stripe all the way around the jar. The stripe is for the Tree of Life seeds. Only I know.

Soon I have many fittings—for sandals of reed and leather, for robes that open in front or go over the head, for hairdressings of silver and gold and beads. I have to stand still for so long that I have to cross my legs so my pee-pee won't come out. All I want to do is to go with Balili to where he teaches, so that maybe when he has other things to do, he will hand me the tablet and say, "Well, my star pupil, teach them well." Then he will disappear, and I will have the attention of all the children. It is the best feeling in all the world to be the teacher.

When I told Aya all about it, Aya moved her nose like a rabbit and said, "This writing, what does it look like? Will you teach me?"

I said yes, but I have not been home in a long time, and Aya has not come to visit me in the city. Naava has, but Balili says she is too busy to see me.

One day, only seven days until the festival, I am showing Puabi how to hold a stylus. We are sitting cross-legged in the rectangle of shade made by the prince's house, our backs up against the cool mud bricks. I demonstrate, then Puabi takes the stylus and tries to copy me.

"No," I say, pushing Puabi's thumb down. "Like this. Good. Now draw *water*."

Puabi does, except her lines are straight like a stick.

"Like this," I correct her, taking the stylus and drawing two waves, one on top of the other.

Just then the prince walks around the corner.

Puabi stands and hands me the stylus. She runs to greet the prince, yelling, "Papa, Papa."

The prince laughs and swings her up into his arms.

I remember my father doing that to me, and I smile.

The prince turns to me and speaks in his own language, now that I know it. "I have something to ask you," he says. "It is of critical importance." He sets Puabi down and squeezes her cheeks. Looking down at her, he says, "I am thirsty, what *will* your poor father do?" and Puabi jumps up and down and says, "I get it. I get it."

The prince nods and watches as Puabi runs back around the corner.

I straighten my robe and lay the wet tablet and stylus in my lap.

The prince sits down next to me and wraps his arms around his knees. He's wearing a huge gold star around his neck, and it swings back and forth when he moves. I cannot take my eyes off it for a long time.

"Your sister Naava," the prince says.

I look at the prince's smooth face. It reminds me of Turtle's wide round shell. I want to touch it, to feel its softness. But I do not.

"She has not been with a man, no?" says the prince.

I think this is a funny question. Of course Naava has been with lots of men—Father, Cain, and Abel—oh, yes, Jacan too. And she must have been with some of the men in the marketplace, because Balili said she visits the city.

The prince's eyes look like the clay pellets that I make for Abel's and Jacan's slingshots—round and big. He laughs nervously and says, "What I mean is, has she lain with a man?"

I am happy to give the prince any information he's looking for. After all, I do not want to give him or Ahassunu any reason to throw me out into the desert where I could be eaten by the wicked lion. "Well, she sleeps with me and Jacan and—"

The prince interrupts. "Jacan is . . ." He pauses for me to answer.

"My brother," I answer. "My *twin* brother. He came out first, then it was me. Mama says that I was very kind to her when I was born—"

"You were saying about your sister, whom she has lain with," says the prince.

I think the prince is rude to interrupt me. I am telling him very important things about myself, things that he should know if I am taking care of his children.

"Cain and Abel sleep outside mostly, so I don't know if she ever sleeps with them," I tell him.

"Mmm," says the prince.

I shake my head. I don't think that Naava has ever spent the night in the city.

"What about the blood between her legs?" says the prince.

My mouth goes like this: O. "Is something the matter with Naava?" I ask.

The prince laughs. "No, certainly not, I am just wondering if she has had her first month yet."

"She has had many months," I tell him. "She is older than Aya, and Aya is older than me. Wait a moment, I will tell you how many months Naava is." I take up the stylus and make bird scratches in the wet clay, moving my lips as I count. I look up.

The prince is studying my face, his lips twitching like Mongoose's tail when Mongoose is getting ready to pounce on a snake.

"She is about one six . . . um, one hundred and sixty-eight months." I hold up the tablet to show my countings to the prince. Balili would be proud of me.

Puabi comes around the corner with a mug in the shape of a lion in her hands. She walks slowly, so as not to spill anything.

The prince takes the mug and says to me, "You've been most helpful. I'll tell Zenobia that you deserve a sweet."

Puabi looks up. "Me too?" she says.

"You too, little one," says the prince. He sips his beer through a reed stalk and waves good-bye.

Puabi and I wave back. Puabi says, "Mama say your sister is a rat. She will be sorry if she comes here."

Eve

Adam's fever broke after two days.

Abel made Adam a cane out of a small poplar tree, and Adam walked with it every morning, grimacing and grunting like a boar. It was painful to watch.

Adam remembered nothing I had said to him in those first few dark hours, and I did not reiterate my feelings.

I felt it a continual challenge to hold on to the few lucid memories of that night; everything seemed so different and harder to sort out when I was in the thick of my normal routine.

Abel, the dear heart, was with us more in those difficult times. He returned home each night rather than staying out on the steppes with his flocks. He was concerned, I knew, about the lion's presence and what harm it could do to me and his sisters.

On the night that Adam's fever broke, as I was blowing out the oil lamps and checking on the girls, I heard, from the stables, Abel singing in his low voice. I stopped, stood still, and the melody washed over me like a much-needed cool breeze. Oh, how I had missed his singing!

Tears sprang up in my eyes, and I sat down slowly upon the dirt, to let his song fill me. I lifted my wet face up to the dark luminous sky pocked with stars and felt such an overwhelming oneness with everything around me that I could not stop crying.

Call me a fool, but then you have never been overwhelmed with wonder like that. It was enough to make me believe in Elohim, enough to make me feel there was a higher purpose for my life than the drudgery, the everydayness I so dreaded.

Well, almost.

Aya

So many betrayals, like bolts of lightning. How savage and ruthless they can be.

Tell me this, if you can: How do you stop a river once it has the force of melting snows behind it? So determined is Cain to have his revenge, so determined is Naava to be loved, so determined is Dara to belong, so determined is Mother to find happiness, so determined is Father to unify his family, that their rushing river is bound to overflow its banks and sweep all the trust and loyalty away.

Ah, me. So it is. I am called upon once more to right the wrongs of a thoughtless family member.

After all, if it's not me, no one else will do it. I must deliver Mother from an ill done to her, for Father has not once uttered an apology for selling Mother's garden. Thank the starry heavens, he did not think to barter for my herb plot! He has accepted Mother's ministrations with not one grateful word or even a single regretful look. He is blind not to see Mother's love. He is deaf not to hear her words of apology for a misdirected life.

So. I must resort to stealing. Not by choice, but by necessity.

I am the steady hand of punishment. I am the consistent provider of food. I am the knowledgeable mender of ailments. I am the merciless killer of snakes. I am the girl who will not learn her limits. Ever.

This is *my* story, whether I like it or not. Do not pity me. I rather like the challenge.

In the end, I had to tell Mother everything, for she wouldn't have known where all the seeds came from, and in mentioning it to Father, she would have been informed that it was because of the good hand of Elohim. Now, I do not mind if Elohim gets praise and adoration for the things *He* has done, but if He receives recognition for something *I* have done, that is where I draw the line.

I chose the cover of night, when the last person had departed Mother's garden to return to the city. The line of torches was a yellow snake winding northward toward the main gates. I caught faint bits of conversation and laughter upon the breeze when it was blowing my way, but other than that, the torches looked like strange little unassisted flames dancing above the plains. I watched until the last bobbing light became a vague circle of brightness on the horizon, then made my way past the garden's boulders—which the men from the city had rolled thunderously off their carts to enforce their admonishments to "stay away"—and entered the chatter of the garden. So many noises—frogs, birds, crickets, leaves, and water. I should have liked to rest my head awhile, but, no, I had come on a mission, and I was going to see it through. I am Aya the Brave, Aya the Stouthearted, Aya the Persistent, but you already knew that.

I set my oil lamp down on the ground and lit it with glowing embers from a clay pot. This way, if I could not see by the light of the moon—which was growing each night to its fullness for the festival—I could bring my collections back to the lamp to identify them before placing them in my baskets, so as to assure an even assortment of seeds.

The fragrance of the flowering trees and shrubs was like the sweetest of rains. So many plants and trees were fruiting now, their pods bursting open, their fruit ripe and broken upon the ground, that I was able to fill my baskets with a wide selection of seeds, all waiting to be dried and planted in Mother's new garden.

My leg bothered me little while I was there, for I was keenly aware of the hallowedness of the place. Most seeds had come from the Garden of Elohim.

Every plant spoke of its Creator. This was what I missed most, the awe that flowed through my body when I entered this place. It was a green-leafed respite away from the harshness and bitterness of life.

Except that the city people had cut some of the vegetation back, ravaging the sheer wildness of it. They had trimmed and shaped some of the bushes. I found several birds' nests, torn apart and discarded, on one of the paths. I discovered a hare, bloodied and fly-covered, caught in a woven reed trap, that they had forgotten. The waste! The profanity! They gave no regard or respect to their environment. Woe be to them when Elohim finds out. That is all I will say on the matter.

All in all, I gathered enough seeds to have difficulty carrying them back. It was then that my leg ached and my shoulders cried out. I hummed Mother's and Father's song—not loudly, of course, because I could not keep a tune— and somehow it bolstered me up so that I could make it back to the courtyard without mishap.

When I woke on the morrow, I overheard Mother and Naava talking. I sat up and strained to hear what they were saying.

Mother said, "Well, you must tell him, and in the meantime I will talk to your Father. This is a difficult situation, but maybe it is only because I did not see it happening this way."

I stood and went to the doorway. I peered out.

Mother touched Naava's belly briefly, then embraced Naava. Naava was crying. "There now," said Mother, wiping the tears away.

Well, if I had not seen it myself, Naava would never have told me, for I had been right. In some way, she was getting her comeuppance.

I entered the courtyard, yawning. I did not want either of them to think I'd been spying.

Just then Mother saw the abundance of seeds piled high in the baskets. She clapped her hands and said, "Oh." She moved closer and began to sort through them. "Oh, where did these come from? Who has given us such a grand gift?" She turned to me. "Do you think it is Abel's doing?" she said. All good things came from Abel, in Mother's opinion. *Was I not capable of giving her a gift?*

I shook my head and told her that she could start over with these seeds from Elohim's Garden. That they were a gift from me.

I am part of the rushing river I have spoken about. I am not without blame. I know this. Despite the fact that I have acted as the judgment of Elohim by slashing down Cain's dates, others, if they knew of my actions, would not approve. Mother would say, "Aya, you have endangered us all," and Father would say, "Only Elohim can judge."

But as I see it, none of my interests interferes with anyone else's. I am determined for Elohim to hear me. I am determined that my leg will be healed. Neither of these things requires the help of someone other than Elohim, so I am freed from the workings of my family, unless someone has sabotaged another, as Father and Naava have done to Mother and as Cain has done to Dara and Goat. Then I am called upon to administer justice.

Do you not think this is a fair arrangement?

This word *fair* is not without its problems. When we speak of fair weather or a fair price or a fair fight or someone who is fair, do we mean *agreeable* and, if so, to whom?

For example, I would say the following circumstance is *un*fair. Our river's shores have grown marshlike, and the stench of rot has become unbearable, because the city, which lies upriver, has slowly diverted more water to their irrigation channels, to their cisterns. This is agreeable only to them, and both Father and Cain have talked late into the night of how to remedy the situation. Act now, and the city people could overcome us by force. Act later, and we shall have nothing left. Poor us.

Certainly our going to the festival will show the city people that we are an amiable folk, and having Dara working for the prince gives us some degree of freedom in our interactions. The prince, it seems, has allowed Naava a role in their festival, and this can only mean that they want an ongoing relationship with our family—or Naava alone.

The wager that Cain entered into was not wise, and although he has already failed at it, he is determined that he will overcome it by offering the best of his other crops. What I would like to ask is: *What about the offering to Elohim?* But this will be Cain's dilemma, not mine.

Naava

The beating of the drums and the blowing of the horns sounded unceasingly now from the north. The rhythms had swelled over the past days—it was the city's New Year's festival, the time of autumn's harvest. Everything was dry and parched from the summer sun, and now, the city people believed, the god Enki had died and gone to the underworld. He would rise once more when the steppes and plains greened and blossomed again. This was the season of Inanna, Queen of Heaven, and they celebrated her and asked her to bless their fields and their wombs.

Now, at last, the day had come when Naava was to visit the city with her family. All summer long she had dreamed of such an occasion and her spectacular entrance into the city, ever since Adam and Cain came back in early summer, dizzy with the city's beer.

Her robe was ready, her hair had been hennaed, and her nails had been decorated. She had taken no small amount of ribbing for this, by Adam and her brothers, because she had had to labor out in the fields with the rest of the family—harvesting—and with all the threshing, winnowing, and washing of the grain, it had been a constant trial to remain presentable.

The prince had dispatched one of his wagons and servants to escort Naava and her family into the city. Cain, Abel, and Jacan loaded up cheeses and sweets and beer to take as gifts.

Adam's leg was not yet mended, but still he had insisted upon going. He was curious to see if all Cain had said about the city was true.

Cain and Abel had withheld their first fruits for Elohim, as agreed, and their sacrifices, or offerings, would take place the following evening, to coincide with the city's celebrations and the full moon. Naava was suspicious, though. She saw Cain hefting a mysterious large basket into the rear of the wagon, and she knew that he would be offering something to Inanna, just to make sure that he had covered all the gods. Whenever he and Naava had talked about this, as Cain held her in his arms, Naava had insisted he was being irrational. *If* there were a god—"or goddess," he would chime in—Naava said they would have known already. *Why would a god not have shown himself or herself to people he or she had made?*

At least Naava had been able to convince Cain—after the prince had asked her to warn him—not to take revenge on the city men by releasing aphids into their fields. "Think," she said. "Be not rash. The aphids will only find their way here, to *your* fields."

"I have ladybugs, though, and praying mantises," said Cain.

"It doesn't matter. Whatever you wreak on them will come back to haunt you," said Naava.

Cain agreed, in the long run, and had not lifted his hand against the city men.

At least not yet.

Eve had cleaned up, the best she was able, from the hard work in the fields and orchards. Her face was scrubbed raw, and she had plaited her long hair and wrapped it around her head, securing it with a decorative wood stick in the shape of a twig insect, whittled for her by Jacan. She wore a necklace of white shells and a bracelet of silver. But all in all she was a swollen gourd, ready to be split open, and therefore would not be a threat to Naava. She looked like a servant and nothing more—although Naava felt a twinge of jealousy when she saw the look on Adam's face, the one of bright surprise at seeing Eve so different, so lovely, at least to him. Adam kissed Eve on the cheek and said, "You are wearing my necklace and my bracelet."

Eve nodded shyly and kissed him back.

Aya had bound her hair with grasses and had tucked a lily behind one ear. *How ridiculous*, Naava thought. She looked absolutely primitive, but how would her backward sister have known? She had never been to the city.

When Naava was about to climb into the wagon, Eve said to Adam, "Look. Isn't it spectacular, Naava's robe? Look how she wove the Garden into it."

Naava twirled, smiling, and Adam studied the intricate stitches—the bright sun poking out from white billowing clouds, the blue flowing river, the green bushes, the vibrant reds and yellows of the flowers, even a gazelle and a lion. "It is very accurate," he said softly, then turned away.

The servant was civil but surly, and when he saw Abel helping Aya into the wagon, he barked something that caused Cain to stop what he was doing. Cain and the man bickered like foxes fighting over a hare, before Cain turned to Aya and said, "It is as we feared. Sister, you will have to stay here."

Aya did not move from where she sat. She looked at Abel, then at Cain, and said evenly, "I am going."

Cain said, "You can't. They won't let you in. They think you're bad luck."

Abel said to Cain, "Leave us at the city gate. I will stay with her."

Aya stole a glance at Abel. He smiled at her, and it made Naava want to retch. For a moment she was envious. But the feeling didn't last long. With Cain at her side—his hand reaching surreptitiously into the front of her robe when no one was looking—and with thoughts of seeing the prince again, Naava was well on her way to being the happiest woman alive.

Just one problem pricked her like a thorn. Naava held a secret in her heart, which she had told only Eve. Eve had instructed her to tell Cain, that the right decision might be made. Naava would follow her mother's advice, but not until she had had her fill of the city—and the prince.

And the glorious festival.

Oh, the music, the wondrous music! Naava had never heard anything like it in all her life. Its grandeur and lustiness—the harps and lyres and flutes and clappers and drums and cymbals—mingled so oddly and enchantingly. The belt-attached harps and the ram-shaped lyres had strings of gut and sinew that were plucked, and out came the most soothing sound, like being underwater and hearing the soft muffled sounds of people talking above.

Naava's family had an advantageous view from the wagon. Swarming about them, people danced and shouted, dressed in their scarlet and yellow and orange finery. Banners swayed and snapped in the breeze. They were draped everywhere, in every imaginable color. The smell and smoke of roasting meat and sweet perfume rose thickly in the air, and everywhere there were strange sounds—clangings and clashings and thunkings.

Naava thought she would never find the prince in this mayhem, but she would have all day and all night, so in that long interim, surely he would find her.

The mountain of steps had been washed clean. There was a line of people up to the very top, where the temple shone a brilliant white in the sun as the priestess in her equally white robes and Balili in his gold headdress accepted the people's offerings and libations to Inanna.

Eve and Adam were mute; they were astounded. Never before had they seen such a spectacle. They had heard these things from Cain and Naava certainly, but they had not imagined it quite this way, Naava could tell. Eve stared at the women, all bangled and painted. She looked away when they blinked at her with their blackened eyes and long eyelashes, bashful in the face of their audacity, brashness, and wanton appearance. Naava laughed inside—oh, Eve had so much to learn. Naava saw her mother's eyes shift to Adam, terrified of his response to these strangely exotic women, but they were the least of his concerns.

"I had no idea," he said again and again to Cain, his head swiveling this way and that. "These people are so . . . so advanced, far more than I could ever imagine."

Cain laughed and said, "I told you. You weren't listening."

"The buildings . . . the stalls . . . I could never have fathomed this." Awe and fear flickered across Adam's face.

It was at precisely this point that Naava felt another shift occur, this one between child and parent, parent and child. Now she saw for certain that Cain and she were wiser than their parents and that Adam and Eve would be left behind, abandoned, if they did not change their ways. She knew her father and mother would have called her cruel and insensitive if she were to voice it exactly like that. But her desire was overwhelming, an irresistible yearning to make her own way in the world without having to worry about the primitive customs and practices of her mother and father. It was this last thought that caused her a small amount of consternation, a pang of regret for the loss of something she was leaving behind, and only the magnificent sounds and sights of the city could sweep it away.

"Dara!" Eve stood up shakily in the wagon and waved her hand back and forth. The day marked Dara's homecoming. "Dara," Eve shouted again. Dara would stay until the baby was born, then go back to caring for the city's babies. Eve had been ecstatic about it, getting her littlest back, even if it was for just a short while. "There's Dara," she said, pointing toward a small group of people crowding around the roaring fires that licked at charred boars and gazelles impaled on spits.

"Where?" asked Jacan. His eyes followed Eve's finger, and once he could see Dara he waved furiously at her.

Where Dara is, the prince will be too, thought Naava. She adjusted the bracelet on her wrist, the one the prince had told her to wear, and she sat up straighter, tucking a stray hair behind her ear. She bit her lips to draw the blood into them.

Suddenly the dancing people began parting like water for their wagon. They gawked and stared at Naava and her family and bent their heads in acknowledgment. Naava knew this was because of her great beauty, and instead of bowing her head timidly, she looked them in the eyes, as if to say, *Yes, thank you, I acknowledge your tribute, and I am grateful for it.*

Wherever the wagon went, it created a wake of silence. The instruments pinged slower and slower, like raindrops after a rain, until they faltered, then stopped. The presence of Naava and her family had mesmerized the city people. There was no other explanation for it.

If only Aya and Abel could see this. The servant had done as Abel had requested and left the two of them at the city's entrance. If they had been here, they would have seen that Naava was right all along, that there *was* something special about her. Observe all these people—sophisticated, cultured people—who knew upon first glance. *Why was Naava's family so blind, so stupid?* They worked her fingers to the bone without one thankful remark. They made her toil at sheep-plucking time and harvesttime, and aid in all the undertakings, minor and major, that filled their dull and colorless days. *Why did they constantly fail to acknowledge the treasure they had among them?*

Then the prince was up ahead, like the sun appearing from behind a gray cloud. There was something different about him, but Naava could not place it. He stood up on a box and waved for the music and dancing to resume. The frivolity returned slowly, with snippets of laughter and talk, a note here and there, until the marketplace had returned to its former din and clamor.

The prince approached the wagon with several bare-chested men who were also wearing gold jewelry around their upper arms. Their long black hair had been pulled back and bound. Two of them had paintings on their arms. One had a large black star on his back, which Naava saw as the men helped them each down from the wagon.

The two women who had visited Eve and seen her garden stood off in the distance, watching, waiting. They pushed Dara forward with their hands, and Dara ran to Eve's side. Jacan went to sit by her, clasping Dara's fingers in his own.

The prince bowed to Eve and Adam. He said, "Friends, welcome. Everything you must enjoy. Please, drink, be merry, for tomorrow is no matter to us." He turned to Cain. "Show your father where the girl-houses are. Please, no coin or barter today."

Cain's cheeks and neck turned a pomegranate red. Naava wondered what these girl-houses were and what Cain and Adam could want with them.

The prince looked to Eve. "I need your daughter. She can come with me, no?" He reached out and touched Naava's arm.

Eve looked up, startled, and nodded.

"No," Cain blurted.

"No?" said the prince.

Naava found this amusing, two men fighting over her. Of course, she wanted the prince to win. This is what she had been waiting for. Because she knew that someday, when he would marry her—devote his entire life to her— she would be inexpressibly happier living in the city. If her father knew what she and Cain had done, he would insist that they be married. But he didn't know, and she did not care, anyway. They couldn't force her to do anything.

Cain said, "On this special day, we would like to be together as a *family*."

The prince glared at Cain. Then, in an even voice, he said, "We will ask Naava."

Eve and Adam turned to Naava, questions in their eyes, concern etched on their foreheads. "Naava?" said Adam.

Naava barely heard her father. She had been chosen by the prince, in the presence of her parents. Her heart felt as though it would burst with joy as she blinked and nodded her head.

"Yes?" said Adam. "You want to go?"

Naava said "Yes," but she did not look at the prince directly, for this would have indicated her joy in having her dreams realized. She did not look at Cain either, for she knew what she would see. There would be fire, an all-consuming fire in his eyes, for which she would pay later. But she was not thinking about later.

Cain leaned close to Adam and whispered, loud enough for all to hear, "You do not know what he wants."

Adam dipped his head to the prince to give his permission, then replied to Cain, "Leave your worries behind. The prince is our host. He has promised his protection"—here he glanced at the prince with upraised eyebrows—"has he not?"

The prince nodded. "She will not be harmed."

Cain glared at the prince. His fists were clenched, and a vein throbbed near his temple.

The prince continued, ignoring Cain's anger. "My men will take you to the food stalls first. Fill your bellies. Enjoy the festivities. We will join you later." He led Naava away from the wagon, down an inner street, away from the room where they had previously met.

"Where are we going?" said Naava.

"My house," said the prince.

Naava looked behind her and saw the two familiar women following, with their children, at a distance. "Why are they following us?" said Naava.

The prince did not answer.

Naava wondered at the prince's brusqueness, his hurry. She had time to study his face again, and suddenly it dawned upon her. He had blackened his eyes like the women, and he was painted like them too—rosy cheeks, swollen lips. "What have you done to your face?" she said.

"Soon you will know."

They made their way through the narrow dusty streets, encountering drunken revelers and cavorting couples and mangy dogs lingering along the sides. Everyone else—the families, the children, the shepherds, the farmers, the artisans—had hastened toward the city's middle, the marketplace.

Soon the prince halted in front of a carved wooden door. Naava was astonished, for never before had she seen such a thing. *Where would the prince have gotten such a large piece of wood?* All Naava had seen were the scrawny willow and poplar and tamarisk trees that grew by the river, nothing like this solid piece of whatever-it-was. She reached out to feel it.

"You like it?" said the prince. "It is from the north. Oak."

Naava nodded, allowing herself to be led inside.

The room was not stark and bare-boned like home but splendid. Naava struggled to accustom her eyes to the cool darkness. Woven rugs of reds and blues hung on the walls and covered the dirt floors. Several chairs of the same heft as the door and tables made of wood carved with magnificent beasts had been artfully arranged into small seating areas. A thin wisp of smoke rose from a clay pot, its smell sweet and musky.

But Naava had little time to look, for the prince was dragging her to the back, through other rooms with columns—oh, they were magnificent!—to a staircase. They clambered up, exiting out onto a lush rooftop bordered by green and flowering plants in large clay vases alongside wooden benches. Off to the side was a stack of rolled-up reed mats, similar to the ones Eve made for her own family.

The rooftop was scorching hot, and Naava shielded her eyes from the afternoon sun. She was able to see Inanna's temple from where she stood. Naava turned to the prince. "It's beautiful," she said.

Right then, the two women and their children who had been trailing behind the prince and Naava hurried out onto the rooftop. *What was their business with the prince and her?*

The prince turned to Naava. "They will—how do you call it?—*prepare* you. You must be ready when the sun is three-quarters to the horizon." He pointed to a position in the sky.

Confused, Naava looked at the women, trying to remember their names, then back to the prince. "Do you not like how I look?" she said, the disappointment evident in her voice.

The prince ignored Naava and spoke to the women in his tongue. He grabbed Naava's shoulder and twirled her around, so the women could see her robe. The women nodded and *oohe*d and *ahhe*d, all the while raking their eyes over Naava's entire length. They waved their hands about her face, pinched her cheeks, and brushed her eyebrows with their fingers.

She would not stand for it. "I want to go back," she said to the prince, in the strongest voice she could muster. "Can we not meet later, in the usual place?"

The prince lifted his hands, as if he'd given up. "They will make you Inanna. You want this, no?" He waited for her answer, his eyes imploring.

"Yes," she said slowly. "But won't you be with me?"

The prince leaned close and kissed her, and his lips were wet and soft. He drew back and held her chin but said nothing.

Naava stared at his eyes, black like her mother's Tree of Life seeds, letting this moment sink into her innermost being. She would be Inanna, and she would be adored.

The prince kissed her lightly upon the cheek, like the brush of a butterfly wing, and with that, he was gone, down the stairs.

And then began the most unusual hours of Naava's life. She was leapt upon by those vulgar women, who glared at her like hyenas, and transformed, with many pullings and proddings, into a vision of their design. Naava did not understand their chatter. They seemed oblivious to her protests. They yanked on her hair and pulled on her eyelids and jerked her chin this way and that, grunting either their approval or repugnance.

The women laid out animal-hair brushes and small wooden boxes which, when opened, displayed the most astonishing colors of crushed stone and sparkling minerals. These the women stroked on her face, and Naava began to wonder what she looked like.

There were extraordinarily fine hairpieces made of lapis lazuli and magnetite and coral and agate, laid in fantastic shapes of butterflies and stars and frogs. There were gold and copper and silver bracelets and nose rings and necklaces, all with exquisite etchings.

When they were done with her face and hair, they moved to her hands and arms. Very carefully, the women used henna to paint flourishes and flowers and dots on Naava's palms and fingertips and wrists, turning her hands this way and that to get at them properly. She had to sit for a long time to allow the artwork to dry. When she had sat long enough, they twisted her around and around to see what they might have overlooked.

Obviously the prince had chosen her to play Inanna because she was beautiful.

She only wished she could see what she looked like. She wanted to know what her parents would think when they saw her. *Would they see how wrong they'd been about her?*

If asked, Naava would have said that the most glorious part of that day was when she was led up Inanna's steps the back way. It was the moment when she realized that this was happening—*really* happening. She was going to be presented to all the people of the city—and to her family—as someone special, as someone of splendor.

The women had at last acquiesced and let Naava glimpse herself in a polished silver mirror at the very end of their preparations. What she beheld was a creature beyond her imagination, a woman so completely obliterated by adornment that she could not see any evidence of herself. *This is what it feels like to be Inanna,* she thought. *This is what it feels like to be a goddess.*

So she carried herself like one. She pressed her shoulders back. She held her neck erect and her head high, which was difficult because she wore a heavy crown of wired leaves and butterflies and flowers that sprang exuberantly around her head with each and every step she took.

There were an abundance of steps to Inanna's temple, and Naava felt slightly wilted by the time she reached the top. As she rounded the corner of the temple, she smelled the incense. She saw the sea of waiting people below and immediately felt a wave of dizziness pass over her. She heard the priestess's voice reciting something in a booming voice.

Then, a pause. It was so quiet that Naava could hear a child cry out from below, followed by the parents' whispered scoldings.

Just as quickly there was a rattling—a *shush shush shush* noise—from inside the temple. Naava glimpsed the terror on the people's faces. Again the noise came from inside, and again came the gasps and quick genuflections of the crowd.

Only one small segment of the masses below did not bow, did not gasp. Adam and Eve stood near the front, agape at all the goings-on, not aware they should be afraid. Cain bowed. He understood the priestess's words and the unusual sound. Dara smiled and whispered in his ear. He frowned, and his brow furrowed. He shook his head, lifted her up, and put her on his shoulders. Back and forth they talked, and at one point Cain seemed agitated with her and took her off his shoulders. Naava couldn't see Dara anymore, the crowds were shoving so. When Cain crossed his arms and stared at Naava, she felt the smallest sense of unease wash over her.

She brushed it aside. *Just wait, just wait,* she thought. *The best is yet to come.*

Dara

The only person I tell is Cain. When he bows to Inanna with all the other people, I whisper in his ear about what Balili is doing way up there in the house on top of the steps with his bull rattle, *shush shush shush*. Cain doesn't believe me at first.

"Balili showed it to me," I told him.

Cain shakes his head and points at the little house. "It's the breath of Inanna, come down to visit us."

I shake my head. "No," I say. "Here. Look." I pull one out of my robe. "I was going to show you later." I show him my baby rattle, shaking it close to his ear.

Cain looks around him and says, "You cannot mean all of these people are worshipping a rattle."

I nod and pull on his robe, for him to lift me up.

He frowns and picks me up and puts me on his shoulders, so I can see the heads of all the people, like carrot tops sticking up from the ground. I can even see Zenobia and Puabi and Ahassunu and Shala bowing low to the ground and looking up at Bosom Lady at the top of the steps. And now there's Inanna, the Queen of Heaven, with a crown of springy things around her head.

Cain looks up at me and says, "See? I told you so."

"That's Naava," I say. "She's going to live with the prince."

Cain sets me down real quick and grabs my arm. "What did you say?"

I shrug. "Zenobia says she's going to live with them. To make babies."

Cain looks and looks at me. He chews the inside of his mouth like Naava and Father do when they're thinking about something. He lets me go and stands back up with his arms across his chest.

I tug at his robe again. I can't see anything, except for hands and bellies and feet.

"Not now, Dara," Cain says. His voice is scary angry.

When Mama called me over from Ahassunu and Zenobia, I had so much I had to learn about my family. Jacan had grown taller like me. Father had almost gotten eaten by that bad lion, and Abel and Jacan had saved him. Now he walked around like Aya.

I asked Mama where Aya was.

Mama said, "We had to leave her at the gate. You remember how the women startled at seeing her bad leg?"

I nodded.

Mama said, "Abel stayed with her. He is kind like that, you know."

I nodded again, but then there came Aya, with Abel supporting her with his hand. It didn't even look like Aya was limping! She was wearing a new robe, the color of Mama's and her eyes, and now Aya holds her head up to the sky, instead of down to the ground.

Mama smelled good, like rain and lemons. She laughed and brushed up against Father all the time. I thought Father might tip over, but he didn't, he just smiled and kissed Mama a lot.

Just look, I go away from my family, and they all go to sleep like caterpillars and wake up like butterflies. They are so different.

When the prince first led Naava away, Cain took us all to where two big men with red sweaty faces were roasting a boar and a gazelle over a big fire. Round and round the meat turned, crackling and popping and smelling like garlic and herbs. My insides growled, and my tongue watered. Cain sat everyone down at tables and went back to get some food. Thank the stars and moon that I didn't have to take care of those children for a while. It was just me and Aya taking care of Mama, now that she was going to have the baby.

It was funny. Mama drank too much beer, and the lines around her eyes got all crinkly like sand with ridges. After tasting the meat, she winked at Aya and said, "Well, Aya, I think you could teach them a few things."

Aya looked at Abel really quick, then back at Mama, then she got as red as a fox's tail.

"It's true," said Abel.

Aya hid her face with her hands. But she was smiling, I could tell.

The grown-up people were dancing all around us, round and round like the boar was spinning. A man came up to Mama and told her she was very beautiful; what was her name? She didn't understand, so I told her what he said. Mama giggled and said, "Eve."

"Eve," he said. "Eve." He put his hands on her eyelids, to see if her eyes were real. He told her that they were the lapis lazuli of the desert and kissed her hand. She smiled.

Father reached over and waved the man's hands away.

"Oh, he's not hurting anything," said Mama.

Father frowned and hissed, "Have you forgotten what they did to Aya?"

"Look at him," Mama said. "He's an old man."

"An old man with a penis," said Father.

Jacan laughed, but Father was not amused.

So many men came up to Mama that Father moved over to sit next to her. If he saw anyone come close, he waved them away.

One of the men stopped to talk to Cain about his dates. He wanted to know what Cain was going to offer them now that his dates were gone.

Cain's nose flapped like laundry hanging in the wind, and he put on his angry face. "Wait and see," he said. "Why do you kick a man when he is down?"

Mama turned to me and said, "What does the man want?"

I said, "He wants Cain's dates."

Mama's eyes flitted from Cain to the man, from the man to Cain. "Do you know the *secret* of my son's dates?" Her eyebrows arched like mushroom caps, and she laughed, giddy, and leaned her chin on her hands. "I taught him." She grabbed Father's arm. "*We* taught him. And guess who taught *us*? Elohim. Blessed be the name of Elohim." She raised her beer goblet into the air. "Blessed be the name of Elohim."

"Mother," said Aya sharply. "That's enough."

Still, Mama laughed. She was starting to sound like Cain.

Naava

When Naava was presented to the masses, she understood nothing.
The priestess—the large round woman who had slaughtered the lamb in
Naava's family's courtyard moons ago—addressed the crowd, and the people bowed to her. Suddenly there was a storm of clapping, and there he
was, by her side, steadying her arm with his hand. "You are beautiful," the
prince whispered as he waved to the crowd. Naava sneaked a look at him
and gasped. He had been decorated even more than she. Jewel after jewel
had been piled on his chest, and he wore a skirt covered with shiny disks
that tinkled as he moved. His face was masklike, and a thick gold band en-
circled his head. "Stay," he murmured to Naava. "I must be cleansed."

He left her then and knelt in front of the priestess. One by one, the
priestess removed his jewels and the gold band around his head. Pausing
to inhale, she slapped him across the face, hard, then again, until his tears
flowed like a spring.

How dare she? Naava fought back an urge to throw herself at the
woman. But she had been told to stay, and stay she would, with all those
eyes upon her. She focused on her family below, noticing Aya and Abel
standing not far from Adam and Eve. *How did they manage to get inside the
gate?* Well, good. They, too, would see her in all her glory.

The prince kissed the priestess's feet as his tears continued to flow.
Satisfied, she gave a grand gesture with her hand, made a loud pronounce-

ment, and began to laden him down again with all his jewels and his crown, returning him to his former glory in no time. The crowd stomped their feet and cheered.

The prince held Naava's gaze as he approached her and took her hand. He kissed her tenderly upon her cheek, and she felt the heat rise to her face.

It was what came next that was jumbled up in Naava's mind whenever she tried to tell it later.

The priestess spoke again—it seemed like some kind of blessing—and threw a splash of scented water upon them. The prince smiled and led Naava toward the entrance of Inanna's temple.

All Naava saw was Cain bounding up the steps, two and three at a time, yelling, "Naava, no!" Several of the prince's men ran after him, but not before Cain had reached the top and grabbed Naava and started yanking her down the stairs.

"It's the Sacred Marriage," Cain said to Naava. "He wants to consummate with Inanna. It's a fertility rite."

Naava was confused. So much was happening all at once. "What are you saying?" she said. "He does not love me?"

Then the men were upon Cain, pulling him from Naava and pushing him down the stairs.

"Do not do it, Naava," Cain yelled. "I love you."

So Cain did love her, the wild animal that he was. Naava turned to the prince. "Do you intend to have me?" she said. A slight thrill trembled through her. "Will you discard me afterward, or will you keep me as a wife?"

This is what I asked for, thought Naava. *But is this what I really want?*

"You are my wife," said the prince, as plainly as he might have said that the bracelet on her arm was his oath to her. "That was the marriage ceremony."

Frightened and alone, Naava could not absorb this information quickly enough. *What was happening? And if she refused to go along with the prince, what would he do to her? To her family? What would Inanna do?* Already she had seen Cain seized by the prince's men.

These things flitted through Naava's head, and she saw clearly, all at once, that despite her deep-seated disdain for certain members of her family, they were all she had, and, without question, they loved her and wanted her to be safe.

It was not enough, though. All these unusual and magnificent things that were happening to her were happening because of her association with the *prince*. He thought she was someone special, and he treated her that way. She knew not what he intended at that precise moment, but he would not hurt her or force her to do anything that she didn't want.

Would he? The memory of their first meeting in the city—the feel of him on top of her, overcoming her—rose up, and a feeble wariness set in.

The prince led her through the doorway, into the dark interior lit by hundreds of lamps, across to the far side of the temple, where a great reed mat lay on the swept mud floor. It was surrounded on either side by roughly carved wooden statues of the city's gods. At the foot of the mat stood the largest statue of all, reaching from the floor to the ceiling. It was Inanna, Naava was sure of it, for Inanna's presence filled the whole place. Crude ringlets framed her solid face, and she sat, hands on thighs, staring forward with bulging eyes. It was both eerie and exhilarating.

"Here," said the prince. Their sandals were touching the reed mat. "I will help you." He began by taking off her fancy headdress, then reached down to untie the sash of her robe.

Naava put her hand on his. "Wait," she said calmly, more calmly than she felt.

The prince's mouth opened, then closed. "Our union ensures many crops and strong babies. Inanna demands it."

"Union," said Naava, biting her lip. *So this is it,* she thought. *This is what Cain and I were practicing for.*

Naava was in a daze. It was all happening so fast.

Oddly enough, she longed for Eve's advice, but Eve was not there.

Eve

After we had eaten and drunk our fill in the city, we made our way with the jostling crowds to Inanna's temple, the grand stairs in the middle of the marketplace. It was late afternoon already. The sun's heat was merciless, and we were sticky with sweat. There was little breeze, and the flies were abundant.

I recognized the plump woman at the top as the one who had killed that precious lamb when she visited us, and when I asked Cain about her, he said she was a priestess of Inanna—she took the people's sacrifices and offered them up to the goddess. She would oversee the day's ceremonies.

As she told their grand Epic of Creation, Cain translated for us, and I was glad to hear this account. I had always wondered about the origin of the city people. Their telling was so different from Adam's and mine. In their version, the gods had grown weary of all the work to be done, so they formed man and woman from the clay of the earth to work for them. Indeed, I thought, Elohim had said the same about Adam and me working, but it was not so much an order as a suggestion for living. I would have to think about this.

It also dawned on me, for the first time, what Dara had meant when she said they held Adam and me in high esteem, for if we had lived from the beginning of time in Dilmun—their version of Eden—we would be godlike. But this served only to confuse me, for if we were created *at the beginning of time,* where had *they* come from? And *when?*

I think I knew the truth about my daughter when she appeared at the top of the steps and I recognized the prince at her side, but my heart was slow to understand what my mind was telling it. What was she doing up there? Why was she adorned so? What was the priestess saying? Cain had stopped translating long before then, but I could see he was agitated.

My heart told me that we had been naive not to trust Cain this time.

As Naava and the prince turned their backs, Naava glanced somewhat apprehensively over her shoulder at us, and Cain tore up the stairs, two and three at a time, yelling, and I thought I would die of embarrassment *and* fear. Embarrassment because here we were, guests at a magnificent event, and one of my own was interfering with the sacred celebration. Fear because I knew not what the prince intended with my eldest daughter. *But,* I thought at the time, *Cain must know something we do not.*

The prince's men bounded up the stairs after Cain and seized him at the top. There was a scuffle as they forced him back down, and I could not distinguish Cain in the blur of limbs. The next thing I knew, Cain was plunging headlong down the stairs, arms and legs askew and head and body pummeled mercilessly by the sun-hardened steps.

I grimaced as he landed in a heap at Dara's feet.

I ran to him. We all ran to him. Everyone was pointing and jabbering. A circle of city people had already formed around my son, as if Cain were a stone dropped from the sky into a river and they were the ripples.

Cain groaned and tried to get up, but he could not. Wildly, he looked around at all of us, his eyes meeting Abel's. "Brother," he said. "You must save our sister. The prince will take away her honor."

No, it couldn't be. Certainly Cain was wrong. Naava would be sworn to Cain, now that they had lain together. Elohim had said that Adam and I were to cleave to each other—as man and woman, as one being—and I assumed this would be the case for my children once they found their complements.

Abel leaned over his brother. "How do you know this?"

Too anguished to explain, Cain fell back upon the ground. "Go. Now." Then he whimpered and held his head. "I would do it for you," he said.

Abel and Adam looked at each other, taking stock of the situation. Together they started up the stairs, where their path was immediately barred by the prince's men. I watched their hands and their faces, knowing they were explaining they wanted Naava back. They wanted to settle this reasonably, but of course, without Cain, neither side could understand the other, and time began to slip away. I clung to the twins, fearful of what might happen next, and felt Aya's protective arm on my shoulder. Naava and the prince had already entered the temple at the top of the steps, and the door had closed behind them. Adam and Abel's distress became more apparent, and eventually they reached down to withdraw their daggers from the straps on their legs.

A riot followed. The prince's men retaliated by drawing their daggers, and they set upon Adam and Abel, jabbing and slashing the air with their weapons. Adam didn't last long—he couldn't have, with his recent injuries—and very quickly he suffered a severe wound to the upper arm, which sent him sprawling down the steps to a place not far from where Cain lay. I thrust the twins into Aya's arms and ran to him.

"Cain," I cried. "Get up. Help them. They cannot do it alone."

Abel was steadfast in his defense, but the men were advancing upon him, and soon he would falter simply because he was outnumbered. I bent over Cain and shook him.

He did not respond.

A voice from the crowd yelled something.

"Mama," yelled Dara. "Run!"

I couldn't leave my sons and my husband. I knelt and put my ear over Cain's mouth. His breath was warm, but he had lost consciousness. I slapped him across the cheek. "Cain!" I screamed. "Cain!"

His eyelids fluttered open, and as he struggled to focus on my face, he groaned.

The crowd closed in then, tightly. Their faces were grim and accusatory. Several roughshod men pushed their way into the inner circle and spit on Cain.

"Aya," I cried. I scanned the crowd all around me frantically, hoping that my children were close. "Dara! Jacan! Aya!"

I heard Dara scream, then a man's exclamation of surprise.

I saw Aya briefly through the crowd. She was being dragged along the ground, kicking and protesting. "Elohim! Elohim!" she screamed.

I stood and saw that two men were hovering over Adam, one with a knife pressed against his throat. Abel was nowhere to be seen, in the midst of the men surrounding him. I thrust myself into the crowd, but their reaching, gripping hands held me fast. I heard myself screaming my husband's name. I scratched at my captors' faces; I clawed their arms; I would stop at nothing to get to Adam. Someone grabbed my arms firmly and brought them around to my back. They yanked up on them, and I bent over, crying out in pain. "My husband," I cried. My face was now wet with tears, and I could no longer see Adam. "Please. My husband. My sons."

It was too late. Quickly, I was bound and gagged and thrown upon the ground, with two brutish men to stand watch over me. One picked his teeth and watched Abel continue to fight; the other leered at me.

Naava

The prince slipped Naava's robe off her shoulders and pulled it away from her, so she could get her arms out. Freed of its burden, she was naked, standing in the middle of a beautiful and terrifying place, surrounded by all sorts of ceremonial articles clustered along the feet of the statues, some glinting in the flickering light, some smoking with incense.

Naava covered her small breasts with her hands and shivered. Never before had she had so many eyes looking at her.

The prince pulled her hands away. "No," he said. He held her hands out from her body and clicked his tongue with approval. He let go of her arms and began to undress.

Naava watched with interest. She had entered a time and place in her mind where her family did not exist, where Cain did not exist, where no one but she and the prince existed. It was a pleasant place of freedom, this place, and she began to relax.

The prince stood before her, naked. His breath was shallow, like hers. His body shone in the light. His skin had been oiled. He was thinner than Cain, not as built up with work, and though his chest was bare, his loins were not. He was excited, and his black thicket of hair did nothing to disguise it.

Although Naava had tried to block out what was happening outside, she heard a swelling uproar and glanced back to the temple entrance.

The prince came to her. "You worry," he said. "Do not." His fingertips caressed her forehead. He reached for her hand and led her to the center of the reed mat. He motioned for her to lie down on her back, then he positioned himself on top of her. He was heavy, but not as heavy as Cain. Underneath his nose, a fine glisten of sweat had beaded up.

Heavily oiled, the prince felt warm and slippery. He touched her gently and slowly, whereas Cain had always squeezed her roughly and hurriedly. "Inanna," he murmured.

Under her fingers, his banded muscles pushed and pulled against her belly and groin and legs. She wanted to run; she wanted to stay. She tasted the salt on his neck, and he returned her kisses—on her neck and face and breasts and even down below. What he was doing to her felt delicious. She was floating. She was Inanna. She was Power. She had gotten what she wanted. *What had she wanted again? This?* Oh, she didn't want to ponder it. Her belly shuddered when he entered her. Her legs clenched, her insides fell away, and she rocked back and forth with the prince. His groans made her groan, and when he rose up on his hands at the end, arching his back, his body tense as a piece of driftwood, she felt something surge inside her, and she was happy.

If she had tried to pick through all the threads of what she felt precisely at that moment, she would have said her happiness was a result of several things. First, she had acquired the prince's love. Second, she had learned much from Cain, for her lovemaking with the prince was a success. Third, she had been honored in front of her family, so they could no longer ignore her uniqueness. All in all, she had been raised up to the heavens for all to see.

Now her life could truly begin.

When Naava was again presented to the people, dressed once more in her jewels and bangles and robe, she felt strange that all these cheering people knew what she had done.

The prince wrapped his arm around her waist, and the people cheered louder.

The priestess anointed them with more words, and finally the prince and she were allowed down the steps, toward the adoring crowd.

Naava strained to see her family, but they were nowhere to be found. Not even Cain.

The prince supported her arm as they descended and moved forward, and as they did, the crowd bowed and parted as they passed. All the people seemed to understand the prince's marriage before Naava herself had understood it.

An old woman who had lost all her teeth touched Naava's robe as she passed, mumbling a plea. Her lips cupped her gums like seed pods, and her words were slurred.

Naava stopped. The prince waited. Naava put her hand on the woman's brow and said, "Be well, mother." When Naava thought of this later, she did not know what had compelled her. It was truly a kind gesture, one far outside the boundaries of her nature. Maybe she had become Inanna after all.

The word that the prince's men brought was that Naava's family had been forcibly removed from the city after her father and brothers had taken up arms against them.

Surprised, the prince turned to Naava and said, "Your family is not pleased with our alliance?"

"They do not understand," said Naava. "*I* did not understand . . . until I went into the temple with you. They did not know I would marry you . . . Be One with you. It is a sacred thing—something that exists between only one woman and one man." She saw the prince's face darken with confusion.

"But we are one woman"—he pointed at her—"and one man"—he pointed to himself.

She frowned and felt a trickle of sweat roll down her forehead. How could she explain about Cain, whom she had already lain with? She put her hand gently on his arm. "Do not worry. I will go to them, placate them, get them to agree to my union with you."

"How will you do this?" said the prince skeptically.

Naava had to keep him listening, keep him on the topic at hand. "I will go, get my things, talk to them, make them understand. Then I will come back to live with you. That *is* what you want?"

The prince nodded. "Yes," he said. "That is what I want." He smiled, yet his eyes portrayed distrust, and she knew it was because her expression must have matched the turmoil she felt inside. "You talk to them. I will come for you. The day after tomorrow." He kissed her and turned to go, but then he paused and looked back at her. "Tell your brother we expect him to fulfill his oath."

She could not risk it—the prince meeting Cain again. She grabbed his arm and pleaded with him, "I shall return on my own. My brother Jacan will come with me so I am safe. Please, there's no need for you to retrieve me. Who knows what my brothers and father may do to you?"

The prince did not like this answer. "I will go to your house. I will bring gifts—marriage gifts. I will take Cain's offerings. All will go well, don't worry."

There was nothing Naava could do or say that would change the prince's mind.

She remembered things that the prince had whispered to her on the reed mat, that her stars were in alignment, that she was very lucky indeed. Then she had felt that way, but now she only felt a growing sense of unease in her belly.

Eve

I feared for Adam's life, not knowing what the men had done to him. My two strong sons had disappeared too amid the men who had overwhelmed them, and I had completely lost track of Jacan, Dara, and Aya. I was dragged across the marketplace and hurled into a wagon. There my three poor lambs were cowering in the corner, huddled into one another, bound and gagged as I had been. Dara whined into her gag and scooted, with great effort, toward me. She laid her little head in my lap, and it was only then that I saw she was trailing blood along the rough wooden boards.

I could not tell how badly she was hurt.

It was much later, when darkness had already descended, that Adam and Abel and Cain, bleeding from multiple wounds—thank Elohim they were spared!—were thrown in beside us. Cain would not look at any of us. Adam gazed at me, tears streaming down his face. I knew he loved me just then; he would have given his life for me.

The same servant who brought us to the city delivered us back home. He pushed the oxen hard, so that we rattled and bounced like dried seeds.

The servant halted at last a great distance from our house—he would go no farther—and we were made to stumble toward our abode, not daring to look back or to free ourselves until he was well out of sight.

It was not until the next morning that Naava was returned to us. She came in a cloud of dust evident from a long way off, and I feared what we would see. *What had they done to her? Would they have taken care of her? Protected her? How many of them were with her?*

Jacan pointed and said, "It's the city people." His arm trembled, and his voice wavered. He ran to retrieve his slingshot.

"Stay close, you hear?" I said, but he ignored me.

"I don't want to go back," said Dara. She winced from her cuts and scrapes and clung to my skirts.

I had not the heart to reassure her, for we had to prepare for the worst.

Abel—with one arm and leg girded tightly with Aya's mendings—gathered heavy implements down off the wall and set them by the gate for easy access. Cain grabbed the torches slathered with bitumen and stood in the courtyard, ready to plunge them into Aya's fire at the slightest provocation. Adam was too weak to stand; he called out from our room, "Someone help me up. Please."

There was no time to help Adam join the fray. He would have been a liability. We had to defend ourselves, the best we could.

I stood with Jacan, a slingshot in one hand and a fistful of pellets in the other.

As it turned out, there was no reason to be alarmed. Naava arrived alone, with a male servant who had been charged with delivering her to us safely. She seemed unhurt but was especially sullen and refused to speak to any of us. Once the servant turned his oxen around to go back to the city, she disappeared into her weaving room and came out only for more baskets to pack up her things.

I tried to talk to her. I placed my hand on her shoulder and said, "Naava, are you all right? Were you hurt in any way?"

She skimmed away, like a bug upon the surface of the water. Up close she looked like a badger, with those black-lined eyes, although when the sunlight hit her just so, her face sparkled like a meadow of poppies under a blazing sun, and with a jolt I suddenly understood that she had become a woman. I had not been blind. It was simply a matter of finally glimpsing something new out of the corner of my eye, rather than gazing upon it directly.

"Where do you think you are going?" I said.

She gave me an incredulous look. "What does it matter?" she said.

"You have responsibilities here."

"If you must know, I have married the prince, and I am going to live with him. He loves me, and I love him."

I contemplated this turn of events. "What of Cain, daughter? You have Been One with him; you cannot Be One with another man. It is forbidden."

Naava laughed derisively. "But I already have, Mother. You cannot stop me."

"What of your secret, then?" I whispered, grabbing her arm and forcing her to look at me.

Her face fell, and she began gnawing on the insides of her cheeks—her telltale nervous gesture. "No one need know right now," she said slowly. "And you must not tell anyone."

My little girl was no longer. Indeed, she had known the truth before I did.

Now I come to the most difficult part of my telling. It is fraught with holes, I am afraid, for in the end, I know only what Cain confided in me and what Aya told me afterward. I fear Cain was not in his right mind—he seemed to have jumped off a cliff. He blundered through his words, clawed at the air. It was as though he heard voices in his head and he was trying to strike them away. And Aya . . . well, she was delirious for some time after.

So I tell you these things because it feels good to give life and credence to the truth of what happened.

I will begin with the offerings. Those fateful offerings. Mind you, I had thought nothing would come of them, as Elohim had not seen fit up to this point to either validate or disprove His existence after our expulsion from the Garden. True, He had spoken to Aya in the garden and to Abel and Jacan from the rocks, but He had not sought me out.

I was not expecting much.

Except maybe the reconciliation of my sons through this act of camaraderie, as forced as it was.

If you remember, it was Cain's idea to offer the harvest's first fruits to
Elohim. He was the most adamant about following the city's lead, and,
truly, this sacrifice was everything we had observed at the city's New Year's
festival—libations of beer and wine and offerings of figs and bread and
olives, all for the gods and goddesses to enjoy. Certainly I had felt a twinge
of guilt at the people's overwhelming display of respect and gratitude. We
had not thought to do this for Elohim, at least not in such an exuberant
fashion.

As arranged beforehand, we had already finished the harvesting and
Abel and Cain had selected their first fruits—Abel from his flocks and
Cain from his harvest. During the weeks preceding the city's celebra-
tion, Cain had begun calling the sacrifices he and Abel would make The
Ceremony.

Abel made one modification.

On the morning of our departure for the city, Abel sat down at the
morning repast and said, "There seems to be a question of whether or not
Elohim exists, whether or not He cares for us. It's an old question, one that
needs to be answered once and for all." With his finger, he spread ghee on
a chunk of barley bread. He looked up at each of us and said, "I want you
to know that Elohim is all around, that the absence of Elohim might be
your perception, not Elohim's." He paused, took a bite, and chewed.

We were silent, waiting.

He continued, "I propose that Cain and I set up our offerings over a
pile of brushwood. We will not light the fire. Instead, we will implore
Elohim to light it for us, if He is well-pleased with our offerings. That way
there can be no question of His existence. He either answers or He
doesn't."

Cain was the first to speak. He held out his hand, and Abel shook it.
"Done," he said. We all were astonished, I think, that Abel and Cain could
come to such an understanding so simply, so easily. None of us uttered a
word.

In my heart, of course, I was protesting. *What if Elohim fails the test? If
Elohim does not exercise His powers and prove His existence, what then?*

Naava refused to be a part of The Ceremony. All that day after her return, while we finished our preparations, she lingered in the courtyard, elbows resting on the wall, shouting after us in that obstinate, arrogant voice of hers, "Inanna will be angry. Beware."

Cain muttered to Adam, "Maybe she is right."

Adam sighed. "Naava thinks only of herself."

Cain was not convinced. "Inanna is a jealous god."

"So is Elohim," said Adam. His voice grew softer. "Let us try just this once to please Elohim, to do this thing that is right."

Cain gave Adam a doubtful look, but nodded.

Just before sunset, when the sun was an orange lamp hung in the western sky, we stood as a family—Naava excluded—in front of two circles scratched into the ground with a stick. Each circle bore a neat pile of bramble and brushwood and the first fruits chosen by Abel, from his flock, and Cain, from his harvest. It was Cain, of course, who had insisted on the separate pyres. Each was bordered by lit torches, which smoked black in the cool evening air.

The sacrifices were a combination of the most precious and pleasing animals' body parts and the choicest fruits and vegetables—and delicacies made from them.

Abel had killed two goats and three sheep, in perfect form and health, for the occasion. Aya and I had used one goat for the lentil stew and one sheep steeped in cumin and bay leaves from her herb plot. Abel had skinned the others and displayed the organs and fat in a flat open clay pot, to show Elohim there was no other purpose for these animals beyond pleasing Him.

Aya had caught seven fish that afternoon and split and cleaned and salted them. She had cooked them over a brushwood and date-palm-leaf fire, until the tender meat slid off the backbones. This, too, was offered to Elohim, alongside a spicy dipping sauce made from pickled raw fish.

Cain had gathered together baskets of chickpeas, squash, barley, wheat, apples, pears, grapes, and olives. Aya had helped Cain too, bless her heart. She had pressed figs and extracted their sweet syrups. These she presented to Cain in narrow-necked clay jars. She baked barley bread, made a paste of honey and cream, filled jars with beer and milk, and braised onion and garlic bulbs and placed them on Cain's wood pile in wide flat bowls.

"The smell," she said, as she handed it to Cain. "It will please Elohim."

Cain shrugged, but I could tell he was thankful.

The crickets whirred, and the torches flickered.

Abel and Jacan stood in front of their offerings. Cain stood in front of his.

Adam and I held hands—Adam holding Dara's hand, me holding Aya's.

The sun dipped lower and lower, expanding around its middle, then lessening, until finally it slipped like a fat egg yolk over the horizon. The sky overhead was a dusky blue, and our faces grew dim in the twilight. The world blackened slowly, as the full moon rose in the eastern sky, along with the familiar smattering of stars.

Abel lifted up his voice and sang the song of the Garden. The song rose on the waves of heat and circled up around the moon. It sent shivers over my skin. Truly, I felt blessed, and I know Adam did too, because he squeezed my hand and his eyes were shining.

Abel turned to Cain when he was done, and Cain cleared his throat and raised his hands to the sky, palms turned upward, much like the city's priestess had done over Naava and the prince.

"Elohim," Cain began. "Father of all gods . . ." Cain glanced at Abel, and Abel nodded, as if to verify that Cain's supplication was a proper one. "To You we give these first fruits of our bounty, to You who holds life in His hands, whose divinity fills the sky and sea and land, we offer these, our offerings. May they be pleasing to You. Give us Your blessing, we pray. Answer us, O Elohim. Answer us, so that we might know You are the one whom we should serve."

Then it was quiet. Interminably quiet. There were no signs or sounds of wildlife, not even a breath of wind. I looked up to the growing swath of stars above me, and I saw that I was a speck upon this great earth, that I did not understand the universe as Elohim had explained it, and that my mind and heart would never fully understand.

I remembered Elohim's tears upon our expulsion. *If He cared for us and missed us, why did He not meet us here, in this wild, unfortunate place?*

Then a great sound shattered the night.

"Look," Dara cried, pointing to the sky.

With a terrifying roar, a streak of fire shot from heaven, struck squarely upon Abel's offerings, and consumed them. We sprang back from the blaze, or it would have devoured us too. In an instant our faces grew warm; we dripped with sweat.

Oh, the wonder of it! The exhilaration—to receive a sign from Elohim, who had been silent so long. Abel and Jacan were laughing. We all were laughing. We hugged one another, kissed one another. It was truly miraculous. *Oh, thank You, Elohim!*

The air reeked of charred animal skins, roasted meat, and herbs. Everything in Abel's circle was burned to a gray ash flecked with glowing coals that poured light into each of our beings, pointing the way to Elohim, conjuring Him up where He could not be seen before.

This was Abel's answer, *our* answer.

Then. In the midst of our joy, we realized that Cain was still and silent. From his circle, there was nothing. No fire, no wind. Nothing. *Had Elohim forgotten there were two offerings?*

Cain began to pace back and forth between his circle and Abel's. "Sparks from your torch must have fallen into your offering," he said to Abel.

Abel shook his head.

"They must have," said Cain.

"There's been a mistake," I said.

Adam frowned. "I don't think so," he said.

"My fire came from heaven," said Abel. He did *not* voice the question in all of our minds: *Would Elohim play favorites?* Truth be told: I had learned early on that to favor one child over the other only led to disaster. Elohim would have known this.

When Cain began to rant, we gave him distance. He cupped his head in his hands. "No," he said. "No." He fell to his knees. "I gave You everything I had."

Adam went to him. He set his hand upon his shoulder. "Son," he said.

Cain twisted violently, shoved Adam to the ground, and backed away from us, crouching as though he were under attack by a wild beast. "Get back," he said. His face was twisted in pain and confusion. It was as though he no longer recognized any of us; he saw us as threatening and dangerous.

Aya squeezed my hand with the same force she used to wring a bird's neck for cooking. I think she did not recognize her own fear.

"Cain," I said, releasing Aya's hand. "We will try again. Surely Elohim will bless you too." I approached him warily, speaking softly and tenderly, as I would to an injured animal.

"Don't," said Cain, tearing one of Abel's burning torches out of the ground and shoving it toward me.

The flames leapt out at me, nearly singeing my hair and scorching my face. I retreated, knowing my son had gone completely mad. *Elohim,* I prayed, *Where are You? My son Cain needs You. Please accept his gifts.*

Cain turned on Abel. "You," he said. Spit rained from him, and drool dripped from his chin. "You," he said again, jabbing the air with his torch. "You knew this would happen."

Abel held up his hands, wanting peace. "Cain, I knew not what would happen, truthfully."

"*You* cut down my dates," said Cain.

"No," said Abel. "And I know not who did it. I am sorry for it, though."

There was a heavy pause where all that could be heard was the crackling of burning wood.

Aya stepped forward, breaking the moment. She spoke firmly. "I did it."

Cain shifted back and forth on his feet, his upper body bent over in a crouch. He said nothing, contemplating this turn of events.

"Aya, *what* did you do?" I said. Desperately, I wanted to bring peace where there was none.

Aya kept her eyes on Cain. "I cut them down," she said.

Cain straightened. He stared at her. He laughed. His laughter was a waterfall crashing into a tumultuous pool of anguish, hate, and bitterness. "You?" he said. "You cannot even walk properly. How would you climb my date palms? Don't think I don't notice how you look at Abel. What? You think to save him now? You think that by standing there and shifting the blame, you will save him? You will not. He will be punished for his misdeeds, just as you will be punished for your lies." Cain lowered his torch and set the flame atop his circle's brushwood. He held it there, turning it so that it would set the whole pile ablaze.

I held my breath. *Let there be flame,* I thought.

It did not light. It *would not* light.

Cain drew his torch out so roughly that his offerings tumbled down the pile in wrathful disarray. He threw himself down in their midst, head tilted back and mouth contorted as he howled. It was a purple torrent of rage, of misunderstanding and loneliness.

Naava came then into the light. "What has happened?" she said, looking with horror upon Cain's prostrate form.

No one answered.

We left Cain there, surrounded by the ruin of his work. He continued to rage at Elohim until the early-morning hours. Needless to say, sleep never came. Our ears were full of Cain's bottomless anger and discontent.

And then. My water broke.

Dara

I wanted to help Mama when she had her baby, but she kept screaming at me to get away. I watched Aya pour a little puddle of oil into her hands and rub Mama's belly with it. She cooed to her, "Think of the Garden, Mother. It'll be over soon." When I started crying, Aya shooed me outside. I went to where Father and Abel were sitting around the fire and said, "The baby won't come out."

Abel stood up. "It might be feetfirst." He left to go help Aya.

Father stared at the fire and chewed the insides of his cheek. He could barely sit upright, he was hurting that badly from his cuts. He muttered under his breath, "If only they hadn't come, if only they hadn't come." *Who,* I wanted to ask. *Who? Me?*

In the distance, Cain still cried out to the sky and pulled at his hair. I could see his dark shadow alongside Abel's glowing fire.

I thought very hard then. I did not have all of the five things I was collecting for the baby, because Turtle had died, the butterfly had shriveled up, and the pomegranate was rotten. I had dropped the rattle I showed Cain in the city, and I didn't think Father would let me go back and get it.

The only thing left that I had to offer was the agate. *If Aya likes rocks,* I thought, *then the baby might too.*

Mama screamed again, and Father put his head in his hands. He said, "A little piece of my heart breaks off when Mama does that."

"I know," I said. I walked over to him. "I will kiss it, like Aya does her foods." Then I leaned down and kissed his heart, so he would get better.

Father's eyes were leaking, his nose too.

I wiped all his tears away and said that I loved him and that Mama would be all right. I told Father that when Abel's offering lit, I saw a star shoot across the sky. That meant that something important would happen. "That's what Zenobia says," I said.

"Hmmm," he said, putting his hand on my head and pressing down on it.

Father pulled me into his lap. He grimaced. "You have grown up. What do you make of all this, Dara? Why did Elohim send fire down on Abel's offerings but not on Cain's?"

I was glad he was asking me this. "Maybe the star was supposed to be for Cain's fire, but it went the wrong way." I stroked his beard. I liked how it moved when he talked.

"Maybe," said Father. He looked at me then, and I could see the fire-light behind me in his eyes. *Isn't that strange,* I thought, *that there are two fires, one behind me and one in Father's eyes?* "Do you believe in Elohim?" Father asked me in a serious voice.

"There are many gods up in the sky," I said. I thought hard. "Maybe thirty-two."

"There are not that many!" exclaimed Father.

"Yes," I told him. "I think there are many."

Father looked down like Goat did when she was sad. "Do you *really* not believe in Elohim? Because there is only one Elohim, and I have met Him."

"I know," I said. "What did He look like?"

Father smiled, just a little. He said, "He was beyond description. He could take any form, although I have to be honest with you, we never saw Him in any other form than something that looked like us, except bigger, more glorious."

"Like Inanna?" I said. "Like her statue?"

"Inanna does not exist," said Father. He leaned his head to one side. "Even though the city people made quite a spectacle yesterday."

Oops. I covered my mouth with my hand. "Who told you?" I whispered. "I didn't say anything. Please don't tell."

Father looked at me, pushed me away from him, put his hands on my shoulders. "What are you saying? That you knew too?"

I nodded. "I gave Balili the idea."

"For the sound?" said Father.

I nodded again. Father was impressed, I thought. He cleared his throat. "Then why do you believe in so many gods? You know of their trickery, and still you believe?"

"Zenobia says that if we don't give Inanna gifts, she will create a disaster."

Mother screamed again, and I thought that maybe Inanna was punishing us.

"But," said Father, "if she exists, why do they have to make sounds for her?"

"I don't know," I said. "I have to think about that."

"Elohim sent the fire," said Father.

I whispered, "What if it was Inanna?"

"Inanna wouldn't answer a prayer to Elohim, now, would she? That would only further convince us that Elohim exists," said Father.

Why doesn't Elohim come out of hiding so we can see Him? Then we would know who is the right one to worship.

Naava

Naava felt strangely saddened to leave her family. Part of her wanted to say, "Good riddance." Another wanted to say, "I'm sorry." The events of the last two days and nights had flown by like a band of locusts, and she was still trying to make sense of it all. Her thoughts would not rest; they bit at her like fleas. She was relieved to be leaving the bickering and the unhappiness, but she was frightened by the black unknown that awaited her.

When she had returned to the house, her family's treatment of her had not changed.

No bowing, of course. Not even the slightest deference or acknowledgment of her new status.

No *Naava, dear, please sit, and let us get you some sweets and wine.*

No *What should we call you now, dear Naava, now that you have become—what have you become? Princess? Queen?*

No.

Instead, Naava's family had all but ignored her, so determined were they to offer up Cain's and Abel's sacrifices to Elohim. Right after they had *heard* Inanna, Queen of Heaven, whisper from the temple, right after they had *heard* the priestess speak the holy words. Could they not see that the city people—more prolific than Naava's parents and siblings would ever be—had come upon a satisfactory solution to keeping the gods and goddesses happy? Did they not want to be a part of it?

When something is working, why alter it? Naava wanted nothing to do with her brothers' sacrifices to Elohim. She was the city people's princess, and she would not betray them or the prince, who had seen her true beauty and celebrated it. No, she would be faithful and loyal to their practices and their religion. To Inanna, *her* queen.

Only when she had heard Cain shouting and screaming did she run to the site of the sacrifices. He was like a rabid dog, he was so far gone. Naava half-thought Adam would strike Cain down for his blasphemous words, but no, Adam stood and watched and said nothing.

Any lingering doubts about committing herself wholly to the prince vanished as she watched her brother rave. She would forget their kissing and lovemaking and sweet talks. Cain was too uncontrollable, had even struck her at times, just for disagreeing with him. Her future was with the prince, his city, and his gods.

Eve had cried out in the early-morning hours, in the midst of Cain's weepings, that her water had broken and the baby was coming.

Except the baby held fast to Eve's womb. It would not come.

Naava felt useless when it came to birthing babies. She did not relish the sight of blood or the cries that pierced the night, and she knew Aya would take the situation into her capable hands. And so she sat in the courtyard, knees pulled into her chest, rocking back and forth. She listened intently to the whispers and cries that came from Eve's room, and she felt unmoored.

She had to go to the city. She was to be princess and live with the prince.

She had to stay at home. She shared a secret with Cain, one that, soon enough, would be obvious to all. Her mother needed her. Her family needed her.

Which was more important?

Immediately Naava felt her face grow hot and her conscience grow black. She saw two choices before her—the difference between them like that of night and day.

If she went to the city, she would be ensuring good relations with its people for all time. She would be giving her family access to their advances—the how-tos of metalworking, the import of stone and timber, even the commerce along the river. All these things would be at her family's disposal, thanks to Naava.

But if she stayed here, she would only invite more trouble with Cain, who had seen her go into the temple with the prince. And with her mother. Her attempts to communicate with Eve always ended with exasperated cries or irritated retorts, and this confused Naava, for it was as though she was a moth inexplicably drawn to Eve's light. A sudden thought struck her and astonished her.

She did not want anything bad to happen to Eve.

It was as this realization bloomed in her head that Adam approached her and pressed her shoulder gently with his hand. "Did the prince hurt you?" Grunting in pain, he tried to maneuver himself into a sitting position next to her.

Naava shook her head. "No," she said. She bit her lip. "Father—" Adam looked at her with such tenderness that she faltered. "Never mind."

"What is it, my child?" he said, taking her hand. "You can tell me."

Naava waited. Her mouth felt dry and thick. "Father," she began, and then it all came out in a rush. "I have married the prince, and he wants me to come live with him in the city as his wife. He is coming tomorrow morning . . . *this* morning . . . to offer you gifts, if you'll have them."

"You have married? But when?" The confusion in his eyes suddenly cleared, but rather than anger she saw only sadness. He shook his head. "Ah, yes, it was this ceremony that you were a part of. It is as Cain feared, then."

Naava nodded again. "I should like to go with the prince." She looked beseechingly at her father. "When he comes," she added.

He released her hand and stood, with difficulty. "If this is what you wish, then you shall have it," he said quietly.

"Thank you, Father," she said. "There is one more thing."

Adam waited. Eve's screams rose again, interrupting the silence.

"The prince is expecting the wager payment from Cain," said Naava. "Will you tell him?"

Adam stood there, hunched over in pain. Naava knew she was asking him to do the impossible. When finally he spoke, his voice seemed drained of all joy. "For every action, there is a consequence. I hope you know what you are playing at."

Aya emerged from Eve's room then. "Naava," she said. She looked stunned to see Adam standing there. "You must lie down, Father, or you will not mend properly."

Adam nodded and limped off to the fire again.

"Please," Aya said, pulling on Naava's arm. "Just hold her hand while I prepare something to soothe her. Talk to her. Wipe her forehead." Naava could see the fear on her sister's face as Aya explained that the baby was not moving and that she feared that both Eve and the baby . . . Well, it was best not to think of those things. Naava felt a sudden surge of anger, which must have been obvious because Aya spat out, "However much you hate Mother, please do this one last thing for the family."

"I don't hate her," said Naava.

So she would have one more chance to redeem herself.

As Naava entered her mother's room, Eve was panting and pleading for death. Naava went to her and stroked her arm. She watched Eve's torment and told herself that disaster could not strike twice in a day, and since her family had already been thrown out of the city, she knew, in her heart, that Eve would be fine.

"Shhh," said Naava, running her hands through her mother's hair, teasing out the sweaty knots. "I'm here."

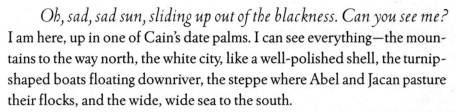

Aya

Oh, sad, sad sun, sliding up out of the blackness. Can you see me? I am here, up in one of Cain's date palms. I can see everything—the mountains to the way north, the white city, like a well-polished shell, the turnip-shaped boats floating downriver, the steppe where Abel and Jacan pasture their flocks, and the wide, wide sea to the south.

I can see the smoke from Abel's sacrifice. It smells of ashes and singed fur.

Cain had been punished. That, anyone could see. I was glad of it that Elohim had agreed with me.

At the foot of my tree, Goat brays.

"Shhh," I say. "I'll be down soon."

Beneath me, the yellow river teems with cranes and herons and egrets. They call to their mates. The sound of their wings flapping and lifting upon the steamy air lodges in my ears, and I wish to be one of them. I wish to soar upon the wind and fly to the mountains, to find Elohim.

For now I know that He exists. Now I know that He listens. After all, He sent fire down from the sky. *Did He not?*

I squint in the morning grayness and see Cain heading to the stables. I see Abel and Jacan milking the goats. I see Father limping off to the fields, to check the soil for replanting. Mother is still sleeping. She bore my baby brother last night in a delirious rant, and when he emerged like one of

Abel's stubborn ewes, all blubbering and blue and cold, she refused to feed him. She fell asleep not long after, and though I tried to coax her to bare a breast for the baby, she shifted and turned her body from me. I got Jacan to help me extract a bit of milk from a willing goat, and this we used to tempt the baby's palate. My brother—Mother has not named him yet— latched on to my finger and sucked as though everything he needed was contained within it.

I do not know what is wrong with Mother. If anything, she received a response to her life's prayer last night, but this seems not to matter to her.

Soon, I know, I shall have to help with the morning repast, but I want to linger here awhile longer, feel the breeze on my face, and smell the occasional whiff of Abel's dying fire. The fire that spoke of Elohim.

So Cain had noticed my affections for Abel. I did not think to be so obvious. I shall have to correct that.

And Mother. She muttered over and over, "Why would Elohim do that? Honor Abel and not Cain? They both worked so hard. Why, Aya, why?"

Finally I said, "Cain performs a duty he only half-believes in, Mother. He isn't entirely sure Inanna the Queen of Heaven isn't a real deity. It's his heart that's different than Abel's."

It did not appease her. She repeated the question over and over again in the next few hours, as Cain continued to rage on into the night, and when I lay down, next to Dara, I could still hear her pleading voice. *Why?*

I thought back to Mother's stories of the Garden. In my head, I recounted the details that Mother had thought to include in each telling— her love for Elohim, the deceit of Lucifer, and her and Father's subsequent decision to eat of the fruit. *What was missing? Why was Elohim's punishment so severe for so minor an infraction?* And now Elohim had disregarded Cain's sacrifice.

I had already considered, for a fleeting moment, that maybe Cain's offerings were ignored because of *my* contributions. Perhaps Elohim did not appreciate broken people either. But then I remembered that I had helped Abel with his offerings. This relieved me, as you can imagine.

Oh, what a strange deity, this Elohim.

As I told Mother, I had decided that Elohim somehow regarded the *intent* and *attitude* of the heart, not the deed itself, as the significant thing.

Maybe.

Cain's anger last night was but one grain of sand compared to the whirlwind of his anger today. He overheard Naava speaking to Father about her leaving for the city to be with the prince. Only through threats was Father able to keep him away from her, even though she had fallen asleep next to Mother.

I see Cain sidle out from behind the stable and join Abel and Jacan on their way back to the house. They lean into their headbands, into the weight of their milk jars. Cain gestures wildly as he talks. Abel looks at Cain only once. Jacan kicks at plants and pebbles as they walk along.

They reach the courtyard, and that's when Cain sees Naava standing in the doorway of her weaving room, and he leaps toward her, fists raised to strike. She is carrying my baby brother on her hip, nestled in a length of wool wrapped about her shoulder. She cries out, and Abel grabs him from behind. Abel has him down on the ground in a flash, and Cain holds up his hands in mock surrender. Abel releases him, wary, and beckons him to come with him, away from Naava.

Abel waits until Cain gets up and leaves the courtyard, then he follows.

There is something not right about Cain's posturing. Even I can see that from here. He is too excited, too animated. He jabs at the air with his hands, gesturing urgently, stumbling several times because he pays no heed to where he's walking. Abel says something, and Cain stops and turns to him, jabbing him in the chest. Abel swipes his hand away and keeps walking. Cain follows, his face red and his arms pumping.

He and Abel approach the river and the grove of date palms, moving directly toward where I am sitting, high up in Cain's tree.

I adjust my position, making sure I am hidden behind plenty of palm fronds. Cain continues to gesticulate. Abel listens but does not respond. Soon they are standing beneath me, a way off but not so far that I cannot hear them. They can go no farther west, unless they want to swim the breadth of the river.

"Brother, I am warning you. Do not do this thing. We shall not escape like we did yesterday. They will kill us this time," Abel says.

Cain paces. "He cannot lay claim to my sister. She is *mine*. She will be *my* wife."

"So it *is* true, then, about you and Naava," Abel says quietly.

"Of course it's true. Why else—" But he didn't finish his statement; he was too agitated. "My head," he says. "I think I'm going crazy. I hear a . . . voice."

"A voice?" Abel repeats.

"That is what I am trying to tell you," says Cain vehemently.

Abel turns to face Cain. His stance is wide, a defensive posture. "I am innocent. I did not cut them down," he says.

"You are not listening," screams Cain. "Elohim has spoken to me in the night."

Abel's eyebrows raise. "I am not surprised," says Abel. "He speaks to me all the time."

Cain's lips curl like the sun-baked reeds that are strewn along the shoreline. He sneers, "I know, you say this always. Are you trying to provoke me?"

"No, brother," says Abel. "I only wish you could believe in Elohim as I do."

Cain scratches his ear. Puzzlement washes over his face. "He asked why I was angry, why my countenance had fallen. If I did well, I would be glad. If I did not do well, sin would crouch at my door. In fact, its desire would be for me, and I would have to conquer it." He rubs his forehead. "What do you make of that?"

Abel is silent a moment. Then he says slowly, "I think Elohim wants your heart."

"My heart?" says Cain. "My *heart*? Did my offerings not show Him my heart?" He bends down to pick up a ripened coconut, washed down from upriver, and juggles it back and forth in his hands. A ray of light passes across his cheeks, and he smiles suddenly. "Do you remember when you bashed out my teeth?"

Abel nods. "You asked me to."

"Yes," says Cain. Then his smile disappears, and he is brooding once more, picking at the coconut fibers with his fingers.

"I am sorry about the dates," says Abel. "I know how important they were to you."

Cain's face rears up like the hood of a snake, like the face of Lucifer himself. It hovers and sways back and forth. His fingers stretch wide around the coconut, poised and ready.

I see Cain's face, the determination, the coldness, and my mouth opens to scream, to warn Abel of Cain's intentions, but when I do, nothing comes out, not even a squeak. My innards clamp up, and for a moment I cannot move. I cannot breathe.

Abel seems not to notice that Cain's purpose is to hurt him. He turns to go. Then, oddly enough, he thinks of something and turns back to Cain, saying, "I shall help you with the dates next—" But Cain is upon him, and even before Abel can cry out, Cain is striking him on the head with the coconut, over and over again.

Abel has had no time to reach for the dagger tied to his leg, and now his robe is awry, the sharp blade exposed in the morning light. He had not expected to be cut down like a tree in the middle of life. He had not expected to be plucked of his fruits before he was ripe. The blows continue to rain down until Abel, with his crushed head and his astonished eyes and opened mouth, slumps to the ground, unmoving. His face is immobilized, fixed fast like the traces of life in the fossils he had collected for me.

"Abel," I cry out finally, my scream finding its way out of my mouth.

Cain stops, stares at his hands, at the coconut. He looks around and does not see me. Then he looks up, slowly, to the top of the date palm.

"You," he says weakly. Again he looks at his hands and at Abel at his feet. He drops the coconut.

He looks back at me, his face unreadable. "It was you," he says.

"What have you done?" I cry out. I begin to shinny down the tree. "Help him," I scream. "*Do* something."

Cain seems confused. He grabs his head in his hands and drops to his knees. He does nothing.

I call Goat, and she comes bounding. It is I who must run as fast as a rabbit now. It is I who must save Abel.

It is as I am running that I hear a tremendous growl and snuffling off to my right side, and I glimpse a blur of yellow, a blur of fur, chasing me, breathing on me, and I want to scream, I want to cry out, but my throat is dry and will not cooperate. The earth trembles underneath the lion's giant paws, and I throw back my head and think that now would be a good time for Elohim to show His power. Answer my prayer. *Please, Elohim, make me as swift as the wind.*

I think it is Jacan's lion, the lion who killed the little boy from the city, the one who felled Father, the one who will kill me now, a crippled girl who is not his match. I think these are my last steps, my last breath . . .

But the lion's breath is gone—it has vanished—and I look behind, thinking that I am in the space between the lion breathing and the lion pouncing, and I cannot believe my eyes. The lion has Goat pinned beneath his great paw.

She cries out for me.

The lion blinks nonchalantly, then bends down and tears Goat's head from her body.

I run like the wind. I imagine flying, my wings outstretched. I find that I am sobbing and choking on my tears. It is like this that I run to Abel's stable and collapse among his ewes. I cannot think. I do not want to think what it is that I have done.

PART FOUR

Strangers
in the
Land

Eve

Could it be that I had been so blinded and so hard of hearing that I had not seen Elohim's hand until then? Until that fiery bolt of light descended upon us from the starry heavens to light Abel's sacrifice?

That is what it took for me to be awakened, and instead of pleasing me, it caused me dread. For I had lived many years under the pretense that Elohim had forgotten us, forgotten *me,* and if it were not so, I had wasted many moons in self-imposed misery.

Of course, I could have convinced myself that Elohim's sign was simply a bolt of lightning, one of those odd occurrences in the summer months and nothing else. Or I could have said that Abel had knocked a spark from one of the torches surrounding his offerings, causing his sacrifices to go up in flames. Oh, there were so many ways of inventing plausible explanations for what I saw, or felt, or heard. I had done it for so long; to doubt was ingrained within me. If I had done it to Elohim, how many times had I done it to Adam and my children?

I love Elohim. There, I have said it.

Every day I pine to see Elohim once again. Every day I *have* seen Him. Only not in the way I thought I should have. He is in the sweet grasses, the pink sunrises. He is in the shining clouds and the rain showers and the pale sunlight. He is in the crevices: between dark and first light; between the petals of an iris; between a man and a woman. All things sing of Him, only we must listen.

I had wasted so much time. Elohim's first question to us in the Garden after we had eaten was, "Where are you, my children? Why do you hide from me?"

It was never a little thing. I hid because I could not believe He could forgive me.

The baby in my womb was like a rock wedged between two boulders, and he would not come easily. My visions of death and release came in waves, in full color and vividly. I was convinced that my son and I would join the others in their earth graves.

Adam heard my screams and came to me. The only other births he had been present at were Cain's and Abel's. The other children, whole and not, came when he was out in the fields. Aya had learned to help me, to do what I needed.

Adam was sweetly tender. He brought me a little wine mixed with milk and held the cup as I drank. He held out his fingers so that I might squeeze them when the pain grew too great. He stroked my hair and looked upon me as a mother would her newborn child. He kissed my forehead.

And I wept. For all the times we had misunderstood each other. For all the times I was selfish and extracted from him only what I needed. For all the times I gave more love to my children, thinking he no longer needed it.

That night Elazar was born. In my heart, I named him *Elohim helps*.

Aya, my dear daughter, begged for me to take him. "He needs you," she said, holding him out. "He needs your milk."

I was too tired, too weary to look upon another face that needed me. The sky pressed down upon me, and I grieved. One of my children had been ignored—rejected—by Elohim. Cain, of all my children, who sought praise and acceptance from anything he latched on to.

I turned toward the wall and slept.

It was morning. Cain knelt at my pallet. He was crying. His fists were whitened along the knuckles, and he blubbered like a newborn child. I could not see his eyes; they were squeezed shut.

I studied his reddened face and searched for my little boy, the one who had played Mama Fish and Baby Fish with me, the one who had named all the plants and discovered how best to use them. How had he arrived at this desperate, inconsolable state? What could I do to ease his pain?

I reached out to lay my hand on his brow, to soothe the ridges in his face, and as I did so, I was startled to see a star emblazoned on his forehead, half hidden under a shock of hair. It was like a birthmark but darker, its border reddened—fresher somehow. I pulled my hand away and marveled at this man about whom I knew so little.

"Cain," I said. "How did you get this mark upon your forehead?"

Cain's eyelids flew open, and his hands went instinctively to his face. He found the star and traced its edges, his eyes downcast and searching for an answer, *any* answer. He looked up at me incredulously and said, "He said He would, and He has."

He seemed to think I knew what he was talking about, but his utterances only convinced me further that he had truly gone mad, that he had found a reason to score this symbol upon himself as a mark of defiance or devotion or both.

"What have you done?" I asked, still thinking that he would be able to explain.

"I am sorry, Mother," he sobbed, reaching for my hands and putting one on each of his cheeks. "I have sinned. I need your forgiveness."

I was astonished by this admission. *Had my son Cain come home?* No more arguments. No more rantings and ravings. No more hateful looks. The possibility stunned me.

I looked at him tenderly and raised my head the best I could. I was still so exhausted, so weak. "Cain, my son, my first, you have the smell of the field, which Elohim has blessed," I murmured. "May Elohim give you the dew of heaven, the fat of the earth, a plethora of grain and new wine. He searches for your heart, and you have given it. Be fruitful and multiply. Blessed be those who bless you. Cursed be those who curse you." I let my head fall back. "Your mother blesses you. Go, do well now. I must rest."

Again Cain cried out. He pulled my hands from his cheeks. "No, Mother, I have done a grievous deed. You do not understand. You bless me, but I should be cast from your sight. I should be ground under your heel. I am not worthy of your love. I am not worthy of your blessing."

Alarmed at his words, I struggled to sit up. "Do not talk this way," I said. "Look at me."

He stared at me, and his words poured forth. "Elohim has cursed me! My brother's blood cries out to Him from the ground, and the earth has opened its mouth to drink it from my hand. The earth will no longer yield its fruit to me, and I am doomed to wander the earth as a vagrant. I . . . I cannot bear it." He was sobbing. "Help me. Please help me."

It was then that I knew the truth.

A mother knows.

He had done irredeemable harm. I could see it in the way his eyes sparked open, then constricted shut, squeezing the life out of Abel, who was choking and suffering at that very moment, as Cain held my hands in his. I could not breathe; I could not move. I wanted to get away from him, from Cain, but my body was too weak. I *willed* it to move—there, one foot at a time—away from such evil. I gripped the sides of the doorway; my chest struggled to fill with air. My rage boiled within me, and I thought I should like to strangle my firstborn for the pain he had caused me and the grief I would have to bear because of him. I turned to him, and yet I could not find my voice. I doubled over and retched. With the bitter taste still in my mouth, I said these words, chilling even to me, a mother who was losing a son: "You have done a vile thing. I cannot imagine what you have done. You shall be cursed by Elohim—"

"Already He has done so!" he cried.

"Go away from here, my wicked son. You cannot stay."

"Mother, please," he said, whimpering. "I will change. You will see."

I shuddered. I knew I had to find Abel before it was too late. "Go," I said again. "The prince is coming for you." I studied my son's bowed head and felt nothing but loathing for him. "And the marking?"

Cain mumbled, but I caught his words anyway. "Elohim appointed a sign for me, that whoever should kill me, vengeance will be taken on him sevenfold."

I knew not what to make of this. Elohim saw fit to speak to this killer *and* protect him? Outrageous, no? I struggled for some last scrap of tenderness and spoke in a softer voice. I knew what I was about to say was new to him. "Take Naava with you, for she is with child."

Cain's face rose up, anguish writ upon it, and he was up on his feet in moments. "Pregnant?" he said. "Pregnant?"

I lingered not. I had another son to tend to. My Abel. My dear, dear Abel. I stumbled out into the green-gray day, calling for Adam, calling for anyone who would listen.

Aya

I think a body can fill up with only a fixed measure of madness, like a cup holds only a finite amount of milk. If poured to overflowing, the insanity manifests itself as a cruel joke, something so horrendous and terrible that one can only laugh at it instead of cry.

How fragile we all were. How easily we toppled, like grasses weighted with rain. I could not help but smile, thinking that if *one* of us had stood up, *one* of us had said "Stop!" it might have turned out differently. Abel was already dead. I knew that. My friend Goat was dead too. But the horrors did not cease.

I will tell you what happened in that courtyard, after I made my way back.

Mother emerged from her room, bleary-eyed and asking for Abel. "Where is he?" she demanded of no one.

Mother held her head in her hands. Her eyes were unfocused, her gait uneven. She saw me sitting by my fire, numb and unmoving. "Tell me," she said. Then, "Aya, take me to him."

How she knew that something was wrong with Abel, I'll never know. She was not herself that day.

Without a word, I took her hand and led her out of the courtyard, across the scrubby plain between the house and the river, toward Cain's date palms, which towered over the newly harvested vegetable gardens and fruit orchards. The wind picked up and blew sheets of dust at us. We covered our faces with the sleeves of our robes.

I realized soon that Dara had followed us, humming a nervous tune.

I watched Mother closely—she had been so unresponsive the previous night after birthing my brother—but she said naught. I had to release her hand finally, for she was digging her fingernails into my flesh. I looked down to see several crescent moons of blood oozing from my palm.

I stopped and watched her go, stumbling along, clutching her midsection, oblivious that I was no longer with her. Dara, ever the forlorn little lamb, trailed after her.

I could not look again upon Abel, my brother, my friend.

I have sweet memories, of course, and those I will carry with me until the day I die.

He had been the only one to stand with me outside the city when my family discarded me like plucked wool. He had given his hand to me when we sneaked through the entry, so it might appear that I did not limp. It was because of him that I was able to see all that was within the walls, and for that, I was grateful.

He told me that my new robe reminded him of the top of the sky at midday. Sometimes, he said, he would nap for a few moments while Jacan looked after the flocks. One time he had lain back, and right before he fell into a brief slumber, he had noticed a wonderful thing. He pointed it out to Jacan. "Isn't it interesting that straight up from us—no, up there, follow my finger—the sky is a deep blue, then you drop all the way down, to where the edge of the earth is, and the color changes, from blue to light blue, then to white. Isn't that amazing? I will wager that if someone tried to capture that or use it in a story, no one would believe him."

On the day Abel stayed with me outside the city gate, he told me he cared for me—and by this, he was insinuating something more than for a sister, I'm sure of it—and that someday, who knew what would happen? He appreciated that I was a thinker, like him, and he knew that we would be able to solve the problems of life together, for we both knew Elohim.

I had not the gumption to ask *when* and *how*, but I do know that he loved me, as no one else did.

Just as I returned to the house, the prince arrived with his wagon, piled high with gifts and teetering precariously underneath the weight of them all. Naava and I were the only ones in the courtyard to greet him. Naava went to him, kissed him. The prince asked her how we all had fared, and Naava told him of Mother's difficult birth and of the horrible night of offerings.

The prince acted like a young boy, one eager to please. He began unloading the gifts for our family—for Naava's hand in marriage—chests made of oak and walnut, inlaid with mother-of-pearl and rosewood; linen of all colors; gold bracelets and silver rings and headbands with multicolored stones in them; oranges and lemons that had been stored in cool places; dates in abundance; jams and jellies and syrups and vinegars; flat and raised barley breads; beer and wine and cheese.

I almost asked him why he bothered, knowing that Cain owed him some of our harvest wealth.

Suddenly Cain stumbled out of Mother's room into the green-gray light. He was shouting, "It is too much to bear. You have hidden Your face from me, and now You drive me from the very ground I work. Truly I shall die!"

No one answered. I think we were too shocked at his appearance, his demeanor, his surpassing rage.

Cain fell upon his face and wept like a child. "I cannot go on," he said. "I cannot live this way."

The prince, shielded by his wagon, looked at Naava, his eyebrows raised.

My sister could only shrug. "Cain," she said. She walked over to where he was sprawled on the earth. "Where are your stores for the city, the things you owe them, to fulfill your oath?"

Cain froze. Slowly, ominously, rising up from the hollowed depths of the cave he'd created for himself, we heard, "Where is he?"

"Whom do you seek?" Naava said, already backing away. She went to stand in the doorway of her weaving room. Her face was hidden in the shadows.

Cain stood. He swiveled toward her. "There you are, you harlot," he said. "Where's your lover?"

Naava's face drained of color. She did not move.

Cain blundered toward her, holding his arms out at chest height. His massive hands, callused with field labor and strengthened by hate, clasped around her neck.

The prince sprang forward, launching himself at Cain, grabbing at his hands.

I was too shocked to move at first.

Naava gasped and pawed at her throat. She dropped to her knees, still pawing, still choking.

It was then that I ran to Cain and strained with the prince to pull him off Naava. "Cain, you imbecile," I screeched. "You have murdered once already."

Cain released his grasp and wheeled around to me. "What did you say?" he roared.

"You are a murderer," I said.

Abruptly, he became a child and began murmuring to himself. He tore at his hair and said, "I cannot go on. I cannot go on." He put his fingers in his ears, pulled at his lobes, and slowly realized that the prince himself was standing within arm's reach. His nose twitched, and his lips curled.

The prince reached down for his dagger. He held it out in front of him, indicating he would not use it, and said, "Cain, I mean no harm."

Cain laughed—this is what I mean by laughter coming so close upon the heels of madness. "You have dishonored my sister," he said. "And you, better than anyone, know what the penalty is."

The prince shifted back and forth, so as to confuse Cain's advances. "I took her in a marriage ceremony, before Inanna. How is that a dishonor?"

Cain spat on the ground. "She is with child," he said.

I heard Naava gasp behind me.

The prince turned to Naava. He looked confused. I imagined he was thinking, *How could she be with child? Was it not just yesterday that I lay with her?*

Cain continued. "I see you blanch. She is *mine*. Do you hear me?" He looked at me, then the prince, then Naava.

"Does your brother speak the truth?" said the prince to Naava.

Naava stared at him.

"Of course it's true, you boar. She is carrying my child. *My* child," said Cain.

Naava shook her head no but did nothing more. It was as though her words had been stolen away, her tongue cut out.

"What is that mark upon your forehead?" said the prince.

Cain's hands fluttered to his face, his forehead.

With a flash of recognition, the prince said, "A star." His face became as white as Abel's horizon sky. He dropped his dagger, and it fell to the ground. "Inanna's star," he said breathlessly.

"It was not Inanna," said Cain, reaching for the dagger upon his shin.

"Her sign," said the prince. "Her sign of protection." The prince seemed struck with awe.

I was dumbfounded too. Elohim had chosen a symbol that He knew most people would recognize.

"You will not fight me?" said Cain. He pointed his dagger at the prince.

"I cannot," said the prince.

I found my voice. "He means to kill you," I shouted, reaching my hand out toward the prince. "You have to fight. You don't know him. He will kill you."

The prince looked at me in astonishment. "He would not," he said, but even as he said it, Cain was coming for him, and his look turned to one of terror.

"This will be easy," said Cain, leaping forward.

The prince held his hands out in petition. "Please," he said.

Cain was the stronger man, a man of the fields and of hard labor. The first stab was an undercut to the belly. I heard the crack and crunch of ribs and the belated *oomph* that leaked out of the prince's mouth—his lips opened in an astonished and petrified oval.

"Stop!" I said, hobbling to Cain's side, trying to put myself between the prince and Cain.

The prince's fingers clasped around my arm. Stiffly, he turned to me and whispered, "He is cursed." The veins in his face swelled up. His eyes bulged.

Quickly, Cain circled around the prince, grabbed the prince's chin, yanked his head back, and, with a flick of his wrist, made one clean slice across his slender neck. Blood poured forth from the wound, and the head dangled to one side. The prince slumped and fell like a sack of gourds. His limbs twitched violently, then grew still.

There was a moment of silence. Naava began to pummel Cain with her fists. "Do you know what you have done?" she screamed. "Do you?" She was spitting at him, her eyes awash in fury. "They will kill you. They will hunt you down and kill you, you stupid, stupid man. And then they'll kill the rest of us."

I ran to the prince and felt his neck. *Please let there be something,* I thought. *Please let him live. Please.* I saw the prince's eyes, wide and vacant, and I reached up to close them. I straightened his robes about him and covered his face with a cloth, so the flies wouldn't land on him. I felt strangely numb, strangely absent, as though these things could not possibly be happening to me, to us. I would wake up, and all would be well.

Cain had captured Naava's flailing arms, like a frog does a bug, a smile flickering about his lips. I thought of the asp I had killed—here was Lucifer's spirit embodied in another.

Naava finally got her words out. "The baby. I wish it were anyone's but yours." She sank down before him and crumpled into a heap at his feet, sobbing.

Eve

There I was, on the other side of love. I could no sooner alter my children's behavior than Elohim could alter mine or Adam's. How strange and unreal it felt.

In the gathering dust storm, I held Abel's head, bloodied beyond recognition and crawling with flies. The wicked vultures hovered, drifting overhead, their wings trembling upon the wind currents. I would *not* let them have him! I thought that something had to happen, something had to occur, that Elohim would show Himself and breathe life into my boy, as He had breathed life into Adam and me. My son would live again. He *had* to live again.

Elohim could not have meant to allow Cain to do this awful thing. Surely it must have been a mistake, and Elohim would rectify it. I simply had to wait. But waiting was what I'd always done, as though in the waiting I had given myself over to forces stronger than myself. I had surrendered the *living* of my life.

Elohim *had* promised that things would go awry and that we would be furious with the *nature* of it all.

And I *was* furious. Livid beyond anything I had yet experienced.

How could this striving, this death, be a natural thing? It was so final. I didn't want to ponder His reasoning—that it was the order of things, to lay down at the end of one's life, to return to the earth from which it was made.

I wanted Elohim to be wrong.

I wanted to find Abel when I went back to the courtyard. He would be sitting there, playing his flute or laughing with Jacan or helping Aya with the meal. He would hug me and tell me what a wonderful mother I've been and tell me all that he had learned from Elohim.

You see where Cain got his madness.

Dara

Abel's head is bloody. Mama kneels beside him, and I whisper, "Abel, get up. What's wrong, Abel?" Mama puts her hand over my mouth and says, "Shhh, he cannot hear you, child."

"Why not?" I bend down over Abel's face and peer into his eyes.

Mama reaches over to close his eyelids.

"He's sleeping, is all," I say, trying to help, but I know whatever Abel's doing, he's not sleeping. All the lights in Abel's body have been snuffed out, leaving behind just his shell.

"Shhh," says Mama, placing her fingers lightly on my lips. She leans over his body and grabs him up like a baby, rocking him. She doesn't cry. Instead, she sings him the Garden song. She caresses his sticky matted hair, and she brushes his feathery eyelashes with her finger. I think she is trying to remember his face, what he looked like when he was here.

I'm as quiet as a mouse, because somehow I know that Mama is changed, and I am too. We've lost something so big and beautiful, and we'll never get it back.

Later, Father tells me, "You cannot go back to the city to watch the children, because Cain has done a wicked thing." He sighs and goes back to packing our baskets. "We have to flee because of him."

Aya says, "Cain did not care about his heart, and that's the most important thing in all the world, Dara. Remember that." Then she's crying into the stew, and when I say, "Aya, I can help you," in a soft voice, she says, "Poor Goat. She never saw it coming. Neither did Abel, and what did I do? . . . I ran away." Her chin is raining teardrops.

I say, "Maybe Goat and Turtle and Abel live together in the sky now," and Aya laughs even though she's crying.

Mama will not speak to Cain. She won't even sit around the fire at repast; she asks Aya to bring it to her room.

Jacan does not act like himself anymore. He is tougher, meaner. I heard him say to Father, "We were stupid. All along we were worried about the lion, when really it was Cain. But still, I don't understand, because Abel can kill with one shot. How did Cain get the better of him?"

And Aya, who was throwing her dough onto the sides of the *tinûru*, snorted and said, "He was ambushed, that's how."

And Jacan spit on the ground and said, "I *hate* Cain," and Father said, "Hate only hurts you, not the person that it's intended for," and Jacan said, "But he's a bad man, and he's taken"—he began to choke on his sobs—"my brother . . . away . . . and now I am alone up in the hills . . . and I keep hearing his voice in the wind."

I took the agate that I was going to give to the baby and went to Jacan and slipped it in between his fingers. He startled and stared down at my stone, but he had no smiles for me. He handed it back and said, "Dara, how can you think about stones when the most awful thing has happened?" and I thought he was probably right. Still, I did not want to spend my days crying, making my eyes and cheeks and stomach hurt. There was no point in doing that. I had to make everyone happy again.

All the butterflies are gone. I cannot find one single one.

I know because I've looked, to replace the dead one for Elazar. He is a funny-looking baby with red spots on his cheeks and hair that is red. He sleeps constantly, and he will not open his eyes to let me see what color they are.

Abel had red-brown eyes, like the clay I used for my pottery.
I remember.

I am sad because I don't know where we are going and what we will do for
a house and stables and cistern like ours. Where will I get my clay, and will
Turtle, my buried Turtle, be lonely, be washed away by the rains?

If Abel is dead only for a short time, and his eyes open and he starts
breathing again, how will he find us?

Maybe we will go to Elohim's Garden, where Mama and Father are
from. *Then* Abel will know right where to find us.

Aya

I have solved Abel's dream, but I am too late. It is Cain's dark face over the cistern. Cain's evil intentions. And yet. Is my face there too? Because I stirred the waters of Cain's wrath?

Cain and Naava fled in the night, taking only meager bits of food and water with them. Intentionally, they did not tell us where they were going, so that when the men from the city appeared, we would not know how to direct them.

We stood in the courtyard as they prepared to leave. Mother refused to say good-bye to Cain. Father tried to draw her outside, pleading with her, saying that it was the last time she might see her son. She hissed at him, "He is no son of mine."

Cain heard it all, and his countenance fell. "Let us go," he said to Naava gruffly.

"Wait," said Naava. She went inside to Mother then, and soon Mother emerged in the lamplight, her face swollen and red.

"Well, then," she said, smacking her hands together, as if to wash her hands clean of them. But she didn't have a chance to finish her thought, because Cain fell before her, groveling. He kissed her feet.

"Mother," he said. "I . . . I'm sorry. Please"—he raised his pleading face to hers—"if you can find it in your heart to forgive me, I would be grateful. Please, Mother." The stillness thudded around us. "I have been damned by Elohim," he croaked. "Not you too. I could not bear it."

After a long drawn-out silence, Mother finally said, "Forgive? How can I forgive such a thing?" Her words hung like little clouds in the air. It was as though she were saying them just to see them, savor them, contemplate them.

Naava knelt too, beside Cain. To see these two—Cain and Naava—in this fashion gave us all pause, and the image would stick in our memories forever.

Naava blurted out, "Elohim forgave you and Father, did He not? He would want you to forgive us . . . to give us your blessing."

Naava's words stung Mother—we could all see it. Mother put her hand up to her throat, as though she were choking. "Elohim," she finally said, as though she had misplaced Him. She reached down slowly and put her hands on Cain's and Naava's heads. "My children . . . my sweet children, I will do what you've asked. I can only forgive you as Elohim has forgiven your father and me. I bless you." She paused and seemed to search for words. "May you find life that sustains, companionship that keeps giving, and children who love you." She lifted her hands quickly and darted back inside.

Cain stood and went to Father, to kiss him on both cheeks. "I am sorry," he said, "to have caused you so much pain." Father nodded but said nothing. Instead, he hung his head and wept silently. Every once in a while he would glance up, squint into the distance, then look back to the parting couple.

Despite her humble gestures, Naava seemed almost herself, but slightly blunted. Her eyes and nose were red with weeping. When I hugged her good-bye, she whispered in my ear, "I will still become great. Just you watch."

I couldn't help myself. "You've made a good start," I said, pulling away from her.

Aside from his brief apologies to our parents, Cain's demeanor had hardened like Dara's clay pots. As they left, he yelled back, "You can have your God who plays favorites. I shall find my own." And as the yellow moon rose in the sky, Cain and Naava vanished like dark shadows into the night. The air grew as heavy as bread dough, and the silence pounded in my ears.

I never saw Cain again.

I did on one occasion see Cain and Naava's son, Enoch, from a distance, when I visited the city Cain had named after him. I knew who Enoch was only because he was pointed out to me as Cain's son. He had the wild hair and nervous habits of his father. I thought of engaging him in conversation and introducing myself, but he was berating another man for not carving quickly enough, and I did not want to interfere or discover with certainty that he was as ill-tempered as Cain.

It is strange how traits like this are seen for many generations, even though one does not intentionally pass them on to sons and daughters and grandsons and granddaughters.

The sudden absence of our lost ones was overwhelmingly difficult—emotionally, of course, but more than that, logistically. The hours needed to pack up all our belongings, prepare the necessary foodstuffs, and keep the animals milked and fed made us all intolerant of one another.

In the end, Father shooed three-quarters of the flocks into the steppes, because we could not maintain them. He said, "Maybe they will accept this gift as payment for the prince's death." He ran his hands through his hair and beard, and I looked at Mother, and Mother looked at me. We knew he did not truly believe that we would be forgiven that easily, but just his saying it made it seem real. It was a severe loss for us.

Elohim has answered my prayer. Oh, no, I have not been healed. I am still crooked. But I am confident that He has shown me that I am as He intended me to be. I do not understand it, for I would have liked *not* to be crooked, but after all that has transpired I am better able to be content.

Not every day, mind you, but *most* days.

I have an idea, which I very much like, and as I ponder it I think it a viable thought that simply reinforces all the pieces of Mother's story.

Here's what I think. The Garden was not a place of perfection—*perfect* meaning no death, no crookedness, no anything-that-we-perceive-as-bad—as Mother described it. Elohim had said that Father and Mother would have to *subdue* the earth. The word *subdue* indicates to me that there were hardships that needed to be overcome—sicknesses and pain, maybe? I remember too that Elohim had said to Mother that her pain in childbirth would *increase,* meaning that there was already a bit of pain to begin with.

Oh, I am reticent to say these things—after all, am I simply believing it because I *want* it to be so?

Maybe Elohim created the world in great diversity, *including* the crippled and the blind and the deaf, *including* creatures that would be born and experience pain and die, and He said it was *good*. Then, in the Great Disconnect, when Mother and Father desired wisdom, their *perceptions* of what was and was not acceptable changed and dimmed.

Elohim did not desire for Mother and Father to see or experience evil, but in their choosing, they now *knew* evil, and it colored how they saw, felt, tasted, heard, and touched.

And more fantastically—bear with me—*if* this were true, *if* it is our vision that is discolored, then, oh joy, we might be able to regain what we have lost, by altering the way we see the world, the recognition that it is much bigger and brighter than we realize. Life can be *better*.

So. This is what it means for me.

Elohim thinks I am beautiful the way I am. I cannot change my parents' or siblings' thoughts or manner toward me. In fact, I should not try but should rest in the knowledge that Elohim created me this way for a purpose, just like He has made others for a different purpose.

I should like to know what prayer is, because it seems a tedious thing when I am the only one talking. And I should like to know also how you know when it's been answered, if the answer is simply a *realization* like the one above, of which I've just spoken. It is not so clear as I would like it to be.

I might have been expected to choose one of the following explanations: 1) The lion did not kill me because I ran faster than Goat; 2) The lion did not kill me because Elohim willed it; 3) The lion did not kill me because Elohim *made* me run faster than Goat (or *made* Goat run slower); 4) Everything has a greater purpose: For instance, by maiming Goat, Cain unwittingly saved me from the lion.

These choices only knot up my thoughts.

True, I had been trying to *change* Elohim's heart in my prayers—the fact that He may yield to my request, or at least consider it, is a hopeful thing, don't you think? Then to pray makes sense to me.

But sometimes I wonder if it works both ways—while I am asking Him to *change* His heart, He is wanting me to *know* His heart, and where the two merge, there I have been given my answer.

Naava

Cain and Naava were shooting stars, fallen to earth. Naava knew this.

One thing had led to another. She connected herself to Cain, and Cain had been damned, so they were inextricably linked in a mire they couldn't climb out of.

She never could convince Cain that what she had done with the prince was legitimate—after all, they *had* been married. Cain heard only what he wanted to hear, saw only what he wanted to see, and that was the way it was. Always. Never, in all the years Cain and she were together, had she seen him alter from that path. It was a nuisance—*more* than a nuisance, to be sure, for he looked at her in only one way, as a traitor. He punished her for it.

That black night, lit by a yellow moon, Cain and Naava escaped downriver, wading along the shore among the bulrushes and cattails for an unbearable distance and coming out on the opposite shore to throw their pursuers off.

Naava's heart and mind were numb. She was no longer beloved princess of the city, and now she followed a murderer—a murderer who was the father of her child. Naava knew that Adam and Eve would take the brunt of Cain's punishment, and she was glad of it. To say all of this happened because of Adam and Eve was simplifying things, but for a long time Naava blamed her parents. Eve was especially to blame for giving Naava's secret away before she could say it on her own.

Cain and Naava traveled south to the sea, thinking that they would follow its coastline, that where there was water, they could live. Unfortunately, the sea was rife with salt. They could not even drink it. What they thought would nourish their plants did nothing but cause them to wilt and die.

Cain and Naava then moved eastward, toward the Tigris River, forever hungry and always thirsty.

Naava had a girl child and named her Miri, *bitterness*. Miri's head was covered with black down, and her eyes were her grandmother's—blue like the uninhibited sky. She screamed constantly, and Naava cried along with her many a night because Miri was so wearying, so demanding. Naava, in a half-delirious moment, remembered Aya saying that dill tea was good for a colicky baby, and it was this that saved Naava from her great depression.

Naava wanted then to return home—in fact, she begged Cain to do this one thing for her—but Cain was adamant that her family had moved on and it would be futile to try to find them.

Cain talked incessantly about building a city and naming it after the son she would bear. Naava told him she did not want to have more children. They were a headache and a heartache. Cain did not listen, of course, and in due time, Naava was again with child.

Then Naava had a boy child and named him Enoch, *to dedicate* or *to begin,* for she and Cain were beginning a life together, for better or for worse—mostly worse.

To think that Aya, crippled Aya, may have had a better life than she did made Naava want to bite her nails.

Naava saw Aya two more times in the years before she returned to Eve's bedside. The first was when Cain and Naava were living in the southern plains, near the sea, in tents made from dyed hides, with their three children—they had added a girl by the name of Shachar, because she was born at *dawn*. This was before they had settled down in one place, and truly they were an unsophisticated lot. Later they lived in their northeast city of Enoch, in rooms adorned with basalt columns and limestone carvings and luscious silks and decorated walls. But back then, Naava was still tending the fire, cradling her littlest in a shoulder hammock, when up from the desert arose a dust cloud so thick, Naava thought an army of people were approaching.

Cain went out to greet them.

He said later that he spoke to a man, a man who claimed to be the leader of his clan, a shepherd of many flocks, carrying on a lucrative business with the cities to the north. The shepherd wanted to know if Cain had any need for plucked wool, and Cain, in true form, had declined the offer. *What was he thinking?* Naava had built a makeshift loom, and she needed more wool, to be sure, but her husband did not consider this. He had been thinking only of his infernal city. With a stick, he continually scratched plans of walls and buildings and temples into the sand outside their tents, plans that were erased when the winds came. When Naava asked him, half jokingly, how he was going to build a city on rubbed-out dreams, he said, as he tapped his head with his forefinger, "It's all in here."

Naava had gone into the tent with the children, remembering Adam's long-ago warning that you never knew if a stranger was friend or foe. Upon pushing aside the door flap and peering out, Naava saw her sister. Aya's face had grown long and more narrow, like a gazelle's. The skin around her eyes showed her age, but the thing Naava noticed most was that Aya had a peaceful glow, almost as if she was glad of her life, glad of her circumstances. Naava had never known Aya to be glad of anything, and it made her wonder what exactly Aya possessed.

The second time Naava saw Aya was several years later, at a distance, when Aya visited the city of Enoch. Aya had four children about her, all ages. Naava would have guessed they were twelve, maybe, ten, eight, and four. Aya was haggling over the cost of barley flour and sweet cakes. Her children gazed wide-eyed at the goings-on around them. Naava was sure all the sights were new to them. Going from a nomadic lifestyle to a city lifestyle was definitely eye-opening—the din and laughter of the workers, the wares and chatter of the merchants, the hollering and bantering of the children, the pleasant and maliferous odors—Naava remembered well how overwhelming they could be. Since moving to a city palace, she'd reflected on how hard she and Cain had worked on the plains and how much of their life had centered on survival only.

Aya's hair was graying a little around her hairline. She smiled even while bartering, and all the merchants seemed to defer to her, like oil to a container, their faces aglow in her radiance, soaking up little pieces of her falling on them, gracing them. At least that's how it seemed to Naava.

Naava thought of going to Aya, embracing her, calling her "Sister," but the thought of Aya's obvious happiness paralyzed her. Would Aya see Naava's unhappiness as easily as Naava could see Aya's happiness? Would Aya mock Naava, as she once did, for Naava's hard-heartedness, her selfishness?

Better that Aya thought Naava was a rich wife of a city-builder. Better that Aya thought Naava was satisfied with her life.

Appearance was everything.

Eve

Adam and I ended up staying, though we paid dearly for the prince's murder.

After Adam released many of the animals, and before we could flee as Cain and Naava had done, the men from the city descended upon us, demanding to know where Cain was and when he would fulfill his debt. We fell on our faces, of course—what else could we do?—and confessed everything with Dara's help. We took the men to where we had laid the prince and covered him with frankincense and galbanum and stacte, to cover the stink.

We drew up a pact with them that we would work seven years to pay off Cain's debt and the prince's death. They threatened many things but never followed through with them, probably in the end coming to regard us as pesky parasites that could do them no real harm.

They would continue to search for Cain. I never knew whether or not they had succeeded until I heard, from a stone trader who landed his vessel at our docks, looking to sell his wares, that a great city was being built to the northeast, and that a man named Cain was building it. The city was called Enoch.

I had the Tree of Life seeds in my possession again. After Naava and Cain had gone, Dara came to me with a small leather pouch. "I'm sorry," Dara said. "Ahassunu made me take them." I'm sure my face showed mixed emotions—astonishment that she took them, anger that she hadn't told me, then gladness that she had given them back. Their importance to me had diminished, for I realized it wasn't the seeds that had mattered, it was my response that had been the key.

We planted them in our new garden, along with the seeds Aya had collected under the cover of night. It could never be *the* Garden, but by then, we weren't attempting to make it so.

Still, it was resplendent when it was finished.

My children: What can I say about them?

I forgave Cain and Naava, quickly and rashly, although I am grateful I did, for even if I felt nothing at the time—in fact, I was quite numb—I knew it was significant for *them*. I never saw Cain again, although I heard great things. But I wanted badly to see Naava, my beautiful girl. When I knew I was dying, I sent word by the traders that I should like to see her to ask her forgiveness for my oversights, for my harshness toward her. I was somewhat surprised when she appeared in the courtyard, timid and worn and, I believe, frightened to see her mother again.

Aya married a shepherd of many flocks, who bartered profitably with the people from the mountainous north. She visited frequently, whenever their caravan would pass through. She brought me trinkets and stones and told me grand stories of the people they'd met, the sights they'd seen. She had had seven children when she returned the last time, before these, my last days. She had left them behind, cared for by other women in her clan, as she called it, but the way she described each one, in such detail, was a gift in and of itself. *To be so loved,* I thought. *I wish I would have had her grace.* She remained true to Elohim and told me on several occasions that she had dreams of flying with Him. "I can't explain it, Mother," she said. "I lift up. With wings. I soar and circle over the plains. He is above me, beside me, under me." The lines in her face relaxed, and her eyes became soft. "It is the most wonderful—and peaceful—feeling."

I know what she meant.

Dara, my funny little Dara, is grown and gone. She married a man from the city, a merchant who specializes in saffron and for whom she does the accounting. She told me once, laughing, that when she had been caring for the city's little ones, she had seen an orange-dusted man selling saffron in one of the stalls, and not knowing what saffron was at the time, she thought he had purposefully sprinkled it over everything, finding it attractive. She has nine of her own little ones—they are not so little anymore!—and she taught each to read and write. She lives in one of the city's mud houses, and although it doesn't look like much from the outside, inside it is magnificent—cedar furniture, woven rugs, and beaded hangings. Adam and I would visit her every month when we needed to stock up on supplies—after all, we *did* get the saffron at a discount price.

Jacan became embittered—the poor soul, my brave boy. He was like a fish out of water after Abel died, burying himself in the animals as Abel had done, but differently, in that he began to withdraw from us, even from Dara, his sweet twin. For days he would disappear with the flocks, and when he returned, he slept in the stables. He left us when he was fifteen, I believe. We knew not to where, but every once in a while we would get word that a man by the name of Jacan, with his small band of scoundrels, had robbed a house or burned down a ship or thieved a herd of cattle. My son had become a renowned villain with a sizable bounty upon his head. I do not know if he continued to speak to Elohim as Abel had taught him—probably not, since he had chosen such a reckless path. How would he have reconciled the two?

I miss Abel every day. Often, I visit the steppes where we buried him, especially in the spring, when they are profuse with bloom—poppies, tulips, yellow stars, dandelions, buttercups, and lavender. The heather—the color of wine—is sweet-smelling, and the mere sight of it reminds me of my darling son and how he would make wreaths of it for me when he was little. He'd say, "Bend down," then lay the circle of flowers on top of my head. I was always reminded of the Garden and how Adam used to do the same thing. Is it not strange how things come full circle?

The question I have asked of myself is this: What was Abel here to teach me, that only in his death he could show me? I have only one answer. I believe he taught me to embrace life. In the here and now. Not in how I *want* things to be, but how things *are*.

Every guest we entertained—traders and merchants from faraway cities coming through—I thought: *Is it he, come back to his mother?*

As I speak of lineage, I am reminded to add one more item of note.

I gave birth to another son several years later, to fill the void left by Abel. I named him Seth, *the appointed one*. Seth was a meek-mannered child, beautiful of face and spirit, and I should have loved him as much as I loved Abel, but Abel's memory never faded. Truth be told, I always loved Abel best out of all the children I bore, nineteen in all.

A final story.

Later, when Adam was glimpsing the face of death more and more each day, I asked him, "Husband, why did you blame me for eating the fruit?"

Adam smiled. He was a man beyond his prime, and the strength of his body was ebbing away. I believe his eyes twinkled. He said, "I ate too, of course, but I was afraid. You were so brave, so brash. You were so . . . so curious, and I saw that Elohim loved that about you." He paused and drew in another breath. "I *wanted* to experience new things with you . . . but did not want the blame. Yes, I think that was it." He put his hand upon mine. "I am sorry for that. It has been hard for me to say I was wrong. I didn't *want* to be wrong, if it meant that I had hurt Elohim so."

I was quiet a moment. "Lucifer spoke the truth," I said slowly. "We *did* gain wisdom, but I'm not sure it was the wisdom we longed for. It has brought as much pain as it has delight, and I am afraid we've hurt our children by it, because of our not-knowing what to tell them about Elohim."

Adam squeezed my hand gently. "We should leave that to Elohim. Who are we to control our children's minds and thoughts like a dam controls the river? Elohim was not even able to control us." His eyes were full of sadness, but mixed in there somewhere was hope—undeniable hope. "He gave us a gift—although we did not understand at the time—by allowing us to choose Him *or* something else. Then, I suppose, He would know where our loyalties lay."

I laid my cheek on our linked fingers. "I chose you," I whispered. "After that summer."

Adam lifted me up, held my chin. "Isn't it beautiful to know that mistakes can be mended?" He traced the outline of my lips. "My dear Eve, you are the light of my life. I carry you in my bones and sinews. You are me, and I am you. I will always love you, and you alone."

My eyes brimmed with tears, and I leaned down to kiss his nose. "I love you more than you'll ever know," I whispered.

We were a tragic pair, Adam and I, but let me tell you this: We loved each other with a deep ferocity. More than either of us could ever express. We knew labor and pain and sorrow and dissonance, and this had only served to enrich and strengthen our marriage.

Adam's words bolstered me the rest of my living days.

Epilogue

Your tears are as a flood, my child. There, now. Let me embrace you, daughter of mine. Has life been so difficult, so tiresome to you? I wish, my love, that you could stay until Aya and Dara arrive. They will embrace you, give you solace, for your thoughts are not altogether wrong, I'm afraid. They will give credence to what you had to endure from me, and they would ask you to see, really see, how I have changed, how *they* have changed.

Dearest Naava, I see you have made the same mistakes I have. Oh, woe is me, if it were not for your quick flight, I would have had time to show you a different path. Know this, daughter of my heart, I am at peace now. My hands and feet and eyes and heart see Elohim every day, maybe not in the way I expect, but He *is* there, waiting to be discovered. Your father and I had our differences, true, but after that heartbreaking summer we came together again, like many strands of a rope plaited together, rendering it stronger, tougher.

Adam reminded me of an incident once, and I shall tell it to you now. You will find it funny and sad at the same time, I think.

Once, after a rainstorm in the Garden, we saw the need to repair our bower, for it had acquired a large gaping hole in one side. I handed Adam twig after twig, so he could weave them together in a way that he saw fit. Later, we would place palm fronds and fig leaves over the top, but first we had to secure a platform underneath, so that the leaves would endure, providing us with sufficient cover.

Well, I did not see that one of the twigs I handed him was afflicted with splinters. One of them lodged in your father's finger, and as he cried out, he was not upset with the splinter or the twig. No, he was yelling, "Eve, you goat, you have handed me a bad branch. What were you thinking? Now I have this infernal—ow!—splinter, and I can't get it out." He danced about, with his finger in his mouth, trying to ease the pain. "Go away from here. I do not want to look at you."

I protested, of course, saying that he was silly and that he should direct his anger at the twig, not at me.

We laughed about it later, when he reminded me of it, but I have thought upon it since and realized that I had been doing the same thing to Elohim all those years. I pointed my finger at Elohim, demanding an explanation for His absence and His punishment, when all along I did not see my own fault. It was not He who did not draw nigh to me; it was I who did not draw nigh to Him.

Elohim's ears and eyes were not closed.

Mine were.

Belief is not always easy.

It is equal parts doubt and astonishment and gratitude and confusion.

And then you see how deeply colored the sky is, how the grass is so sharply fragrant, how the fields are a dazzling gold, and you have to step back and breathe in this wild fabulous world. We live in the space of abundant questions and inadequate answers. How else can we live?

Open your heart, and all the uncertainty fills it—the dimpled earth, the generous sky, the shaking flowers—all of it crowding into your grateful heart. Don't you see?

Everything ordinary is extraordinary and points to one luminous thing, to a love that has already given its response. You have only to receive it.

Afterword

Eve: A Novel is a work of fiction, inspired by the Genesis account and Mesopotamian history. As you might have already guessed, I had to answer many questions for myself, which for some in the religious community might be considered borderline blasphemous and somewhat sacrilegious. I will try to explain.

It has long been thought that the Torah—or the first five books of the Old Testament: Genesis, Exodus, Leviticus, Numbers, and Deuteronomy—was written by a handful of authors. Biblical scholars base this hypothesis on the divine names used, the diction and style, the comparison of accounts, the political agenda, and the personality of the writers. If you're curious about this notion, look at the first two chapters of Genesis. You'll find two separate creation accounts. The first is a lush, almost poetic rendering, in which man and woman are created together, at the same time. The second is a rather dry accounting of how things occurred and how Eve was created from Adam's rib—you'll hear more about the difficulties of this word *rib* later. Harold Bloom, a literary critic who's not immune to controversy, proposed the radical idea, in his *Book of J,* that one of the writers may have been female. We can only speculate, of course.

Did Adam and Eve exist? Or were they part of a larger creation myth, whose traces are found even in Sumerian and Babylonian literature? Faithful readers of the Genesis account will insist Adam and Eve were real people. I, myself, am not so sure. They may have been characters placed in a moral tale. Or perhaps they were the first *Hebrew* people. As a side note to those of you who love history and would like to delve into this further, search out the creation story in Sumerian and Babylonian literature. They even have a flood story. Stephen Bertman's *Handbook to Life in Ancient Mesopotamia* has a nice summary of both.

As an aside, I have remained true to the Genesis accounting, in which Adam and Eve were made by God in a sudden and abrupt way. For the evolutionists—theistic or not—this will be disappointing because they want to know, *Couldn't God have chosen to breathe spirit or breath into an apelike creature, at a certain point in time?* Yes, He could have. I have no problem with that. I do not want to limit God, for I believe He is capable of anything, so that was not my intention. I simply chose to stay close to the poetic Genesis story.

The problem for me became: Where in history do I place Adam and Eve? Again, readers of the Genesis account will insist, "Well, at the very beginning of time, of course!" but what makes this difficult is that scientists and archaeologists disagree on *when* the beginning of humankind actually was, anywhere from fifteen thousand years ago to hundreds of thousands of years ago. Biblical researchers have placed Adam and Eve's creation at about 4000 BC, but other researchers and archaeologists date the Sumerians even earlier, based on archaeological excavations by J. E. Taylor, R. Campbell Thompson, Dr. H. R. Hall, and Sir Leonard Woolley, among myriad other archaeologists. I am not an expert on prehistoric times. All I know is that scientists seem to agree that the Fertile Crescent was where civilization rose up, where wheat was planted for the first time, and where cities were established. I know that the Genesis account has Cain building a city and naming it after his son, Enoch. So Mesopotamia is where I placed my Adam and Eve characters, after their "fall" in the Garden. Indeed, if you look closely at Genesis 4:17–22, within several generations of Adam and Eve's family, there were skilled artisans working in musical instruments and bronze and iron, something that in history books takes eons of years to accomplish. History students will balk at how I've combined the Ubaid (4000–3500 BCE), and Uruk (3500–3000 BCE), and Jemdet Nasr (3000–2900 BCE) periods of civilization, based on developments in architecture, writing, seals, metal-working, and pottery. For this I apologize, but since so much is undecided about when and where things came from, I took a smidgen of literary license. What we *do* know, so far, is that originally there was no precious stone or timber or metal in the lower Mesopotamia regions. These things had to be imported from the north, either by land or by *keleks* or boats sailing down the Euphrates and Tigris rivers.

As for the city people, you are probably asking, "If Adam and Eve are the universal father and mother, where are all these other people coming from?" Good question. You might find it fascinating to note that when Cain kills Abel, he is fearful of retaliation by other people. Look at Genesis 4:14 (quoting the NIV translation). Cain says, ". . . I will be hidden from your presence; I will be a restless wanderer on the earth, and whoever finds me will kill me." I am assuming Cain was the oldest child of Adam and Eve, so what other people was he referring to? Is it possible that there were other people inhabiting the earth at the same time as Adam and Eve and their family?

One other curious thing along the same lines, which I have found no satisfactory answer for in all of the books I have read, is: Who are the Nephilim in Genesis 6:1–5? I quote from the NIV Bible:

> When men began to increase in number on the earth and daughters were born to them, the sons of God saw that the daughters of men were beautiful, and they married any of them they chose. Then the Lord said, "My Spirit will not contend with man forever, for he is mortal, his days will be a hundred and twenty years." The Nephilim were on the earth in those days—and also afterward—when the sons of God went to the daughters of men and had children by them. They were the heroes of old, men of renown. The Lord saw how great man's wickedness on the earth had become, and that every inclination of the thoughts of his heart was only evil all the time.

This is important because, although the Nephilim are a quick mention, it somehow affected how evil men became and what they learned.

Certainly there are people with theories, of which the Book of Enoch—a book not included in the Torah or the Old Testament—is one. Readers may want to look at *Forbidden Mysteries of Enoch: Fallen Angels and the Origins of Evil* by Elizabeth Clare Prophet for further enlightenment.

So, all that said, it was with this information in mind that I let my imagination work. Suppose Adam and Eve were influenced by other people? Another culture? Whether or not these people were Nephilim—whoever they might be—or Sumerian-like people was not for me to answer. Having a city nearby gave me my much-needed conflict for an interesting story.

Another verse that influenced me—one that I had never noticed before—gets very little mention, at least in the sermons I've heard. Look at Genesis 4:26 (italics are mine): "Seth also had a son, and he named him Enoch. *At that time* men began to call on the name of the Lord." When I read this, the first thing I wanted to know was: Didn't Adam and Eve worship Elohim? Didn't they teach their children about Elohim? Or did they not know *how*? Better yet: Did they *struggle* with their expulsion and their loyalty to Elohim? I went with the latter.

I am grateful to the authors I used to help me answer important and necessary questions, such as: Did Adam and Eve have sex in the Garden or was the Garden too sacred for such a thing? For this, I turned to *The Genesis of Perfection: Adam and Eve in Jewish and Christian Imagination* by Gary A. Anderson and *The Life Story of Adam and Havah: A New Targum of Genesis 1:26–5:5* by Shira Halevi. Anderson's book also discusses the varying opinions—touted by some rabbis, and only partly used by me—regarding the "garments of skin" Adam and Eve were given by Elohim to cover their nakedness. For those who believe that no animals were slaughtered until after the flood (Genesis 9:1–7), this presents a problem, so they have come up with an alternative meaning. What if Adam and Eve had a garment of light about them in the Garden, and upon their expulsion, Elohim clothed them in garments of skin—their own *human*, mortal skin?

As to what was meant by the serpent and what was meant by Elohim's forbidding of the Tree of the Knowledge of Good and Evil, I used three sources: Gerald J. Blidstein's *In the Rabbi's Garden: Adam and Eve in the*

Midrash, Rabbi David Fohrman's *The Beast That Crouches at the Door,* and Elaine Pagels's *Adam, Eve, and the Serpent.*

Were Adam and Eve created at the same time, or was Eve created from Adam's rib? To carry this further: Is Adam superior and Eve inferior, or are they equal? There are two very different accounts in Genesis, one in which Adam and Eve are referred to as a unit—some scholars say an androgynous being—and the other in which Eve is created from Adam's side. Why? I don't know. I am grateful to Phyllis Trible's article, "Eve and Adam: Genesis 2–3 Reread." In it, she obliterates any need for us to think of men and women as being either *above* or *under* the other. And again, in her engaging *God and the Rhetoric of Sexuality* (p. 128), she encourages us to view Eve's "curse" as a consequence, not as a punishment:

> Hence, the woman is corrupted in becoming a slave, and the man is corrupted in becoming a master. His supremacy is neither a divine right nor a male prerogative. Her subordination is neither a divine decree nor the female destiny. Both their positions result from shared disobedience. God describes this consequence but does not prescribe it as punishment.

Believe it or not, there is a plethora of opinion just on the word *rib.* There seems to be some difficulty in the translation of that pesky Hebrew word.

Eve is fascinated with the fruit-she-cannot-eat. She deems it beautiful and desirable and having all the signs of being delicious. This is important because we see that she is capable of making a good decision. She wants wisdom, certainly. It is interesting that in the Biblical account she asks questions, when given the chance, and considers what to do. Adam, on the other hand, simply takes it from his wife's hand and eats it (Genesis 3:6).

It was in researching the Garden that I became intrigued with the Garden itself. Where might it be located? Is it buried underneath the waters of the Persian Gulf? Again there is a lot of conjecture on this point and not a lot of answers. I took the opinion of William Willcocks, in his article, "The Garden of Eden and Its Restoration," as published in *The*

Geographical Journal, Vol. 40, No. 2 (August 1912). He places the Garden of Eden "on the upper Euphrates between Anah and Hit. Here must have been the first civilized settlement of the Semites, the ancestors of the children of Israel, as they moved down from the north-west." In the Biblical account, Eden is located at the source of a river whose four headwaters include the Tigris and the Euphrates rivers.

Was the Garden a perfect paradise with no sickness, disease, or pain—as I was taught as a child—or was it a world like ours today, and it is only our minds that have changed? For this, I used the thought-provoking book *Mosquitoes in Paradise: A New Look at Genesis, Jesus and the Meaning of Life* by John R. Aurelio, in which he suggests that it is our minds and our visions that have been altered. Read Elohim's wording carefully. Elohim commands Adam and Eve to work the Garden: "The Lord God took the man and put him in the Garden of Eden to work it and take care of it." To many people, this would not signify a perfect place. After all, who wants to work? Now pay attention to Elohim's language when he curses Adam and Eve, after they've eaten of the forbidden fruit. He says to Eve (italics mine), "I will *greatly increase* your pains in childbearing; with pain you will give birth to children. . . ." In my mind, this means that she had already experienced pain in the Garden. To Adam, Elohim says, "By the sweat of your brow you will eat your food until you return to the ground. . . ." Did Adam's work in the Garden not cause him to sweat? Or was it simply easier in the Garden? As my reader will note, all I could do was wonder.

With great interest, I read Jean Bottéro's *Everyday Life in Ancient Mesopotamia,* translated by Antonia Nevill. He discusses "Dilmun, the lost paradise," which Ahassunu references in my story. According to the Sumerians' creation myth, Dilmun is where the gods and goddesses were formed and given their divine functions. Dilmun is a pure and clean and perfect land where there is no death or illness—similar to how the Garden of Eden has been portrayed in literature, art, and theology.

For hashing out the *why* of Adam and Eve's expulsion for such a seemingly minor offense, I relied heavily on Rabbi David Fohrman's *The Beast That Crouches at the Door: Adam & Eve, Cain & Abel, and Beyond.* His book is warm and conversational. He takes an unflinching look at some of the most confusing passages of this famous story.

You may be wondering: Wasn't the forbidden fruit of the Tree of the Knowledge of Good and Evil an apple? Well, no. It has become an apple in illustrations and paintings by artists who needed to paint *something,* so they made it an apple. No one knows what the fruit looked like, although, again, there is much speculation.

If you've read carefully, you may have noticed that Eve changes Elohim's commandment by adding the fact they may not *touch* the Tree of the Knowledge of Good and Evil. This is curious to me. Why would she have done this? It is a point that is much debated in the literature on Adam and Eve.

Regarding the serpent in Eden: Who was this creature? Simply a snake who could talk? One of the angels? Maybe Satan? Again, it's not simple. Reams of books have been written on Satan. Elaine Pagels's book, *The Origin of Satan,* is a great one to start with. Here is a teaser:

> In the Hebrew Bible, as in mainstream Judaism to this day, Satan never appears as Western Christendom has come to know him, as the leader of an "evil empire," an army of hostile spirits who make war on God and humankind alike. As he first appears in the Hebrew Bible, Satan is not necessarily evil, much less opposed to God. . . . In biblical sources the Hebrew term *satan* describes an adversarial role. It is not the name of a particular character. . . . The *satan*'s presence in a story could help account for unexpected obstacles or reversals of fortune. Hebrew storytellers often attribute misfortunes to human sin.

In deciding how I would describe the city people, I came upon the Sumerians' fascinating culture—at the Ancient Near Eastern Art Exhibit in the Metropolitan Museum of Art, in Susan Pollock's *Ancient Mesopotamia,* Karen Rhea Nemet-Nejat's *Daily Life in Ancient Mesopotamia,* and Jean Bottéro's *Everyday Life in Ancient Mesopotamia* (translated by Antonia Nevill), and Leonard Cottrell's *The Quest for Sumer.* Absolutely delightful was Samuel Noah Kramer's *History Begins at Sumer.* Readers might be interested in the Sumerian CD collection from the California Museum of Ancient Art—talks given by Dr. Samuel Noah

Kramer, Dr. Wolfgang Heimpel, and Dr. William Fulco—on everything from astronomy to Inanna to shepherds. Although I do not call my city people *Sumerians,* they carry numerous similarities.

When Balili the priest tells Dara and the children about Inanna and the *huluppu*-tree, he says that Inanna made a *pukku* and a *mikku* for Gilgamesh, who had saved her. Opinions range widely on what those objects were. Some conjectures: a drum and drumstick, a hockey stick and puck, or a ball and stick.

Again, when Dara uses a word she doesn't know—*gidim*—she likes the effect it has on Shala, her naughty little charge. What she doesn't know is that the *gidim* were the Sumerians' unburied and wandering dead.

On the character of Eve, I consulted numerous books on how Eve is seen in various cultures and how she has been portrayed in history and literature, for I wanted an Eve who seemed achingly real. Someone with whom I could identify. Someone for whom I was rooting. I relied on Mishael M. Caspi's *Eve in Three Traditions and Literatures: Judaism, Christianity, and Islam* (in collaboration with Mohammad Jiyad), Pamela Norris's *Eve: A Biography,* and Carol Meyers's *Discovering Eve: Ancient Israelite Women in Context.* But mostly Eve comes from my heart and from the experiences of my women friends. After all, if she is human, then she has felt everything we feel.

As you already know, the skeleton of the Adam and Eve story is there in Genesis. I have had to bulk it up with fat and bones. *Fictional* fat and bones. Eve's daughters have emerged from my imagination, as does the reason why Elohim rejected Cain's offering. I have had to concoct a solution to the puzzle of why Elohim would reward one child and not the other, when they both were being dutiful in their offerings—externally, anyway. I used Rabbi David Fohrman's *The Beast That Crouches at the Door* to sort out, in my mind, why Cain would kill Abel and what would lead him to do such a thing.

I think the most difficult thing about the writing of the story was how to portray Elohim—how He spoke, what He looked like. I ran the risk of making Him appear like Bob Newhart, and that, I didn't want, as you can imagine—my sincerest apologies to Bob Newhart. Eve is at a loss for words, as I was too.

It was in the researching of Sumeria that I discovered the sensual Inanna. Cities in Sumeria were often dedicated to one god over all others—and indeed this was the case in the ancient city of Erech, of which she had divine rulership—thus I made Inanna my city's primary goddess. Texts differ on what, exactly, she is the goddess of, but according to the wonderfully translated *Inanna: Queen of Heaven and Earth* by Diane Wolkstein and Samuel Noah Kramer, Inanna is the Goddess of Love and Procreation, worshipped in a "Sacred Marriage" ceremony at the New Year's festival in the fall. The reigning monarch "marries" Inanna, which ensures the fertility of the soil and the fecundity of the womb. Naava is Inanna's substitute, in this case. Neither Naava nor her family—except Cain—understands the significance of this rite. Hence the chaotic aftermath. In later years, the poets continued composing songs for this female goddess, but sang them to Ishtar, Inanna's Semitic name.

One of the outstanding features of a Sumerian city is its ziggurat—the tall, stepped, pyramidlike structure with a temple at the top. No one knows why the Sumerians built them. We might surmise they wanted to reach the heavens, where their gods existed. I discovered that the first city of Sumeria, Eridu, had a small one. In Eridu's earliest phases—dating back to approximately 5500 BC—its ziggurat measured about twelve by fifteen feet. It was made of mud brick and had a niche made for a god's statue and a single altar upon which sacrifices were laid. What a quandary Adam and Eve would be in if confronted with such idolatry! What would they have made of it?

Amazingly enough, the crops and cuisine of the Mesopotamian region today—present-day Iraq—are similar to what they were back in ancient times. I consulted two fine books—one scientific, the other contemporary—on Mesopotamian eating habits. The first was Jean Bottéro's *The Oldest Cuisine in the World: Cooking in Mesopotamia* (translated by Teresa Lavender Fagan), and the second was Nawal Nasrallah's *Delights from the Garden of Eden: A Cookbook and a History of the Iraqi Cuisine.*

Cuneiform writing was introduced by the Sumerians. It began as simple symbols for objects, etched into wet clay with a reed stylus. Later, the symbols were transformed into more elaborate drawings that could substitute for a situation or a phrase. Often, these drawings can only be translated *in context.* Priest-scribes were usually the ones who taught cuneiform in the schools, but overall, cuneiform writing was used for business transactions and archival records and storytelling. Dara learns the most primitive of this cuneiform, in which one might be able to guess immediately what the picture stands for.

Tentative in my usage of the elements of time, *day* and *year,* I was astonished to discover that the Sumerians had already figured out the patterns of the months and seasons. In following the moon's phases, they were continually short about eleven and three-quarters of a day, so they adjusted their "lunar-year calendar" to account for lost time. I refer to the day and night cycle being like our own, but to the Mesopotamians, the day cycle began at sunset. A day lasted from sunset to sunset.

In deciding how Eve and her daughters would render their speech, I fell back on the fact that even historians have difficulty deciphering Sumerian cuneiform texts. I did not want the language to be jolting or archaic in any way. I did not want my reader to stumble upon the prose and grow frustrated with it. As you know, the English language is replete with words that are derived from other languages, so I became flummoxed with which words I could use, which words I should avoid. In the end, the only thing I avoided was to use terms they might not understand at the time. What this means is that Eve could not have talked about a "steel-gray sky" because steel did not yet exist. She *does* use the word *plagued* because, although we relate that particular word to bubonic plague, there certainly were other plagues at the time—animal plagues, such as locusts, or biological plagues, such as sickness and disease. When Eve is in the Garden, she refers to Lucifer's many colors in terms of precious stones, which she could not have known at the time, but remember, she is looking back on her life, *after* she has grown familiar with the precious stones introduced by the city people.

Eve's voice comes from a culmination of sources—Job, certainly, wailing against Elohim's injustice to him and his family; Song of Songs, yes, those wonderfully metaphoric ways of describing the marriage bed; and the Psalms, in which David begs for Elohim's attention and mourns that his body is wasting away with grief.

For Dara's sweet response to Aya's insistence that she learn to talk to

Elohim—"Maybe Elohim is wild, like the hedgehog," I say. "You can't count on Him"—I have Philip Yancey to thank. In his book Prayer: Does It Make Any Difference? he tells of a fox den behind his house and how, when he has visitors, he takes them to the fox den, hoping for an appearance of their litter of kits. Yancey warns his guests in advance, "They are wild animals, you know. . . . We're not in charge. It's up to them whether they make an appearance or not." After a particularly exciting viewing, one of Yancey's guests, who had been going through a difficult time, wrote him a letter saying, "He is wild, you know. . . . We're not in charge."

My sentiments, exactly.

Acknowledgments

For the fine bookstores and libraries I used to research this book, I am extremely grateful. The Rochester Public Library is an invaluable help when I need obscure texts and out-of-date books. To the many librarians who had to search for and shelve hundreds of books for me, especially those in the interlibrary loan department, I say, "Thank you from the bottom of my heart."

I would like to thank my editors, Tracy Devine and Kerri Buckley, and my agent, Daniel Lazar—to whom I owe everything for the idea of *Eve;* Kathy Lord, Virginia Norey, and Marietta Anastassatos for their exquisite expertise; my friend Nancy Salvo, who listens to all my rash ideas and encourages me to keep writing; John Wilson, who graciously allows me to write book reviews for his magazine *Books & Culture,* and his lovely wife, Wendy; the Loft Literary Center, which supports Minnesota writers so abundantly, and Jerod Santek, who was so gracious to me during the Loft Mentor Series; the Church of the Open Door and Dave Johnson, who both fed my husband and me for three years now.

For help with researching archives for illustrations, I want to thank Wayne Mareci in the Nolen Library of the Metropolitan Museum and Margaret Schroeder, Archival and Photo Services Assistant at the Oriental Institute of the University of Chicago, both of whom were extraordinarily nice to me.

And to all my friends who accept that life is rife with more questions than answers: thank you. Your willingness to discuss, debate, and hold differing opinions—in a congenial way—is very rare.

Lastly, I would like to steal from Candice Bergen and say, "I used to believe that marriage would diminish me, reduce my options. That you had to be someone less to live with someone else when, of course, you have to be someone more." I'm not sure when it happened—that I did not feel this way anymore—but I do know that my life has expanded, beyond what I thought possible, with a husband in my life. Thank you, Dan, for allowing me to question and giving me the room and space in which to explore them.

DA Mar 2 5 2019

DA ✓ MAR 2 3 2009